PENGUIN MODERN CLASSICS

*Fifth Business*

ROBERTSON DAVIES (1913–1995) was born and raised in Ontario, and was educated at a variety of schools, including Upper Canada College, Queen's University, and Balliol College, Oxford. He had three successive careers: as an actor with the Old Vic Company in England; as publisher of the *Peterborough Examiner;* and as university professor and first master of Massey College at the University of Toronto, from which he retired in 1981 with the title of master emeritus.

He was one of Canada's most distinguished men of letters, with several volumes of plays and collections of essays, speeches, and belles lettres to his credit. As a novelist, he gained worldwide fame for his three trilogies: the Salterton Trilogy, the Deptford Trilogy, and the Cornish Trilogy, and for later novels *Murther & Walking Spirits* and *The Cunning Man.*

His career was marked by many honours: He was the first Canadian to be made an honorary member of the American Academy of Arts and Letters, he was a companion of the Order of Canada, and he received honorary degrees from twenty-six American, Canadian, and British universities.

M.G. VASSANJI is the author of seven novels, two collections of stories, a travel memoir about India, a memoir of East Africa, and a biography of Mordecai Richler. He is a winner of the Giller Prize for fiction (twice), the Governor General's Award for non-fiction, the Harbourfront Festival Prize, the Commonwealth First Book Prize (Africa), and the Bressani Prize. He is a member of the Order of Canada and has been awarded several honorary doctorates. He lives in Toronto.

## *Also by Robertson Davies*

NOVELS

Tempest-Tost
Leaven of Malice
A Mixture of Frailties
The Manticore
World of Wonders
The Rebel Angels
What's Bred in the Bone
The Lyre of Orpheus
Murther & Walking Spirits
The Cunning Man

SHORT FICTION

High Spirits

CRITICISM

A Voice from the Attic

ESSAYS AND DIARY

One Half of Robertson Davies
The Enthusiasms of Robertson Davies
The Merry Heart
Happy Alchemy
Selected Works on the Art of Writing
Selected Works on the Pleasures of Reading
A Celtic Temperament

PLAYS

Selected Plays

# ROBERTSON DAVIES

## *Fifth Business*

*With an Introduction by M.G. Vassanji*

PENGUIN

an imprint of Penguin Canada Books Inc., a Penguin Random House Company

Published by the Penguin Group
Penguin Canada Books Inc.,
320 Front Street West, Suite 1400, Toronto, Ontario M5V 3B6, Canada

Penguin Group (USA) LLC, 375 Hudson Street, New York, New York 10014, U.S.A.
Penguin Books Ltd, 80 Strand, London WC2R 0RL, England
Penguin Ireland, 25 St Stephen's Green, Dublin 2, Ireland (a division of Penguin Books Ltd)
Penguin Group (Australia), 707 Collins Street, Melbourne, Victoria 3008, Australia
    (a division of Pearson Australia Group Pty Ltd)
Penguin Books India Pvt Ltd, 11 Community Centre, Panchsheel Park, New Delhi – 110 017, India
Penguin Group (NZ), 67 Apollo Drive, Rosedale, Auckland 0632, New Zealand
    (a division of Pearson New Zealand Ltd)
Penguin Books (South Africa) (Pty) Ltd, 24 Sturdee Avenue, Rosebank, Johannesburg 2196, South Africa

Penguin Books Ltd, Registered Offices:  80 Strand, London WC2R 0RL, England

First published in the U.S.A. by The Viking Press, 1970. Published in Canada by Macmillan Company of
Canada Limited, 1970. Published in paperback by Penguin Canada Books Inc., 1977, 1996, 2005, 2014.
Published in this edition, 2015.

 3  4  5  6  7  8  9  10   (RRD)

Copyright © Robertson Davies, 1970
Introduction copyright © M.G. Vassanji, 2005

LIBRARY AND ARCHIVES CANADA CATALOGUING IN PUBLICATION

Davies, Robertson, 1913–1995, author
Fifth business / Robertson Davies ; with an introduction by M.G. Vassanji.

(Penguin modern classics)
Originally published: 2005.
ISBN 978-0-14-319824-6 (paperback)

I. Vassanji, M. G., writer of introduction  II. Title.
III. Series: Modern classics (Toronto, Ont.)

PS8507.A67F5 2015         C813'.54         C2015-905150-9

Visit the Penguin Canada website at **www.penguin.ca**

Special and corporate bulk purchase rates available; please see **www.penguin.ca/corporatesales** or
call 1-800-810-3104.

# Contents

*Fifth Business* … Definition

Those roles which, being neither those of
Hero nor Heroine, Confidante nor Villain,
but which were none the less essential to
bring about the Recognition or the dénouement
were called the Fifth Business in drama
and opera companies organized according
to the old style; the player who acted these
parts was often referred to as Fifth Business.
                              —Tho. Overskou, *Den Danske Skueplads*

# Introduction

*by M.G. Vassanji*

He was beloved in his lifetime and became an icon of Canadian high culture, yet Robertson Davies's proclivities as a writer were far from the trendy or fashionable. He even called himself a moralist, balking only slightly at this uncool term of description for anybody, especially in the sixties. Of course he astutely defined the term "moralist" to suit his purpose. When the prevailing literary view of man or woman was that of a creature caught in a despair not of his or her making; when that creature was held up as merely an involuntary blink of consciousness, or as someone pitted in a struggle against an over-bearing world, or as a victim of historical circumstance, Davies wrote a novel about moral responsibility. That novel was *Fifth Business*. Overnight it became a bestseller and a classic of modern literature.

On a winter's day in Deptford, a village of five hundred in southern Ontario, Percy Boyd Staunton, a boy of about eleven, throws a barrage of snowballs out of spite at his friend and rival Dunstan Ramsay, who is on his way home for dinner following an afternoon of sledding. The last snowball contains hidden in it a stone. Dunstan ducks the ball and it hits the young bride Mrs. Dempster, out on a walk with her husband, the Baptist minister. The pregnant Mrs. Dempster gives birth prematurely by three months; the baby, Paul, barely survives; and the woman becomes "simple." Dunstan Ramsay is wracked with guilt.

The throw of a stone, literally and metaphorically, sets the novel in motion; a trilogy is born. But in the universe that unfolds for us, this simple act is seen as nothing comparable to the proverbial butterfly's innocent flutter that will cause an atmospheric disturbance halfway round the world. It is wilful, childishly cruel, and thoughtless. It determines the life trajectories of two of the Deptford boys, Dunstan Ramsay and Paul Dempster, and it will return to demand a reckoning from the third, the privileged "Boy" Staunton.

*Fifth Business* has the most powerfully haunting prelude one is ever to find in a modern novel. "I began it," Davies said, "because for many years I had been troubled by a question: to what extent is a man responsible for the outcome of his actions, and how early in life does the responsibility begin?"

We are all responsible for our actions, even as children, the book suggests; no, it proclaims. Our deeds bear consequences, trivial or profound, and we are accountable. However, what is proposed is not retribution or punishment, justice in a simple sense. We are given a simple observation. But while we may not be judged by a higher court—parental, religious, or state—we may judge ourselves. And this is what Ramsay does: he did not throw the stone, but he moved aside and it hit someone else who suffered instead. The Christian symbolism therein is unmistakable.

It should come as no surprise to find in a writer's work various forms of the more enduring myths and symbols of our shared humanity, especially a writer brought up on popular theatre and fairy tale and the Bible. Davies himself made much of myth and fairy tale, calling them "the distilled truth about what we call 'real life,'" meaning that they illustrate the significant events of our lives in pure imaginative form; which, in a sense, is what a work of fiction often also does. In exploring his personal experiences and traumas, Davies took a keen interest in Freud, and a greater one in Jung, who explained the development of human personality in terms of universal archetypes. He found Jung particularly useful in understanding the transformations of middle age. But it would be misleading to conclude that he simply pegged his plots to a series of archetypes and myths, or that his writerly importance lies merely in his making use of them, however wonderfully. He was far too serious and conscious a writer to be reducible to a one-trick magician.

Davies's somewhat Magian appearance in old age, his sense of humour, and his forthrightness may have created the impression of a likeable, idiosyncratic, and out-of-fashion old uncle; a woman sighting him in a public place, for example, is said to have grabbed his abundantly flowing white beard, assuming thereby a certain familiarity. But behind that jolly facade—for he was first a man of the theatre, an actor, playwright, and director—lurked a complex personality, fighting many demons. He trawled his life's experiences for the substance of his novels and delved deep into what he called his "writer's conscience" for the psychological depth and the moral dilemmas he depicted. This conscience, he said in a revealing essay, "is the writer's inner struggle toward self-knowledge and self-recognition, which he makes manifest through his art." It is, said Davies, quoting Ibsen's chilling description of the writer's calling, "a man's self-judgment / As Doom shall judge the Dead."

Robertson Davies did not come from a privileged background or even a very happy family. He would recall his father's "appalling black moods which were terrifying—utterly terrifying." "All Welshmen are manic depressives," he said, and admitted to his own depressions—as which writer hasn't? He remained haunted by certain childhood traumas, for example when he had to physically abase himself before his mother for impudence, a scene that finds a strong and touching parallel in *Fifth Business*. He could never forgive his parents for having him late, and his mother for having been so old (she was forty-three, and nine years older than his father). He was never sure he had been wanted. In a 1966 diary entry he wrote, "My deep buried anxiety manifests itself in dreams of loss, of rejection, of love denied."

Life in school had its successes and its failures. He loved drama, and his knowledge of it was prodigious. At Upper Canada College, which he attended during his later years of schooling, he was a fascinating character unforgettable to his contemporaries; but this was the carefully cultivated persona of a gifted young actor who worked at his speech and demeanour. He performed brilliantly at the school's drama productions, became editor of the school paper and a prefect. But he was awful at sports, made much of at this boys' college even to this day, and prone to illnesses, and he could not pass mathematics, even after great effort. According to his biographer, this failure continued to haunt him into his later years. Without the requisite credits, he could not attend a degree program at any Ontario university, and Queen's accepted him only as a special, non-degree student. Salvation came when he was admitted to Oxford on the recommendation of his professors. He was now at the centre of the universe, as it were, and it came as a liberating, exhilarating experience, as it has done for many a colonial from the outer reaches of the Empire. He comported himself with elegance and style, and was an exuberant success in dramatics, but this persona, an extension of the one at UCC, hid a deeper problem. At the end of his first year he was diagnosed with a "severe nervous breakdown" and a heart condition. The depression was partly brought on by rejection in love; but the psychiatrist who treated him, and apparently alleviated his suffering, discovered another source for his condition, concluding, "You have been disastrously badly brought up."

His childhood was perhaps no more disastrous than many others; it was also, in many ways, privileged. Good and bad, it was experienced by a remarkable child, and it is from that childhood that Robertson Davies drew the core material for his Deptford novels.

Deptford is based on the town of Thamesville, Ontario, where Davies spent the first five years of his life. His father, Rupert, born a Welshman, published the local weekly newspaper, which he initially rented using all the money he had saved, having worked previously as a tailor, an errand boy, and a typesetter. Davies's two elder brothers helped part-time in the press, and his mother with keeping the accounts, setting type, and proofreading. When Davies was five, the family moved north to Renfrew, a larger town, where Rupert again published the local weekly. The family's fortunes were now on the rise. Still later they moved to Kingston, where Rupert took over the *Daily British Whig*, which combined with another paper to become the *Kingston Whig-Standard*.

The Deptford that Davies portrays was perhaps not untypical of a fairly prosperous Canadian village of those times (the trilogy begins in 1908); nowhere has he suggested that it was an exaggeration, and critics have hailed his faithful depictions of Canadian life. It was, on the one hand, a small, intimate place in which a sensitive child, a future author, could observe all the vagaries of human existence at close range and store them away for future use. It was, on the other hand, a village of narrow-minded and bigoted Christian sects where the public show of emotion or joy, a strand of hair out of place, even the bloom on the pregnant young Mrs. Dempster's face, were regarded as unbecoming. In Deptford you were Anglican, Baptist, Methodist, Presbyterian, Roman Catholic; each group a distinct identity and in its own eyes superior to the rest. "The Scots, I believed until I was aged at least twenty-five," writes Ramsay, "were the salt of the earth." A Presbyterian child, in particular, "knew a good deal about damnation." A Dante's *Inferno*, with lurid illustrations of hell's tortures, was a popular household object, "and probably none of us was really aware that Dante was an R.C." Deviancy in Deptford was meted out with harsh, unmitigated cruelty. Two of the victims of such cruelty were Paul Dempster and his mother.

"That horrid little village" is how one of the characters, Liesl, describes Deptford in the third book, *World of Wonders*. It is a place that has maimed the three men united by that fateful snowball, and to which none of them has formed an attachment: Ramsay and Staunton return only for brief periods initially, and Paul Dempster stops over once, just long enough to jump out onto the railway platform and spit twice in "loathing" in the direction of the village. All three change their names, thus giving themselves a second birth. Staunton and Ramsay abandon the Presbyterian Church, the former to join the Anglicans and the latter by discovering his own form of religious worship. Dempster seems to be an atheist, though he can quote passages from the Bible in profusion, thanks to the fanatical injunctions received in childhood from his father, the Reverend Amasa Dempster.

But of course, the central point of *Fifth Business* is that, as he admits, Ramsay never leaves Deptford in spirit. The incident of the stone weighs him with guilt; and guilt is imbibed with mother's milk in a town like Deptford. Ramsay's sense of sin and guilt has been compounded by Mrs. Dempster's dreadful fate subsequent to his departure. As a boy and later as an adult he attributes intercessional powers to her and comes to believe that she is a saint. Once, at a critical moment during his service in the Great War, he even sees her face on a statue of the Madonna. Later, when he is working as a teacher, he goes off on various sojourns in Europe in search of that statue, and finally becomes a full-fledged hagiologist, a specialist in European saints.

The second novel of the trilogy, *The Manticore*, is a charming, Jungian journey of a well-known middle-aged Toronto lawyer into his own psyche; it begins with the impact of a stone—the same fateful object that launched its predecessor. After a traumatic incident in which this stone prominently figures, Boy Staunton's son, David, sets off to Zürich's Jung Institute to undergo treatment. As the attractive Swiss doctor Johanna von Haller walks him through his life's experiences, we are given another perspective on Boy Staunton's career, and the effect his dominating personality has had upon his family, especially David. We also catch another look at Deptford, and meet the world of upper-class Toronto, for the Stauntons have done exceedingly well. In the process of this examination, David is made to acknowledge all the archetypes that have shaped his personality. However, just as for Ramsay, it is the European "ogress" Liesl who provides David with his epiphany, in this case when he acknowledges his ancestors: the ancient people who inhabited the caves of Europe, and also, significantly, Maria Dymock, an English servant girl who emigrated with her bastard son to Canada, having named him Staunton after her native village.

Finally, in *World of Wonders* it is Paul Dempster's turn to tell his story. He is now Magnus Eisengrim, the world's most accomplished magician—a career in which Ramsay as "fifth business" has also played a part. Dempster is a charismatic, self-made, and arrogant man, having transformed himself from the prematurely born weakling son of a tragic village woman. But he is not free of his wounds. In his creation, Robertson Davies has used his knowledge and experience of popular theatre to provide a vivid description of the travelling entertainment scene before the intrusion of television. It is with him that we first meet Liesl, and it is she who enables him to realize his full potential with the new name that she selects for him.

In this artfully layered trilogy, the impact of a single event reverberates throughout. The past is continually revisited and reinformed; the pursuit of a hobby—the study of saints—becomes in a sense a pursuit of Deptford. Ramsay finds Deptford in himself, and also in Dempster and Staunton; and in a far-off mountain retreat in Switzerland we leave this gentle man who was not a mover but a facilitator, now older and wiser.

DAVIES'S WORLD IS DEPTFORD and the other Canadian towns of his novels, based on the places he has known; it includes certain aspects of Toronto, where he spent a large portion of his life. This is the world of "English" (meaning British and all that entails) Canada. There is to it, in my reading of this world, a distinct sensibility of the other, the colonial, manifest in a cultural nostalgia, a longing for what is authentically European and British. "I think it was loneliness," says Magnus Eisengrim, of the Canadians he sees during his tour of the country, "not just for England ... but for some faraway and long-lost Europe."

Davies's Thamesville was a village close in recent memory to the British roots of its people. Besides its own weekly paper, it had music and drama societies and the Ferguson Opera House. Theatrical pictures adorned his father's study, including those of the famous theatre personality Sir Thomas Irving. Rupert Davies, who had first arrived in Canada at fifteen, felt deeply nostalgic about his native Wales, and Robertson spent many hours hearing stories about that land. In his old age, Rupert finally accomplished his dream of buying himself a house in Wales. His famous son never considered himself as anything but Canadian; he had wise words to say about that. Yet as a student at Upper Canada College he had worked assiduously to rid himself of his Ontario accent. How familiar that sounds in the annals of empire.

In *Fifth Business* Davies describes the mindset of many a Canadian lad who went off to the Great War. It was not to save the world, as wishful—though understandable—modern hindsight would have it. It was to fight for England against Germany that they went. "None had any clear idea what the war was about, though many felt that England had been menaced and had to be defended...." Simultaneously, the demonization of the Germans and the Kaiser was complete: "These Germans, I gathered, were absolute devils; not winning campaigns, but maiming children, ravishing women...."

This connectedness to Britain perhaps might embarrass a new Canadian sensibility, groomed on a more modern sense of the nation. But it can be freely admitted in a world that is, as we now realize, so interconnected and filled with memories of departure and arrival.

Robertson Davies was of the generation previous to the one that in the seventies rallied against British and (especially) American cultural domination to promote an independent Canadian culture. Davies himself, having written at that time one of the defining books of Canadian literature, felt comfortable with American and British admirers. American readers seem to have loved him. Speaking to an American audience, he compared Canada to the daughter who stayed behind with Mother while Columbia went away, became independent, and prospered. Mother and the renegade later formed a close bond. What of the stay-at-home? She grew up and went her own way, discovered herself. The Deptford Trilogy is one of those moments during her maturing, when an author held up a mirror of some complexity for her to look at.

My point in pursuing Davies's Anglo-rootedness, and the Anglo and Euro cultural nostalgia of his books, is to hold them up as an example of the cultural multiplicities that our world has become aware of. In his imaginative exploring of where he came from, he becomes remarkably contemporary, joining the company of many a writer who arrives at new shores (often from a colony) to dissect the life and place he or she has left behind. As such, Davies is not from the mainstream of a once-dominant, now receding, irrelevant, and quaint past, but from a larger, diverse mainstream of the present-day.

---

For details about Robertson Davies's private life I am indebted to the excellent biography *Robertson Davies: Man of Myth* by Judith Skelton Grant. Many of Davies's own comments on his life and work have been collected in *One Half of Robertson Davies* and *The Enthusiasms of Robertson Davies* (edited by J.S. Grant). The quotations employed here have been taken from these books as well as the Trilogy.

*Fifth Business*

# 1

## *Mrs Dempster*

### ( 1 )

My lifelong involvement with Mrs Dempster began at 5:58 o'clock p.m. on 27 December 1908, at which time I was ten years and seven months old.

I am able to date the occasion with complete certainty because that afternoon I had been sledding with my lifelong friend and enemy Percy Boyd Staunton, and we had quarrelled, because his fine new Christmas sled would not go as fast as my old one. Snow was never heavy in our part of the world, but this Christmas it had been plentiful enough almost to cover the tallest spears of dried grass in the fields; in such snow his sled with its tall runners and foolish steering apparatus was clumsy and apt to stick, whereas my low-slung old affair would almost have slid on grass without snow.

The afternoon had been humiliating for him, and when Percy was humiliated he was vindictive. His parents were rich, his clothes were fine, and his mittens were of skin and came from a store in the city, whereas mine were knitted by my mother; it was manifestly wrong, therefore, that his splendid sled should not go faster than mine, and when such injustice showed itself Percy became cranky. He slighted my sled, scoffed at my mittens, and at last came right out and said that his father was better than my father. Instead of hitting him, which might have started a fight that could have ended in a draw or even a defeat for me, I said, all right, then, I would go home and he could have the field to himself. This was crafty of me, for I knew it was getting on for suppertime, and one of our home

3

rules was that nobody, under any circumstances, was to be late for a meal. So I was keeping the home rule, while at the same time leaving Percy to himself.

As I walked back to the village he followed me, shouting fresh insults. When I walked, he taunted, I staggered like an old cow; my woollen cap was absurd beyond all belief; my backside was immense and wobbled when I walked; and more of the same sort, for his invention was not lively. I said nothing, because I knew that this spited him more than any retort, and that every time he shouted at me he lost face.

Our village was so small that you came on it at once; it lacked the dignity of outskirts. I darted up our street, putting on speed, for I had looked ostentatiously at my new Christmas dollar watch (Percy had a watch but was not let wear it because it was too good) and saw that it was 5:57; just time to get indoors, wash my hands in the noisy, splashy way my parents seemed to like, and be in my place at six, my head bent for grace. Percy was by this time hopping mad, and I knew I had spoiled his supper and probably his whole evening. Then the unforeseen took over.

Walking up the street ahead of me were the Reverend Amasa Dempster and his wife; he had her arm tucked in his and was leaning towards her in the protective way he had. I was familiar with this sight, for they always took a walk at this time, after dark and when most people were at supper, because Mrs Dempster was going to have a baby, and it was not the custom in our village for pregnant women to show themselves boldly in the streets—not if they had any position to keep up, and of course the Baptist minister's wife had a position. Percy had been throwing snowballs at me, from time to time, and I had ducked them all; I had a boy's sense of when a snowball was coming, and I knew Percy. I was sure that he would try to land one last, insulting snowball between my shoulders before I ducked into our house. I stepped briskly—not running, but not dawdling—in front of the Dempsters just as Percy threw, and the snowball hit Mrs Dempster on the back of the head. She gave a cry and, clinging to her husband, slipped to the ground; he might have caught her if he had not turned at once to see who had thrown the snowball.

I had meant to dart into our house, but I was unnerved by hearing Mrs Dempster; I had never heard an adult cry in pain before and the sound was terrible to me. Falling, she burst into nervous tears, and suddenly there she was, on the ground, with her husband kneeling beside her, holding her in his arms and speaking to her in terms of endearment that were strange and embarrassing to me; I had never heard married people—or any people—speak unashamedly loving words before. I knew that I was watching a "scene," and my parents had always warned against scenes as very serious breaches of propriety. I stood gaping, and then Mr Dempster became conscious of me.

"Dunny," he said—I did not know he knew my name—"lend us your sleigh to get my wife home."

I was contrite and guilty, for I knew that the snowball had been meant for me, but the Dempsters did not seem to think of that. He lifted his wife on my sled, which was not hard because she was a small, girlish woman, and as I pulled it towards their house he walked beside it, very awkwardly bent over her, supporting her and uttering soft endearment and encouragement, for she went on crying, like a child.

Their house was not far away—just around the corner, really—but by the time I had been there, and seen Mr. Dempster take his wife inside, and found myself unwanted outside, it was a few minutes after six, and I was late for supper. But I pelted home (pausing only for a moment at the scene of the accident), washed my hands, slipped into my place at table, and made my excuse, looking straight into my mother's sternly interrogative eyes. I gave my story a slight historical bias, leaning firmly but not absurdly on my own role as the Good Samaritan. I suppressed any information or guesswork about where the snowball had come from, and to my relief my mother did not pursue that aspect of it. She was much more interested in Mrs Dempster, and when supper was over and the dishes washed she told my father she thought she would just step over to the Dempsters' and see if there was anything she could do.

On the face of it this was a curious decision of my mother's, for of course we were Presbyterians, and Mrs Dempster was the wife of the Baptist parson. Not that there was any ill-will among the denominations in our village, but it was understood that each looked after its own, unless a situation got too big, when outside help might be called in. But my mother was, in a modest way, a specialist in matters relating to pregnancy and childbirth; Dr McCausland had once paid her the great compliment of saying that "Mrs Ramsay had her head screwed on straight"; she was ready to put this levelness of head at the service of almost anybody who needed it. And she had a tenderness, never obviously displayed, for poor, silly Mrs Dempster, who was not twenty-one yet and utterly unfit to be a preacher's wife.

So off she went, and I read my Christmas annual of the *Boy's Own Paper*, and my father read something that looked hard and had small print, and my older brother Willie read *The Cruise of the "Cachalot,"* all of us sitting round the baseburner with our feet on the nickel guard, till half-past eight, and then we boys were sent to bed. I have never been quick to go to sleep, and I lay awake until the clock downstairs struck half-past nine, and shortly after that I heard my mother return. There was a stovepipe in our house that came from the general living-room into the upstairs hall, and it was a fine conductor of sound. I crept out into the hall—Willie slept like a bear—put my ear as near to it as the heat permitted and heard my mother say:

"I've just come back for a few things. I'll probably be all night. Get me all the baby blankets out of the trunk, and then go right down to Ruckle's and make him get you a big roll of cotton wool from the store—the finest he has—and bring it to the Dempsters'. The doctor says if it isn't a big roll to get two."

"You don't mean it's coming now?"

"Yes. Away early. Don't wait up for me."

But of course he did wait up for her, and it was four in the morning when she came home, self-possessed and grim, as I could tell from her voice as I heard them talking before she returned to the Dempsters'—why, I did not know. And I lay awake too, feeling guilty and strange.

That was how Paul Dempster, whose reputation is doubtless familiar to you (though that was not the name under which he gained it), came to be born early on the morning of 28 December in 1908.

## ( 2 )

In making this report to you, my dear Headmaster, I have purposely begun with the birth of Paul Dempster, because this is the cause of so much that is to follow. But why, you will ask, am I writing to you at all? Why, after a professional association of so many years, during which I have been reticent about my personal affairs, am I impelled now to offer you such a statement as this?

It is because I was deeply offended by the idiotic piece that appeared in the *College Chronicle* in the issue of midsummer 1969. It is not merely its illiteracy of tone that disgusts me (though I think the quarterly publication of a famous Canadian school ought to do better), but its presentation to the public of a portrait of myself as a typical old schoolmaster doddering into retirement with tears in his eyes and a drop hanging from his nose. But it speaks for itself, and here it is, in all its inanity:

### FAREWELL TO THE CORK

A feature of "break-up" last June was the dinner given in honour of Dunstan ("Corky") Ramsay, who was retiring after forty-five years at the school, and Assistant Head and Senior History Master for the last twenty-two. More than 168 Old Boys, including several MPs and two Cabinet Ministers, were present, and our able dietician Mrs Pierce surpassed herself in providing a truly fine spread for the occasion. "Corky" himself was in fine form despite his years and the coronary that laid him up following the death of his lifelong friend, the late Boy Staunton, D.S.O., C.B.E., known to us all as an Old Boy and Chairman of the Board of Governors of this school. He spoke of his long years as a teacher and friend to innumerable boys, many of whom now occupy positions of influence and prominence, in firm tones that many a younger man might envy.

"Corky's" career may serve both as an example and a warning to young masters for, as he said, he came to the school in 1924 intending to stay only a few years and now he has completed his forty-fifth. During that time he has taught history, as he sees it, to countless boys, many of whom have gone on to a more scientific study of the subject in the universities of Canada, the U.S., and the U.K. Four heads of history departments in Canadian universities, former pupils of "Corky's," were head-table guests at the dinner, and one of them, Dr E.S. Warren of the University of Toronto, paid a generous, non-critical tribute to "The Cork," praising his unfailing enthusiasm and referring humorously to his explorations of the borderland between history and myth.

This last subject was again slyly hinted at in the gift presented to "Corky" at the close of the evening, which was a fine tape recorder, by means of which it is hoped he may make available some of his reminiscences of an earlier and undoubtedly less complicated era of the school's history. Tapes recording the Headmaster's fine tribute to "Corky" were included and also one of the School Choir singing what must be "The Cork's" favourite hymn—never more appropriate than on this occasion!—"For all the saints, Who from their labours rest." And so the school says, "Good-bye and good luck, Corky! You served the school well according to your lights in your day and generation! Well done, thou good and faithful servant!"

THERE YOU HAVE IT, Headmaster, as it came from the pen of that ineffable jackass Lorne Packer, M.A. and aspirant to a Ph.D. Need I anatomize my indignation? Does it not reduce me to what Packer unquestionably believes me to be—a senile, former worthy who has stumbled through forty-five years of teaching armed only with a shallow, *Boy's Book of Battles* concept of history, and a bee in his bonnet about myth—whatever the dullard Packer imagines myth to be?

I do not complain that no reference was made to my V.C.; enough was said about that at the school in the days when such decorations were thought to add to the prestige of a teacher. However, I think something might have been said about my ten books, of which at least one has circulated in six languages and has sold over three-quarters of a million copies, and another exerts a widening influence in the realm of mythic history about which Packer attempts to be jocose. The fact that I am the only Protestant contributor to *Analecta*

*Bollandiana,* and have been so for thirty-six years, is ignored, though Hippolyte Delehaye himself thought well of my work and said so in print. But what most galls me is the patronizing, dismissive tone of the piece—as if I had never had a life outside the classroom, had never risen to the full stature of a man, had never rejoiced or sorrowed or known love or hate, had never, in short, been anything except what lies within the comprehension of the donkey Packer, who has known me slightly for four years. Packer, who pushes me toward oblivion with tags of Biblical quotation, the gross impertinence of which he is unable to appreciate, religious illiterate that he is! Packer and his scientific view of history! Oh God! Packer, who cannot know and could not conceive that I have been cast by Fate and my own character for the vital though never glorious role of Fifth Business! Who could not, indeed, comprehend what Fifth Business is, even if he should meet the player of that part in his own trivial life-drama!

So, as I feel my strength returning in this house among the mountains—a house that itself holds the truths behind many illusions—I am driven to explain myself to you, Headmaster, because you stand at the top of that queer school world in which I seem to have cut such a meagre figure. But what a job it is!

Look at what I wrote at the beginning of this memoir. Have I caught anything at all of that extraordinary night when Paul Dempster was born? I am pretty sure that my little sketch of Percy Boyd Staunton is accurate, but what about myself? I have always sneered at autobiographies and memoirs in which the writer appears at the beginning as a charming, knowing little fellow, possessed of insights and perceptions beyond his years, yet offering these with a false naïveté to the reader, as though to say, "What a little wonder I was, but All Boy." Have the writers any notion or true recollection of what a boy is?

I have, and I have reinforced it by forty-five years of teaching boys. A boy is a man in miniature, and though he may sometimes exhibit notable virtue, as well as characteristics that seem to be charming because they are childlike, he is also schemer, self-seeker, traitor, Judas, crook, and villain—in short, a man. Oh, these autobiographies in which the writer postures and simpers as a David Copperfield or a Huck Finn! False, false as harlots' oaths!

Can I write truly of my boyhood? Or will that disgusting self-love which so often attaches itself to a man's idea of his youth creep in and falsify the story? I can but try. And to begin I must give you some notion of the village in which Percy Boyd Staunton and Paul Dempster and I were born.

( 3 )

Village life has been so extensively explored by movies and television during recent years that you may shrink from hearing more about it. I shall be as brief as I can, for it is not by piling up detail that I hope to achieve my picture, but by putting the emphasis where I think it belongs.

Once it was the fashion to represent villages as places inhabited by laughable, lovable simpletons, unspotted by the worldliness of city life, though occasionally shrewd in rural concerns. Later it was the popular thing to show villages as rotten with vice, and especially such sexual vice as Krafft-Ebing might have been surprised to uncover in Vienna; incest, sodomy, bestiality, sadism, and masochism were supposed to rage behind the lace curtains and in the haylofts, while a rigid piety was professed in the streets. Our village never seemed to me to be like that. It was more varied in what it offered to the observer than people from bigger and more sophisticated places generally think, and if it had sins and follies and roughnesses, it also had much to show of virtue, dignity, and even of nobility.

It was called Deptford and lay on the Thames River about fifteen miles east of Pittstown, our county town and nearest big place. We had an official population of about five hundred, and the surrounding farms probably brought the district up to eight hundred souls. We had five churches: the Anglican, poor but believed to have some mysterious social supremacy; the Presbyterian, solvent and thought—chiefly by itself—to be intellectual; the Methodist, insolvent and fervent; the Baptist, insolvent and saved; the Roman Catholic, mysterious to most of us but clearly solvent, as it was frequently and, so we thought, quite needlessly repainted. We supported one lawyer, who was also the magistrate, and one banker in a private bank, as such things still existed at that time. We had two doctors: Dr McCausland who was reputed to be clever, and Dr Staunton, who was Percy's father and who was also clever, but in the realm of real estate—he was a great holder of mortgages and owned several farms. We had a dentist, a wretch without manual skill, whose wife underfed him, and who had positively the dirtiest professional premises I have ever seen; and a veterinarian who drank but could rise to an occasion. We had a canning factory, which operated noisily and feverishly when there was anything to can; also a sawmill and a few shops.

The village was dominated by a family called Athelstan, who had done well out of lumber early in the nineteenth century; they owned Deptford's only three-storey house, which stood by itself on the way to the cemetery; most of our houses were of wood, and some of them stood on piles, for the Thames had a trick of flooding. One of the remaining Athelstans lived across the street from us, a poor demented old woman who used from time to time to escape from her nurse-housekeeper and rush into the road, where she threw herself down, raising a cloud of dust like a hen having a dirt-bath, shouting loudly, "Christian men, come and help me!" It usually took the housekeeper and at least one other person to pacify her; my mother often assisted in this way, but I could not do so for the old lady disliked me—I seemed to remind her of some false friend in the past. But I was interested in her madness and longed to talk with her, so I always rushed to the rescue when she made one of her breaks for liberty.

My family enjoyed a position of modest privilege, for my father was the owner and editor of the local weekly paper, *The Deptford Banner*. It was not a very prosperous enterprise, but with the job-printing plant it sustained us and we never wanted for anything. My father, as I learned later, never did a gross business of $5000 in any year that he owned it. He was not only publisher and editor, but chief mechanic and printer as well, helped by a melancholy youth called Jumper Saul and a girl called Nell Bullock. It was a good little paper, respected and hated as a proper local paper should be; the editorial comment, which my father composed directly on the typesetting machine, was read carefully every week. So we were, in a sense, the literary leaders of the community, and my father had a seat on the Library Board along with the magistrate.

Our household, then, was representative of the better sort of life in the village, and we thought well of ourselves. Some of this good opinion arose from being Scots; my father had come from Dumfries as a young man, but my mother's family had been three generations in Canada without having become a whit less Scots than when her grandparents left Inverness. The Scots, I believed until I was aged at least twenty-five, were the salt of the earth, for although this was never said in our household it was one of those accepted truths which do not need to be laboured. By far the majority of the Deptford people had come to Western Ontario from the south of England, so we were not surprised that they looked to us, the Ramsays, for common sense, prudence, and right opinions on virtually everything.

Cleanliness, for example. My mother was clean—oh, but she was clean! Our privy set the sanitary tone of the village. We depended on wells in Deptford, and water for all purposes was heated in a tank called a "cistern" on the side of the kitchen range. Every house had a privy, and these ranked from dilapidated, noisome shacks to quite smart edifices, of which our own was clearly among the best. There has been much hilarity about privies in the years since they became rarities, but they were not funny buildings, and if they were not to become disgraceful they needed a lot of care.

As well as this temple of hygiene we had a "chemical closet" in the house, for use when someone was unwell; it was so capricious and smelly, however, that it merely added a new misery to illness and was rarely set going.

That is all that seems necessary to say about Deptford at present; any necessary additional matter will present itself as part of my narrative. We were serious people, missing nothing in our community and feeling ourselves in no way inferior to larger places. We did, however, look with pitying amusement on Bowles Corners, four miles distant and with a population of one hundred and fifty. To live in Bowles Corners, we felt, was to be rustic beyond redemption.

( 4 )

The first six months of Paul Dempster's life were perhaps the most exciting and pleasurable period of my mother's life, and unquestionably the most miserable of mine. Premature babies had a much poorer chance of surviving in 1908 than they have now, but Paul was the first challenge of this sort in my mother's experience of childbirth, and she met it with all her determination and ingenuity. She was not, I must make clear, in any sense a midwife or a trained person—simply a woman of good sense and kindness of heart who enjoyed the authority of nursing and the mystery which at that time still hung about the peculiarly feminine functions. She spent a great part of each day and not a few nights at the Dempsters' during that six months; other women helped when they could, but my mother was the acknowledged high priestess, and Dr McCausland was good enough to say that without her he could never have pulled little Paul safely up onto the shores of this world.

I learned all the gynaecological and obstetrical details as they were imparted piecemeal to my father; the difference was that he sat comfortably beside the living-room stove, opposite my mother, while I stood barefoot and in my nightshirt beside the stovepipe upstairs, guilt-ridden and sometimes nauseated as I heard things that were new and terrible to my ears.

Paul was premature by some eighty days, as well as Dr McCausland could determine. The shock of being struck by the snowball had brought Mrs Dempster to a series of hysterical crying fits, with which her husband was clumsily trying to cope when my mother arrived on the scene. Not long afterward it had become clear that she was about to bear her child, and Dr McCausland was sent for, but as he was elsewhere making a call he did not arrive until a quarter of an hour before the birth. Because the child was so small it came quickly, as the time for first children goes, and looked so wretched that the doctor and my mother were frightened, though they did not admit it to one another until some weeks afterward. It was characteristic of the time and the place that nobody thought to weigh the child, though the Reverend Amasa Dempster christened it immediately, after a brief wrangle with Dr McCausland. This was by no means in accord with the belief of his faith, but he was not himself and may have been acting in response to promptings stronger than seminary training. My mother said Dempster wanted to dip the child in water, but Dr McCausland brusquely forbade it, and the distracted father had to be content with sprinkling. During the ceremony my mother held the child—now named Paul, as it was the first name that came into Dempster's head—as near the stove as she could, in the hottest towels she could provide. But Paul must have weighed something in the neighbourhood of three pounds, for that was what he still weighed ten weeks later, having gained little, so far as the eye could judge, in all that time.

My mother was not one to dwell on unsightly or macabre things, but she spoke of Paul's ugliness to my father with what was almost fascination. He was red, of course; all babies are red. But he was wrinkled like a tiny old man, and his head and his back and much of his face were covered with weedy long black hair. His proportions were a shock to my mother, for his limbs were tiny and he seemed to be all head and belly. His fingers and toes were almost without nails. His cry was like the mewing of a sick kitten. But he was alive, and something had to be done about him quickly.

Dr McCausland had never met with a baby so dismayingly premature as this, but he had read of such things, and while my mother held Paul as near the fire as was safe, he and the badly shaken father set to work to build a nest that would be as much as possible like what the infant was used to. It underwent several changes, but in the end it was an affair of jeweller's cotton and hot-water bottles—assisted at the beginning by a few hot bricks—with a tent over it into which the steam from a kettle was directed; the kettle had to be watched carefully so that it might neither boil dry nor yet boil the baby. The doctor did not know what to do about feeding the child, but he and my mother worked out a combination of a glass fountain-pen filler and a scrap of soft cotton, through which they pumped diluted, sweetened milk into Paul, and Paul feebly pumped it right back out again. It was not for two days that he kept any perceptible portion of the food, but his vomiting gained a very little in strength; it was then that my mother decided that he was a fighter and determined to fight with him.

Immediately after the birth the doctor and my mother were busy with the baby. Mrs Dempster was left to the care of her husband, and he did the best he knew how for her, which was to kneel and pray out loud by her bedside. Poor Amasa Dempster was the most serious of men, and his background and training had not provided him with tact; he besought God, if He must take the soul of Mary Dempster to Him, to do so with gentleness and mercy. He reminded God that little Paul had been baptized, and that therefore the soul of the infant was secure and would be best able to journey to Heaven in the company of its mother. He laboured these themes with as much eloquence as he could summon, until Dr McCausland was compelled to read the Riot Act to him, in such terms as a tight-lipped Presbyterian uses when reading the Riot Act to an emotional Baptist. This term— "reading the Riot Act"—was my mother's; she had thoroughly approved of the doctor's performance, for she had the real Scots satisfaction in hearing somebody justifiably scolded and set to rights. "Carrying on like that, right over the girl's bed, while she was fighting for her life," she said to my father, and I could imagine the sharp shake of the head that accompanied her speech.

I wonder now if Mrs Dempster was really fighting for her life; subsequent circumstances proved that she was stronger than anybody knew. But it was an accepted belief at that time that no woman bore a child without walking very close to the brink of death, and, for anything I know to the contrary, it may have been true at that stage of medical science. But certainly it must have seemed to poor Dempster that his wife was dying. He had hung about all through the birth; he had seen his hideous, misshapen child; he had been pushed about and bustled by the doctor and the good neighbour. He was a parson, of course, but at root he was a frightened farmer lad, and if he lost his head I cannot now blame him. He was one of those people who seem fated to be hurt and thrown aside in life, but doubtless as he knelt by Mary's bed he thought himself as important an actor in the drama as any of the others. This is one of the cruelties of the theatre of life; we all think of ourselves as stars and rarely recognize it when we are indeed mere supporting characters or even supernumeraries.

What the following months cost in disorganization of our household you can imagine. My father never complained of it, for he was devoted to my mother, considered her to be a wonderful woman, and would not have done anything to prevent her from manifesting her wonderfulness. We ate many a scratch meal so that little Paul might not miss his chance with the fountain-pen filler, and when the great day came at last when the infant retained a perceptible part of what it was given, I think my father was even more pleased than my mother.

The weeks passed, and Paul's wrinkled skin became less transparent and angry, his wide-set eyes opened and roamed about, unseeing but certainly not blind, and he kicked his feet just a little, like a real baby. Would he ever be strong? Dr McCausland could not say; he was the epitome of Scots caution. But my mother's lionlike spirit was already determined that Paul should have his chance.

It was during these weeks that I endured agony of mind that seems to me, looking back over more than sixty years, to have been extraordinary. I have had hard times since then, and have endured them with all the capability for suffering of a grown man, so I do not want to make foolish and sentimental claims for the suffering of a child. But even now I hesitate to recall some of the nights when I feared to go to sleep and prayed till I sweated that God would forgive me for my mountainous crime.

I was perfectly sure, you see, that the birth of Paul Dempster, so small, so feeble and troublesome, was my fault. If I had not been so clever, so sly, so spiteful in hopping in front of the Dempsters just as Percy Boyd Staunton threw that snowball at me from behind, Mrs Dempster would not have been struck. Did I never think that Percy was guilty? Indeed I did. But a psychological difficulty arose here. When next I met him, after that bad afternoon, we approached each other warily, as boys do after a quarrel, and he seemed disposed to talk. I did not at once speak of the birth of Paul, but I crept up on the subject and was astonished to hear him say, "Yes, my Pa says McCausland has his hands full with that one."

"The baby came too soon," said I, testing him.

"Did it?" said he, looking me straight in the eyes.

"And you know why," I said.

"No I don't."

"Yes you do. You threw that snowball."

"I threw a snowball at you," he replied, "and I guess it gave you a good smack."

I could tell by the frank boldness of his tone that he was lying. "Do you mean to say that's what you think?" I said.

"You bet it's what I think," said he. "And it's what you'd better think too, if you know what's good for you."

We looked into each other's eyes and I knew that he was afraid, and I knew also that he would fight, lie, do anything rather than admit what I knew. And I didn't know what in the world I could do about it.

So I was alone with my guilt, and it tortured me. I was a Presbyterian child and I knew a good deal about damnation. We had a Dante's *Inferno* among my father's books, with the illustrations by Doré, such books were common in rural districts at that time, and probably none of us was really aware that Dante was an R.C.; it had once been a shivery pleasure to look at those pictures. Now I knew that they showed the reality of my situation, and what lay beyond this life for such a boy as I. I was of the damned. Such a phrase seems to mean nothing to people nowadays, but to me it was utterly real. I pined and wasted to some extent, and my mother was not so taken up with the Dempsters that she failed to dose me regularly with cod-liver oil. But though I did not really suffer much physically I suffered greatly in my mind, for a reason connected with my time of life. I was just upon eleven, and I matured early, so that some of the earliest changes of puberty were beginning in me.

How healthy-minded children seem to be nowadays! Or is it just the cant of our time to believe so? I cannot tell. But certainly in my childhood the common attitude towards matters of sex was enough to make a hell of adolescence for any boy who was, like myself, deeply serious and mistrustful of whatever seemed pleasurable in life. So here I was, subject not only to the smutty, whispering speculations of the other boys I knew, and tormented by the suspicion that my parents were somehow involved in this hog-wallow of sex that had begun to bulk so large in my thoughts, but I was directly responsible for a grossly sexual act—the birth of a child. And what a child! Hideous, stricken, a caricature of a living creature! In the hot craziness of my thinking, I began to believe that I was more responsible for the birth of Paul Dempster than were his parents, and that if this were ever discovered some dreadful fate would overtake me. Part of the dreadful fate would undoubtedly be rejection by my mother. I could not bear the thought, but neither could I let it alone.

My troubles became no less when, at least four months after Paul's birth, I heard this coming up the stovepipe—cooler now, for spring was well advanced:

"I think little Paul is going to pull through. He'll be slow, the doctor says, but he'll be all right."

"You must be pleased. It's mostly your doing."

"Oh no! I only did what I could. But the doctor says he hopes somebody will keep an eye on Paul. His mother certainly can't."

"She isn't coming around?"

"Doesn't appear so. It was a terrible shock for the poor little thing. And Amasa Dempster just won't believe that there's a time to talk about God and a time to trust God and keep your mouth shut. Luckily she doesn't seem to understand a lot of what he says."

"Do you mean she's gone simple?"

"She's as quiet and friendly and sweet-natured as she ever was, poor little soul, but she just isn't all there. That snowball certainly did a terrible thing to her. Who do you suppose threw it?"

"Dempster couldn't see. I don't suppose anybody will ever know."

"I've wondered more than once if Dunstable knows more about that than he's letting on."

"Oh no, he knows how serious it is. If he knew anything he'd have spoken up by now."

"Whoever it was, the Devil guided his hand."

Yes, and the Devil shifted his mark. Mrs Dempster had gone simple! I crept to bed wondering if I would live through the night, and at the same time desperately afraid to die.

18

( 5 )

Ah, if dying were all there was to it! Hell and torment at once; but at least you know where you stand. It is living with these guilty secrets that exacts the price. Yet the more time that passed, the less I was able to accuse Percy Boyd Staunton of having thrown the snowball that sent Mrs Dempster simple. His brazen-faced refusal to accept responsibility seemed to deepen my own guilt, which had now become the guilt of concealment as well as action. However, as time passed, Mrs Dempster's simplicity did not seem to be as terrible as I had at first feared.

My mother, with her unfailing good sense, hit the nail on the head when she said that Mrs Dempster was really no different from what she had been before, except that she was more so. When Amasa Dempster had brought his little bride to our village the spring before the Christmas of Paul's untimely birth, the opinion had been strong among the women that nothing would ever make a preacher's wife out of that one.

I have already said that while our village contained much of what humanity has to show, it did not contain everything, and one of the things it conspicuously lacked was an aesthetic sense; we were all too much the descendants of hard-bitten pioneers to wish for or encourage any such thing, and we gave hard names to qualities that, in a more sophisticated society, might have had value. Mrs Dempster was not pretty—we understood prettiness and guardedly admitted it as a pleasant, if needless, thing in a woman—but she had a gentleness of expression and a delicacy of colour that was uncommon. My mother, who had strong features and stood for no nonsense from her hair, said that Mrs Dempster had a face like a pan of milk. Mrs Dempster was small and slight, and even the clothes approved for a preacher's wife did not conceal the fact that she had a girlish figure and a light step. When she was pregnant there was a bloom about her that seemed out of keeping with the seriousness of her state; it was not at all the proper thing for a pregnant woman to smile so much, and the least she could have done was to take a stronger line with those waving tendrils of hair that seemed so often to be escaping from a properly severe arrangement. She was a nice little thing, but was that soft voice ever going to dominate a difficult meeting of the Ladies' Aid? And why did she laugh so much when nobody else could see anything to laugh at?

Amasa Dempster, who had always seemed a level-headed man, for a preacher, was plain silly about his wife. His eyes were always on her, and he could be seen drawing pails of water from their outside well, for the washing, when this was fully understood to be woman's work, right up to the last month or so of a pregnancy. The way he looked at her would make you wonder if the man was soft in the head. You would think they were still courting, instead of being expected to get down to the Lord's work and earn his $550 *per annum;* this was what the Baptists paid their preacher, as well as allowing him a house, not quite enough fuel, and a ten-percent discount on everything bought in a Baptist-owned store—and a few other stores that "honoured the cloth," as the saying went. (Of course he was expected to give back an exact tenth of it to the church, to set an example.) The hope was widely expressed that Mr Dempster was not going to make a fool of his wife.

In our village hard talk was not always accompanied by hard action. My mother, who could certainly never have been accused of softness with her family or the world, went out of her way to help Mrs Dempster—I will not say, to befriend her, because friendship between such unequal characters could never have been; but she tried to "show her the ropes," and whatever these mysterious feminine ropes were, they certainly included many good things that my mother cooked and just happened to leave when she dropped in on the young bride, and not merely the loan, but the practical demonstration of such devices as carpet-stretchers, racks for drying lace curtains, and the art of shining windows with newspaper.

Why had Mrs Dempster's mother never prepared her for these aspects of marriage? It came out she had been brought up by an aunt, who had money and kept a hired girl, and how were you to forge a preacher's wife from such weak metal as that? When my father teased my mother about the amount of food she took the Dempsters, she became huffy and asked if she was to allow them to starve under her nose while that girl was learning the ropes? But the girl was slow, and my mother's answer to that was that in her condition she couldn't be expected to be quick.

Now it did not seem that she would ever learn the craft of housekeeping. Her recovery from Paul's birth was tardy, and while she grew strong again her husband looked after the domestic affairs, helped by neighbour women and a Baptist widow for whose occasional services he was able to eke out a very little money. As spring came Mrs Dempster was perfectly able-bodied but showed no signs of getting down to work. She did a little cleaning and some inept cooking, and laughed like a girl at her failures. She hovered over the baby, and as he changed from a raw monster to a small but recognizably Christian-looking infant she was as delighted as a little girl with a doll. She now breast-fed him—my mother and all the neighbours had to admit that she did it well—but she lacked the solemnity they expected of a nursing mother; she enjoyed the process, and sometimes when they went into the house there she was, with everything showing, even though her husband was present, just as if she hadn't the sense to pull up her clothes. I happened upon her once or twice in this condition and gaped with the greedy eyes of an adolescent boy, but she did not seem to notice. And thus the opinion grew that Mrs Dempster was simple.

There was only one thing to be done, and that was to help the Dempsters as much as possible, without approving or encouraging any tendencies that might run contrary to the right way of doing things. My mother ordered me over to the Dempsters' to chop and pile wood, sweep away snow, cut the grass, weed the vegetable patch, and generally make myself handy two or three times a week and on Saturdays if necessary. I was also to keep an eye on the baby, for my mother could not rid herself of a dread that Mrs Dempster would allow it to choke or fall out of its basket or otherwise come to grief. There was no chance of such a thing happening, as I soon found, but obeying my instructions brought me much into the company of Mrs Dempster, who laughed at my concern for the baby. She did not seem to think that it could come to any harm in her keeping, and I know

now that she was right, and that my watchfulness must have been intrusive and clumsy.

Caring for a baby is one thing, and the many obligations of a parson's wife are another, and for this work Mrs Dempster showed no aptitude at all. By the time a year had passed since Paul's birth her husband had become "poor Reverend Dempster" to everybody, a man burdened with a simple-minded wife and a delicate child, and it was a general source of amazement that he could make ends meet. Certainly a man with $550 a year needed a thrifty wife, and Mrs Dempster gave away everything. There was a showdown once when she gave an ornamental vase to a woman who had taken her a few bakings of bread; the vase was part of the furnishings of the parsonage, not the personal property of the Dempsters, and the ladies of the church were up in arms at this act of feckless generosity and demanded of Amasa Dempster that he send his wife to the neighbour's house to ask for the vase back, and if this meant eating crow she would have to eat crow. But he would not humiliate his wife and went on the distasteful errand himself, which everyone agreed was weakness in him and would lead to worse things. One of my jobs, under instruction from my mother, was to watch for chalk marks on the Dempsters' verandah posts, and rub them out when I saw them; these chalk marks were put there by tramps as signals to one another that the house was good for a generous handout, and perhaps even money.

After a year or so most of the women in our village grew tired of pitying the Baptist parson and his wife and began to think that he was as simple as she. Like many ostracized people, they became more marked in their oddity. But my mother never wavered; her compassion was not of the short-term variety. Consequently, as they became, in a sense, charges of my family, my jobs for the Dempsters grew. My brother Willie did very little about them. He was two years older than I and his schoolwork was more demanding; further, after school hours he now went to the *Banner* printing plant to make himself useful and pick up the trade. But my mother was as watchful as ever, and my father, in whose eyes she could do nothing wrong, approved completely of all that was done.

( 6 )

Being unofficial watchdog to the Dempster family was often a nuisance to me and did nothing for my popularity. But at this time I was growing rapidly and was strong for my age, so not many of the people with whom I went to school liked to say too much to my face; but I knew that they said enough behind my back. Percy Boyd Staunton was one of these.

He had a special place in our school world. There are people who, even as boys, assume superior airs and are taken as grandees by those around them. He was as big as I, and rather fleshy; without being a fat boy he was plump. His clothes were better than ours, and he had an interesting pocket-knife, with a chain on it to fasten to his knicker-bockers, and an ink-bottle you could knock over without spilling a drop; on Sundays he wore a suit with a fashionable half-belt at the back. He had once been to Toronto to the Exhibition, and altogether breathed a larger air than the rest of us.

He and I were rivals, for though I had none of his graces of person or wealth I had a sharp tongue. I was raw-boned and wore clothes that had often made an earlier appearance on Willie, but I had a turn for sarcastic remarks, which were known to our group as "good ones." If I was pushed too far I might "get off a good one," and as our community had a long memory such dour witticisms would be remembered and quoted for years.

I had a good one all ready for Percy, if ever he gave me any trouble. I had heard his mother tell my mother that when he was a dear little fellow, just learning to talk, his best version of his name, Percy Boyd, was Pidgy Boy-Boy, and she still called him that in moments of unbuttoned affection. I knew that I had but once to call him Pidgy Boy-Boy in the schoolyard and his goose would be cooked; probably suicide would be his only way out. This knowledge gave me a sense of power in reserve.

I needed it. Some of the oddity and loneliness of the Dempsters was beginning to rub off on me. Having double chores to do kept me out of many a game I would have liked to join; dodging back and forth between their house and ours with this, that, and the other thing, I was sure to meet some of my friends; Mrs Dempster often stood in the door when I was running home, waving and thanking me in a voice that seemed to me eerie and likely to bring mockery down on my head, not hers, if anybody overheard her, as they often did. I knew that some of them had nicknamed me Nursie. They did not call me that to my face, however.

My position here was worst of all. I wanted to be on good terms with the girls I knew; I suppose I wanted them to admire me and think me wonderful in some unspecified way. Enough of them were silly about Percy and sent him mash Valentines on February 14, without any names on them but with handwriting that betrayed the sender. No girl ever sent me a Valentine except Elsie Webb, known to us all as Spider Webb because of her gawky, straddling walk. I did not want Spider Webb, I wanted Leola Cruikshank, who had cork-screw curls and a great way of never meeting your eyes. But my feeling about Leola was put askew by my feeling about Mrs Dempster. Leola I wanted as a trophy of success, but Mrs Dempster was beginning to fill my whole life, and the stranger her conduct became, and the more the village pitied and dismissed her, the worse my obsession grew.

I thought I was in love with Leola, by which I meant that if I could have found her in a quiet corner, and if I had been certain that no one would ever find out, and if I could have summoned up the courage at the right moment, I would have kissed her. But, looking back on it now, I know I was in love with Mrs Dempster. Not as some boys are in love with grown-up women, adoring them from afar and enjoying a fantasy life in which the older woman figures in an idealized form, but in a painful and immediate fashion; I saw her every day, I did menial tasks in her house, and I was charged to watch her and keep her from doing foolish things. Furthermore, I felt myself tied to her by the certainty that I was responsible for her straying wits, the disorder of her marriage, and the frail body of the child who was her great delight in life. I had made her what she was, and in such circumstances I must hate her or love her. In a mode that was far too demanding for my age or experience, I loved her.

Loving her, I had to defend her, and when people said she was crazy I had to force myself to tell them that they were crazy themselves and I would knock their blocks off if they said it again. Fortunately one of the first people with whom I had such an encounter was Milo Papple, and he was not hard to deal with.

Milo was our school buffoon, the son of Myron Papple, the village barber. Barbers in more sophisticated communities are sometimes men with rich heads of hair, or men who have given a special elegance to a bald head, but Myron Papple had no such outward grace. He was a short, fat, pear-shaped man with the complexion and hair of a pig of the Chester White breed. He had but one distinction; he put five sticks of gum into his mouth every morning and chewed the wad until he closed his shop in the evening, breathing peppermint on each customer as he shaved, clipped, and talked.

Milo was his father in miniature, and admitted by us all to be a card. His repertoire of jokes was small but of timeless durability. He could belch at will, and did. He could also break wind at will, with a prolonged, whining note of complaint, and when he did so in class and then looked around with an angry face, whispering, "Who done that?" our mirth was Chaucerian, and the teacher was reduced to making a refined face, as if she were too good for a world in which such things were possible. Even the girls—even Leola Cruikshank— thought Milo was a card.

One day I was asked if I would play ball after school. I said I had to do some work.

"Sure," said Milo, "Dunny's got to get right over to the bughouse and cut the grass."

"The bughouse?" asked a few who were slow of wit.

"Yep. The Dempsters'. That's the bughouse now."

It was now or never for me. "Milo," I said, "if you ever say that again I'll get a great big cork and stick it up you, and then nobody'll ever laugh at you again." As I said this I walked menacingly towards him, and as soon as Milo backed away I knew I was the victor, for the moment. The joke about Milo and the cork was frugally husbanded by our collectors of funny sayings, and he was not allowed to forget it. "If you stuck a cork in Milo nobody would ever laugh at him again," these unashamed gleaners of the fields of repartee would say and shout with laughter. Nobody said "bughouse" to me for a long time, but sometimes I could see that they wanted to say it, and I knew they said it behind my back. This increased my sense of isolation—of being forced out of the world I belonged to into the strange and unchancy world of the Dempsters.

## ( 7 )

The passing of time brought other isolations. At thirteen I should have been learning the printing business; my father was neat-handed and swift, and Willie was following in his steps. But I was all thumbs in the shop, slow to learn the layout of the frames in which the fonts of type were distributed, clumsy at locking up a forme, messy with ink, a great spoiler of paper, and really not much good at anything but cutting reglet or reading proof, which my father never trusted to anyone but himself in any case. I never mastered the printer's trick of reading things upside down and backward, and I never properly learned how to fold a sheet. Altogether I was a nuisance in the shop, and as this humiliated me, and my father was a kindly man, he sought some other honourable work to keep me from under his feet. It had been suggested that our village library should be open a few afternoons a week so that the more responsible schoolchildren might use it, and somebody was needed to serve as under-librarian, the real librarian being busy as a teacher during the daytime and not relishing the loss of so much of her free time. I was appointed to this job, at a salary of nothing at all, the honour being deemed sufficient reward.

This suited me admirably. Three afternoons a week I opened our one-room library in the upstairs of the Town Hall and lorded it over any schoolchildren who appeared. Once I had the dizzy pleasure of finding something in the encyclopaedia for Leola Cruikshank, who had to write an essay about the equator and didn't know whether it went over the top or round the middle. More afternoons than not, nobody appeared, or else those who came went away as soon as they found what they wanted, and I had the library to myself.

It was not much of a collection—perhaps fifteen hundred books in all, of which roughly a tenth part were for children. The annual budget was twenty-five dollars, and much of that went on subscriptions to magazines that the magistrate, who was chairman of the board, wanted to read. Acquisitions, therefore, were usually gifts from the estates of people who had died, and our local auctioneer gave us any books that he could not sell; we kept what we wanted and sent the rest to the Grenfell Mission, on the principle that savages would read anything.

The consequence was that we had some odd things, of which the oddest were kept in a locked closet off the main room. There was a medical book, with a frightful engraving of a fallen womb, and another of a varicocele, and a portrait of a man with lavish hair and whiskers but no nose, which made me a lifelong enemy of syphilis. My special treasures were *The Secrets of Stage Conjuring* by Robert-Houdin and *Modern Magic* and *Later Magic* by Professor Hoffmann; they had been banished as uninteresting—uninteresting!—and as soon as I saw them I knew that fate meant them for me. By studying them I should become a conjurer, astonish everybody, win the breathless admiration of Leola Cruikshank, and become a great power. I immediately hid them in a place where they could not fall into the hands of unworthy persons, including our librarian, and devoted myself to the study of magic.

I still look back upon those hours when I acquainted myself with the means by which a French conjurer had astonished the subjects of Louis-Napoleon as an era of Arcadian pleasure. It did not matter that everything about the book was hopelessly old-fashioned; great as the gap between me and Robert-Houdin was, I could accept his world as the real world, so far as the wonderful art of deception was concerned. When he insisted on the necessity of things that were unknown to Deptford, I assumed that it was because Deptford was a village and Paris was a great and sophisticated capital, where everybody who was anybody was mad for conjuring and wanted nothing more than to be delightfully bamboozled by an elegant, slightly sinister, but wholly charming master of the art. It did not surprise me in the least that Robert-Houdin's Emperor had sent him on a special diplomatic mission to Algiers, to destroy the power of the marabouts by showing that his magic was greater than theirs. When I read of his feat on the Shah of Turkey's yacht, when he hammered the Shah's jewelled watch to ruins in a mortar, then threw the rubbish overboard, cast a line into the sea, pulled up a fish, asked the Shah's chef to clean it, and stood by while the chef discovered the watch, quite unharmed, enclosed in a silk bag in the entrails of the fish, I felt that this was life as it ought to be lived. Conjurers were obviously fellows of the first importance and kept distinguished company. I would be one of them.

The Scottish practicality that I had imitated from my parents was not really in grain with me; I cared too little for difficulties. I admitted to myself that Deptford was unlikely to yield a conjurer's table—a gilded *guéridon*, with a cunning *servante* on the back of it for storing things one did not wish to have seen, and a *gibecière* into which coins and watches could noiselessly be dropped; I had no tailcoat, and if I had I doubt if my mother would have sewn a proper conjurer's *profonde* in the tails, for disappearing things. When Professor Hoffmann instructed me to fold back my cuffs, I knew that I had no cuffs, but did not care. I would devote myself to illusions that did not require such things. These illusions, I discovered, called for special apparatus, always described by the Professor as "simple," which the conjurer was advised to make himself. For me, a boy who always tied his shoelaces backward and whose Sunday tie looked like a hangman's noose, such apparatus presented a problem that I had to admit, after a few tries, was insuperable. Nor could I do anything about the tricks that required "a few substances, easily obtainable from any chemist," because Ruckle's drugstore had never heard of any of them. But I was not defeated. I would excel in the realm which Robert-Houdin said was the truest, most classical form of conjuring: I would be a master of sleight-of-hand, a matchless *prestidigitateur*.

It was like me to begin with eggs—or, to be precise, one egg. It never occurred to me that a clay egg, of the kind used to deceive hens, would do just as well. I hooked an egg from my mother's kitchen and when the library was empty began to practise producing it from my mouth, elbow, and back of the knee; also putting it into my right ear and, after a little henlike clucking, removing it from my left. I seemed to be getting on splendidly, and when the magistrate made a sudden appearance to get the latest of *Scribner's* I had a mad moment when I thought of amazing him by taking an egg out of his beard. Of course I did not dare to go so far, but the delightful thought that I could if I wanted to put me into such a fit of giggles that he looked at me speculatively. When he was gone I handled the egg with greater boldness until, disappearing it into my hip pocket, I put my thumb through it.

Ha ha. Every boy has experiences of this kind, and they are usually thought to be funny and childlike. But that egg led to a dreadful row with my mother. She had missed the egg—it never occurred to me that anybody counted eggs—and accused me of taking it. I lied. Then she caught me trying to wash out my pocket, because, in a house with no running water, washing cannot be a really private business. She exposed my lie and demanded to know what I wanted with an egg. Now, how can a boy of thirteen tell a Scotswoman widely admired for her practicality that he intends to become the world's foremost *prestidigitateur*? I took refuge in mute insolence. She stormed. She demanded to know if I thought she was made of eggs. Visited unhappily by a good one, I said that was something she would have to decide for herself. My mother had little sense of humour. She told me that if I thought I had grown too old to be beaten she would show me I was mistaken, and from the kitchen cupboard she produced the pony whip.

It was not for ponies. In my boyhood such pretty little whips were sold at country fairs, where children bought them, and flourished them, and occasionally beat trees with them. But a few years earlier my mother had impounded such a whip that Willie had brought home, and it had been used for beatings ever since. It had been at least two years since I had had a beating, but now my mother flourished the whip, and when I laughed she struck me over the left shoulder with it.

"Don't you dare touch me," I shouted, and that put her into such a fury as I had never known. It must have been a strange scene, for she pursued me around the kitchen, slashing me with the whip until she broke me down and I cried. She cried too, hysterically, and beat me harder, storming about my impudence, my want of respect for her, of my increasing oddity and intellectual arrogance—not that she used these words, but I do not intend to put down what she actually said—until at last her fury was spent, and she ran upstairs in tears and banged the door of her bedroom. I crept off to the woodshed, a criminal, and wondered what I should do. Become a tramp, perhaps, like the shabby, sinister fellows who came so often to our back door for a handout? Hang myself? I have been very miserable since— miserable not for an hour but for months on end—but I can still feel that hour's misery in its perfect desolation, if I am fool enough to call it up in my mind.

My father and Willie came home, and there was no supper. Naturally he sided with her, and Willie was very officious and knowing about how intolerable I had become of late, and how thrashing was too good for me. Finally it was settled that my mother would come downstairs if I would beg pardon. This I had to do on my knees, repeating a formula improvised by my father, which included a pledge that I would always love my mother, to whom I owed the great gift of life, and that I begged her—and secondarily God—to forgive me, knowing full well that I was unworthy of such clemency.

I rose from my knees cleansed and purged, and ate very little supper, as became a criminal. When it came time for me to go to bed my mother beckoned me to her, and kissed me, and whispered, "I know I'll never have another anxious moment with my own dear laddie."

I pondered these words before I went to sleep. How could I reconcile this motherliness with the screeching fury who had pursued me around the kitchen with a whip, flogging me until she was gorged with—what?—Vengeance? What was it? Once, when I was in my thirties and reading Freud for the first time, I thought I knew. I am not so sure I know now. But what I knew then was that nobody—not even my mother—was to be trusted in a strange world that showed very little of itself on the surface.

( 8 )

Instead of sickening me of magic, this incident increased my appetite for it. It was necessary for me to gain power in some realm into which my parents—my mother particularly—could not follow me. Of course, I did not think about the matter logically; sometimes I yearned for my mother's love and hated myself for having grieved her, but quite as often I recognized that her love had a high price on it and that her idea of a good son was a pretty small potato. So I drudged away secretly at the magic.

It was card tricks now. I had no trouble getting a pack of cards, for my parents were great players of euchre, and of the several packs in the house I could spirit away the oldest for a couple of hours any afternoon, if I replaced it at the back of the drawer where it was kept, as being too good to throw away but too slick and supple to use. Having only the one pack, I could not attempt any tricks that needed two cards of the same suit and value, but I mastered a few of those chestnuts in which somebody chooses a card and the conjurer finds it after much shuffling; I even had a beauty, involving a silk thread, in which the chosen card hopped from the deck as the conjurer stood nonchalantly at a distance.

I needed an audience, to judge how well I was doing, and I found one readily in Paul Dempster. He was four, and I was fourteen, so on the pretext of looking after him for an hour or two I would take him to the library and entertain him with my tricks. He was not a bad audience, for he sat solemn and mute when he was bidden, chose cards at my command, and if I presented the deck to him with one card slightly protruding, while I held the deck tight, that was the card he invariably chose. He had his faults; he could neither read nor count, and so he did not relish the full wonder of it when I produced his card triumphantly after tremendous shufflings, but I knew that I had deceived him and told him so. In fact, my abilities as a teacher had their first airing in that little library, and as I was fond of lecturing I taught Paul more than I suspected.

Of course he wanted to play too, and it was not easy to explain that I was not playing but demonstrating a fascinating and involved science. I had to work out a system of rewards, and as he liked stories I read to him after he had watched me do my tricks.

Luckily we both liked the same book. It was a pretty volume I found in the cupboard of banished books, called *A Child's Book of*

*Saints.* It was the work of one William Canton, and it began with a conversation between a little girl and her father, which I thought a model of elegant writing. I can quote passages from it still, for I used to read and reread them to Paul, and he, with the memory of a non-reader, could repeat them by heart. Here is one, and I am sure that though I have not read it for fifty years, I have it right:

Occasionally these legends brought us to the awful brink of religious controversies and insoluble mysteries, but, like those gentle savages who honour the water-spirits by hanging garlands from tree to tree across the river, W.V.—[W.V. was the little girl]—could always fling a bridge of flowers over our abysses. "Our sense," she would declare, "is nothing to God's; and though big people have more sense than children, the sense of all the big people in the world put together would be no sense to His." "We are only little babies to Him; we do not understand Him at all." Nothing seemed clearer to her than the reasonableness of one legend which taught that though God always answers our prayers, He does not always answer in the way we would like, but in some better way than we know. "Yes," she observed, "He is just a dear old Father." Anything about our Lord engrossed her imagination; and it was a frequent wish of hers that He would come again. "Then,"—poor perplexed little mortal! whose difficulties one could not even guess at—"we should be quite sure of things. Miss Catherine tells us from books: He would tell us from His memory. People would not be so cruel to Him now. Queen Victoria would not allow any one to crucify Him."

There was a picture of Queen Victoria hanging in the library, and one look at her would tell you that anybody under her protection was in luck.

Thus for some months I used Paul as a model audience, and paid him off in stories about St Dorothea and St Francis, and let him look at the pretty pictures, which were by Heath Robinson.

I progressed from cards to coins, which were vastly more difficult. For one thing, I had very few coins, and when my books of instructions said, "Secure and palm six half-crowns," I was stopped dead, for I had no half-crowns or anything that looked like them. I had one handsome piece—it was a brass medal that the linotype company had prepared to advertise its machines, which my father did not want—and as it was about the size of a silver dollar I practised with that. But oh, what clumsy hands I had!

I cannot guess now how many weeks I worked on the sleight-of-hand pass called The Spider. To perform this useful bit of trickery, you nip a coin between your index and little fingers, and then revolve it by drawing the two middle fingers back and forth, in front or behind it; by this means it is possible to show both sides of the hand without revealing the coin. But just try to do it! Try it with red, knuckly Scots hands, stiffened by grass-cutting and snow-shovelling, and see what skill you develop! Of course Paul wanted to know what I was doing, and, being a teacher at heart, I told him.

"Like this?" he asked, taking the coin from me and performing the pass perfectly.

I was stunned and humiliated, but, looking back on it now, I think I behaved pretty well.

"Yes, like that," I said, and though it took me a few days to realize it, that was the moment I became Paul's instructor. He could do anything with his hands. He could shuffle cards without dropping them, which was something I could never be sure of, and he could do marvels with my big brass medal. His hands were small, so that the coin was usually visible, but it was seen to be doing something interesting; he could make it walk over the back of his hand, nipping it between the fingers with a dexterity that left me gasping.

There was no sense in envying him; he had the hands and I had not, and although there were times when I considered killing him, just to rid the world of a precocious nuisance, I could not overlook that fact. The astonishing thing was that he regarded me as his teacher because I could read and tell him what to do; the fact that he could do it did not impress him. He was grateful, and I was in a part of my life where gratitude and admiration, even from such a thing as Paul, were very welcome.

If it seems cruel to write "such a thing as Paul," let me explain myself. He was an odd-looking little mortal, with an unusually big head for his frail body. His clothes never seemed to fit him; many of them were reach-me-downs from Baptist families, and because his mother was so unhandy they always had holes in them and were ravelled at the edges and ill-buttoned. He had a lot of curly brown hair, because his mother kept begging Amasa Dempster to put off the terrible day when Paul would go to Myron Papple for the usual boy's scalping. His eyes seemed big in his little face, and certainly they were unusually wide apart, and looked dark because his thin skin was so white. My mother was worried about that pallor and occasionally took charge of Paul and wormed him—a humiliation children did not seem to need any more. Paul was not a village favourite, and the dislike so many people felt for his mother—dislike for the queer and persistently unfortunate—they attached to the unoffending son.

( 9 )

My own dislike was kept for Amasa Dempster. A few of his flock said that he walked very closely with God, and it made him spooky. We had family prayers at home, a respectful salute to Providence before breakfast, enough for anybody. But he was likely to drop on his knees at any time and pray with a fervour that seemed indecent. Because I was often around their house I sometimes stumbled on one of these occasions, and he would motion me to kneel with them until he was finished—which could be as much as ten or fifteen minutes later. Sometimes he mentioned me; I was the stranger within their gates, and I knew he was telling God what a good job I did on the grass and the woodpile; but he usually got in a dig at the end, when he asked God to preserve me from walking with a froward mouth, by which he meant my little jokes to coax a laugh or a smile from his wife. And he never finished without asking God for strength to bear his heavy cross, by which I knew that he meant Mrs Dempster; she knew it too.

This was the only unkindness he ever offered her. In everything else he was patient and, so far as his spirit permitted, loving. But before Paul's birth he had loved her because she was the blood of his heart; now he seemed to love her on principle. I do not think he knew that he was hinting to God to notice the meek spirit in which he bore his ill luck, but that was the impression his prayers left on my mind.

He was no skilled rhetorician, and the poor man had nothing much in the way of brains, so very often what he felt came out more clearly than what he meant to say.

His quality of feeling was weighty. I suppose this is what made him acceptable to the Baptists, who valued feeling very highly—much more highly than we Presbyterians, who were scared of it and tried to swap it for intellect. I got the strength of his feeling one awful day when he said to me:

"Dunny, come with me to my study in the church. I want a word with you."

Wondering what on earth all this solemnity was about, I tagged along with him to the Baptist church, where we went to the tiny parson's room beside the baptismal tank. The first thing he did was to drop to his knees and ask God to assist him to be just but not unkind, and then he went to work on me.

I had brought corruption into the innocent world of childhood. I had offended against one of God's little ones. I had been the agent—unknowingly, he hoped—by means of which the Evil One had trailed his black slime across a pure life.

Of course I was frightened. There were boys and girls known to me who made occasional trips to the groves of trees in the old gravel pit that lay to the west of our village and gave themselves up to exploratory pawing. One of these, a Mabel Heighington, was rumoured to have gone the limit with more than one boy. But I was not of this group; I was too scared of being found out, and also, I must say in justice to my young self, too fastidious, to want the pimply Heighington slut; I preferred my intense, solitary adoration of Leola Cruikshank to such frowzy rough-and-tumble. But all boys used to be open to accusation on matters of sex; their thoughts alone, to say nothing of half-willing, half-disgusted action, incriminated them before themselves. I thought someone must have given him my name to divert attention from the others.

I was wrong. After the preliminary mysterious talk it came out that he was accusing me of putting playing-cards—he called them the Devil's picture-book—into the hands of his son Paul. But worse—much worse than that—I had taught the boy to cheat with the cards, to handle them like a smoking-car gambler, and also to play deceptive tricks with money. That very morning there had been three cents' change from the baker's visit, and Paul had picked them up from the table and caused them to vanish! Of course he had restored them—utter corruption had not yet set in—and after a beating and much prayer it had all come out about the cards and what I had taught him.

This was bad enough, but worse was to follow. Papistry! I had been telling Paul stories about saints, and if I did not know that the veneration of saints was one of the vilest superstitions of the Scarlet Woman of Rome, he was going to have a word with the Presbyterian minister, the Reverend Andrew Bowyer, to make sure I found out. Under conviction of his wickedness Paul had come out with blasphemous stuff about somebody who had spent his life praying on a pillar forty feet high, and St Francis who saw a living Christ on a crucifix, and St Mary of the Angels, and more of the same kind, that had made his blood freeze to hear. Now—what was it to be? Would I take the beating I deserved from him, or was he to tell my parents and leave it to them to do their duty?

I was a boy of fifteen at this time, and I did not propose to take a beating from him, and if my parents beat me I would run away and become a tramp. So I told him he had better tell my parents.

This disconcerted him, for he had been a parson long enough to know that complaints to parents about their children were not always gratefully received. I was bold enough to say that maybe he had better do as he threatened and speak to Mr Bowyer. This was good argument, for our minister was not a man to like advice from Amasa Dempster, and though he would have given me the rough side of his tongue, he would first have eaten the evangelistic Baptist parson without salt. Poor Dempster! He had lost the fight, so he took refuge in banishing me. I was never to set foot in his house again, he said, nor speak to any of his family, nor dare to come near his son. He would pray for me, he concluded.

I left the church in a strange state of mind, for a Deptford boy, though I learned later in life that it was common enough. I did not feel I had done wrong, though I had been a fool to forget how dead set Baptists were against cards. As for the stories about saints, they were tales of wonders, like *Arabian Nights,* and when the Reverend Andrew Bowyer bade all us Presbyterians to prepare ourselves for the Marriage Feast of the Lamb, it seemed to me that *Arabian Nights* and the *Bible* were getting pretty close—and I did not mean this in any scoffing sense. I was most hurt that Dempster had dragged down my conjuring to mere cheating and gambling; it had seemed to me to be a splendid extension of life, a creation of a world of wonder, that hurt nobody. All that dim but glittering vision I had formed of Paris, with Robert-Houdin doing marvels to delight grand people, had been dragged down by this Deptford parson, who knew nothing of such things and just hated whatever did not belong to life at the $550-a-year level. I wanted a better life than that. But I had been worsted by moral bullying, by Dempster's conviction that he was right and I was wrong, and that gave him an authority over me based on feeling rather than reason: it was my first encounter with the emotional power of popular morality.

In my bitterness I ill-wished Amasa Dempster. This was a terrible thing to do, and I knew it. In my parents' view of life, superstition was trash for ignorant people, but they had a few reservations, and one was that it was very unlucky to ill-wish anybody. The evil wish would surely rebound upon the wisher. But I ill-wished Dempster; I begged Somebody—some God who understood me—that he should be made very sorry for the way he had talked to me.

He said nothing to my parents, nor yet to Mr Bowyer. I interpreted his silence as weakness, and probably that was an important element in it. I saw him now, a few times each week, at a distance, and it seemed to me that the burdens of his life were bearing him down. He did not stoop, but he looked gaunter and crazier. Paul I saw only once, and he turned away from me and ran towards his home, crying; I was terribly sorry for him. But Mrs Dempster I saw often, for she had intensified her roaming and would spend a whole morning wandering from house to house—"traipsing" was the word many of the women now used—offering bunches of wilted rhubarb, or some rank lettuce, or other stuff from her garden, which was so ill tended without me that nothing did well in it. But she wanted to give things away and was hurt when neighbours refused these profferings. Her face wore a sweet but woefully un-Deptford expression; it was too clear that she did not know where she was going next, and sometimes she would visit one house three times in a morning, to the annoyance of a busy woman who was washing or getting a meal for her husband and sons.

When I think of my mother now, I try to remember her as she was in her dealings with Mrs Dempster. A poor actress, she nevertheless feigned pleasure over the things that were given and always insisted that something be taken in return, usually something big and lasting. She always remembered what Mrs Dempster had brought and told her how good it had been, though usually it was only fit to be thrown away.

"The poor soul dearly loves to give," she said to my father, "and it would be wicked to deny her. The pity is that more people with more to give don't feel the same way."

I avoided direct meetings with Mrs Dempster, for she would say, "Dunstable Ramsay, you've almost grown to be a man. Why don't you come to see us any more? Paul misses you; he tells me so."

She had forgotten, or perhaps she never knew, that her husband had warned me away. I never saw her without a pang of guilt and concern about her. But for her husband I had no pity.


( 10 )


Mrs Dempster's wanderings came to an end on Friday 24 October 1913. It was almost ten o'clock at night and I was reading by the stove, as was my father; my mother sewed—something for the Mission Circle bazaar—and Willie was at a practice of a Youth Band a local enthusiast had organized; Willie played the cornet and had his eye on the first flute, one Ada Blake. When the knock came at the door my father went, and after some quiet muttering asked the callers to come in while he put on his boots. They were Jim Warren, who was our part-time village policeman, and George and Garnet Harper, a couple of practical jokers who on this occasion looked unwontedly solemn.

"Mary Dempster's disappeared," my father explained. "Jim's organizing a hunt."

"Yep, been gone since after supper," said the policeman. "Reverend come home at nine and she was gone. Nowheres round the town, and now we're goin' to search the pit. If she's not there we'll have to drag the river."

"You'd better go along with your father," said my mother to me. "I'll get right over to Dempsters' and keep an eye on Paul, and be ready when you bring her home."

Much was implied in that speech. In the instant my mother had acknowledged me as a man, fit to go on serious business. She had shown also that she knew that I was as concerned about the Dempsters, perhaps, as herself; there had been no questions about why I had not been going there to do the chores for the past few months. I am sure my parents knew Amasa Dempster had warned me away and had assumed that it was part of the crazy pride and self-sufficiency that had been growing on him. But if Mrs Dempster was lost at night, all daylight considerations must be set aside. There was a good deal of the pioneer left in people in those days, and they knew what was serious.

I darted off to get the flashlight; my father had recently bought a car—rather a daring thing in Deptford at that time—and a large flashlight was kept in the tool-kit on the runningboard, in case we should be benighted with a flat tire.

We made for the pit, where ten or twelve men were already assembled. I was surprised to see Mr Mahaffey, our magistrate, among them. He and the policeman were our law, and his presence meant grave public concern.

This gravel pit was of unusual importance to our village because it completely blocked any normal extension of streets or houses on our western side; thus it was a source of indignation to our village council. However, it belonged to the railway company, which valued it as a source of the gravel they needed for keeping their roadbed in order, and which they excavated and hauled considerable distances up and down the track. How big it was I do not accurately know, but it was big, and prejudice made it seem bigger. It was not worked consistently and so was often undisturbed for a year or more at a time; in it there were pools, caused by seepage from the river, which it bordered, and a lot of scrub growth, sumac, sallow, Manitoba maple, and such unprofitable things, as well as goldenrod and kindred trashy weeds.

Mothers hated it because sometimes little children strayed into it and were hurt, and big children sneaked into it and met the like of Mabel Heighington. But most of all it was disliked because it was a refuge for the tramps who rode the rods of the railway. Some of these were husky young fellows; others were old men, or men who seemed old, in ragged greatcoats belted with a piece of rope or a strap, wearing hats of terrible dilapidation, and giving off a stench of feet, sweat, faeces, and urine that would have staggered a goat. They were mighty drinkers of flavouring extracts and liniments that had a heavy alcohol base. All of them were likely to appear at a back door and ask for food. In their eyes was the dazed, stunned look of people who live too much in the open air without eating properly. They were generally given food and generally feared as lawless men.

In later life I have been sometimes praised, sometimes mocked, for my way of pointing out the mythical elements that seem to me to underlie our apparently ordinary lives. Certainly that cast of mind had some of its origin in our pit, which had much the character of a Protestant Hell. I was probably the most entranced listener to a sermon the Reverend Andrew Bowyer preached about Gehenna, the hateful valley outside the walls of Jerusalem, where outcasts lived, and where their flickering fires, seen from the city walls, may have given rise to the idea of a hell of perpetual burning. He liked to make his hearers jump, now and then, and he said that our gravel pit was much the same sort of place as Gehenna. My elders thought this far-fetched, but I saw no reason then why hell should not have, so to speak, visible branch establishments throughout the earth, and I have visited quite a few of them since.

Under the direction of Jim Warren and Mr Mahaffey it was agreed that fifteen of us would scramble down into the pit and form a line, leaving twenty or thirty feet between each man, and advance from end to end. Anybody who found a clue was to give a shout. As we searched there was quite a lot of sound, for I think most of the men wanted any tramps to know we were coming and get out of the way; nobody liked the idea of coming on a tramps' bivouac—they were called "jungles," which made them seem more terrible—unexpectedly. We had seen only two fires, at the far end of the pit, but there could be quite a group of tramps without a fire.

My father was thirty feet on my left, and a big fellow named Ed Hainey on my right, as I walked through the pit. In spite of the nearness of the men it was lonely work, and though there was a moon it was waning and the light was poor. I was afraid and did not know what I feared, which is the worst kind of fear. We might have gone a quarter of a mile when I came to a clump of sallow. I was about to skirt it when I heard a stirring inside it. I made a sound—I am sure it was not a yell—that brought my father beside me in an instant. He shot the beam of his flashlight into the scrub, and in that bleak, flat light we saw a tramp and a woman in the act of copulation. The tramp rolled over and gaped at us in terror; the woman was Mrs Dempster.

It was Hainey who gave a shout, and in no time all the men were with us, and Jim Warren was pointing a pistol at the tramp, ordering him to put his hands up. He repeated the words two or three times, and then Mrs Dempster spoke.

"You'll have to speak very loudly to him, Mr Warren," she said, "he's hard of hearing."

I don't think any of us knew where to look when she spoke, pulling her skirts down but remaining on the ground. It was at that moment that the Reverend Amasa Dempster joined us; I had not noticed him when the hunt began, though he must have been there. He behaved with great dignity, leaning forward to help his wife rise with the same sort of protective love I had seen in him the night Paul was born. But he was not able to keep back his question.

"Mary, what made you do it?"

She looked him honestly in the face and gave the answer that became famous in Deptford: "He was very civil, 'Masa. And he wanted it so badly."

He put her arm under his and set out for home, just as if they were going for a walk. Under Mr Mahaffey's direction, Jim Warren took the tramp off to the lock-up. The rest of us dispersed without a word.

( 11 )

Dempster visited Mr Mahaffey early on Saturday and said that he would lay no charge and take part in no trial, so the magistrate took council with my father and a few other wise heads and told Jim Warren to get the tramp off the village bounds, with a warning never to be seen there again.

The real trial would come on Sunday, and everybody knew it. The buzzing and humming were intense all day Saturday, and at church on Sunday everybody who was not a Baptist was aching to know what would happen at the Baptist service. The Reverend Andrew Bowyer prayed for "all who were distressed in spirit, and especially for a family known to us all who were in sore travail," and something of a similar intention was said in the Anglican and Methodist churches. Only Father Regan at the Catholic church came out flat-footed and said from his pulpit that the gravel pit was a disgrace and a danger and that the railway had its nerve not to clean it up or close it up. But when we heard about that, everybody knew it was beside the point. Mrs Dempster had given her consent. That was the point. Supposing she was a little off her head, how insane had a woman to be before it came to that? Dr McCausland, appealed to on the steps of our church by some seekers after truth, said that such conduct indicated a degeneration of the brain, which was probably progressive.

We soon knew what the Baptist parson said that morning: he went into his pulpit, prayed silently for a short time, and then told his congregation that the time had come for him to resign his charge, as he had other duties that were incapable of being combined with it. He asked for their prayers, and went into his study. A prominent member of the congregation, a baker, took charge and turned the service into a meeting; the baker and a few other men were asking the parson to wait a while, but the majority was against them, especially the women. Not that any of the women spoke; they had done their speaking before church, and their husbands knew the price of peace. So at last the baker and one or two others had to go into the study and tell Amasa Dempster that his resignation was accepted. He left the church without any prospects, a crazy and disgraced wife, a delicate child, and six dollars in cash. There were several men who wanted to do something for him, but the opinion of their wives made it impossible.

There was a terrible quarrel in our household—the more terrible because I had never heard my parents disagree when they knew that Willie and I could hear them; what I heard by way of the stovepipe sometimes amounted to disagreement but never to a quarrel. My father accused my mother of wanting charity; she replied that as the mother of two boys she had standards of decency to defend. That was the meat of the quarrel, but before it had gone very far it reached a point where she said that if he was going to stand up for filthy behaviour and adultery he was a long way from the man she had married, and he was saying that he had never known she had a cruel streak. (I could have told him something about that.) This battle went on at Sunday dinner and drove Willie, who was the least demonstrative of fellows, to throw down his napkin and exclaim, "Oh, for the love of the crows!" and leave the table. I dared not follow, and as my parents' wrath grew I was numbed with misery.

Of course my mother won. If my father had not given in he would have had to live with outraged female virtue for—perhaps the rest of his life. As things were, I do not believe that she ever gave up a suspicion that he was not as firm in his moral integrity as she had once believed. Mrs Dempster had transgressed in a realm where there could be no shades of right and wrong. And the reason she had offered for doing so—!

That was what stuck in the craws of all the good women of Deptford: Mrs Dempster had not been raped, as a decent woman would have been—no, she had yielded because a man wanted her. The subject was not one that could be freely discussed even among intimates, but it was understood without saying that if women began to yield for such reasons as that, marriage and society would not last long. Any man who spoke up for Mary Dempster probably believed in Free Love. Certainly he associated sex with pleasure, and that put him in a class with filthy thinkers like Cece Athelstan.

Cecil Athelstan—always known as Cece—was the black sheep of our ruling family. He was a fat, swag-bellied boozer who sat in a chair on the sidewalk outside the Tecumseh House bar when the weather was fine, and on the same chair inside the bar when it was not. Once a month, when he got his cheque, he went for a night or two to Detroit, across the border, and, according to his own account, he was the life and soul of the bawdy houses there. Foul-mouthed bum though he was, he had enough superiority of experience and native wit to hold a small group of loafers in awe, and his remarks, sometimes amusing, were widely quoted, even by people who disapproved of him.

Mrs Dempster's answer was a gift to a man like Cece. "Hey!" he would shout across the street to one of his cronies, "you feeling civil today? I feel so God-damned civil I got to get to Detroit right away— or maybe just up to You Know Who's!" Or as some respectable woman passed on the other side of the street from the hotel he would sing out, just loud enough to be heard, "I wa-a-ant it! Hey, Cora, I want it so-o-o!" The strange thing was that the behaviour of this licensed fool made the enormity of Mrs Dempster's words greater, but did not lower the town's esteem of Cece Athelstan—probably because it could go no lower.

At school there were several boys who pestered me for descriptions, with anatomical detail, of what I had seen in the pit. I had no trouble silencing them, but of course Cece and his gang lay beyond my power. It was Cece, with some of his crowd, and the Harper boys (who ought to have known better) who organized the shivaree when the Dempsters moved. Amasa Dempster got out of the Baptist parsonage on the Tuesday after his resignation and took his wife and son to a cottage on the road to the school. The parsonage had been furnished, so they had little enough to move, but a few people who could not bear to think of them in destitution mustered furniture for the new place, without letting it be too clearly known who had done it. (I know my father put up some of the money for this project, very much on the quiet.)

At midnight a gang with blackened faces beat pans and tooted horns outside the cottage for half an hour, and somebody threw a lighted broom on the roof, but it was a damp night and no harm was done. Cece's voice was heard half over the town, shouting, "Come on out, Mary! We want it!" I wish I could record that Amasa Dempster came out and faced them, but he did not.

I never saw a man change so much in so short a time. He was gaunt and lonely before, but there had been fire in his eyes; in two weeks he was like a scarecrow. He had a job; George Alcott, who owned the sawmill, offered Dempster a place as a bookkeeper and timekeeper at twelve dollars a week, which was not a bad wage for the work and in fact made the Dempsters slightly better off than they had been, for there was no church tithe expected out of it. But it was the comedown, the disgrace, that broke Dempster. He had been a parson, which was the work dearest to his heart; now he was nothing in his own eyes, and clearly he feared the worst for his wife.

What passed between them nobody knew, but she was not seen in the village and very rarely in the little yard outside the cottage. There was a rumour that he kept her tied to a long rope inside the house, so that she could move freely through it but not get out. On Sunday mornings, her arm in his, she went to the Baptist church, and they sat in a back pew, never speaking to anyone as they came and went. She began to look very strange indeed, and if she was not mad before, people said, she was mad now.

I knew better. After a few weeks during which I was miserable because of the village talk, I sneaked over there one day and peeped in a window. She was sitting on a chair by a table, staring at nothing, but when I tapped on the pane she looked at me and smiled in recognition. In an instant I was inside, and after a few minutes of uneasiness we were talking eagerly. She was a little strange because she had been so lonely, but she made good sense, and I had enough gumption to keep on general topics. I soon found out that she knew nothing of what was going in the world because the Dempsters took no newspaper.

After that I went there two or three times a week, with a daily paper, or a copy of our own *Banner,* and I read things to her that I knew would interest her, and kept her up on the gossip of the town. Often Paul was with us, because he never played with other children, and I did what I could for him. It was well understood that these visits were not to be mentioned to Dempster, for I was sure he still thought me a bad influence.

I began this deceitful line of conduct—for my mother would have been furious, and I thought anybody who had seen me going there would have spread the word—hoping I could do something for Mrs Dempster, but it was not long before I found that she was doing much for me. I do not know how to express it, but she was a wise woman, and though she was only ten years older than myself, and thus about twenty-six at this time, she seemed to me to have a breadth of outlook and a clarity of vision that were strange and wonderful; I cannot remember examples that satisfactorily explain what I mean, and I recognize now that it was her lack of fear, of apprehension, of assumption that whatever happened was inevitably going to lead to some worse state of affairs, that astonished and enriched me. She had not been like this when first I knew her, after Paul's birth, but I see now that she had been tending in this direction. When she had seemed to be laughing at things her husband took very seriously, she had been laughing at the disproportion of his seriousness, and of course in Deptford it was very easy to understand such laughter as the uncomprehending gigglings of a fool.

It would be false to suggest that there was anything philosophical in her attitude. Rather, it was religious, and it was impossible to talk to her for long without being aware that she was wholly religious. I do not say "deeply religious" because that was what people said about her husband, and apparently they meant that he imposed religion as he understood it on everything he knew or encountered. But she, tied up in a rotten little house without a friend except me, seemed to live in a world of trust that had nothing of the stricken, lifeless, unreal quality of religion about it. She knew she was in disgrace with the world, but did not feel disgraced; she knew she was jeered at, but felt no humiliation. She lived by a light that arose from within; I could not comprehend it, except that it seemed to be somewhat akin to the splendours I found in books, though not in any way bookish. It was as though she were an exile from a world that saw things her way, and though she was sorry Deptford did not understand her she was not resentful. When you got past her shyness she had quite positive opinions, but the queerest thing about her was that she had no fear.

This was the best of Mary Dempster. Of the disorder and discomfort of that cottage I shall not speak, and though little Paul was loved and cherished by his mother he was in his appearance a pitifully neglected child. So perhaps she was crazy, in part, but it was only in part; the best side of her brought comfort and assurance into my life, which badly needed it. I got so that I did not notice the rope she wore (it was actually a harness that went around her waist and shoulders, with the horse-smelling hemp rope knotted to a ring on one side, so that she could lie down if she wanted to), or the raggedness of her clothes, or the occasional spells when she was not wholly rational. I regarded her as my greatest friend, and the secret league between us as the tap-root that fed my life.

Close as we grew, however, there was never any moment when I could have asked her about the tramp. I was trying to forget the spectacle, so horrible in my visions, of what I had seen when first I happened on them—those bare buttocks and four legs so strangely opposed. But I could never forget. It was my first encounter with a particular kind of reality, which my religion, my upbringing, and the callowly romantic cast of my mind had declared obscene. Therefore there was an aspect of Mary Dempster which was outside my ken; and, being young and unwilling to recognize that there was anything I did not, or could not know, I decided that this unknown aspect must be called madness.

( 12 )

The year that followed was a busy one for me, and, except for my visits to Mrs Dempster, lonely. My school friends accused me of being a know-all, and with characteristic perversity I liked the description. By searching the dictionary I discovered that a know-all was called, among people who appreciate knowledge and culture, a polymath, and I set to work to become a polymath with the same enthusiasm that I had once laboured to be a conjurer. It was much easier work; I simply read the encyclopaedia in our village library. It was a *Chambers'*, the 1888 edition, and I was not such a fool as to think

I could read it through; I read the articles that appealed to me, and when I found something particularly juicy I read everything around it that I could find. I beavered away at that encyclopaedia with a tenacity that I wish I possessed now, and if I did not become a complete polymath I certainly gained enough information to be a nuisance to everybody who knew me.

I also came to know my father much better, for after the search for Mrs Dempster in the pit he put himself out to make a friend of me. He was an intelligent man and well educated in an old-fashioned way; he had gone to Dumfries Academy as a boy, and what he knew he could marshal with a precision I have often envied; it was he and he alone who made the study of Latin anything but a penance to me, for he insisted that without Latin nobody could write clear English.

Sometimes on our Sunday walks along the railroad track we were joined by Sam West, an electrician with a mind above the limitations of his work; as a boy he had been kept hard at the *Bible*, and not only could he quote it freely, but there was not a contradiction or an absurdity in it that he did not know and relish. His detestation of religion and churches was absolute, and he scolded about them in language that owed all its bite to the *Old Testament*. He was unfailingly upright in all his dealings, to show the slaves of priestcraft and superstition that morality has nothing to do with religion, and he was an occasional attendant at all our local churches, in order to wrestle mentally with the sermon and confute it. His imitations of the parsons were finely observed, and he was very good as the Reverend Andrew Bowyer: "O Lord, take Thou a live coal from off Thine altar and touch our lips," he would shout, in a caricature of our minister's fine Edinburgh accent; then, with a howl of laughter, "Wouldn't he be surprised if his prayer was answered!"

If he hoped to make an atheist of me, this was where he went wrong; I knew a metaphor when I heard one, and I liked metaphor better than reason. I have known many atheists since Sam, and they all fall down on metaphor.

At school I was a nuisance, for my father was now Chairman of our Continuation School Board, and I affected airs of near-equality with the teacher that must have galled her; I wanted to argue about everything, expand everything, and generally turn every class into a Socratic powwow instead of getting on with the curriculum. Probably I made her nervous, as a pupil full of green, fermenting information is so well able to do. I have dealt with innumerable variations of my young self in classrooms since then, and I have mentally apologized for my tiresomeness.

My contemporaries were growing up too. Leola Cruikshank was now a village beauty, and well understood to be Percy Boyd Staunton's girl. Spider Webb still thought me wonderful, and I graciously permitted her to worship me from a distance. Milo Papple had found that a gift for breaking wind was not in itself enough for social success, and he learned a few things from the travelling salesmen who were shaved by his father that gave him quite a new status. It was an era when parodies of popular songs were thought very funny, and when conversation flagged he would burst into:

> I had a dewlap,
> A big flabby dewlap,
> And you had
> A red, red nose.

Or perhaps:

> I dream of Jeannie
> With the light brown hair,
> Drunk in the privy
> In her underwear.

These fragments were always very brief, and he counted on his hearers bursting into uncontrollable laughter before they were finished. Nuisance that I was, I used to urge him to continue, for which he very properly hated me. He also had a few pleasantries about smelly feet, which went well at parties. I refused to laugh at them, for I was jealous of anybody who was funnier than I. The trouble was that my jokes tended to be so complicated that nobody laughed but Spider Webb, who obviously did not understand them.

The great event of the spring was the revelation that Percy Boyd Staunton and Mabel Heighington had been surprised in the sexual act by Mabel's mother, who had tracked them to Dr Staunton's barn and pounced. Mrs Heighington was a small, dirty, hysterical woman whose own chastity was seriously flawed; she had been a grass-widow for several years. What she said to Percy's father, whom she insisted on seeing just as he got nicely off into his after-dinner nap one day, was so often repeated by herself on the streets that I heard it more than once. If he thought because she was a poor widow her only daughter could be trampled under foot by a rich man's son and then flung aside, by Jesus she would show him different. She had her feelings, like anybody else. Was she to go to Mr Mahaffey right then and get the law to work, or was he going to ask her to sit down and talk turkey?

What turkey amounted to remained a mystery. Some said fifty dollars, and others said a hundred. Mrs Heighington never revealed the precise sum. There were those who said that twenty-five cents would have been a sufficient price for Mabel's virtue, such as it was; she consistently met the brakeman of a freight train that lay on a siding near the gravel pit for half an hour every Friday, and he enjoyed her favours on some sacks in a freight car; she had also had to do with a couple of farmhands who worked over near the Indian Reservation. But Dr Staunton had money—reputedly lots of money—for he had built up substantial land holdings over the years and was doing very well growing tobacco and sugar-beet, which was just coming into its own as an important crop. The doctoring was a second string with him, and he kept it up chiefly for the prestige it carried. Still, he was a doctor, and when Mrs Heighington told him that if there was a baby she would expect him to do something about it, she struck a telling blow.

For our village, this amounted to scandal in high society. Mrs Staunton was elaborately pitied by some of the women; others blamed her for letting Percy have his own way too much. Some of the men thought Percy a young rip, but the Cece Athelstan crowd acclaimed him as one of themselves. Ben Cruikshank, a tough little carpenter, stopped Percy on the street and told him if he ever came near Leola again he would cripple him; Leola wore a stricken face for days, and it was known that she was pining for Percy and forgave him in spite of everything, which made me cynical about women. Some of our more profound moralists harked back to the incident of Mrs Dempster and said that if a parson's wife behaved like that, it was no wonder young ones picked up notions. Dr Staunton kept his own counsel, but it became known that he had decided to send Percy away to school, where he would not have his mother to baby him. And that, Headmaster, is how Percy came to be at Colborne College, of which in time he became a distinguished Old Boy, and Chairman of the Board of Governors.

( 13 )

The autumn of 1914 was remarkable in most places for the outbreak of the war, but in Deptford my brother Willie's illness ran it close as a subject of interest.

Willie had been ill at intervals for four years. His trouble began with an accident in the *Banner* plant when he had attempted to take some rollers from the big press—the one used for printing the newspaper—without help. Jumper Saul was absent, pitching for the local baseball team. The rollers were not extremely heavy but they were awkward, and one of them fell on Willie and knocked him down. At first it seemed that nothing would come of it except a large bruise on his back, but as time wore on Willie began to have spells of illness marked by severe internal pain. Dr McCausland could not do much for him; X-ray was unheard of in our part of the world, and the kind of exploratory operations that are so common now were virtually unknown. My parents took Willie to Pittstown a few times to see a chiropractor, but the treatments hurt Willie so much that the chiropractor refused to continue them. Until the autumn of 1914, however, Willie had come round after a few days in bed, with a light diet and a quantity of Sexton Blake stories to help him along.

This time he was really very ill—so ill that he had periods of delirium. His most dramatic symptom, however, spoken of around the village in hushed tones, was a stubborn retention of urine that added greatly to his distress. Dr McCausland sent to Toronto for a specialist—an alarming move in our village—and the specialist had very little to suggest except that immersions in warm water at four-hour intervals might help; he did not advise an operation yet, for at that time the removal of a kidney was an extremely grave matter.

As soon as the news of what the specialist had said got around we had a group of volunteers to assist with the immersions. These were bound to be troublesome, for we had no bathtub except a portable one, which could be put by the bed, and to which all the warm water had to be carried in pails. I have already said that our village had a kind heart, and practical help of this kind was what it understood best; six immersions a day were nothing, in the light of their desire to lend a hand. Even the new Presbyterian minister, the Reverend Donald Phelps (come to replace the Reverend Andrew Bowyer, retired in the spring of 1914), was a volunteer, comparative stranger though he was; more astonishing, Cece Athelstan was one of the group, and was cold sober every time he turned up. Getting Willie through this bad time became a public cause.

The baths certainly seemed to make Willie a little easier, though the swelling caused by the retention of urine grew worse. He had been in bed for more than two weeks when the Saturday of our Fall Fair came and brought special problems with it. My father had to attend; not only had he to write it up for the *Banner,* but as Chairman of our Continuation School Board he had to judge two or three contests. My mother was expected to attend, and wanted to attend, because the Ladies' Aid of our church was offering a Fowl Supper, and she was a noted organizer and pusher of fancy victuals. The men who would give Willie his six-o'clock plunge bath would arrive in plenty of time, but who was to stay with him during the afternoon? I was happy to do so; I would go to the Fair after supper, because it always seemed particularly gay and romantic as darkness fell.

From two until three I sat in Willie's room, reading, and between three and half-past I did what I could for Willie while he died. What I could do was little enough. He became restless and hot, so I put a cold towel on his head. He began to twist and moan, so I held his hands and said what I could think of that might encourage him. He ceased to hear me, and his twisting became jerking and convulsion.

He cried out five or six times—not screaming, but spasmodic cries—and in a very few minutes became extremely cold. I wanted to call the doctor, but I dared not leave Willie. I put my ear to his heart: nothing. I tried to find his pulse: nothing. Certainly he was not breathing, for I hurried to fetch my mother's hand mirror and hold it over his mouth: it did not cloud. I opened one eye: it was rolled upward in his head. It came upon me that he was dead.

It is very easy to say now what I should have done. I can only record what I did do. From the catastrophe of realizing that Willie was dead—it was the psychological equivalent of a house falling inward upon itself, and I can still recall the feeling—I passed quickly into strong revolt. Willie could not be dead. It must not be. I would not have it. And, without giving a thought to calling the doctor (whom I had never really liked, though it was the family custom to respect him), I set out on the run to fetch Mrs Dempster.

Why? I don't know why. It was not a matter of reason—not a decision at all. But I can remember running through the hot autumn afternoon, and I can remember hearing the faint music of the merry-go-round as I ran. Nothing was very far away in our village, and I was at the Dempsters' cottage in not much more than three minutes. Locked. Of course. Paul's father would have taken him to the Fair. I was through the living-room window, cutting Mrs Dempster's rope, telling her what I wanted, and dragging her back through the window with me, in a muddle of action that I cannot clearly remember at all. I suppose we would have looked an odd pair, if there had been anyone to see us, running through the streets hand in hand, and I do remember that she hoisted up her skirts to run, which was a girlish thing no grown woman would ever have done if she had not caught the infection of my emotion.

What I do remember was getting back to Willie's room, which was my parents' room, given up to the sick boy because it was the most comfortable, and finding him just as I had left him, white and cold and stiff. Mrs Dempster looked at him solemnly but not sadly, then she knelt by the bed and took his hands in hers and prayed. I had no way of knowing how long she prayed, but it was less than ten minutes. I could not pray and did not kneel. I gaped—and hoped.

After a while she raised her head and called him. "Willie," said she in a low, infinitely kind, and indeed almost a cheerful tone. Again, "Willie." I hoped till I ached. She shook his hands gently, as if rousing a sleeper. "Willie."

Willie sighed and moved his legs a little. I fainted.

When I came round, Mrs Dempster was sitting on Willie's bed, talking quietly and cheerfully to him, and he was replying, weakly but eagerly. I dashed around, fetched a towel to bathe his face, the orange and albumen drink he was allowed in very small quantities, a fan to create a better current of air—everything there was that might help and give expression to my terrible joy. Quite soon Willie fell asleep, and Mrs Dempster and I talked in whispers. She was deeply pleased but, as I now remember it, did not seem particularly surprised by what had happened. I know I babbled like a fool.

The passing of time that afternoon was all awry, for it did not seem long to me before the men came to get Willie's six-o'clock plunge ready, so it must have been half-past five. They were astonished to find her there, but sometimes extraordinary situations impose their own tactful good manners, and nobody said anything to emphasize their first amazement. Willie insisted that she stand by him while he was being plunged, and she helped in the difficult business of drying him off, for he was tender all around his body. Therefore I suppose it must have been close to half-past six when my mother and father arrived home, and with them Amasa Dempster. I don't know what sort of scene I expected; something on Biblical lines would have appeared appropriate to me. But instead Dempster took his wife's arm in his, as I had seen him do it so often, and led her away. As she went she paused for an instant to blow a kiss to Willie. It was the first time I had ever seen anybody do such a thing, and I thought it a gesture of great beauty; to Willie's everlasting credit, he blew a kiss back again, and I have never seen my mother's face blacker than at that moment.

When the Dempsters were gone, and the men had been thanked, and offered food, which they refused (this was ritual, for only the night plungers, at two and six in the morning, thought it right to accept coffee and sandwiches), there was a scene downstairs which was as bad, though not as prolonged, as anything I later experienced in the war.

What did I mean by failing to send for Dr McCausland and my parents at the first sign of danger? What under Heaven had possessed me to turn to that woman, who was an insane degenerate, and bring her, not only into our house but to the very bedside of a boy who was dangerously ill? Did all this cynical nonsense I had been talking, and the superior airs I had been assuming, mean that I too was going off my head? How did I come to be so thick with Mary Dempster in her present condition? If this was what all my reading led to, it was high time I was put to a job that would straighten the kinks out of me.

Most of this was my mother, and she performed variations on these themes until I was heartsick with hearing them. I know now that a lot of her anger arose from self-reproach because she had been absent, making a great figure of herself in the Ladies' Aid, when duty should have kept her at Willie's bedside. But she certainly took it out of me, and so, to a lesser degree, did my father, who felt himself bound to back her up but who plainly did not like it.

This would have gone on until we all dropped with exhaustion, I suppose, if Dr McCausland had not arrived; he had been in the country and had just returned. He brought his own sort of atmosphere, which was cold and chilly and smelled of disinfectant, and took a good look at Willie. Then he questioned me. He catechized me thoroughly about what symptoms Willie had shown, and how he had behaved before he died. Because I insisted that Willie had indeed died. No pulse; no breathing.

"But clenched hands?" said Dr McCausland. "Yes," said I, but did that mean that Willie could not have been dead? "Obviously he was not dead," said the doctor; "if he had been dead I would not have been talking to him a few minutes ago. I think you may safely leave it to me to say when people are dead, Dunny," he continued, with what I am sure he meant as a kindly smile. It had been a strong convulsion, he told my parents; the tight clenching of the hands was a part of it, and an unskilled person could not be expected to detect very faint breathing, or heartbeat either. He was all reason, all reassurance, and the next day he came early and did an operation on Willie called "tapping"; he dug a hollow needle into his side and drew off an astonishing quantity of bloody urine. In a week Willie was up and about; in four months he had somehow lied his way into the Canadian Army; in 1916 he was one of those who disappeared forever in the mud at St Eloi.

I wonder if his hands were clenched after death? Later on I saw more men than I could count die, myself, and a surprising number of the corpses I stumbled over, or cleared out of the way, had clenched hands, though I never took the trouble to write to Dr McCausland and tell him so.

For me, Willie's recall from death is, and will always be, Mrs Dempster's second miracle.

( 14 )

The weeks following were painful and disillusioning. Among my friends I dropped from the position of polymath to that of a credulous ass who thought that a dangerous lunatic could raise the dead. I should explain that Mrs Dempster was now thought to be dangerous, not because of any violence on her part, but because fearful people were frightened that if she were to wander away again some new sexual scandal would come of it; I think they really believed that she would corrupt some innocent youth or bewitch some faithful husband by the unreason of her lust. It was widely accepted that, even if she could not help it, she was in the grip of unappeasable and indiscriminate desire. Inevitably it came out that I had been visiting her on the sly, and there was a lot of dirty joking about that, but the best joke of all was that I thought she had brought my brother back to life.

The older people took the matter more seriously. Some thought that my known habit of reading a great deal had unseated my reason, and perhaps that dreaded disease "brain fever," supposed to attack students, was not far off. One or two friends suggested to my father that immediate removal from school, and a year or two of hard work on a farm, might cure me. Dr McCausland found a chance to have what he called "a word" with me, the gist of which was that I might become queer if I did not attempt to balance my theoretical knowledge with the kind of common sense that could be learned from—well, for instance, from himself. He hinted that I might become like Elbert Hubbard if I continued in my present course. Elbert Hubbard was a notoriously queer American who thought that work could be a pleasure.

Our new minister, the Reverend Donald Phelps, took me on and advised me that it was blasphemous to think that anyone—even someone of unimpeachable character—could restore the dead to life. The age of miracles was past, said he, and I got the impression that he was heartily glad of it. I liked him; he meant it kindly, which McCausland certainly did not.

My father talked to me several times in a way that gave me some insight into his own character, for though he was a man of unusual courage as an editor, he was a peace-at-any-pricer at home. I would do best, he thought, to keep my own counsel and not insist on things my mother could not tolerate.

I might even have done so—if she had been content to let the subject drop. But she was so anxious to root out of my mind any fragment of belief in what I had seen, and to exact from me promises that I would never see Mrs Dempster again and furthermore would accept the village's opinion of her, that she kept alluding to it darkly, or bringing it out for full discussion, usually at meals. It was clear that she now regarded a hint of tenderness toward Mrs Dempster as disloyalty to herself, and as loyalty was the only kind of love she could bring herself to ask for, she was most passionate when she thought she was being most reasonable. I said very little during these scenes, and she quite rightly interpreted my silence as refusal to change my mind.

She did not know how much I loved her, and how miserable it made me to defy her, but what was I to do? Deep inside myself I knew that to yield, and promise what she wanted, would be the end of anything that was any good in me; I was not her husband, who could keep his peace in the face of her furious rectitude; I was her son, with a full share of her own Highland temper and granite determination.

One day, after a particularly wretched supper, she concluded by demanding that I make a choice between her and "that woman."

I made a third choice. I had enough money for a railway ticket, and the next day I skipped school, went to the county town, and enlisted.

This changed matters considerably. I was nearly two years under age, but I was tall and strong and a good liar, and I had no difficulty in being accepted. She wanted to go to the authorities and get me out, but my father put his foot down there. He said he would not permit me to be disgraced by having my mother drag me out of the Army. So now she was torn between a fear that I would certainly be shot dead the day after I began training, and a conviction that there was something even darker between Mrs Dempster and me than she had permitted herself to think.

As for my father, he was disgusted with me. He had a poor opinion of soldiers and as he had run some risks by being pro-Boer in 1901 he had serious doubts about the justice of any war. Feeling about the war in our village was romantic, because it touched us so little, but my father and Mr Mahaffey were better aware of what went into the making of that war and could not share the popular feeling. He urged me to reveal my true age and withdraw, but I was pig-headed and spread the news of what I had done as fast as I could.

What my elders thought I did not know or care, but I regained some of the position I had lost among my contemporaries. I loafed at school, as became a man waiting his call to more serious things. My friends seemed to think I might disappear at any hour, and whenever I met Milo Papple, which was at least once a day, he would seize my hand and declaim passionately:

> Say cuspidor,
>> But not spittoon—

which was the barbershop version of a song of the day that began:

> Say *au revoir*,
>> But not good-bye.

Girls took a new view of me, and to my delighted surprise Leola Cruikshank made it clear that she was mine on loan, so to speak. She still pined for Percy Boyd Staunton, but he was away at school and was a bad and irregular letter-writer, so Leola thought that a modest romance with a hero in embryo could do no harm—might even be a patriotic duty.

She was a delightful girl, pretty, full of sentimental nonsense, and clean about her person—she always smelled of fresh ironing. I saw a great deal of her, persuaded her that a few kisses did not really mean disloyalty to Percy, and paraded her up and down our main street on Saturday nights, wearing my best suit.

I had kept away from Mrs Dempster, partly from obedience and fear and partly because I could not bear to face her when so many hateful opinions about her were ringing in my ears. I knew, however, that I could not go off to war without saying good-bye, and one afternoon, with great stealth, I reached her cottage and climbed through the window for the last time. She spoke to me as if I had visited her as often as usual, and did not seem greatly surprised by the news that I joined the Army. We had talked a great deal about the war when it first broke out, and she had laughed heartily at the news that two Deptford women who liked to dabble in spiritualism went several times a week to the cemetery to read the latest news from France to their dead mother, sitting on her grave, picnic-style. When I had to leave she kissed me on both cheeks—a thing she had never done before—and said, "There's just one thing to remember; whatever happens, it does no good to be afraid." So I promised not to be afraid, and may even have been fool enough to think I could keep my promise.

In time my call came. I climbed on to the train, proud of my pass to the camp, and waved from the window to my almost weeping mother, and my father, whose expression I could not interpret. Leola was in school, for we had agreed that it would not do for her to come to the station—too much like a formal engagement. But the night before I left she had confided that in spite of her best efforts to keep the image of Percy bright in her heart she had discovered that she really loved me, and would love me forever, and wait until I returned from the battlefields of Europe.

# 2

# *I Am Born Again*

( 1 )

I shall say little about the war, because though I was in it from early 1915 until late 1917 I never found out much about it until later. Commanders and historians are the people to discuss wars; I was in the infantry, and most of the time I did not know where I was or what I was doing except that I was obeying orders and trying not to be killed in any of the variety of horrible ways open to me. Since then I have read enough to know a little of the actions in which I took a part, but what the historians say throws no great light on what I remember. Because I do not want to posture in this account of myself as anything other than what I was at the time of my narrative, I shall write here only of what I knew when it happened.

When I left Deptford for the training camp I had never been away from home alone before. I found myself among men more experienced in the world than I, and I tried not to attract attention by any kind of singular behaviour. Some of them knew I was desperately homesick and were kindly; others jeered at me and the other very young fellows. They were anxious to make men of us, by which they meant making us like themselves. Some of them were men indeed— grave, slow young farmers and artisans with apparently boundless resources of strength and courage; others were just riffraff of the kind you get in any chance collection of men. None of them had much education; none had any clear idea what the war was about, though many felt that England had been menaced and had to be defended; perhaps the most astonishing thing was that none of us had much notion of geography and thought that going to fight in France might involve almost any kind of climate, from the Pole to the Equator. Of course some of us had some geography in school and had studied maps, but a school map is a terribly uncommunicative thing.

I was a member of the Second Canadian Division, and later we were part of the Canadian Corps, but such descriptions meant little to me; I was aware of the men directly around me and rarely had a chance to meet any others. I might as well say at once that although I was on pretty good terms with everybody I made no lasting friends. There were men who formed strong friendships, which sometimes led to acts of bravery, and there were men who were great on what they called "pals" and talked and sang loudly about it. Those now living are still at it. But I was a lonely creature, and although I would have been very happy to have a friend I just never happened to meet one.

Probably my boredom was to blame. For I was bored as I have never been since—bored till every bone in my body was heavy with it. This was not the boredom of inactivity; an infantry trainee is kept on the hop from morning till night, and his sleep is sound. It was the boredom that comes of being cut off from everything that could make life sweet, or arouse curiosity, or enlarge the range of the senses. It was the boredom that comes of having to perform endless tasks that have no savour and acquire skills one would gladly be without. I learned to march and drill and shoot and keep myself clean according to Army standards; to make my bed and polish my boots and my buttons and to wrap lengths of dung-coloured rag around my legs in the approved way. None of it had any great reality for me, but I learned to do it all, and even to do it well.

Thus, when I went home for my leave before going abroad, I was an object of some wonderment. I was a man, in appearance. My mother was almost silenced, so far as her customary criticism went; she made a few attempts to reduce me to the status of her own dear laddie, but I was not willing to play that game. Leola Cruikshank was proud to be seen with me, and we got a little beyond the kissing stage in our last encounter. I desperately wanted to see Mrs Dempster, but it was impossible, for in my uniform I was unable to go anywhere without being noticed, and though I would have died rather than admit it, I was still too much afraid of my mother to defy her openly. Paul I saw once, but I do not think he knew me, for he stared and passed by.

So off I went on a troopship, lectured by officers who were anxious to harden us with tales of German atrocities. These Germans, I gathered, were absolute devils; not winning campaigns, but maiming children, ravishing women (never less than ten to a single victim), and insulting religion were the things they had gone to war to accomplish; they took their tone from their Kaiser, who was a comic, mad monster; they had to be shown that decency still ruled the world, and we were decency incarnate. I had by that time seen enough of Army life to think that if we were decency the Germans must be rough indeed, for a more foul-mouthed, thieving, whoring lot of toughs than some of the soldiers I met it would be hard to imagine. But I was not discontented with soldiering; I was discontented with myself, with my loneliness and boredom.

In France, though my boredom was unabated, loneliness was replaced by fear. I was, in a mute, controlled, desperate fashion, frightened for the next three years. I saw plenty of men whose fear found vent; they went mad, or they shot themselves (dead or badly enough to get out of service), or they were such nuisances to the rest of us that they were got rid of in one way or another. But I think there were many in my own case; frightened of death, of wounds, of being captured, but most frightened of admitting to fear and losing face before the others. This kind of fear is not acute, of course; it is a constant, depleting companion whose presence makes everything gray. Sometimes fear could be forgotten, but never for long.

I saw a good deal of service, for I was strong, did not break down, and miraculously suffered no wounds. I had leaves, when it was possible to grant them, but for months on end I was at what was called the Front. What it was the Front of I never really knew, for there were always men who were ready to tell—God knows how accurately—where the Allied troops were disposed, and where we were in relation to the British and the French, and from what they said it seemed the Front was everywhere. But certainly we were often only a few hundred yards from the German lines and could see the enemy, in their cooking-pot helmets, quite clearly. If you were such a fool as to show your head they might put a bullet through it, and we had men detailed for the same ugly work.

It seems now to have been a very odd war, for we have had another since then, which has set the standard for modernity of fighting. I saw things that now make my pupils regard me as comparable to one of Wellington's men, or perhaps Marlborough's. My war was greatly complicated by horses, for motor vehicles were useless in Flanders mud; if one was among the horses during a bombardment, as I once chanced to be, the animals were just as dangerous as the German shells. I even saw cavalry, for there were still generals who thought that if they could once get at the enemy with cavalry the machine-guns would quickly be silenced. These cavalrymen were as wondrous to me as Crusaders, but I would not have been on one of their horses for the earth. And of course I saw corpses, and grew used to their unimportant look, for a dead man without any of the panoply of death is a desperately insignificant object. Worse, I saw men who were not corpses but who would be soon and who longed for death.

It was the indignity, the ignominy, the squalor, to which war reduced a wounded man that most ate into me. Men in agony, smashed so that they will never be whole again even if they live, ought not to be something one ignores; but we learned to ignore them, and I have put my foot on many a wretched fellow and pushed him even deeper into the mud, because I had to get over him and onto some spot that we had been ordered to achieve or die in trying.

This was fighting, when at least we were doing something. But for days and weeks there was not much fighting, during which we lived in trenches, in dung-coloured mud into which dung and every filth-iness had been trodden, in our dung-coloured uniforms; we were cold, badly fed, and lousy. We had no privacy whatever and began to doubt our individuality, for we seemed to melt into a mass; this was what the sergeants feared, and they did astonishing work in keeping that danger at bay, most of the time; occasionally the horrible loss of personality, the listlessness of degradation, got beyond them, and then we had to be sent to the rear to what were called rest camps; we never rested in them, but at least we could draw a full breath without the lime-and-dung stench of the latrines in it.

In spite of the terribly public quality of a soldier's life, in which I ate, slept, stood, sat, thought, voided my bowels, and felt the dread of death upon me, always among others, I found a little time for reading. But I had only one book, a *New Testament* some well-meaning body had distributed in thousands to the troops. It would never have been my choice; if it had to be the *Bible* I would have taken the *Old Testament* any day, but I would rather have had some big, meaty novels. But where could a private soldier keep such things? I have read often since those days of men who went through the war with books of all sorts, but they were officers. Once or twice on leaves I got hold of a book or two in English but lost them as soon as we had to fight. Only my *Testament* could be kept in my pocket without making a big bulge, and I read it to the bone, over and over.

This gained me a disagreeable reputation as a religious fellow, a Holy Joe, and even the chaplain avoided that kind, for they were sure trouble, one way or another. My nickname was Deacon, because of my *Testament* reading. It was useless to explain that I read it not from zeal but curiosity and that long passages of it confirmed my early impression that religion and *Arabian Nights* were true in the same way. (Later I was able to say that they were both psychologically rather than literally true, and that psychological truth was really as important in its own way as historical verification; but while I was a young soldier I had no vocabulary for such argument, though I sensed the truth of it.) I think *Revelation* was my favourite book; the Gospels seemed less relevant to me then than John's visions of the beasts and the struggle of the Crowned Woman, who had the moon beneath her feet, with the great Red Dragon.

The nickname Deacon stuck to me until, in one of the rest camps, word went out that an impromptu show was being organized, and men were called on to volunteer if they would do something to amuse the troops. With a gall that now staggers me, I forced myself to offer an imitation of Charlie Chaplin, whom I had seen exactly twice in film shows for the troops behind the lines. I managed to get the right kind of hat from a Frenchman in the nearby village, I cut myself a little cane from a bush, and when the night came I put on a burnt-cork moustache and shuffled onto the platform; for twelve minutes

I told the dirtiest jokes I knew, attaching them to all the officers—including the chaplain—and all the men who had some sort of public character. I now blush at what I remember of what I said, but I drew heavily on the repertoire of Milo Papple and was astonished to find myself a great hit. Even the former vaudevillian (who could sing *If You Were the Only Girl in the World and I Were the Only Boy* in a baritone-and-falsetto duet with himself) was less admired. And from that time forth I was called, not "Deacon," but "Charlie."

What really astonished me was the surprise of the men that I could do such a thing. "Jesus, the old Deacon, eh—getting off that hot one about the Major, eh? Jesus, and that riddle about Cookie, eh? Jesus!" They could hardly conceive that anybody who read the *Testament* could be other than a Holy Joe—could have another, seemingly completely opposite side to his character. I cannot remember a time when I did not take it as understood that everybody has at least two, if not twenty-two, sides to him. Their astonishment was what astonished *me*. Jesus, eh? People don't look very closely at other people, eh? Jesus!

I did not philosophize in the trenches; I endured. I even tried to make a good job of what I had to do. If I had not been so young and handicapped by lack of education—measured in school terms, for the Army did not know that I was a polymath and would not have cared—I might have been sent off for training as an officer. As it was, I eventually became a sergeant; casualties were heavy—which is the Army way of saying that men I had known and liked were exploded like bombs of guts almost under my nose—and my success in hiding my fear was enough to get me a reputation for having a cool head; so a sergeant I became, as well as a veteran of Sanctuary Wood and Vimy Ridge, before I was twenty. But I think my most surprising achievement was becoming Charlie.

( 2 )

My fighting days came to an end somewhere in the week of 5 November 1917, at that point in the Third Battle of Ypres where the Canadians were brought in to attempt to take Passchendaele. It was a

Thursday or Friday; I cannot be more accurate because many of the details of that time are clouded in my mind. The battle was the most terrible of my experience; we were trying to take a village that was already a ruin, and we counted our advances in feet; the Front was a confused mess because it had rained every day for weeks and the mud was so dangerous that we dared not make a forward move without a laborious business of putting down duckboards, lifting them as we advanced, and putting them down again ahead of us; understandably this was so slow and exposed that we could not do much of it. I learned from later reading that our total advance was a little less than two miles; it might have been two hundred. The great terror was the mud. The German bombardment churned it up so that it was horribly treacherous, and if a man sank in much over his knees his chances of getting out were poor; a shell exploding nearby could cause an upheaval that overwhelmed him, and the likelihood even of recovering his body was small. I write of this now as briefly as I may, for the terror of it was so great that I would not for anything arouse it again.

One of the principal impediments to our advance was a series of German machine-gun emplacements. I suppose they were set out according to some plan, but we were not in a position to observe any plan; in the tiny area I knew about there was one of these things, and it was clear that we would get no farther forward until it was silenced. Two attempts were made at this dangerous job, with terrible loss to us. I could see how things were going, and how the list of men who might be expected to get to that machine-gun nest was dwindling, and I knew it would come to me next. I do not remember if we were asked to volunteer; such a request would have been merely formal anyhow; things had reached a point where pretence of choice disappeared. Anyhow, I was one of six who were detailed to make a night raid, in one of the intervals of bombardment, to see if we could get to the machine-guns and knock them out. We were issued the small arms and other things we needed, and when the bombardment had stopped for five minutes we set out, not in a knot, of course, but spaced a few yards apart.

The men in the nest were expecting us, for we were doing exactly what their side would have done in the same situation. But we crawled forward, spread-eagled in the mud so as to spread out total weight over as wide an area as possible. It was like swimming in molasses, with the additional misery that it was molasses that stank and had dead men in it.

I was making pretty good progress when suddenly everything went wrong. Somebody—it could have been someone on our side at a distance or it could have been one of the Germans in the nest—sent up a flare; you do not see where these flares come from, because they explode in the air and light up the landscape for a considerable area. When such a thing happens and you are crawling toward an objective, as I was, the proper thing to do is to lie low, with your face down, and hope not to be seen. As I was mud from head to foot and had blackened my face before setting out, I would have been hard to see, and if seen I would have looked like a dead man. After the flare had died out I crept forward again and made a fair amount of distance, so far as I could judge; I did not know where the others were, but I assumed that like me they were making for the gun nest and waiting for a signal from our leader, a second lieutenant, to do whatever we could about it. But now three flares exploded, and immediately there began a rattle of machine-gun fire. Again I laid low. But it is the nature of flares, when they are over the arc of their trajectory, to come down with a rush and a characteristic loud hiss; if you are hit by one it is a serious burn, for the last of the flare is still a large gob of fire, and between burning to death or drowning in mud the choice is trivial. Two of these spent flares were hissing in the air above me, and I had to get out of where I was as fast as I could. So I got to my feet and ran.

Now, at a time when we had counted on at least a half-an-hour's lull in the bombardment, it suddenly set up again, and to my bleak horror our own guns, from a considerable distance to the left, began to answer. This sort of thing was always a risk when we were out on small raids, but it was a risk I had never met before. As the shells began to drop I ran wildly, and how long I wallowed around in the dark I do not know, but it could have been anything between three minutes and ten. I became aware of a deafening rattle, with the rhythm of an angry, scolding voice, on my right. I looked for some sort of cover, and suddenly, in a burst of light, there it was right in front of me—an entry concealed by some trash, but unmistakably a door over which hung a curtain of muddy sacking. I pushed through it and found myself in the German machine-gun nest, with three Germans ahead of me firing busily.

I had a revolver, and I shot all three at point-blank range. They did not even see me. There is no use saying any more about it. I am not proud of it now and I did not glory in it then. War puts men in situations where these things happen.

What I wanted to do most of all was to stay where I was and get my breath and my wits before starting back to our line. But the bombardment was increasing, and I knew that if I stopped there one of our shells might drop on the position and blow me up, or the Germans, whose field telephone was already signalling right under my nose, would send some men to see what had happened, and that would be the end of me. I had to get out.

So out I crawled, into mud below and shells above, and tried to get my bearings. As both sides were now at the peak of a bombardment, it was not easy to tell which source of death I should crawl toward, and by bad luck I set out toward the German lines.

How long I crawled I do not know, for I was by this time more frightened, muddled, and desperate than ever before or since. "Disorientation" is the word now fashionable for my condition. Quite soon I was worse than that; I was wounded, and so far as I could tell, seriously. It was shrapnel, a fragment of an exploding shell, and it hit me in the left leg, though where I cannot say; I have been in a car accident in later life, and the effect was rather like that—a sudden shock like a blow from a club; and it was a little time before I knew that my left leg was in trouble, though I could not tell how bad it was.

Earlier I said that I had not been wounded; there were a surprising number of men who escaped the war without a wound. I had not been gassed either, though I had been twice in areas where gas was used nearby. I had dreaded a wound, for I had seen so many. What is a wounded man to do? Crawl to shelter and hope he may be found by his own people. I crawled.

Some men found that their senses were quickened by a wound; their ingenuity rose to exceptional heights under stress of danger. But I was one of the other kind. I was not so much afraid as utterly disheartened. There I was, a mud man in a confusion of noise, flashing lights, and the stink of gelignite. I wanted to quit; I had no more heart for the game. But I crawled, with the increasing realization that my left leg was no good for anything and had to be dragged, and the awful awareness that I did not know where I was going. After a few minutes I saw some jagged masonry on my right and dragged toward it. When at last I reached it I propped myself up with my back to a stone wall and gave myself up to a full, rich recognition of the danger and hopelessness of my position. For three years I had kept my nerve by stifling my intelligence, but now I let the intelligence rip and the nerve dissolve. I am sure there has been worse wretchedness, fright, and despair in the world's history, but I set up a personal record that I have never since approached.

My leg began to declare itself in a way that I can only describe in terms of sound; from a mute condition it began to murmur, then to moan and whine, then to scream. I could not see much of what was wrong because of the mud in which I was covered, but my exploring hand found a great stickiness that I knew was blood, and I could make out that my leg lay on the ground in an unnatural way. You will get tetanus, I told myself, and you will die of lockjaw. It was a Deptford belief that in this disease you bent backward until at last your head touched your heels and you had to be buried in a round coffin. I had seen some tetanus in the trenches, and nobody had needed a round coffin even if one had been available; still, in my condition, the belief was stronger than experience.

I thought of Deptford, and I thought of Mrs Dempster. Particularly of her parting words to me: "There's just one thing to remember; whatever happens, it does no good to be afraid." Mrs Dempster, I said aloud, was a fool. I was afraid, and I was not in a situation where doing good, or doing evil, had any relevance at all.

It was then that one of the things happened that make my life strange—one of the experiences that other people have not had or do not admit to—one of the things that makes me so resentful of

Packer's estimate of me as a dim man to whom nothing important has ever happened.

I became conscious that the bombardment had ceased, and only an occasional gun was heard. But flares appeared in the sky at intervals, and one of these began to drop toward me. By its light I could see that the remnant of standing masonry in which I was lying was all that was left of a church, or perhaps a school—anyhow a building of some size—and that I lay at the foot of a ruined tower. As the hissing flame dropped I saw there about ten or twelve feet above me on an opposite wall, in a niche, a statue of the Virgin and Child. I did not know it then but I know now that it was the assembly of elements that represent the Immaculate Conception, for the little Virgin was crowned, stood on a crescent moon, which in its turn rested on a globe, and in the hand that did not hold the Child she carried a sceptre from which lilies sprang. Not knowing what it was meant to be, I thought in a flash it must be the Crowned Woman in *Revelation*—she who had the moon beneath her feet and was menaced by the Red Dragon. But what hit me worse than the blow of the shrapnel was that the face was Mrs Dempster's face.

I had lost all nerve long before. Now, as the last of the flare hissed toward me, I lost consciousness.

( 3 )

"May I have a drink of water?"

"Did you speak?"

"Yes. May I have a drink, Sister?"

"You may have a glass of champagne, if there is any. Who are you?"

"Ramsay, D., Sergeant, Second Canadian Division."

"Well, Ramsay-Dee, it's marvellous to have you with us."

"Where is this?"

"You'll find out. Where have *you* been?"

Ah, where *had* I been? I didn't know then and I don't know yet, but it was such a place as I had never known before. Years later, when for the first time I read Coleridge's *Kubla Khan* and came on—

Weave a circle round him thrice,
And close your eyes with holy dread,
For he on honey-dew hath fed,
And drunk the milk of Paradise

—I almost jumped out of my skin, for the words so perfectly described my state before I woke up in hospital. I had been wonderfully at ease and healingly at peace; though from time to time voices spoke to me I was under no obligation to hear what they said or to make a reply; I felt that everything was good, that my spirit was wholly my own, and that though all was strange nothing was evil. From time to time the little Madonna appeared and looked at me with friendly concern before removing herself; once or twice she spoke, but I did not know what she said and did not need to know.

But here I was, apparently in bed, and a very pretty girl in a nurse's uniform was asking me where I had been. Clearly she meant it as a joke. She thought she knew where I had been. That meant that the joke was on her, for no one, not I myself, knew that.

"Is this a base hospital?"

"Goodness, no. How do you feel, Ramsay-Dee?"

"Fine. What day is this?"

"This is the twelfth of May. I'll get you a drink."

She disappeared, and I took a few soundings. It was not easy work. The last time I had been conscious of was November; if this was May I had been in that splendid, carefree world for quite a while. I wasn't in such a bad place now; I couldn't move my head very much, but I could see a marvellously decorated plaster ceiling, and such walls as lay in my vision were panelled in wood; there was an open window somewhere, and sweet air—no stink of mud or explosive or corpses or latrines—was blowing through it. I was clean. I wriggled appreciatively—and wished I hadn't, for several parts of me protested. But here was the girl again, and with her a red-faced man in a long white coat.

He seemed greatly elated, especially when I was able to remember my Army number, and though I did not learn why at once I found out over a few days that I was by way of being a medical pet, and my recovery proved something; being merely the patient, I was never given the full details, but I believe I was written up in at least two medical papers as a psychiatric curiosity, but as I was referred to only as "the patient" I could never identify myself for sure. The red-faced man was some sort of specialist in shell-shock cases, and I was one of his successes, though I rather think I cured myself, or the little Madonna cured me, or some agencies other than good nursing and medical observation.

Oh, I was a lucky man! Apparently the flare did hit me, and before it expired it burned off a good part of my clothes and consumed the string of my identification disks, so that when I was picked up they were lost in the mud. There had been some doubt as to whether I was dead or merely on the way to it, but I was taken back to our base, and as I stubbornly did not die I was removed eventually to a hospital in France, and as I still refused either to die or live I was shipped to England; by this time I was a fairly interesting instance of survival against all probabilities, and the red-faced doctor had claimed me for his own; I was brought to this special hospital in a fine old house in Buckinghamshire, and had lain unconscious, and likely to remain so, though the red-faced doctor stubbornly insisted that some day I would wake up and tell him something of value. So here it was May, and I was awake, and the hospital staff were delighted, and made a great pet of me.

They had other news for me, not so good. My burns had been severe, and in those days they were not so clever with burns as they are now, so that quite a lot of the skin on my chest and left side was an angry-looking mess, rather like lumpy sealing wax, and is so still, though it is a little browner now. In the bed, on the left side, was an arrangement of wire, like a bee-skip, to keep the sheets from touching the stump where my left leg had been. While my wits were off on that paradisal holiday I had been fed liquids, and so I was very thin and weak. What is more, I had a full beard, and the pretty nurse and I had a rare old time getting it off.

Let me stop calling her the pretty nurse. Her name was Diana Marfleet, and she was one of those volunteers who got a proper nursing training but never acquired the full calm of a professional nursing sister. She was the first English girl I ever saw at close range, and a fine specimen of her type, which was the fair-skinned, dark-haired, brown-eyed type. Not only was she pretty, she had charm and an easy manner and talked amusingly, for she came of that class of English person who thinks it bad manners to be factual and serious. She was twenty-four, which gave her an edge of four years over me, and it was not long before she confided to me that her fiancé, a Navy lieutenant, had been lost when the *Aboukir* was torpedoed in the very early days of the war. We were on tremendous terms in no time, for she had been nursing me since I had come to the hospital in January, and such nourishment as I had taken had been spooned and poured into me by her; she had also washed me and attended to the bedpan and the urinal, and continued to do so; a girl who can do that without being facetious or making a man feel self-conscious is no ordinary creature. Diana was a wonderful girl, and I am sure I gained strength and made physical progress at an unusual rate, to please her.

One day she appeared at my bedside with a look of great serious-ness and saluted me smartly.

"What's that for?"

"Tribute of humble nursing sister to hero of Passchendaele."

"Get away!" (This was a great expression of my father's, and I have never wholly abandoned it.)

"Fact. What do you think you've got?"

"I rather think I've got you."

"No cheek. We've been tracing you, Sergeant Ramsay. Did you know that you were officially dead?"

"Dead! Me?"

"You. That's why your V.C. was awarded posthumously."

"Get away!"

"Fact. You have the V.C. for, with the uttermost gallantry and disregard of all but duty, clearing out a machine-gun nest and thereby ensuring an advance of—I don't know how far but quite a bit. You were the only one of the six who didn't get back to the line, and one of the men saw you—your unmistakable size anyhow—running right towards the machine-gun nest; so it was clear enough, even though they couldn't find your body afterward. Anyway you've got it, and Dr Houneen is making sure you do get it and it isn't sent home to depress your mother."

The other three men in the room gave a cheer—an ironic cheer. We all pretended we didn't care about decorations, but I never heard of anybody turning one down.

Diana was very sorry in a few days that she had said what she did about the medal going home to my mother, for a letter arrived from the Reverend Donald Phelps, in reply to one Dr Houneen had sent to my parents, saying that Alexander Ramsay and his wife, Fiona Dunstable Ramsay, had both died in the influenza epidemic of early 1918, though not before they had received news of my presumed death at Passchendaele.

Diana was ashamed because she thought she might have hurt my feelings. I was ashamed because I felt the loss so little.

( 4 )

It was years before I thought of the death of my parents as anything other than a relief; in my thirties I was able to see them as real people, who had done the best they could in the lives fate had given them. But as I lay in that hospital I was glad that I did not have to be my mother's own dear laddie any longer, or ever attempt to explain to her what war was, or warp my nature to suit her confident demands. I knew she had eaten my father, and I was glad I did not have to fight any longer to keep her from eating me. Oh, these good, ignorant, confident women! How one grows to hate them! I was mean-spiritedly pleased that my mother had not lived to hear of my V.C.; how she would have paraded in mock-modesty as the mother of a hero, the very womb and matrix of bravery, in consequence of my three years of degradation in the Flanders mud!

I confided none of this to Diana, of course. She was intensely curious about my war experience, and I had no trouble at all in talking to her about it. But as I gave her my confidence and she gave me her sympathy, I was well aware that we were growing very close and that some day this would have to be reckoned with. I did not care. I was happy to be living at all, and lived only for the sweetness of the moment.

She was a romantic, and as I had never met a female romantic before it was a delight to me to explore her emotions. She wanted to know all about me, and I told her as honestly as I could; but as I was barely twenty, and a romantic myself, I know now that I lied in every word I uttered—lied not in fact but in emphasis, in colour, and in intention. She was entranced by the idea of life in Canada, and I made it entrancing. I even told her about Mrs Dempster (though not that I was the cause of her distracted state) and felt let down that she did not respond very warmly. But when I told her about the little Madonna at Passchendaele and later as a visitor to my long coma, she was delighted and immediately gave it a conventionally religious significance, which, quite honestly, had never occurred to me. She returned to this theme again and again, and often I was reminded of the introduction to *A Child's Book of Saints* and little W.V., for whom those stories had been told. Personally I had come to think of little W.V. as rather a little pill, but I now reserved my judgement, for Diana was little W.V. to the life, and I was all for Diana.

Gradually it broke in upon me that Diana had marked me for her own, and I was too much flattered to see what that might mean. A lot of the nurses in that hospital were girls of good family, and though they worked very hard and did full nursing duty they had some privileges that cannot have been common. Most of them lived nearby, and they were able to go home in their time off.

When Diana returned from these off-duty jaunts she spoke about her home and her parents, and they seemed to be people unlike parents as I knew them. Her father, Canon Marfleet, was a domestic chaplain at Windsor as well as a parish clergyman; I had little notion what a domestic chaplain might be, but I assumed he jawed the Royal Family about morals, just as the parsons jawed us at home. Her mother was an Honourable, though the Canon was not, which surprised me, and she had been born a De Blaquiere, which, as Diana pronounced it D'Blackyer, I did not get straight for some time. Because of the war the Marfleets were living very simply—only two servants and a gardener three times a week—and the Canon had followed royal example and forbidden alcoholic liquors in his house-hold for the duration, except for a glass or two of port when he felt peaky. They restricted their daily bath-water to three inches, to save fuel for Our Cause; I had never in my life known anyone who bathed every day and assumed that the hospital daily bath was some sort of curative measure that would eventually cease.

Diana was a very educative experience. As she gradually took me over she began to correct me about some of my usages, which she thought quaint—not wrong, just quaint. Fortunately, because I had a good measure of Scots in my speech, we did not have the usual haggle of Old and New World couples about pronunciations, though she was hilarious about me calling a reel of cotton a spool of thread and assured me that pants were things one wore under trousers. But she made it clear that one tore bread, instead of cutting it neatly, and buttered it only in bites, which I thought a time-wasting affectation; she also stopped me from eating like a man who might not live until his next mouthful, a childhood habit that had been exaggerated in the trenches and that still overcomes me when I am nervous. I liked it. I was grateful. Besides, she did it with humour and charm; there was not a nagging breath in her.

Of course this did not happen all at once. It was some time after I woke from my coma before I could get out of bed, and quite a while after that before I could begin experimenting with the succession of artificial legs that came before my final one. I had to learn to walk with crutches, and because so many of my muscles, especially in the left arm, were scarred or reduced to very little, this took time and hurt. Diana saw me through it all. Literally, I leaned on her, and now and then I fell on her. She was a wonderful nurse.

When it was at last possible to do so she took me home, and I met the Canon and the Honourable. The best I can say about them is that they were worthy to be Diana's parents. The Canon was a charming man, quite unlike any clergyman I had ever known, and even at the Sunday midday meal he never talked about religion. Like a good Presbyterian, I tried once or twice to pass him a compliment on his discourse at morning service and pursue its theme, but he wanted none of that. He wanted to talk about the war, and as he was well informed and a Lloyd George supporter it was not the usual hate session in which he invited me to engage; there must have been a lot like him in England, though you would never have known it from the peace we finally made. The Honourable was a wonder, not like a mother at all. She was a witty, frivolous woman of a beauty congruous with her age—about forty-seven, I suppose—and talked as if she hadn't a brain in her head. But I was not deceived; she was what Diana would be at that age, and I liked every bit of it.

How my spirit expanded in the home of the Marfleets! To a man who had been where I had been it was glorious. I only hope I behaved myself and did not talk like a fool. But when I remember those days I remember the Canon and the Honourable and Diana and what I felt about them, but little of what I did or said.

( 5 )

The patchy quality of my recollection of this period is owing, I suppose, to the exhaustion of three years of war. I was out of it at last, and I was happy to take pleasure in security and cleanliness, without paying too close attention to what went on. Now and then it was possible to hear the guns in France; food was short but better than I had had in the trenches; the news came in ominous newspaper dispatches. Nevertheless I was happy and knew that for me, at least, the war was over. My plans were simple—to learn to walk with a crutch, and later with an artificial leg and a cane. Without being positively in love with Diana, I was beglamoured by her and flattered by her attention. I had fought my war and was resting.

We did win it at last, and there was a great hullabaloo in the hospital, and on the day after November 11, Dr Houneen got a car and drove me and another man who was fit for it, and Diana and another nurse, to London to see the fun. The rejoicing was a little too much like an infantry attack for my taste; I had not been in a crowd since I was wounded, and the noise and crush were very alarming to me. Indeed, I have never been much good at enduring noise and crush since late 1917. But I saw some of the excitement and a few things that shocked me; people, having been delivered from destruction, became horribly destructive themselves; people, having been delivered from license and riot, pawed and mauled and shouted dirty phrases in the streets. Nor am I in any position to talk; it was on the night of November 12, in a house in Eaton Square belonging to one of her De Blaquiere aunts, that I first slept with Diana, the aunt giving her assent by silence and discreet absence; to me at least there seemed something unseemly about the union of my scarred and maimed body with her unblemished beauty. Unseemly or not, it was my first experience of anything of the kind, for I had never been able to bring myself to make use of soldiers' brothels or any of the casual company that was available to men in uniform. Diana was not a novice—the fiancé who went down on the *Aboukir*, I suppose—and she initiated me most tenderly, for which I shall always be grateful. Thus we became lovers in the fullest sense, and for me the experience was an important step towards the completion of that manhood which had been thrust upon me so one-sidedly in the trenches.

The next night, because Diana had luck as well as influence, we had tickets for *Chu-Chin-Chow* at His Majesty's, and this was a great experience too, in quite a different way, for I had never seen any theatre more elaborate than a troop show. On one of my two very brief leaves in Paris I had sought out the site of Robert-Houdin's theatre, but it was no longer there. I must have been an odd young man to have supposed that it might still be in existence. But my historical sense developed later.

I see that I have been so muddle-headed as to put my sexual initiation in direct conjunction with a visit to a musical show, which suggests some lack of balance perhaps. But, looking back from my present age, the two, though very different, are not so unlike in psychological weight as you might suppose. Both were wonders, strange lands revealed to me in circumstances of great excitement. I suppose I was still in rather delicate health, mentally as well as physically.

The next great moment in my life was the reception of my Victoria Cross, from the King himself. Dr Houneen had established that I was really alive, and so the award that had been published as posthumous was repeated on one of the lists, and in due course I went to

Buckingham Palace in a taxi, on a December morning, and got it. Diana was with me, for I was allowed to invite one guest, and she was the obvious choice. We were looked at with sentimental friendliness by the other people in the room, and I suppose an obviously wounded soldier, accompanied by a very pretty nurse, was about as popular a sight as the time afforded.

Most of the details are vague, but a few remain. A military band, in an adjoining room, played Gems from *The Maid of the Mountains* (it was Diana who told me), and we all stood around the walls until the King and some aides entered and took a place in the centre. When my turn came I stumped forward on my latest metal leg, making rather a noisy progress, and got myself into the right position, directly in front of the King. Somebody handed him the medal, and he pinned it on my tunic, then shook my hand and said, "I am glad you were able to get here after all."

I can still remember what a deep and rather gruff voice he had, and also the splendid neatness of his Navy beard. He was a good deal shorter than I, so I was looking down into his very blue, rather glittering eyes, and I thought I had better smile at the royal joke, so I did, and retreated in good order.

There was a moment, however, when the King and I were looking directly into each other's eyes, and in that instant I had a revelation that takes much longer to explain than to experience. Here am I, reflected, being decorated as a hero, and in the eyes of everybody here I am indeed a hero; but I know that my heroic act was rather a dirty job I did when I was dreadfully frightened; I could just as easily have muddled it and been ingloriously killed. But it doesn't much matter, because people seem to need heroes; so long as I don't lose sight of the truth, it might as well be me as anyone else. And here before me stands a marvellously groomed little man who is pinning a hero's medal on me because some of his forebears were Alfred the Great, and Charles the First, and even King Arthur, for anything I know to the contrary. But I shouldn't be surprised if inside he feels as puzzled about the fate that brings him here as I. We are public icons, we two: he an icon of kingship, and I an icon of heroism, unreal yet very necessary; we have obligations above what is merely personal, and to let personal feelings obscure the obligations would be failing in one's duty.

This was clearer still afterward, at lunch at the Savoy, when the Canon and the Honourable gave us a gay time, with champagne; they all seemed to accept me as a genuine hero, and I did my best to behave decently, neither believing in it too obviously, nor yet protesting that I was just a simple chap who had done his duty when he saw it—a pose that has always disgusted me. Ever since, I have tried to think charitably of people in prominent positions of one kind or another; we cast them in roles, and it is only right to consider them as players, without trying to discredit them with knowledge of their off-stage life—unless they drag it into the middle of the stage themselves.

( 6 )

The business of getting used to myself as a hero was only part of the work I had on hand during my long stay in the hospital. When first I returned to this world—I will not say to consciousness because it seemed to me that I had been conscious on a different level during what they called my coma—I had to get used to being a man with one leg and a decidedly weakened left arm. I was not so clever at managing these handicaps as were some of the men in that hospital who had lost limbs; I have always been clumsy, and though Diana and the doctor assured me that I would soon walk as well as if I had a real leg I had no belief in it, and indeed I have never managed to walk without a limp and feel much happier with a cane. I was very weak physically, to begin with, and although I was perfectly sane I was a little light-headed for several months, and all my recollections of that period are confused by this quality of light-headedness. But I had to get used to being a hero—that is, not to believe it myself but not to be insulting to those who did so—and I also had to make up my mind about Diana.

There was an unreality about our relationship that had its roots in something more lasting than my light-headedness. I will say nothing against her, and I shall always be grateful to her for teaching me what the physical side of love was; after the squalor of the trenches her beauty and high spirits were the best medicine I got. But I could not be blind to the fact that she regarded me as her own creation. And why not? Hadn't she fed me and washed me and lured me back into this world when I was far away? Didn't she teach me to walk, showing the greatest patience when I was most clumsy? Was she not anxious to retrain me about habits of eating and behaviour? But even as I write it down I know how clear it is that what was wrong between Diana and me was that she was too much a mother to me, and as I had had one mother, and lost her, I was not in a hurry to acquire another—not even a young and beautiful one with whom I could play Oedipus to both our hearts' content. If I could manage it, I had no intention of being anybody's own dear laddie, ever again.

That decision, made at that time, has shaped my life and doubtless in some ways it has warped it, but I still think I knew what was best for me. In the long periods of rest in the hospital I thought as carefully as I could about my situation, and what emerged was this: I had made a substantial payment to society for anything society had given me or would give me in future; a leg and much of one arm are hard coin. Society had decided to regard me as a hero, and though I knew that I was no more a hero than many other men I had fought with, and less than some who had been killed doing what I could not have done, I determined to let society regard me as it pleased; I would not trade on it, but I would not put it aside either. I would get a pension in due time, and my Victoria Cross carried a resounding fifty dollars a year with it; I would take these rewards and be grateful. But I wanted my life to be my own; I would live henceforth for my own satisfaction.

That did not include Diana. She seemed to assume that it did, and perhaps I was unfair to her in not checking her assumptions as soon as I became aware of them. But, to be frank, I liked having her in love with me; it fed my spirit, which was at a low ebb. I liked going to bed with her, and as she liked it too I thought this a fair exchange. But a life with Diana was simply not for me. As girls do, she assumed that we were drifting towards an engagement and marriage; though she never said so in plain words it was clear she thought that when I was strong enough we would go to Canada, and if I did not mistake her utterly, she had in her mind's eye a fine big wheat farm in the West, for she had the English delusion that farming was a great way to live. I knew enough about farming to be sure it was not a life for amateurs or wounded men.

Every two weeks Diana would appear, looking remote and beautiful, and hand me a letter from Leola Cruikshank. These were always difficult occasions because the letters embarrassed me; they were so barren of content, so ill-expressed, so utterly unlike the Leola, all curls and soft lips and whispers, that I remembered. How, I wondered, had I been so stupid as to get myself mixed up with such a pinhead? Diana knew the letters were from a girl, for Leola's guileless writing could not have belonged to any other section of humanity, and intuition told her that, as they were almost the only letters I received, the girl was a special one. I could not have told her how special, for I could no longer remember precisely what pledges I had made to Leola; was I engaged to her or was I not? The letters I wrote in reply, and painstakingly smuggled into the post so Diana should not see them, were as noncommittal as I had the heart to make them; I tried to write in such a way as to evoke from Leola some indication of what she believed our relationship to be, without committing myself. This meant subtlety of a kind that was far outside Leola's scope; she was no hand with the pen, and her flat little letters gave Deptford gossip (with all the spice left out) and usually ended, "Everybody looks forward to your coming home and it will be lovely to see you again, Love, Leola." Was this coolness or maidenly reserve? Sometimes I broke out in a sweat, wondering.

One of Leola's letters came just before Christmas, which I had leave to spend with Diana's family. The Canon had celebrated the Armistice by abandoning the no-alcohol vow and it looked like being a jolly occasion. I had learned to drink neat rum in the Army and was ready for anything. But, on Christmas Eve, Diana contrived a private talk between us and asked me straight out who the girl was who wrote to me from Canada and was I involved with her. *Involved* was her word. I had been dreading this question but had no answer ready, and I havered and floundered and became aware that Leola's name had an uncouth sound when spoken in such circumstances, and hated myself for thinking so. My whole trouble, jackass that I was, sprang from the fact that I tried to be decently loyal to Leola without hurting Diana, and the more I talked the worse mess I made of things. In no time Diana was crying, and I was doing my best to comfort her. But I managed to keep uppermost in my mind the determination I had formed not to get engaged to her, and this led me into verbal acrobatics that quickly brought on a blazing row.

Canadian soldiers had an ambiguous reputation in England at that time; we were supposed to be loyal, furious, hairy fellows who spat bullets at the enemy but ate women raw. Diana accused me of being one of these ogres, who had led her on to reveal feelings I did not reciprocate. Like a fool, I said I thought she was old enough to know what she thought. Aha, she said, that was it, was it? Because she was older than I, she was a tough old rounder who could look out for herself, was she? Not a bit tough, I countered, frank with a flat-footedness that now makes me blush, but after all she had been engaged, hadn't she? There it was again, she countered; I thought she was damaged goods; I was throwing it in her face that she had given herself to a man who had died a hero's death in the very first weeks of the war. I looked on her simply as an amusement, a pastime; she had loved me in my weakness, without knowing how essentially coarse-fibred I was. And much more to the same effect.

Of course this gave way in time to much gentler exchanges, and we savoured the sweet pleasures of making up after a fight, but it was not long before Diana wanted to know, just as someone who wished me well, how far I was committed to Leola. I didn't dare tell her that I wanted to know precisely the same thing; I was too young to be truthful about such a matter. Well then, she continued, was I in love with Leola? I was able to say with a good conscience that I was not. Then I was in love with herself after all, said Diana, making one of those feminine leaps in logic that leave men breathless. I made a long speech about never knowing what people meant when they said they were in love with someone. I loved Diana, I said; I really did. But as for "being in love"—I babbled a good deal of nonsense that I cannot now recall and would not put down if I did.

Diana changed her tactics. I was too intellectual, she said, and analyzed matters on which feeling was the only true guide. If I loved her, she asked no more. What did the future hold for us?

I do not want to make Diana seem crafty in my record of this conversation, but I must say that she had a great gift for getting her own way. *She* had strong ideas on what the future held for us, and I had none, and I am certain she knew it. Therefore she was putting forward this question not to hear from me but to inform me. But I had my little store of craft too. I said that the war had been such a shake-up for me that I had no clear ideas about the future, and certainly had not considered asking her to marry anybody as badly crippled as I.

This proved to be a terrible mistake. Diana was so vehement about what a decent woman felt for a man who had been wounded and handicapped in the war—not to speak of a man who had been given the highest award for bravery—that I nearly lost my head and begged her to be my wife. I cannot look back on my young self in this situation without considerable shame and disgust. So far I had been able to reject this girl's love, but I was nearly captured by her flattery. Not that she meant it insincerely; there was nothing insincere about Diana. But she had been raised on a mental diet of heroism, Empire, decency, and the emotional superiority of womanhood, and she could talk about these things without a blush, as parsons talk about God. And I was only twenty.

What a night that was! We talked till three o'clock, complicating our situation with endless scruple, as young people are apt to do, and trying not to hurt each other's feelings, despite the fact that Diana wanted to get engaged to me and I was fighting desperately to prevent any such thing. But I have said before, and I repeat, Diana was really an exceptional girl, and when she saw she was not going to get her way she gave in with grace.

"All right," she said, sitting up on the sofa and tidying her hair (for we had been very much entangled during parts of our argument, and my latest artificial leg had been giving some ominous croaks); "if we aren't going to be married, that's that. But what *are* you going to do, Dunny? Surely you aren't going to marry that girl with a name like a hair tonic and go on editing your father's potty little paper, are you? There's more to you than that."

I agreed that I was sure there was more to me than that, but I didn't know what it was and I needed time to find out. Furthermore, I knew that the finding out must be done alone. I did not tell Diana that there was the whole question of the little Madonna to be gone into, because I knew that with her conventional Christian back-ground and her generous sentimentality she would begin then and there to explain it for me, and every scrap of intuition I possessed told me that her explanation would be the wrong one. But I did tell her that I was strongly conscious that my lack of formal education was the greatest handicap I had and that I felt that somehow I must get to a university; if I went back to Canada and explored all the possibilities I could probably manage it. It is not easy to put down what one says to a girl in such circumstances, but I managed to make it clear that what I most wanted was time to grow up. The war had not matured me; I was like a piece of meat that is burned on one side and raw on the other, and it was on the raw side I needed to work. I thanked her, as well as I could, for what she had done for me.

"Let me do one thing more for you," she said. "Let me rename you. How on earth did you ever get yourself called Dunstable?"

"My mother's maiden name," said I. "Lots of people in Canada get landed with their mother's maiden name as a Christian name. But what's wrong with it?"

"It's hard to say, for one thing," said she, "and it sounds like a cart rumbling over cobblestones for another. You'll never get anywhere in the world named Dumbledum Ramsay. Why don't you change it to Dunstan? St Dunstan was a marvellous person and very much like you—mad about learning, terribly stiff and stern and scowly, and an absolute wizard at withstanding temptation. Do you know that the Devil once came to tempt him in the form of a fascinating woman, and he caught her nose in his goldsmith's tongs and gave it a terrible twist?"

I took her nose between my fingers and gave it a twist. This was very nearly the undoing of all that I had gained, but after a while we were talking again. I liked the idea of a new name; it suggested new freedom and a new personality. So Diana got some of her father's port and poured it on my head and renamed me. She was an Anglican, of course, and her light-minded attitude toward some sacred things still astonished the deep Presbyterian in me; but I had not waded through the mud-and-blood soup of Passchendaele to worry about foolish things; blasphemy in a good cause (which usually means one's own cause) is not hard to stomach. When at last we went to bed two splendid things had happened: Diana and I were friends instead of lovers, and I had an excellent new name.

Christmas Day was even better than I had foreseen. I am sure Diana's parents knew what was in the wind and were game enough not to stand in the way if we had really wanted to marry. But they were much relieved that we had decided against it. How they knew I cannot say, but parents are often less stupid than their children suppose, and I suspect the Honourable smelled it in the morning air. After all, what satisfaction would it have been to them to have their daughter marry a man in my physical state, of very different background, and four years younger than herself, in order to go off to seek a fortune in a country of which they knew nothing? So they were happy, and I was happy, and I suspect that Diana was a good deal happier than she would ever have admitted.

She had fallen in love with me because she felt she had made whatever I was out of a smashed-up and insensible hospital case; but I don't think it was long before she was just as sure as I that our marriage would never have worked. So I lost a possible wife and gained three very good friends that Christmas.

( 7 )

Getting back to Canada took some time because of the complication of Army necessities and my supposedly fragile state, but early in the following May I got off the train at Deptford, was greeted by the reeve, Orville Cave, and ceremonially driven around the village as the chief spectacle in a procession.

This grandeur had been carefully planned beforehand, by letter, but it was nonetheless astonishing for that. I had little idea of what four years of war had done in creating a new atmosphere in Deptford, for it had shown little interest in world affairs in my schooldays. But here was our village shoe-repair man, Moses Langirand, in what was meant to be a French uniform, personating Marshal Foch; he had secured this position on the best possible grounds, being the only French-speaking Canadian for miles around, and having an immense grey moustache. Here was a tall youth I did not know, in an outfit that approximated that of Uncle Sam. There were two John Bulls, owing to some misunderstanding that could not be resolved without hurt feelings. There were Red Cross nurses in plenty—six or seven of them. A girl celebrated in my day for having big feet, named Katie Orchard, was swathed in bunting and had a bandage over one eye; she was Gallant Little Belgium. These, and other people dressed in patriotic but vague outfits, formed a procession highly allegorical in its nature, which advanced down our main street, led by a band of seven brass instruments and a thunderous drum. I rode after them in an open Gray-Dort with the reeve, and following us was what was then called a Calithumpian parade, of gaily dressed children tormenting and insulting Myron Papple, who was identifiable as the German Emperor by his immense, upturned false moustache. Myron hopped about and feigned madness and deprivation very amusingly, but with such vigour that we wondered how a fat man could keep it up for long. As ours was a small village we toured through all the streets, and went up and down the main street no less than three times. Even at that we had done our uttermost by 2:45, and I had clumped down off the train at 1:30. It was the strangest procession I have ever seen, but it was in my honour and I will not laugh at it. It was Deptford's version of a Roman Triumph, and I tried to be worthy of it, looked solemn, saluted every flag I saw that was 12-by-8 inches or over, and gave special heed to elderly citizens.

The procession completed, I was hidden in the Tecumseh House until 5:30, when I was to have a state supper at the reeve's house. When I write "hidden" I mean it literally. My fellow townsmen felt that it would be unseemly for me to stroll about the streets, like an ordinary human being, before my apotheosis that night, so I was put in the best bedroom in our hotel, upon the door of which a Canadian Red Ensign had been tacked, and the barman, Joe Gallagher, was given strict orders to keep everyone away from me. So there I sat by my window, looking across a livery-stable yard toward St James' Presbyterian Church, occasionally reading *War and Peace* (for I was now well embarked on the big, meaty novels I had longed for at the Front), but mostly too excited to do anything but marvel at myself and wonder when I would be free to do as I pleased.

Freedom was certainly not to be mine that day. At six I supped ceremonially at the reeve's; there were so many guests that we ate on the lawn from trestle tables, consuming cold chicken and ham, potato salad and pickles in bewildering variety, and quantities of ice cream, pie, and cake. We then set the whole banquet well awash inside ourselves with hot, strong coffee. Our progress to the Athelstan Opera House was stately, as befitted the grandees of the occasion, and we arrived ten minutes before the scheduled proceedings at 7:30.

If you are surprised that so small a place should have an Opera House, I should explain that it was our principal hall of assembly, upstairs in the Athelstan Block, which was the chief business premises of our village, and built of brick instead of the more usual wood. It was a theatre, right enough, with a stage that had a surprising roller curtain, on which was handsomely painted a sort of composite view, or evocation, of all that was most romantic in Europe; it is many years since I saw it, but I clearly remember a castle on the shores of a lagoon, where gondolas appeared amid larger shipping, which seemed to be plying in and out of Naples, accommodated at the foot of snowtopped Alps. The floor of the Opera House was flat, as being more convenient for dancing, but this was compensated for by the fact that the stage sloped forward toward the footlights, at an angle which made sitting on chairs a tricky and even perilous feat. I do not know how many people it seated, but it was full on this occasion, and people stood or sat in the aisles on extra chairs, borrowed from an undertaker.

The reeve and I and the other notables climbed a back stairs and pushed our way through the scenery to the chairs that had been set for us on the stage. Beyond the curtain we heard the hum of the crowd above the orchestra of piano, violin, and trombone. A little after the appointed time—to allow for latecomers, said the reeve, but no latecomer could have squeezed in—the curtain rose (swaying menacingly inward toward us as it did so), and we were revealed, set off against a set of scenery that portrayed a dense and poisonously green forest. Our chairs were arranged in straight rows behind a table supporting two jugs of water and fully a dozen glasses, to succour the speakers in their thirst. We were a fine group: three clergymen, the magistrate, the Member of Parliament and the Member of the Legislature, the Chairman of the Continuation School Board, and seven members of the township council sat on the stage, as well as the reeve and myself. I expect we looked rather like a minstrel show. I was the only man in uniform on the stage itself, but in the front row were six others, and on the right-hand end of this group sat Percy Boyd Staunton, in a major's uniform, and at his side was Leola Cruikshank.

On the fourth finger of Leola's left hand was a large diamond ring. Diana had taught me something of these refinements and I got the message at once, as that ring flashed its signals to me during the applause that greeted our appearance. Was I stricken to the heart? Did I blench and feel that all my glory was as dross? No; I was rather pleased. There was one of my homecoming problems solved already, I reflected. Nevertheless I was a little put out and thought that Leola was a sneak not to have informed me of this development in one of her letters.

The purpose of the gathering was plainly signalled by the Union Jack that swathed the speaker's table and a painted streamer that hung above our heads in the toxic forest. "Welcome To Our Brave Boys Back From The Front," it shouted, in red and blue letters on a white ground. We stood solemnly at attention while the piano, violin, and trombone worked their way through *God Save the King, O Canada,* and, for good measure, *The Maple Leaf Forever.* But we did not then rush greedily upon the noblest splendours of the evening. We began with a patriotic concert, to hone our fervour to a finer edge.

Muriel Parkinson sang about the *Rose that Blows in No-Man's Land,* and when she shrieked (for her voice was powerful rather than sweet) that "midst the war's great curse stood the Red Cross Nurse," many people mopped their eyes. She then sang a song about Joan of Arc, which was a popular war number of the day, and thus a delicate compliment was paid to France, our great ally. Muriel was followed by a female child, unknown to me, who recited Pauline Johnson's poem *Canadian Born,* wearing Indian dress; it was at this point that I became aware that one of our Brave Boys, namely George Muskrat the Indian sniper, who had picked off Germans just as he used to pick off squirrels, was not present. George was not a very respectable fellow (he drank vanilla extract, which was mostly alcohol, to excess, and shouted in the streets when on a toot), and he had not been given any medals.

The female child reciter had an encore and was well into it before the applause for her first piece had quite subsided. Then, for no perceptible reason, another girl played two pieces on the piano, not very well; one was called *Chanson des Fleurs* and the other *La Jeunesse,* so perhaps they were further compliments to the French. Then a fellow with a local reputation as a wit, named Murray Tiffin, "entertained"; he was often asked to "entertain" at church evenings, but this was his greatest opportunity so far, and he toiled like a cart horse to divert us with riddles, jokes, and imitations, all of some local application.

"What's the bravest thing a man can do?" he demanded. "Is it go right out to Africa and shoot a lion? No! *That's* not the bravest thing a man can do! Is it capture a German machine-gun nest single-handed?" (Great applause, during which I, the worst actor in the world, tried to feign a combination of modesty and mirth.) "No! The bravest thing a man can do is go to the Deptford Post Office at one minute past six on a Saturday night and ask Jerry Williams for a one-cent stamp!" (Uncontrollable mirth, and much nudging and waving at the postmaster, who tried to look like a man who dearly loved a joke against his cranky self.)

Then Murray got off several other good ones, about how much cheaper it was to buy groceries in Bowles Corners than it was even to steal them from the merchants of Deptford, and similar local wit of the sort that age cannot wither nor custom stale; I warmed to Murray, for although his jokes were clean they had much of the quality that had assured my own rest-camp success as Charlie Chaplin.

When Murray had offended individually at least half the people present and delighted us all collectively, the reeve rose and began, "But to strike a more serious note—" and went on to strike that note for at least ten minutes. We were gathered, he said, to honour those of our community who had risked their lives in defence of liberty. When he had finished, the Methodist parson told us, at some length, how meritorious it was to risk one's life in defence of liberty. Then Father Regan solemnly read out the eleven names of the men from our little part of the world who had been killed in service; Willie's was among them, and I think it was in that moment that I really understood that I would never see Willie again. The Reverend Donald Phelps prayed that we might never forget them, at some length; if God had not been attending to the war, He knew a good deal more about it, from our point of view, by the time Phelps had finished. The Member of the Legislature told us he would not detain us long and talked for forty minutes about the future and what we were going to do with it, building on the sacrifices of the past four years, particularly in the matter of improving the provincial road system. Then the Member of Parliament was let loose upon us, and he talked for three minutes more than one hour, combining patriotism with a good partisan political speech, hinting pretty strongly that although Lloyd George, Clemenceau, and Wilson were unquestionably good men, Sir Robert Borden had really pushed the war to a successful conclusion.

It was by now ten o'clock and even the thirst of a Canadian audience for oratory was almost slaked. Only the great moments that were to follow could have held them. But here it was that the reeve took his second bite at us; in order that Deptford might never forget those who had fought and returned, he said, and in order that our heroes should never lose sight of Deptford's gratitude, every one of us was to receive an engraved watch. Nor was this all. These were no ordinary watches but railway watches, warranted to tell time accurately under the most trying conditions, and probably for all eternity. We understood the merit of these watches because, as we all knew, his son Jack was a railwayman, a brakeman on the Grand Trunk, and Jack swore that these were the best watches to be had anywhere. Whereupon the watches were presented, three by the reeve himself and three by the Member of the Legislature.

As his name and glory were proclaimed, each man in the front row climbed up the steps that led to a pass-door at the side of the stage, squeezed through the green scenery, and made his way to the centre of the platform, while his relatives and townsmen cheered, stamped, and whistled. Percy Boyd Staunton was the sixth, the only officer in the group and the only man who accepted his watch with an air; he had put on his cap before coming to the stage, and he saluted the Member of the Legislature smartly, then turned and saluted the audience; it was a fine effect, and as I grinned and clapped, my stomach burned with jealousy.

I should have been generous, for I was number seven, a V.C., the only man to be given a seat on the stage, and the only man to receive his watch from the hands of our Member of Parliament. He made a speech. "Sergeant Dunstable Ramsay," said he, "I acclaim you as a hero tonight—" and went on for quite a while, though I could not judge how long, because I stood before him feeling a fool and a fake as I had not done when I stood before my King. But at last he handed me the railway watch, and as I had left my hat outside I could not salute, so I had to bob my head, and then bob it at the audience, who cheered and stamped, rather longer than they had done for Percy, I believe. But my feelings were so confused that I could not enjoy it; I heartily wished to get away.

We concluded by singing *God Save the King* again in a classy version in which Muriel Parkinson was supposed to sing some parts alone and the rest of us to join in when she gave a signal; but there were a few people who droned along with her all the way, somewhat spoiling the effect. But when it was done we were free. Nobody seemed inclined to hurry away, and when I had made my way through the green scenery and down the steps by the pass-door I was surrounded by old friends and acquaintances who wanted to talk and shake my hand. I hurried through them as quickly as I could without being rude or overlooking anyone, but I had a little task to perform— a notion I had thought of during the long hour of the Member's speech, and I wanted to be sure I had a good audience. At last I reached Percy and Leola; I seized his hand and shook it vigorously, and then seized Leola in a bear-hug and kissed her resoundingly and at what Deptford would certainly have regarded as a very familiar length.

Leola had always been the kind of girl who closed her eyes when you kissed her, but I kept mine well open and I could see that her eyeballs were rolling wildly beneath her lids; Diana had taught me a thing or two about kisses, and I gave her a pretty good example of that art.

"Darling," I shouted, not letting her go, "you don't know how good it is to see you!"

Percy was grinning nervously. Public kissing was not so common then as it is now, and certainly not in our village. "Dunny, Leola and I have a secret to tell you—not that it will be secret long, of course—but we want you to be the first to hear—outside our families, of course—but we're engaged." And he sprayed his manly grin from side to side, for we were in the middle of a crowd and everybody could hear. There was a happy murmur, and a few people clapped.

I counted three, just to make sure that there was the right sort of pause, then I shook his hand again and roared, "Well, well, the best man has won!"—and kissed Leola again, not so long or so proprietorially, but to show that there had been a contest and that I had been a near winner myself, and had shown some speed in the preliminary heats.

It was a good moment and I enjoyed it thoroughly. Percy was wearing a few medals, the admirable D.S.O. but otherwise minor things, mostly for having been at particular engagements. I have already said that I am not much of an actor, but I gave a powerful, if crude impersonation of the hero who is tremendous on the field of Mars but slighted in the courts of Venus. I am sure that there are people in Deptford to this day who remember it.

I suppose it was mean. But Percy, in his officer's smart uniform, got under my skin just as he had always done, and as for Leola, I didn't particularly want her but resented anybody else having her. I promised that this would be a frank record, so far as I can write one, and God forbid that I should pretend that there is not a generous measure of spite in my nature.

This encounter put us in one of those uneasy situations that are forced on people by fate, for to the crowd—and at that moment Deptford was the whole world—we were the master-spirits of the evening: two men, one of whom was a hero without a left leg and the other a handsome and rich young fellow, only somewhat less a hero, who had aspired to the hand of the prettiest girl in the village, and the winner had been acclaimed; we were a splendidly sentimental story made flesh, and it would have been maladroit in the extreme— a real flying in the face of Providence—if we had not stayed together so people could marvel at us and wonder about us. That was why we went to the bonfire as a threesome.

The bonfire was arranged to take place outside the combination village hall, public library, courthouse, and fire hall; it was to be a gay conclusion, an anti-masque, to the high proceedings in the Opera House. There we had been solemn, acclaiming the heroic young and listening to the wise old: here the crowd was lively and expectant; children dodged to and fro, and there was a lot of laughter about nothing in particular. But not for long. In the distance we heard a great beating on pots and pans and blowing of tin horns, and down our main street came a procession, lit by the flame of brooms dipped in oil—a ruddy, smoky light—accompanying Marshal Foch, the two John Bulls, Uncle Sam, Gallant Little Belgium, the whole gang, dragging at a rope's end Deptford's own conception of the German Emperor, fat Myron Papple, whose writhings and caperings outdid his afternoon efforts as the death aria of an opera tenor outdoes his wooing in Act One.

"Hang him!" we heard the representatives of the Allies shouting as they drew near, and the crowd around the village hall took it up. "Hang him!" they yelled. "Hang the Kaiser!"

Hang him they did. A rope was ready on the flagpole, and during some scrambling preparations a sharp eye would have seen Myron slip away into the darkness as an effigy was tied to the rope by the neck and hauled slowly up the pole. As it rose, one of the Red Cross nurses set fire to it with a broom torch, and by the time it reached the top the figure was burning merrily.

Then the cheers were loud, and the children hopped and scampered round the foot of the flagpole, shouting, "Hang the Kaiser!" with growing hysteria; some of them were much too small to know what hanging was, or what a Kaiser might be, but I cannot call them innocent, for they were being as vicious as their age and experience allowed. And the people in the crowd, as I looked at them, were hardly recognizable as the earnest citizens who, not half an hour ago, had been so biddable under the spell of patriotic oratory, so responsive to *Canadian Born,* so touched by the romantic triangle of Leola, and Percy, and myself. Here they were, in this murky, fiery light, happily acquiescent in a symbolic act of cruelty and hatred. As the only person there, I suppose, who had any idea of what a really bad burn was like, I watched them with dismay that mounted towards horror, for these were my own people.

Leola's face looked very pretty as she turned it upward towards the fire, and Percy was laughing and looking about him for admiration as he shouted in his strong, manly voice, "Hang the Kaiser!"

Myron Papple, an artist to his fingertips, had climbed into the tower of the village hall, so that his screams and entreaties might proceed as near as possible from the height of the burning figure. I could hear him long after I had crept away to my bed in the Tecumseh House. I had not wanted to stay till the end.

( 8 )

The next day was a Saturday, and I had plenty to do. Though still an object of wonder, I was now free to move about as I pleased, and my first move was to get the keys of my old home from the magistrate and make a melancholy tour through its six rooms. Everything was where I knew it should be, but all the objects looked small and dull— my mother's clock, my father's desk, with the stone on it he had brought from Dumfries and always used as a paperweight; it was now an unloved house, and want of love had withered it. I picked up a few things I wanted—particularly something that I had long kept hidden—and got out as fast as I could.

Then I went to see Ada Blake, the girl Willie had been sweet on, and had a talk with her; Ada was a fine girl, and I liked her very much, but of course the Willie she remembered was not the brother I knew. I judge they had been lovers, briefly, and that was what Willie meant to her: to me his chief significance now was that he had died twice, and that the first time Mrs Dempster had brought him back to life. I certainly had no intention of visiting Dr McCausland, to see if he had changed his opinion on that subject, though I did chat with two or three of our village elders before getting my midday dinner at the hotel.

As soon as I had gobbled my greasy stew and apple pie I crossed the street to get a haircut at Papple's. I had already observed that Milo was on the job alone; his father was presumably at home, resting up after his patriotic exertions of the day before, and it was a chance to catch up on the village news. Milo gave me a hero's welcome and settled me in one of the two chairs, under a striped sheet that smelled, in equal portions, of barber's perfumes and the essence of Deptford manhood.

"Jeez, Dunny, this is the first time I ever give you a haircut—you know that? Trimmed your Pa a coupla times after you went to the Front, but never you. Comes of being the same age, I guess, eh? But now I'm taking over more and more from the old man. His heart's not so good now; he says it's breathing up little bits of hair all his life; he says it forms a kind of a hairball in barbers, and a lot of 'em go that way. I don't believe it; unscientific. He never got past third grade—you know that? But jeez, he certainly had 'em laughing yesterday, eh? And last night! But it told on him. Says he can feel the hairball today, just like it was one of his organs.

"You got a double crown. Did you know that? Makes it hard to give you a good cut. What you going to do with the old place? Live there, eh? Nice place to settle down if you was to get married. Your folks always kept it nice. Cece Athelstan always used to say, 'The Ramsays sure are buggers for paint.' But I guess you won't be marrying Leola, eh? Mind you, for them that had eyes to see, there was never an instant's doubt she was Percy's girl—never an instant's. Oh, I know you and her had some pretty close moments before you went to the war; everybody seen that and they kinda laughed. I had to laugh myself. It was just what we called war-fever—you in uniform, you see. But you got to admit she played fair. Wrote to you right up to the end. Jerry Williams used to tell us the letters come through the Post Office every second Monday like clockwork. Because she wrote you every second Sunday, you know that? But when Percy finished up at that school in Toronto in the summer of 'seventeen, he didn't hesitate for a minute—not for a minute. Into training right away, and went over as an officer, and come back a major. And a D.S.O. But you're the V.C., eh, boy? I guess you had a stroke of luck. I never got enlisted: flat feet. But you and Perse had the luck, I guess. He used to come down here as often as he could, and it was easy seen where Leola had give her heart. That's what her old lady used to say. 'Leola's give her heart,' she'd say. Ben Cruikshank wasn't strong on Perse to begin with, but the old lady shut him up. He's pleased now, all right. See him last night? Of course he thinks the sun rises and sets in Leola. It's hard for a father, I guess. But you were the main attraction last night, eh? Yep, you were the Kandy Kid with Gum Feet and Taffy Legs. One Taffy Leg, anyhow. But not with Leola. She's give her heart.

"Jeez the war's made a difference in this little old burg. Unsettled. You know what I mean? Lots of changes. Two fires—bad ones—and Harry Henderson sold his store. But I guess I mean changes in people. Young kids in trouble a lot. And Jerry Cullen—you remember him?—sent to the penitentiary. His daughter squealed on him. Said he was always at her. She was just a kid, mind you. But the cream of it was, I don't think Jerry ever really knew what he done wrong. I think he thought everybody was like that. He was always kinda stupid. About that kinda thing, though, I guess the worst was young Grace Izzard—maybe you don't remember—she's always called Harelip because she's got this funny-looking lip. Well, she got to fourteen and got to guessing, I suppose, but who'd want her with a face like that? So she promises her kid brother Bobby, who's about twelve, a quarter if he'll do it to her, and he does but only if he gets ten cents first, and then, jeez, when he's finished she only gives him another nickel because she says that's all it's worth! Isn't that a corker, eh? These kids today, eh? And then—"

And then two bastards, a juicy self-induced abortion, several jilt-ings, an old maid gone foolish in menopause, and a goitre of such proportions as to make all previous local goitres seem like warts, which Dr McCausland was treating in Bowles Corners. The prurient, the humiliating, and the macabre were Milo's principal areas of enthusiasm, and we explored them all.

"The flu beat everything though. Spanish Influenza, they called it, but I always figured it was worked up by the Huns some ways. Jeez, this burg was like the Valley of the Shadda for weeks. Of course we felt it more than most in here; a barber always has everybody breathing on him, you see. The old man and me, we hung bags of assafoetida around our necks to give the germs a fight. But oh, people just dropped like flies. Like flies. McCausland worked twenty-four hours a day, I guess. Doc Staunton moved out to one of his farms to live and sort of gave up practice. But he'd been mostly a farmer in a big way for years. Rich man now. You remember Roy Janes and his wife, the Anglican minister? They never rested, going around to sick houses, and then both of 'em died themselves within forty-eight hours. The reeve put the town flag at half-mast that day, and everybody said he done right. And your Ma, Dunny—God, she was a wonderful woman! Never let up on nursing and taking soup and stuff around till your Dad went. You know he wouldn't go to bed? Struggled on when he was sick. Of course you could tell. Blue lips. Yeah, just as blue as huckleberries. That was the sign. We give 'em forty-eight hours after that. Your Dad kept on with his lips as blue as a Sunday suit for a day, then he just fell beside the make-up stone, and Jumper Saul got him home on a dray. Your Ma lost heart and she was gone herself before the week was out. Fine folks. Next issue of the *Banner*, Jumper Saul and Nell turned the column rules, and the front page just looked like a big death notice. God, when I saw it I just started bawling like a kid. Couldn't help myself. Do you know, in this little town of five hundred, and the district around, we lost ninety-eight, all told? But the worst was when Jumper turned the column rules. Everybody said he done right.

"You know 'Masa Dempster went? 'Course, he'd been no good for years. Not since his trouble, you remember? Sure you do! We used to see you skin over there after school and climb through the window to see her and Paul. Nobody ever thought there was any wrong going on, of course. We knew your Ma must have sent you. She couldn't do anything for the Dempsters publicly, of course, but she sent you to look after them. Everybody knew it an' honoured her for it. Do you remember how you said Mary Dempster raised Willie from the dead? God, you used to be a crazy kid, Dunny, but I guess the war knocked all that out of you …

"Miz' Dempster? Oh no, she didn't get the flu. That kind is always spared when better folks have to go. But after 'Masa went she was a problem. No money, you see. So the reeve and Magistrate Mahaffey found out she had an aunt somewheres near Toronto. Weston, I believe it was. The aunt come and took her. The aunt had money. Husband made it in stoves, I heard.

"No, Paul didn't go with her. Funny about him. Not ten yet, but he run away. He had a kind of a tough time at school, I guess. Couldn't fight much, because he was so undersized, but kids used to get around him at recess and yell, 'Hey, Paul, does your Ma wear any pants?' and stuff like that. Just fun, you know. The way kids are. But he'd get mad and fight and get hurt, and they just tormented him more to see him do it. They'd yell across the street, 'Hoor yuh today, Paul?' Sly, you see, because he knew damn well they didn't mean 'How are you today, Paul?' but 'Your Ma's a hoor.' Kind of a pun, I guess you'd call it. So when the circus was here, autumn of 'eighteen, he run away with one of the shows. Mahaffey tried to catch up with the circus, but he could never get nowheres with them. Tricky people. Funny, it was the best thing Paul ever done, in a way, because every kid wants to run away with a circus, and it made him kind of a hero after he'd gone. But Mary Dempster took it very bad and went clean off her head. Used to yell out the window at kids going to school, 'Have you seen my son Paul?' It would of been sad if we hadn't of known she was crazy. And it was only two or three weeks after that 'Masa got the flu and died. He certainly had a hard row to hoe. And inside a week the aunt come, and we haven't seen hide nor hair of them since."

By this time the haircut was finished, and Milo insisted on anointing me with every scent and tonic he had in the shop, and stifling me with talcum, as a personal tribute to my war record.

The next day was Sunday, and I made a much appreciated appearance in St James' Presbyterian Church. On Monday, after a short talk with the bank manager and the auctioneer, and a much longer and pleasanter talk with Jumper Saul and Nell, I boarded the train—there was no crowd at the station this time—and left Deptford in the flesh. It was not for a long time that I recognized that I never wholly left it in the spirit.

# 3

# *My Fool-Saint*

( 1 )

In the autumn of 1919 I entered University College, in the University of Toronto, as an Honours student in history. I was not properly qualified, but five professors talked to me for an hour and decided to admit me under some special ruling invoked on behalf of a number of men who had been abroad fighting. This was the first time my boyhood stab at being a polymath did me any good; there was also the fact that it has been my luck to appear more literate than I really am, owing to a cadaverous and scowling cast of countenance and a rather pedantic Scots voice; and certainly my V.C. and general appearance of having bled for liberty did no harm. So there I was, and very pleased about it too.

I had sold the family house for $1200, and its contents, by auction, for an unexpected $600. I had even sold the *Banner,* to a job printer who thought he would like to publish a newspaper, for $750 down and a further $2750 on notes extending over four years; I was an innocent in business, and he was a deadbeat, so I never got all of it. Nevertheless, the hope of money to come was encouraging. I had quite a good pension for my disabilities, and the promise of wooden legs as I needed them, and of course my annual $50 that went with the V.C. I seemed to myself to be the lord of great means, and in a way it proved so, for when I got my B.A. after four years I was able to run to another year's work for an M.A. I had always meant to get a Ph.D. at some later time, but I became interested in a branch of scholarship in which it was not relevant.

During my long summer vacations I worked at undemanding jobs—timekeeper on roadwork and the like—which enabled me to do a lot of reading and keep body and soul together without touching my education money, which was the way I looked on my capital.

I took very kindly to history. I chose it as my special study because during my fighting days I had become conscious that I was being used by powers over which I had no control for purposes of which I had no understanding. History, I hoped, would teach me how the world's affairs worked. It never really did so, but I became interested in it for its own sake, and at last found a branch of it that gripped whatever intelligence I had, and never relaxed its hold. At Varsity I never fell below fifth in my year in anything, and graduated first; my M.A. won me some compliments, though I thought my thesis dull. I gobbled up all the incidentals that were required to give a "rounded" education; even zoology (an introductory course) agreed with me, and I achieved something like proficiency in French. German I learned later, in a hurry, for some special work, and with a Berlitz teacher. I was also one of the handful of really interested students in Religious Knowledge, though it was not much of a course, relying too heavily on St Paul's journeys for my taste, and avoiding any discussion of what St Paul was really journeying in aid of. But it was a pleasure to be inside and warm, instead of wallowing in mud, and I worked, I suppose rather hard, though I was not conscious of it at the time. I made no close friends and never sought popularity or office in any of the student committees, but I got on pretty well with everybody. A dull fellow, I suppose; youth was not my time to flower.

Percy Boyd Staunton, however, flowered brilliantly, and I met him fairly often; brilliant young men seem to need a dull listener, just as pretty girls need a plain friend, to set them off. Like me, he had a new name. I had enrolled in the university as Dunstan Ramsay: Percy, somewhere in his Army experience, had thrown aside that name (which had become rather a joke, like Algernon) and had lopped the "d" off the name that remained. He was now Boy Staunton, and it suited him admirably. Just as Childe Rowland and Childe Harold were so called because they epitomized romance and gentle birth, he was Boy Staunton because he summed up in himself so much of the glory of youth in the postwar period. He gleamed, he glowed; his hair was glossier, his teeth whiter than those of common young men. He laughed a great deal, and his voice was musical. He danced often and spectacularly; he always knew the latest steps, and in those days there were new steps every month. Where his looks and style came from I never knew; certainly not from cantankerous old Doc Staunton, with his walrus moustache and sagging paunch, or from his mother, who was a charmless woman. Boy seemed to have made himself out of nothing, and he was a marvel.

He was a perfectionist, however, and not content. I remember him telling me during his first year as a law student that a girl had told him he reminded her of Richard Barthelmess, the screen star; he would rather have reminded her of John Barrymore, and he was displeased. I was quite a movie-goer myself and foolishly said I thought he was more like Wallace Reid in *The Dancin' Fool,* and was surprised by his indignation, for Reid was a handsome man. It was not until later that I discovered that he coveted a suggestion of aristocracy in his appearance and bearing, and Reid lacked it. He was at that time still casting around for an ideal upon whom he could model himself. It was not until his second year in law that he found it.

This ideal, this mould for his outward man, was no one less than Edward Albert Christian George Andrew Patrick David, the Prince of Wales. The papers were full of the Prince at that time. He was the great ambassador of the Commonwealth, but he had also the common touch; he spoke with what horrified old ladies thought a common accent, but he could charm a bird from a branch; he danced and was reputed to be a devil with the girls; he was said to quarrel with his father (my King, the man with the Navy torpedo beard) about matters of dress; he was photographed smoking a pipe with a distinctive apple-shaped bowl. He had romance and mystery, for over his puzzled brow hung the shadow of the Crown; how would such a dashing youth ever settle himself to the duties of kingship? He was gloated over by old women who wondered what princess he would marry, and gloated over by young women because he thought more of looks and charm than of royal blood. There were rumours of high old times with jolly girls when he had visited Canada in 1919.

Flaming Youth, and yet, withal, a Prince, remote and fated for great things. Just the very model for Boy Staunton, who saw himself in similar terms.

In those days you could not become a lawyer by going to the university—not in our part of Canada. You must go to Osgoode Hall, where the Law Society of Upper Canada would steer you through until at last you were called to the Bar. This worried Boy, but not very much. The university, he admitted to me—I had not asked for any such admission—put a stamp on a man; but if you got that stamp first and studied law later, you would be old, a positive greybeard, before getting into the full tide of life. So far as I could see, the full tide of life had a lot to do with sugar.

Sugar was what old Doc Staunton was chiefly interested in. He had grabbed up a lot of land in the Deptford district and put it all into sugar-beets. The black, deep alluvial soil of the river flats around Deptford was good for anything, and wonderful for beets. Doc was not yet a Sugar-Beet King, but he was well on his way to it—a sort of Sticky Duke. Boy, who had more vision than his father, managed to get the old man to buy into the secondary process, the refining of the sugar from the beets, and this was proving profitable in such a surprising degree that Doc Staunton was rich in a sense far beyond Deptford's comprehension; so rich, indeed, that they forgot that he had skipped town when the flu epidemic struck. As for the present, a very rich man has something better to do than listen to old women's coughs and patch up farmers who have fallen into the chaff-cutter. Doc Staunton never formally dropped practice, and accepted the sanctity that came with wealth in the way he had accepted his prestige as a doctor—with a sour face and a combination of pomposity and grievance that was all his own. He did not move away from Deptford. He did not know of anywhere else to go, I suppose, and the life of a village Rich Man—far outstripping the Athelstans—suited him very well.

The Athelstans did not like it, and Cece got off a "good one" that the village cherished for years. "If Jesus died to redeem Doc Staunton," he said, "He made a damn poor job of it."

So Boy Staunton knew that he too had a crown awaiting him. He did not mean to practise law, but it was a good training for business and, eventually, politics. He was going to be a very rich man—richer than his father by far—and he was getting ready.

He, like his ideal, was not on the best of terms with his father. Doc Staunton gave Boy what he regarded as a good allowance; it was not bad, but it was not ample either, and Boy needed more. So he made some shrewd short-term investments in the stock market and was thus able to live at a rate that puzzled and annoyed the old man, who waited angrily for him to get into debt. But Boy did not get into debt. Debt was for boobs, he said, and he flaunted such toys as gold ciga-rette cases and hand-made shoes under the old man's nose, without explaining anything.

Where Boy lived high, I lived—well, not low, but in the way congenial to myself. I thought twenty-four dollars was plenty for a ready-made suit, and four dollars a criminal price for a pair of shoes. I changed my shirt twice a week and my underwear once. I had not yet developed any expensive tastes and saw nothing wrong with a good boarding-house; it was years before I decided that there is really no such thing as a good boarding-house. Once, temporarily envious of Boy, I bought a silk shirt and paid nine dollars for it. It burned me like the shirt of Nessus, but I wore it to rags, to get my money out of it, garment of guilty luxury that it was.

Here we come to a point where I have to make an admission that will put me in a bad light, considering the story I have to tell. Boy was very good about passing on information to me about investment, and now and then I ventured two or three hundred from my small store, always with heartening results. Indeed, during my university days I laid the foundation for the modest but pleasant fortune I have now. What Boy did in thousands I did in hundreds, and without his guid-ance I would have been powerless, for investment was not in my line; I knew just enough to follow his advice—when to buy and when to sell, and especially when to hang on. Why he did this for me I can only explain on the grounds that he must have liked me. But it was a kind of liking, as I hope will be clear before we have finished, that was not easy to bear.

We were both young, neither yet fully come to himself, and what-ever he may have felt for me, I knew that in several ways I was jealous of him. He had something to give—his advice about how to turn my few hundreds into a few thousands—and I make no apology for benefiting from the advice of a man I sneered at in my mind; I was too much a Scot to let a dollar get away from me if it came within my clutch. I am not seeking to posture as a hero in this memoir. Later, when I had something to give and could have helped him, he did not want it. You see how it was: to him the reality of life lay in external things, whereas for me the only reality was of the spirit—of the mind, as I then thought, not having understood yet what a cruel joker and mean master the intellect can be. So if you choose to see me as a false friend, exploiting a frank and talented youth, go ahead. I can but hope that before my story is all told you will see things otherwise.

We met about once every two weeks, by appointment, for our social lives never intersected. Why would they, especially after Boy bought his car, a very smart affair coloured a rich shade of auburn. He helled around to all the dancing places with men of his own stamp and the girls they liked, drinking a good deal out of flasks and making lots of noise.

I remember seeing him at a rugby game in the autumn of 1923; it was not a year since the Earl of Carnarvon had discovered the tomb of Tutankhamen, and already the gentlemen's outfitters had worked up a line of Egyptian fashions. Boy wore a gorgeous pullover of brownish-red, around which marched processions of little Egyptians, copied from the tomb pictures; he had on the baggiest of Oxford bags, smoked the apple-bowl pipe with casual style, and his demeanour was that of one of the lords of creation. A pretty girl with shingled hair and rolled stockings that allowed you to see delightful flashes of her bare knees was with him, and they were taking alternate pulls at a very large flask that contained, I am sure, something intoxicating but not positively toxic from the stock of the best bootlegger in town. He was the quintessence of the Jazz Age, a Scott Fitzgerald character. It was characteristic of Boy throughout his life that he was always the quintessence of something that somebody else had recognized and defined.

I was filled with a sour scorn that I now know was nothing but envy, but then I mistook it for philosophy. I didn't really want the clothes, I didn't really want the girl or the booze, but it scalded me to see him enjoying them, and I hobbled away grumbling to myself like Diogenes. I recognize now that my limp was always worse when I envied Boy; I suppose that without knowing it I exaggerated my disability so that people would notice and say, "That must be a returned man." God, youth is a terrible time! So much feeling and so little notion of how to handle it!

When we met we usually ended up talking about Leola. It had been agreed by Boy's parents and the Cruikshanks that she should wait until Boy had qualified as a lawyer before they married. There had been some suggestion from Leola that she might train as a nurse in the meanwhile, but it came to nothing because her parents thought the training would coarsen their darling—bedpans and urinals and washing naked men and all that sort of thing. So she hung around Deptford, surrounded by the haze of sanctity that was supposed to envelop an engaged girl, waiting for Boy's occasional weekend visits in the auburn car. I knew from his confidences that they went in for what the euphemism of the day called "heavy petting"—mutual masturbation would be the bleak term for it—but that Leola had principles and they never went farther, so that in a technical, physical sense—though certainly not in spirit—she remained a virgin.

Boy, however, had acquired tastes in the Army that could not be satisfied by agonizingly prolonged and inadequately requited puff-ings and snortings in a parked car, but he had no clarity of mind that would ease him of guilt when he deceived Leola—as he did, with variety and regularity among the free-spirited girls he met in Toronto. He built up a gimcrack metaphysical structure to help him out of his difficulty and appealed to me to set the seal of university wisdom on it.

These gay girls, he explained, "knew what they were doing," and thus he had no moral responsibility toward them. Some of them were experts in what were then called French kisses or soul kisses, which the irreverent called "swapping spits." Though he might "fall" for one of them for a few weeks—even go so far as to have a "pash" for her—he was not "in love" with her, as he was with Leola. I had made this fine philosophical distinction myself in my dealings with Diana, and it startled me to hear it from Boy's lips; noodle that I was, I had supposed this sophistry was my own invention. So long as he truly and abidingly loved none but Leola, these "pashes" did not count, did they? Or did I think they did? Above all things he wanted to be perfectly fair to Leola, who was so sweet that she had never once asked him if he was tempted to fall for any of the girls he went dancing with in the city.

I would have given much for the strength of mind to tell him I had no opinions on such matters, but I could not resist the bittersweet, prurient pleasure of listening. I knew it gave him a pleasure that he probably did not yet acknowledge to himself, to confront me with his possession of Leola. He had wormed it out of her that she had once thought she loved me, and he assured me that all three of us now regarded this as a passing aberration—mere war-fever. I did not deny it, but neither did I like it.

I did not want her, but it annoyed me that Boy had her. I had not only learned about physical love in splendid guise from Diana; I had also acquired from her an idea of a woman as a delightful creature that walked and talked and laughed and joked and thought and understood, which quite outsoared anything in Leola's modest repertoire of charms. Nevertheless—egotistical dog in the manger that I was—I keenly resented the fact that she had thrown me over for Boy and had not had the courage to write and tell me so. I see now that it was beyond Leola's abilities to put anything really important on paper; however much she may have wanted to do so, she could not have found words for what she ought to have said. But at that time, with her parents holding her, as it were, in erotic escrow for Boy Staunton, I was sour about the whole business.

Why did I not find some other girl? Diana, Headmaster, Diana. I often yearned for her, but never to the point where I wrote to ask if we might not reconsider. I knew that Diana would stand in the way of the kind of life I wanted to live and that she would not be content with anything less than a full and, if possible, a controlling share in the life of any man she married. But that did not stop me, often and painfully, from wanting her.

A selfish, envious, cankered wretch, wasn't I?

# ( 2 )

The kind of life I wanted to live—yes, but I was not at all sure what it was. I had flashes of insight and promptings, but nothing definite. So when I was finished at the university, duly ticketed as an M.A. in history, I still wanted time to find my way, and like many a man in my case I took to schoolmastering.

Was it a dead end? Did I thereby join the ranks of those university men of promise whose promise is never fulfilled? You can answer that question as readily as I, Headmaster, and certainly the answer must be no. I took to teaching like a duck to water, and like a duck I never paid exaggerated attention to the medium in which I moved. I applied for a job at Colborne College principally because, being a private school, it did not demand that I have a provincial teacher's training certificate; I didn't want to waste another year getting that, and I didn't really think I would stay in teaching. I also liked the fact that Colborne was a boys' school; I never wanted to teach girls—don't, in fact, think they are best served by the kind of education devised by men for men.

I have been a good teacher because I have never thought much about teaching; I just worked through the curriculum and insisted on high standards. I never played favourites, never tried to be popular, never set my heart on the success of any clever boy, and took good care that I knew my stuff. I was not easily approachable, but if approached I was civil and serious to the boy who approached me. I have coached scores of boys privately for scholarships, and I have never taken a fee for it. Of course I have enjoyed all of this, and I suppose my enjoyment had its influence on the boys. As I have grown older my bias—the oddly recurrent themes of history, which are also the themes of myth—has asserted itself, and why not? But when I first stepped into a Colborne classroom, wearing the gown that we were all expected to wear then, I never thought that it would be more than forty years before I left it for good.

Simply from the school's point of view, I suppose my life has seemed odd and dry, though admittedly useful. As the years wore on I was finally acquitted of the suspicion that hangs over every bachelor schoolmaster—that he is a homosexual, either overt or frying in some smoky flame of his own devising. I have never been attracted to boys. Indeed I have never much liked boys. To me a boy is a green apple whom I expect to expose to the sun of history until he becomes a red apple, a man. I know too much about boys to sentimentalize over them. I have been a boy myself, and I know what a boy is, which is to say, either a fool or an imprisoned man striving to get out.

No, teaching was my professional life, to which I gave whatever was its due. The sources from which my larger life was nourished were elsewhere, and it is to write of them that I address this memoir to you, Headmaster, hoping thereby that when I am dead at least one man will know the truth about me and do me justice.

Did I live chastely—I who have been so critical of Boy Staunton's rough-and-tumble sexual affairs? No memoir of our day is thought complete without some comment on the sex life of its subject, and therefore let me say that during my early years as a schoolmaster I found a number of women who were interesting, and sufficiently interested in me, to give me a sex life of a sort. They were the women who usually get into affairs with men who are not the marrying kind. There was Agnes Day, who yearned to take upon herself the sins of the whole world, and sacrifice her body and mind to some deserving male's cause. She soon became melancholy company. Then there was Gloria Mundy, the good-time girl, who had to be stoked with costly food, theatre tickets, and joyrides of all kinds. She cost more than her admittedly good company was worth, and she was kind enough to break up the affair herself. And of course Libby Doe, who thought sex was the one great, true, and apostolic key and cure and could not get enough of it, which I could. I played fair with all of them, I hope; the fact that I did not love them did not prevent me from liking them very much, and I never used a woman simply as an object in my life.

They all had enough of me quite quickly because my sense of humour, controlled in the classroom, was never in check in the bedroom. I was a talking lover, which most women hate. And my physical disabilities were bothersome. The women were quick to assure me that these did not matter at all; Agnes positively regarded my ravaged body as her martyr's stake. But I could not forget my brownish-red nubbin where one leg should have been, and a left side that looked like the crackling of a roast. As well as these offences against my sense of erotic propriety, there were other, and to me sometimes hilarious, problems. What, for instance, is etiquette for the one-legged philanderer? Should he remove his prosthesis before putting on his prophylactic, or *vice versa?* I suggested to my partners that we should write to Dorothy Dix about it. They did not think that funny.

It was many years before I rediscovered love, and then it was not Love's Old Sweet Song, recalling Diana: no, I drank the reviving drop from the Cauldron of Ceridwen. Very well worth waiting for, too.


( 3 )

At the age of twenty-six I had become an M.A., and the five thousand dollars or so I had begun with had grown, under Boy's counselling, to a resounding eight, and I had lived as well as I wanted to do in the meanwhile on my pension. What Boy had I do not know, for he spoke of it mysteriously as "a plum" (an expression out of his Prince of Wales repertoire), but he looked glossy and knew no care. When he married Leola in St James' Presbyterian Church, Deptford, I was his best man, in a hired morning suit and a top hat in which I looked like an ass. It was the most fashionable wedding in Deptford history, marred only by the conduct of some of the groom's legal friends, who whooped it up in the Tecumseh House when the dry party at Doc Staunton's was mercifully over. Leola's parents were minor figures at the wedding; very properly so, in everybody's opinion, for of course "they were not in a position to entertain." Neither were the Stauntons senior, if they had but known it; they were overwhelmed by the worldliness of Boy's friends, and had to comfort themselves with the knowledge that they could buy and sell all of them, and their parents too, and never feel it. It was clear to my eye that by now Boy had far surpassed his father in ambition and scope. All he needed was time.

Everybody agreed that Leola was a radiant bride; even in the awful wedding rig-out of 1924 she looked good enough to eat with a silver spoon. Her parents (no hired finery for Ben Cruikshank, but his boots had a silvery gleam produced by the kind of blacklead more commonly applied to stoves) wept with joy in the church. Up at the front, and without much to do, I could see who wept and who grinned.

The honeymoon was to be a trip to Europe, not nearly so common then as now. I was going to Europe myself, to blow a thousand out of my eight on a reward to myself for being a good boy. I had booked my passage second class—not then called Tourist—on the C.P.R. ship *Melita;* when I read the passenger list in my first hour aboard I was not pleased to find "Mr and Mrs Boy Staunton" among the First Class. Like so many people, I regarded a wedding as a dead end and had expected to be rid of Boy and Leola for a while after it. But here they were, literally on top of me.

Well, let them find me. I did not care about distinction of classes, I told myself, but it would be interesting to find out if they did. As so often, I underestimated Boy. A note and a bottle of wine—half-bottle, to be precise—awaited me at my table at dinner, and he came down to see me three or four times during the voyage, explaining very kindly that ship's rules did not allow him to ask me to join them in First Class. Leola did not come but waved to me at the Ship's Concert, at which gifted passengers sang *Roses of Picardy,* told jokes, and watched a midshipman—they still had them to blow bugles for meals and so forth—dance a pretty good hornpipe.

Boy met everybody in First Class, of course, including the knighted passenger—a shoe manufacturer from Nottingham—but the one who most enlarged his world was the Reverend George Maldon Leadbeater, a great prophet from a fashionable New York church, who sailed from Montreal because he liked the longer North Atlantic sea voyage.

"He isn't like any other preacher you've ever met," said Boy. "Honestly, you'd wonder how old dugouts like Andy Bowyer and Phelps ever have the nerve to stand up in a pulpit when there are men like Leadbeater in the business. He makes Christianity make sense for the first time, so far as I'm concerned. I mean, Christ was really a very distinguished person, a Prince of the House of David, a poet and an intellectual. Of course He was a carpenter; all those Jews in Bible days could do something with their hands. But what kind of a carpenter was He? Not making cowsheds, I'll bet. Undoubtedly a designer and a manufacturer, in terms of those days. Otherwise, how did He make his connections? You know, when He was travelling around, staying with all kinds of rich and influential people as an honoured guest— obviously He wasn't just bumming his way through Palestine; He was staying with people who knew Him as a man of substance who also had a great philosophy. You know, the way those Orientals make their pile before they go in for philosophy. And look how He appreciated beauty! When that woman poured the ointment on His feet, He knew good ointment from bad, you can bet. And the Marriage at Cana—a party, and He helped the host out of a tight place when the drinks gave out, because He had probably been in the same fix Himself in His days in business and knew what social embarrassment was. And an economist! Driving the money-changers out of the Temple—why? Because they were soaking the pilgrims extortionate rates, that's why, and endangering a very necessary tourist attraction and rocking the economic boat. It was a kind of market discipline, if you want to look at it that way, and He was the only one with the brains to see it and the guts to do something about it. Leadbeater thinks that may have been at the back of the Crucifixion; the priests got their squeeze out of the Temple exchange, you can bet, and they decided they would have to get rid of this fellow who was possessed of a wider economic vision—as well as great intellectual powers in many other fields, of course.

"Leadbeater—he wants me to call him George, and somehow I've got to get rid of this English trick I've got of calling people by their surnames—George simply loves beauty. That's what gets Leola, you know. Frankly, Dunny, as an old friend, I can tell you that Leola hasn't had much chance to grow in that home of hers. Fine people, the Cruikshanks, of course, but narrow. But she's growing fast. George has insisted on lending her this wonderful novel, *If Winter Comes* by A. S. M. Hutchinson. She's just gulping it down. But the thing that really impresses me is that George is such a good dresser. And not just for a preacher—for anybody. He's going to introduce me to his tailor in London. You have to be introduced to the good ones. He says God made beautiful and seemly things, and not to take advantage of them is to miss what God meant. Did you ever hear any preacher say anything like that? Of course he's no six-hundred-dollar-a-year Bible-buster, but a man who pulls down eighty-five hundred from his pulpit alone, and doubles it with lectures and books! If Christ wasn't poor—and He certainly wasn't—George doesn't intend to be. Would you believe he carries a handful of gemstones—semi-precious but gorgeous—in his right-hand coat pocket, *just to feel!* He'll pull them out two or three times a day, and strew them on the madder silk handkerchief he always has in his breast pocket, and let the light play on them, and you should see his face then! "Poverty and sin are not all that God hath wrought," he says with a kind of poetic smile. "Lo, these are beautiful even as His raindrops, and no less His work than the leper, the flower, or woman's smile." I wish you could get up to First Class to meet him, but it's out of the question, and I wouldn't want to ask him to come down here."

So I never met the Reverend George Maldon Leadbeater, though I wondered if he had read the *New Testament* as often as I had. Furthermore, I had read *If Winter Comes* when it first came out; it had been the theme of an extravagant encomium from the Right Honourable William Lyon Mackenzie King, Prime Minister of Canada; he had said it was unquestionably the finest novel of our time, and the booksellers had played it up. It seemed to me that Mr King's taste in literature, like Leadbeater's in religion, was evidence of a sweet tooth, and nothing more.

( 4 )

Boy and Leola left the ship at Southampton. I went on to Antwerp, because the first object of my journey was a tour of the battlefields. Unrecognizable, of course. Neat and trim in the manner of the Low Countries; trenches known to me as stinking mudholes were lined with cement, so that ladies would not dirty their shoes. Even the vast cemeteries woke no feeling in me; because they were so big I lost all sense that they contained men who, had they lived, would have been about my age. I got out as soon as I had scoured Passchendaele for some sign of the place where I had been wounded, and where I had encountered the little Madonna. Nobody I could find was of any use in suggesting where I might have been; the new town had probably buried it under streets and houses. Figures of Our Lady—yes, there were plenty of those, in churches and on buildings, but most of them were new, hideous and unrevealing. None was anything like mine. I would have known her anywhere, as of course I did, many years later.

It was thus my interest in medieval and Renaissance art—especially religious art—came about. The little Madonna was a bee in my bonnet; I wanted to see her again, and quite unreasonably (like a man I knew who lost a treasured walking-stick in the London Blitz and still looks hopefully in every curiosity shop in case it may turn up) I kept hoping to find her. The result was that I saw a great many Madonnas of every period and material and quickly came to know a fair amount about them. Indeed, I learned enough to be able to describe the one I sought as a Virgin of the Immaculate Conception, of poly-chromed wood, about twenty-four inches high, and most probably of Flemish or North German workmanship of the period between 1675 and 1725. If you think I put this together after I had found her, I can only assure you that you are wrong.

First my search, then a mounting enthusiasm for what I saw, led me to scores of churches through the Low Countries, France, Austria, and Italy. I had only afforded myself a few weeks, but I sent for more money and stayed until the latest possible date in August. What are you doing here, Dunstan Ramsay? I sometimes asked myself, and when I had got past telling myself that I was feeding a splendid new enthusiasm for religious art and architecture I knew that I was rediscovering religion as well. Do not suppose I was becoming "religious"; the Presbyterianism of my childhood effectively insulated me against any enthusiastic abandonment to faith. But I became aware that in matters of religion I was an illiterate, and illiteracy was my abhorrence. I was not such a fool or an aesthete as to suppose that all this art was for art's sake alone. It was about something, and I wanted to know what that something was.

As an historian by training, I suppose I should have begun at the beginning, wherever that was, but I hadn't time. Scenes from the Bible gave me no difficulty; I could spot Jael spiking Sisera, or Judith with the head of Holofernes, readily enough. It was the saints who baffled me. So I got to work on them as best I could, and pretty soon knew that the old fellow with the bell was Anthony Abbot, and the same old fellow with hobgoblins plaguing him was Anthony being tempted in the desert. Sebastian, that sanctified porcupine, was easy, and so was St Roche, with the dog and a bad leg. I was innocently delighted to meet St Martin, dividing his cloak, on a Swiss coin. The zest for detail that had first made me want to be a polymath stood me in good stead now, for I could remember the particular attributes and symbols of scores of saints without any trouble, and I found their legends delightful reading. I became disgustingly proud and began to whore after rare and difficult saints, not known to the Catholic faithful generally. I could read and speak French (though never without a betraying accent) and was pretty handy in Latin, so that Italian could be picked up on the run—badly, but enough. German was what I needed, and I determined to acquire it during the coming winter. I had no fear; whatever interested me I could learn, and learn quickly.

At this time it never occurred to me that the legends I picked up were quite probably about people who had once lived and had done something or other that made them popular and dear after death. What I learned merely revived and confirmed my childhood notion that religion was much nearer in spirit to the *Arabian Nights* than it was to anything encouraged by St James' Presbyterian Church. I wondered how they would regard it in Deptford if I offered to replace the captive Dove that sat on the topmost organ pipe with St James' own cockleshell. I was foolish and conceited, I know, but I was also a happy goat who had wandered into the wondrous enclosed garden of hagiology, and I grazed greedily and contentedly. When the time came at last for me to go home, I knew I had found a happiness that would endure.

( 5 )

Schoolmastering kept me busy by day and part of each night. I was an assistant housemaster, with a fine big room under the eaves of the main building, and a wretched kennel of a bedroom, and rights in a bathroom used by two or three other resident masters. I taught all day, but my wooden leg mercifully spared me from the nuisance of having to supervise sports after school. There were exercises to mark every night, but I soon gained a professional attitude towards these woeful explorations of the caves of ignorance and did not let them depress me. I liked the company of most of my colleagues, who were about equally divided among good men who were good teachers, awful men who were awful teachers, and the grotesques and misfits who drift into teaching and are so often the most educative influences a boy meets in school. If a boy can't have a good teacher, give him a psychological cripple or an exotic failure to cope with; don't just give him a bad, dull teacher. This is where the private schools score over state-run schools; they can accommodate a few cultured madmen on the staff without having to offer explanations.

The boys liked me for my wooden leg, whose thuds in the corridor gave ample warning of my approach and allowed smokers, loafers, and dreamers (these last two groups are not the same) to do whatever was necessary before I arrived. I had now taken to using a cane except when I was very much on parade, and a swipe with my heavy stick over the behind was preferred by all sensible boys to a tedious imposition. I may have been the despair of educational psychologists, but I knew boys and I knew my stuff, and it quickly began to show up in examination results.

Boy Staunton was also distinguishing himself as an educator. He was educating Leola, and as I saw them pretty regularly I was able to estimate his success. He wanted to make her into the perfect wife for a rising young entrepreneur in sugar, for he was working hard and fast, and now had a foot in the world of soft drinks, candy, and confectionery.

He had managed brilliantly on a principle so simple that it deserves to be recorded: he set up a little company of his own by borrowing $5000 for four months; as he already had $5000 it was no trouble to repay the loan. Then he borrowed $10,000, and repaid with promptitude. On this principle he quickly established an excellent reputation, always paying promptly, though never prematurely, thereby robbing his creditor of expected interest. Bank managers grew to love Boy, but he soon gave up dealing with branches, and borrowed only at Head Office. He was now a favoured cherub in the heaven of finance, and he needed a wife who could help him to graduate from a cherub to a full-fledged angel, and as soon as possible to an archangel. So Leola had lessons in tennis and bridge, learned not to call her maid "the girl" even to herself, and had no children as the time was not yet at hand. She was prettier than ever, had acquired a sufficient command of cliché to be able to talk smartly about anything Boy's friends were likely to know, and adored Boy, while fearing him a little. He was so swift, so brilliant, so handsome! I think she was always a little puzzled to find that she was really his wife.

It was in 1927 that Boy's first instance of startling good fortune arrived—one of those coincidences that it may be wiser to call synchronicities, which aid the ambitious—something that heaved him, at a stroke, into a higher sphere and maintained him there. He had kept up with his regiment and soldiered regularly; he had thoughts of politics, he told me, and a militia connection would earn a lot of votes. So when the Prince of Wales made his tour of Canada that year, who was more personable, youthful, cheerful, and in every way suited to be one of His Highness's aides-de-camp than Boy Staunton? And not simply for the royal appearance in Toronto, but for the duration of the tour, from sea to sea?

I saw little of this grandeur, except when the Prince paid a visit to the school, for as it has royal patronage he was obliged to do so. We masters all turned out in our gowns and hoods, and sweating members of the Rifle Corps strutted, and yelled, and swooned from the heat, and the slight descendant of King Arthur and King Alfred and Charles the Second did the gracious. I was presented, with my V.C. pinned to the silk of my gown, but my recollection is not of the youthful Prince, but of Boy, who was quite the most gorgeous figure there that day. An Old Boy of the school, and an *aide* to the Prince—it was a great day for him, and the Headmaster of that day doted upon him to a degree that might have seemed a little overdone to a critical eye.

Leola was there too, for though of course she did not go with Boy on the tour, she was expected to turn up now and then at various points across Canada, just as though she happened to be there by chance. She had learned to curtsy very prettily—not easy in the skirts of the period—and eat without seeming to chew, and do other courtier-like things required by Boy. I am sure that for her the Prince was nothing more than an excuse for Boy's brilliant appearances. Never have I seen a woman so absorbed in her love for a man, and I was happy for her and heartily wished her well.

After the Prince had gone home the Stauntons settled down again to be, in a modest manner befitting their youth, social leaders. Boy had a lot of new social usages and took to wearing spats to business. For him and for Leola their Jazz Age period was over; now they were serious, responsible Young Marrieds.

Within a year their first child was born and was conservatively, but significantly, christened Edward David. In due time—how *could* H.R.H. have known?—a christening mug came from Mappin and Webb, with the three feathers and *Ich dien* on it. David used it until he graduated to a cup and saucer, after which it stood on the drawing-room table, with matches in it, quite casually.

( 6 )

Doc Staunton and his wife never visited Boy and Leola, on what I suppose must be called religious grounds. When they came to Toronto, which was rarely, they asked the young Stauntons to their hotel—the cheap and conservative Carls-Rite—for a meal, but declined to set foot in a house where drink was consumed, contrary to the law of the land and against God's manifest will. Another stone that stuck in their crop was that Boy and Leola had left the Presbyterian church and become Anglicans.

In a movement that reached its climax in 1924, the Presbyterians and Methodists had consummated a *mysterium coniunctionis* that resulted in the United Church of Canada, with a doctrine (soother than the creamy curd) in which the harshness of Presbyterianism and the hick piety of Methodism had little part. A few brass-bowelled Presbyterians and some truly zealous Methodists held out, but a majority regarded this union as a great victory for Christ's Kingdom on earth. Unfortunately it also involved some haggling between the rich Presbyterians and the poor Methodists, which roused the mocking spirit of the rest of the country; the Catholics in particular had some Irish jokes about the biggest land-and-property-grab in Canadian history.

During this uproar a few sensitive souls fled to the embrace of Anglicanism; the envious and disaffected said they did it because the Anglican Church was in some way more high-toned than the evangelical faiths, and thus they were improving their social standing. At that time every Canadian had to adhere, nominally, to some church; the officials of the Census utterly refused to accept such terms as "agnostic" or "none" for inclusion in the column marked "Religion," and flattering statistics were compiled on the basis of Census reports that gave a false idea of the forces all the principal faiths could command. Boy and Leola had moved quietly into a fashionable Anglican Church where the rector, Canon Arthur Woodiwiss, was so broadminded he did not even insist that they be confirmed. David was confirmed, though, when his time came, and so was Caroline, who appeared a well-planned two years after him.

My preoccupation with saints was such that I could not keep it out of my conversation, and Boy was concerned for me. "Watch that you don't get queer, Dunny," he would say, sometimes; and, "Arthur Woodiwiss says that saints are all right for Catholics, who have so many ignorant people to deal with, but we've evolved far beyond all that."

As a result I sneaked even more saints into my conversation, to irritate him. He had begun to irritate rather easily, and be pompous. He urged me to get out of schoolmastering (while praising it as a fine profession) and make something of myself. "If you don't hurry up and let life know what you want, life will damned soon show you what you'll get," he said one day. But I was not sure I wanted to issue orders to life; I rather liked the Greek notion of allowing Chance to take a formative hand in my affairs. It was in the autumn of 1928 that Chance did so, and lured me from a broad highway to a narrower path.

Our Headmaster of that day—your predecessor but one—was enthusiastic for what he called "bringing the world to the school and the school to the world," and every Wednesday morning we had a special speaker at Prayers, who told us about what he did in the world. Sir Archibald Flower told us about rebuilding the Shakespeare Memorial Theatre at Stratford-on-Avon and got a dollar from nearly every boy to help do it; Father Jellicoe talked about clearing London slums, and that cost most of us a dollar too. But ordinarily our speakers were Canadians, and one morning the Headmaster swept in—he wore a silk gown, well suited to sweeping—with Mr Joel Surgeoner in tow.

Surgeoner was already pretty well known, though I had not seen him before. He was the head of the Lifeline Mission in Toronto, where he laboured to do something for destitute and defeated people, and for the sailors on the boats that plied the Great Lakes—at that time a very tough and neglected group. He spoke to the school briefly and well, for though it was plain that he was a man of little education he had a compelling quality of sincerity about him, even though I suspected him of being a pious liar.

He told us, quietly and in the simplest language, that he had to run his Mission by begging, and that sometimes begging yielded nothing; when this happened he prayed for help, and had never been refused what he needed; the blankets, or more often the food, would appear somehow, often late in the day, and more often than not, left on the steps of the Mission by anonymous donors. Now, pompous young ass that I was, I was quite prepared to believe that St John Bosco could pull off this trick when he appealed to Heaven on behalf of his boys; I was even persuaded that it might have happened a few times to Dr Barnardo, of whom the story was also told. But I was far too much a Canadian, deeply if unconsciously convinced of the inferiority of my own country and its people, to think it could happen in Toronto, to a man I could see. I suppose I had a sneer on my face.

Surgeoner's back was to me, but suddenly he turned and addressed me. "I can see that you do not believe me, sir," he said, "but I am speaking the truth, and if you will come down to the Lifeline some night I will show you clothes and blankets and food that God has inspired charitable men and women to give us to do His work among His forgotten children." This had an electrical effect; a few boys laughed, the Headmaster gave me a glance that singed my eyebrows, and Surgeoner's concluding remarks were greeted with a roar of applause. But I had no time to waste in being humiliated, for when Surgeoner looked me in the face I knew him at once for the tramp I had last seen in the pit at Deptford.

I lost no time; I was at the Lifeline Mission that very night. It was on the ground floor of a warehouse down by the lakefront. Everything about it was poor; the lower parts of the windows were painted over with green paint, and the lettering on them—"Lifeline Mission, Come In"—was an amateur job. Inside, the electric light was scanty and eked out by a couple of coal-oil lamps on the table at the front; on benches made of reclaimed wood sat eight or ten people, of whom four or five were bums, and the rest poor but respectable supporters of Surgeoner. A service was in progress.

Surgeoner was praying; he needed a variety of things, the only one of which I can remember was a new kettle for soup, and he suggested to God that the woodpile was getting low. When he had, so to speak, put in his order, he began to speak to us, gently and unassumingly as he had done at the school that morning and I was able to observe now that he had a hearing-aid in his left ear—one of the clumsy affairs then in use—and that a cord ran down into his collar and appeared to join a bulge in the front of his shirt, obviously a receiving apparatus. But his voice was pleasant and well controlled; nothing like the ungoverned quack of many deaf people.

He saw me, of course, and nodded gravely. I expected that he would try to involve me in his service, probably to score off me as an educated infidel and mocker, but he did not. Instead he told, very simply, of his experience with a lake sailor who was a notable blasphemer, a man whose every remark carried an insult to God's Name. Surgeoner had been powerless to change him and had left him in defeat. One day Surgeoner had talked with an old woman, desperately poor but rich in the Spirit of Christ, who had at parting pressed into his hand a cent, the only coin she had to give. Surgeoner bought a tract with the cent and carried it absent-mindedly in his pocket for several weeks, until by chance he met the blasphemer again. On impulse he pressed the tract upon the blasphemer, who of course received it with an oath. Surgeoner thought no more of the matter until, two months later, he met the blasphemer again, this time a man transfigured. He had read the tract, he had accepted Christ, and he had begun life anew.

I fully expected that it would prove that the old woman was the blasphemer's aged mother and that the two had been reunited in love, but Surgeoner did not go so far. Was this the self-denying chastity of the literary artist, I wondered, or had he not thought of such a dénouement yet? When the meeting had concluded with a dismal rendition of the revival hymn—

> Throw out the Life Line,
> Throw out the Life Line,
> Someone is drifting away.
> Throw out the Life Line,
> Throw out the Life Line,
> Someone is sinking today.

—sung with the dispirited drag of the unaccompanied, untalented religious, the little group drifted away—the bums to the sleeping quarters next door and the respectable to their homes—and I was alone with Joel Surgeoner.

"Well, sir, I knew you would come, but I didn't expect you so soon," said he and gestured me into a kitchen chair by the table. He frugally turned off the electricity, and we sat in the light of the lamps.

"You promised to show me what prayer had brought," I said.

"You see it around you," he replied, and then, seeing surprise on my face at the wretchedness of the Mission, he led me to a door into the next room—it was in fact a double door running on a track, of the kind you see in old warehouses—and slid it back. In the gloom leaking down through an overhead skylight I saw a poor dormitory in which about fifty men were lying on cots. "Prayer brings me these, and prayer and hard work and steady begging provide for them, Mr Ramsay." I suppose he had learned my name at the school.

"I spoke to our Bursar tonight," I said, "and your talk this morning will bring you a cheque for five hundred and forty-three dollars; from six hundred boys and a staff of about thirty, that's not bad. What will you do with it?"

"Winter is coming; it will buy a lot of warm underclothes." He closed the sliding door, and we sat down again in what seemed to be the chapel, common room, and business office of the Mission. "That cheque will probably be a week getting here, and our needs are daily—hourly. Here is the collection from our little meeting tonight." He showed me thirteen cents on a cracked saucer.

I decided it was time to go at him. "Thirteen cents for a thir-teen-cent talk," I said. "Did you expect them to believe that cock-and-bull story about the cursing sailor and the widow's mite? Don't you underestimate them?"

He was not disconcerted. "I expect them to believe the spirit of the story," he said, "and I know from experience what kind of story they like. You educated people, you have a craze for what you call truth, by which you mean police-court facts. These people get their noses rubbed in such facts all day and every day, and they don't want to hear them from me."

"So you provide romance," I said.

"I provide something that strenghtens faith, Mr Ramsay, as well as I can. I am not a gifted speaker or a man of education, and often my stories come out thin and old, and I suppose unbelievable to a man like you. These people don't hold me on oath, and they aren't stupid either. They know my poor try at a parable from hard fact. And I won't deceive you: there is something about this kind of work and the kind of lives these people live that knocks the hard edge off fact. If you think I'm a liar—and you do—you should hear some of the confessions that come out in this place on a big night. Awful whop-pers, that just pop into the heads of people who have found joy in faith but haven't got past wanting to be important in the world. So they blow up their sins like balloons. Better people than them want to seem worse than they are. We come to God in little steps, not in a leap, and that love of police-court truth you think so much of comes very late on the way, if it comes at all. What is truth? as Pilate asked; I've never pretended that I could have told him. I'm just glad when a boozer sobers up, or a man stops beating his woman, or a crooked lad tries to go straight. If it makes him boast a bit, that's not the worst harm it can do. You unbelieving people apply cruel, hard standards to us who believe."

"What makes you think I'm an unbeliever?" I said. "And what made you turn on me this morning, in front of the whole school?"

"I admit it was a trick," he said. "When you are talking like that it's always a good job near the end to turn on somebody and accuse them of disbelieving. Sometimes you see somebody laughing, but that isn't needful. Best of all is to turn on somebody behind you, if you can. Makes it look as if you had eyes in the back of your head, see? There's a certain amount of artfulness about it, of course, but a greater end has been served, and nobody has been really hurt."

"That's a thoroughly crooked-minded attitude," said I.

"Perhaps it is. But you're not the first man I've used like that, and I promise you won't be the last. God has to be served, and I must use the means I know. If I'm not false to God—and I try very hard not to be—I don't worry too much about the occasional stranger."

"I am not quite so much a stranger as you think," said I. Then I told him that I had recognized him. I don't know what I expected him to do—deny it, I suppose. But he was perfectly cool.

"I don't remember you, of course," he said. "I don't remember anybody from that night except the woman herself. It was her that turned me to God."

"When you raped her?"

"I didn't rape her, Mr Ramsay; you heard her say so herself. Not that I wouldn't have done, the state of mind I was in. I was at the end of my rope. I was a tramp, you see. Any idea what it means to be a tramp? They're lost men; not many people understand them. Do you know, I've heard and read such nonsense about how they just can't stand the chains of civilization, and have to breathe the air of freedom, and a lot of them are educated men with a wonderful philosphy, and they laugh at the hard workers and farmers they beg off of—well, it's all a lot of cock, as they'd put it. They're madmen and criminals and degenerates mostly, and tramping makes them worse. It's the open-air life does it to them. Oh, I know the open air is a great thing, when you have food and shelter to go back to, but when you haven't it drives you mad; starvation and oxygen is a crazy mixture for anybody that isn't born to it, like a savage. These fellows aren't savages. Weaklings, mostly, but vicious.

"I got among them a very common way. Know-it-all lad; quarrelled with my old dad, who was hard and mean-religious; ran away, picked up odd jobs, then began to pinch stuff, and got on the drink. Know what a tramp drinks? Shoe-blacking sometimes, strained through a hunk of bread; drives you crazy. Or he gets a few prunes and lets them stand in the sun in a can till they ferment; that's the stuff gives you the black pukes, taken on a stomach with nothing in it but maybe some raw vegetables you've pulled in a field. Like those sugar-beets around Deptford; fermented for a while, they'd eat a hole in a copper pot.

"And sex too. Funny how fierce it gets when the body is ill fed and ill used. Tramps are sodomites mostly. I was a young fellow, and it's the young ones and the real old ones that get used, because they can't fight as well. It's not kid-glove stuff, like that Englishman went to prison for; it's enough to kill you, you'd think, when a gang of tramps set on a young fellow. But it doesn't, you know. That's how I lost my hearing, most of it; I resisted a gang, and they beat me over the ears with my own boots till I couldn't resist any more. Do you know what they say? "Lots o' booze and buggery," they say. That's their life. Mine too, till the great mercy of that woman. I know now that God is just as near them as He is to you and me at this instant, but they defy Him, poor souls.

"That night we last met, I was crazy. I'd tumbled off the freight in that jungle by Deptford, and found a fire and seven fellows around it, and they had a stew—somebody'd got a rabbit and it was in a pail over a fire with some carrots. Ever eat that? It's awful, but I wanted some, and after a lot of nastiness they said I could have some after they'd had what they wanted of me. My manhood just couldn't stand it, and I left them. They laughed and said I'd be back when I got good and hungry.

"Then I met this woman, wandering by herself. I knew she was a town woman. Women tramps are very rare; too much sense, I guess. She was clean and looked like an angel to me, but I threatened her and asked her for money. She hadn't any; then I grabbed her. She wasn't much afraid and asked what I wanted. I told her, in tramp's language, and I could see she didn't understand, but when I started to push her down and grab at her clothes she said, 'Why are you so rough?' and then I started to cry. She held my head to her breast and talked nicely to me, and I cried worse, but the strange thing is I still wanted her. As if only that would put me right, you see? That's what I said to her. And do you know what she said? She said, 'You may if you promise not to be rough.' So I did, and that was when you people came hunting her.

"When I look back now I wonder that it wasn't all over with me that moment. But it wasn't. No, it was glory come into my life. It was as if I had gone right down into Hell and through the worst of the fire, and come on a clear, pure pool where I could wash and be clean. I was locked in by my deafness, so I didn't know much of what was said, but I could see it was a terrible situation for her, and there was nothing I could do.

"They turned me loose next morning, and I ran out of that town laughing and shouting like the man who was delivered from devils by Our Lord. As I had been, you see. He worked through that woman, and she is a blessed saint, for what she did for me—I mean it as I say it—was a miracle. Where is she now?"

How did I know? Mrs Dempster was often in my mind, but whenever I thought of her I put the thought aside with a sick heart, as part of a past that was utterly done. I had tried to get Deptford out of my head, just as Boy had done, and for the same reason; I wanted a new life. What Surgeoner told me made it clear that any new life must include Deptford. There was to be no release by muffling up the past.

We talked for some time, and I liked him more and more. When at last I left I laid a ten-dollar bill on the table.

"Thank you, Mr Ramsay," said he. "This will get us the soup kettle we need, and a load of wood as well. Do you see now how prayers are answered?"

( 7 )

Back to Deptford, therefore, at the first chance, pretending I wanted to consult Mr Mahaffey about the deadbeat who had bought the *Banner* from me and was still in debt for more than half of the price. The magistrate counselled patience. But I got what I wanted, which was the address of the aunt who had taken Mrs Dempster after the death of her husband. She was not, as Milo Papple thought, a widow, but an old maid, a Miss Bertha Shanklin, and she lived in Weston. He gave me the address, without asking why I wanted it.

"A bad business, that was," he said. "She seemed a nice little person. Then—a madwoman! Struck by a snowball. I don't suppose you have any idea who threw it, have you? No, I didn't imagine you did, or you would have said so earlier. There was guilt, you know; undoubtedly there was guilt. I don't know quite what could have been done about it, but look at the consequences! McCausland says definitely she became a moral idiot—no sense at all of right and wrong—and the result was that terrible business in the pit. I remember that you were there. And the ruin of her husband's life. Then the lad running away when he was really no more than a baby. I've never seen such grief as hers when she finally realized he had gone. McCausland had to give her very heavy morphia before Miss Shanklin could remove her. Yes, there was guilt, whether any kind of charge could have been laid or not. Guilt, and somebody bears it to this day!"

The old man's vehemence, and the way he kept looking at me over and under and around his small, very dirty spectacles, left no doubt that he thought I knew more than I admitted, and might very well be the guilty party myself. But I saw no sense in telling him anything; I still had a grudge against Boy for what he had done, but I remember too that if I had not been so sly Mrs Dempster would not have been hit. I was anxious to regard the whole thing as an accident, past care and past grief.

Nevertheless this conversation reheated my strong sense of guilt and responsibility about Paul; the war and my adult life had banked down that fire but not quenched it. The consequence was that I did something very foolish. I paid a visit to Father Regan, who was still the Catholic priest in Deptford.

I had never spoken to him, but I wanted somebody I could talk to confidentially, and I had the Protestant notion that priests are very close-mouthed and see more than they say. Later in life I got over that idea, but at this moment I wanted somebody who was in Deptford but not wholly of it, and he seemed to be my man. So within fifteen minutes of leaving the magistrate I was in the priest's house, snuffing up the smell of soap, and sitting in one of those particularly uncomfortable chairs that find refuge in priests' parlours all over the globe.

He thought, quite rightly, that I had come fishing for something, and was very suspicious, but when he found out what it was he laughed aloud, with the creaky, short laugh of a man whose life does not afford many jokes.

"A saint, do you say? Well now, that's a pretty tall order. I couldn't help you at all. Finding saints isn't any part of my job. Nor can I say what's a miracle and what isn't. But I don't imagine the bishop would have much to say to your grounds; it'd be his job to think of such things, if anybody did. A tramp reformed. I've reformed a tramp or two myself; they get spells of repentance, like most people. This fella you tell me of, now, seems to be as extreme in his zeal as he was in his sin. I never like that. And this business of raising your brother from his deathbed, as you describe it, was pretty widely talked about when it happened. Dr McCausland says he never died at all, and I suppose he'd know. A few minutes with no signs of life. Well, that's hardly Lazarus, now, is it? And your own experience when you were wounded—man, you were out of your head. I have to say it plainly. You'd better put this whole foolish notion away and forget it.

"You were always an imaginative young fella. It was said of you when you were a lad, and it seems you haven't changed. You have to watch that kinda thing, you know. Now, you tell me you're very interested in saints. Awright, I'm not fishing for converts, but if that's the way it is you'd better take a good look at the religion saints come from. And when you've looked, I'll betcha a dollar you'll draw back like a man from a flame. You clever, imaginative fellas often want to flirt with Mother Church, but she's no flirty lady, I'm telling you. You like the romance, but you can't bear the yoke.

"You're hypnotized by this idea that three miracles makes a saint, and you think you've got three miracles for a poor woman who is far astray in her wits and don't know right from wrong. Aw, go on!

"Look, Mr Ramsay, I'll tell it to you as plain as it comes: there's a lot of very good people in the world, and a lot of queer things happen that we don't see the explanation of, but there's only one Church that undertakes to cut right down to the bone and say what's a miracle and what isn't and who's a saint and who isn't, and you, and this poor soul you speak of, are outside it. You can't set up some kind of a bootleg saint, so take my advice and cut it out. Be content with the facts you have, or think you have, and don't push anything too far— or you might get a little bit strange yourself.

"I'm trying to be kind, you know, for I admired your parents. Fine people, and your father was a fair-minded man to every faith. But there are spiritual dangers you Protestants don't even seem to know exist, and this monkeying with difficult, sacred things is a sure way to get yourself into a real old mess. Well I recall, when I was a seminarian, how we were warned one day about a creature called a fool-saint.

"Ever hear of a fool-saint? I thought not. As a matter of fact, it's a Jewish idea, and the Jews are no fools, y'know. A fool-saint is somebody who seems to be full of holiness and loves everybody and does every good act he can, but because he's a fool it all comes to nothing—to worse than nothing, because it is virtue tainted with madness, and you can't tell where it'll end up. Did you know that Prudence was named as one of the Virtues? There's the trouble with your fool-saint, y'see—no Prudence. Nothing but a lotta bad luck'll rub off on you from one of them. Did you know bad luck could be catching? There's a theological name for it, but I misremember it right now.

"Yes, I know a lot of the saints have done strange things, but I don't recall any of 'em traipsing through the streets with a basketful o' wilted lettuce and wormy spuds, or bringing scandal on their town by shameless goings-on. No, no; the poor soul is a fool-saint if she's anything, and I'd strongly advise you to keep clear of her."

So, back to Toronto with a flea in my ear, and advice from Father Regan so obviously good and kind that I had either to take it or else hate Regan for giving it. Knowing by now what a high-stomached fellow I was, you can guess which I did. Within a week I was at Weston, talking with my fool-saint once again.

( 8 )

She was now forty but looked younger. An unremarkable woman really, except for great sweetness of expression; her dress was simple, and I suppose the aunt chose it, for it was a good deal longer than the fashion of the time and had a homemade air. She had no recollection of me, to begin with, but when I spoke of Paul I roused painful associations, and the aunt had to intervene, and take her away.

The aunt had not wanted to let me in the house, and as I thought this might be so I presented myself at the door without warning. Miss Bertha Shanklin was very small, of an unguessable age, and had gentle, countrified manners. Her house was pretty and suggested an old-fashioned sort of cultivation; much was ugly in the style of fifty years before, but nothing was trashy; there were a few mosaic boxes, and a couple of muddy oil paintings of the Italian Campagna with classical ruins and picturesque peasants, which suggested that somebody had been to Italy. Miss Shanklin let me talk with Mrs Dempster for ten minutes or so, before she took her away. I stayed where I was, though decency suggested that it was time for me to go.

"I am sure you mean this visit kindly, Mr Ramsay," she said when she returned, "but you can see for yourself that my niece is not up to receiving callers. There's not a particle of sense in reminding her of the days past—it frets her and does no good. So I'll say good-afternoon, and thank you for calling."

I talked as well as I could about why I had come, and of my concern for her niece, to whom I owed a great debt. I said nothing of saints; that was not Miss Shanklin's line. But I talked about childhood kindness, and my mother's concern for Mary Dempster, and my sense of guilt that I had not sought her before. This brought about a certain melting.

"That's real kind of you. I know some terrible things went on in Deptford, and it's good to know not everybody has forgotten poor Mary. I suppose I can say to you that I always thought the whole affair was a mistake. Amasa Dempster was a good man, I suppose, but Mary had been used to an easier life—not silly-easy, you understand me, but at least some of the good things. I won't pretend I was friendly towards the match, and I guess I have to bear some of the blame. They didn't exactly run away, but it hurt me the way they managed things, as if there wasn't a soul in the world but themselves. I could have made it easier for her, but Amasa was so proud and even a little mite hateful about Mary having any money of her own that I just said, All right, they can paddle their own canoe. It cost me a good deal to do that. I never saw Paul, you know, and I'd certainly have done anything in the world for him if I could have got things straight with his father. But I guess a little bit of money made me proud, and religion made him proud, and then it was too late. I love her so much, you see. She's all the family I've got. Love can make you do some mean actions when you think it has been snubbed. I was mean, I grant you. But I'm trying to do what I can now, when I guess it's too late."

Miss Shanklin wept, not aloud or passionately, but to the point of having to wipe her eyes and depart for the kitchen to ask for some tea. By the time this tea was brought—by the "hired girl," whose softening influence on Mary Dempster had been so deplored by the matrons of Amasa Dempster's congregation—Miss Shanklin and I were on quite good terms.

"I love to hear you say that Mary was so good and sweet, even after that terrible accident—it was an accident, wasn't it? A blow on the head? From a fall or something?—and that you thought of her even when you were away at the war. I always had such hopes for her. Not just to keep her with me, of course, but—well, I know she loved Amasa Dempster, and love is supposed to excuse anything. But I am sure there would have been other men, and she could hardly have been worse off with one of them, now could she? Life with Amasa seems to have been so dark and wintry and hopeless. Mary used to be so full of hope—before she married.

"Now she remembers so little, and it's better so, because when she does remember she thinks of Paul. I don't even let myself speculate on what would happen to a little fellow like that, running away with show folks. As like as not he's dead long since, and better so, I suppose. But of course she thinks of him as a little boy still. She has no idea of time, you see. When she thinks of him, it's awful to hear her cry and carry on. And I can't get rid of the feeling that if I had just had a little more real sand and horse sense, things would have been very different.

"I'd meant to tell you not to come again, ever, but I won't. Come and see Mary, but promise you'll get to know her again, as a new friend. She hasn't any idea of the past, except for horrible mixed-up memories of being tied up, and Paul disappearing, and Amasa—she always remembers him with a blue mouth, like a rotten hole in his face—telling God he forgave her for ruining his life. Amasa died praying, did you know?"

( 9 )

It was the following May, in the fated year 1929, that I had a call from Boy—in itself an unusual thing, but even more unusual in its message.

"Dunny, don't be in too much of a rush, but you oughtn't to lose more than a couple of weeks in getting rid of some of your things." And he named half-a-dozen stocks he knew I had, because he had himself advised me to buy them.

"But they're mounting every week," I said.

"That's right," said he; "now sell 'em, and get hold of some good hard stuff. I'll see that you get another good block of Alpha."

So that is what I did, and it is to Boy's advice I owe a reputation I acquired in the school as a very shrewd businessman. Just about every master, like some millions of other people on this continent, had money in the market, and most of them had invested on margin and were cleaned out before Christmas. But I found myself pleasantly well off when the worst of the crash came, because Boy Staunton regarded me as in certain respects a responsibility.

My mind was not on money at the time, however, for I was waiting impatiently for the end of term so that I could take ship and set out on a great hunt, starting in England and making my way across France, Portugal, Switzerland, Austria, and at last to Czechoslovakia. This was the first of my annual journeys, broken only by the 1939-45 war, saint-hunting, saint-identifying, and saint-describing; journeys that led to my book *A Hundred Saints for Travellers,* still in print in six languages and a lively seller, to say nothing of my nine other books, and my occasional articles. This time I was after big game, a saint never satisfactorily described and occurring in a variety of forms, whose secret I hoped to discover.

There is a saint for just about every human situation, and I was on the track of a curious specimen whose intercession was sought by girls who wanted to get rid of disagreeable suitors. Her home ground, so to speak, was Portugal, and she was reputed to have been the daughter of a Portuguese king, himself a pagan, who had betrothed her to the King of Sicily; but she was a Christian and had made a vow of virginity, and when she prayed for assistance in keeping it, she miraculously grew a heavy beard; the Sicilian king refused to have her, and her angry father caused her to be crucified.

It was my purpose to visit every shrine of this odd saint, compare all versions of the legend, establish or demolish the authenticity of a prayer reputedly addressed to her and authorized by a Bishop of Rouen in the sixteenth century, and generally to poke my nose into anything that would shed light on her mystery. Her case abounded with the difficulties that people of my temperament love. She was commonly called Wilgefortis, supposed to be derived from Virgo-Fortis, but she was also honoured under the names of Liberata, Kummernis, Ontkommena, Livrade, and in England—she once had a shrine in St Paul's—as Uncumber. The usual fate for Wilgefortis, among the more conservative hagiologists, was dismissal as an ignorant peasant misunderstanding of one of the many paintings of the Holy Face of Lucca, in which a long-haired and bearded figure in a long robe hangs from a cross; it is, of course, Christ, reputedly painted by St Luke himself; but many copies of it might well be pictures of a bearded lady.

I, however, had one or two new ideas about Uncumber, which I wanted to test. The first was that her legend might be a persistence of the hermaphrodite figure of the Great Mother, which was long worshipped in Cyprus and Carthage. Many a useful and popular wonder-working figure had been pinched from the pagans by Christians in early days, and some not so early. My other bit of information came from two physicians at the State University of New York, Dr Moses and Dr Lloyd, who had published some findings about abnormal growth of hair in unusually emotional women; they instanced a number of cases of beard-growing in girls who had been crossed in love; furthermore, two English doctors attested to a thick beard grown by a girl whose engagement had been brutally terminated. Anything here for Uncumber? I was on my way to Europe to find out.

So I jaunted cheerfully about the Continent on my apparently mad mission, hunting up Uncumber in remote villages as well as in such easy and pleasant places as Beauvais and Wissant, and once positively identifying an image that was said to be Uncumber (Wilgeforte, she was locally called, and the priest was rather ashamed of her) as Galla, the patroness of widows, who is also sometimes represented with a beard. It was not until August that I arrived in the Tyrol, searching for a shrine that was in a village about thirty-five miles northwest of Innsbruck.

It was about the size of Deptford, and its three inns did not expect many visitors from North America; this was still before the winter sports enthusiasm opened up every Tyrolean village and forced something like modern sanitation on every inn and guest-house. I settled in at the inevitable Red Horse and looked about me.

I was not the only stranger in the village.

A tent and some faded banners in the market-place announced the presence of *Le grand Cirque forain de St Vite*. I was certainly not the man to neglect a circus dedicated to St Vitus, patron of travelling showmen, and still invoked in country places against chorea and palsy and indeed anything that made the body shake. The banners showed neither the cock nor the dog that the name of St Vitus would have suggested, but they promised a Human Frog, *Le plus grand des Tyroliens*, *Le Solitaire des forêts* and—luck for me—*La Femme à barbe*. I determined to see this bearded lady, and if possible to find out if she had been violently crossed in love.

As a circus it was a pitiable affair. Everything about it stank of defeat and misery. There was no planned performance; now and then, when a sufficient crowd had assembled, a pair of gloomy acrobats did some tumbling and walked a slack wire. The Human Frog sat down on his own head, but with the air of one who took no pleasure in it. The Wild Man roared and chewed perfunctorily on a piece of raw meat to which a little fur still clung; the lecturer hinted darkly that we ought to keep our dogs indoors that night, but nobody seemed afraid. When not on view the Wild Man sat quietly, and from the motion of his jaws I judged that he was solacing himself with a quid of chewing tobacco.

There was an achondroplasic dwarf who danced on broken bottles; his bare feet were dirty, and from repeated dancing the glass had lost its sharpness. Their great turn was a wretched fellow— *Rinaldo the Heteradelphian*—who removed his robe and showed us that below his breast grew a pitiful wobbling lump that the eye of faith, assisted by the lecturer's description, might accept as a pair of small buttocks and what could have been two little legs without feet—an imperfect twin. The bearded lady sat and knitted; her low-cut gown, revealing the foothills of enormous breasts, dispelled any idea that she was a fake. It was upon her that I fixed my attention, for the Heteradelphian and the frowst of Tyrolean *lederhosen* were trying, even for one used to a roomful of schoolboys.

I had had enough of *Le grand Cirque forain de St Vite* and was about to leave when a young man leapt up on the platform beside *Le Solitaire des forêts* and began, rapidly and elegantly, to do tricks with cards. It was Paul Dempster.

I had acquiesced for some time in the opinion put forward by Mr Mahaffey and Miss Shanklin that Paul must be dead, or certainly lost forever. Seeing him now, however, I felt no disbelief and no uncertainty. I had last seen Paul in 1915, when he was seven; fourteen years later many men would have been unrecognizably changed, from child to man, but I knew him in an instant. After all, he had been my pupil in the art of manipulating cards and coins, and I had watched him very closely as he demonstrated his superiority to my clumsy self. His face had changed from child to man, but his hands and his style of using them were not to be mistaken.

He gave his patter in French, dropping occasionally into German with an Austrian accent. He was very good—excellent, indeed, but too good for his audience. Those among them who were card-players plainly belonged to the class who play very slow games at the inns they frequent, laying down each card as if it weighed a pound and shuffling with deliberation. His rapid passes and brilliant manipulations dazzled without enlightening them. So it was when he began to work with coins. "Secure and palm six half-crowns"—the daunting phrase came to my mind again as Paul did precisely that with the big Austrian pieces, plucking them from the beards of grown men or seeming to milk them from the noses of children, or nipping them up with long fingers from the bodices of giggling girls. It was the simplest but also the most difficult kind of conjuring because it depended on the most delicate manual skill; he brought an elegance to it that was as good as anything I had ever seen, for my old enthusiasm had led me to see a conjurer whenever I could.

When he wanted a watch to smash I offered mine, to get his eye, but he ignored it in favour of a large silver turnip handed up by a Tyrolean of some substance. Do what I could, he would not look at me, though I was a conspicuous figure as the only man in the audience not in local dress. When he had beaten the watch to pieces, made the pieces disappear, and invited a large countrywoman to return the watch from her knitting-bag, the performance was over, and the Tyroleans moved heavily towards the door of the tent.

I lingered, and addressed him in English. He replied in French, and when I changed to French he turned at once to German. I was not to be beaten. What passed between us took quite a long time and was slow and uneasy, but in the end he admitted that he was Paul Dempster—or had been so many years before. He had been Faustus Legrand for more years than the ten during which he answered to his earlier name. I spoke of his mother; told him that I had seen her not long before I came abroad. He did not answer.

Little by little, however, I got on better terms with him, principally because the other members of the troupe were curious to know what such a stranger as I wanted with one of them, and crowded around with frank curiosity. I let them know that I was from the village of Paul's birth, and with some of the cunning I had learned when trying to get priests and sacristans to talk about local shrines and the doings of saints, I let it be known that I would consider it an honour to provide the friends of Faustus Legrand with a drink—probably more than one drink.

This eased up the atmosphere at once, and the Bearded Lady, who seemed to be the social leader of *Le grand Cirque forain de St Vite*, organized a party in a very few minutes and closed the tent to business. They all, except *Le Solitaire des forêts* (who had the eyes of a dope-taker), were very fond of drink, and soon we were accommodated with a couple of bottles of that potato spirit sophisticated with brown sugar that goes by the name of Rhum in Austria, but which is not to be confused with rum. I set to work, on this foundation, to make myself popular.

It is not hard to be popular with any group, whether composed of the most conventional Canadians or of Central European freaks, if one is prepared to talk to people about themselves. In an hour I had heard about the Heteradelphian's daughter, who sang in a light opera chorus in Vienna, and about his wife, who had unaccountably wearied of his multiple attractions. The dwarf, who was shy and not very bright, took to me because I saw that he had his fair share of the Rhum. The Human Frog was a German and very cranky about war reparations, and I assured him that everybody in Canada thought they were a crying shame. I was not playing false with these poor people; they were off duty and wanted to be regarded as human beings, and I was quite ready to oblige. I became personal only with the Bearded Lady, to whom I spoke of my search for the truth about Uncumber; she was entranced by the story of the saint and insisted that I repeat it for all to hear; she took it as a tribute to Bearded Ladies in general, and began seriously to discuss having a new banner painted, in which she would advertise herself as Mme Wilgeforte, and be depicted crucified, gazing sternly at the departing figure of a pagan fiancé. Indeed, this was my best card, for the strangeness of my quest seemed to qualify me as a freak myself and make me more than ever one of the family.

When we needed more Rhum I contrived that Paul should go for it; I judged that the time had come when his colleagues would talk to me about him. And so it was.

"He stays with us only because of Le Solitaire," said the Bearded Lady. "I will not conceal from you, Monsieur, that Le Solitaire is not a well man, nor could he travel alone. Faustus very properly acknowledges a debt of gratitude, for before Le Solitaire became so incapable that he was forced to adopt the undemanding role of *un solitaire,* he had his own show of which Faustus was a part, and Faustus regards Le Solitaire as his father in art, if you understand the professional expression. I think it was Le Solitaire who brought him home from America."

It was a very merry evening, and before it was over I had danced with the Bearded Lady to music provided by the dwarf, who whistled a polka and drummed with his feet; the sight of a wooden-legged man dancing seemed hilariously funny to the artistes of the one-eyed little circus as the Rhum got to them. When we broke up I had a short private conversation with Paul.

"May I tell your mother that I have seen you?"

"I cannot prevent it, Monsieur Ramsay, but I see no point in it."

"Grief at losing you has made her very unwell."

"As I mean to remain lost I do not see what good it would do to tell her about me."

"I am sorry you have so little feeling for her."

"She is part of a past that cannot be recovered or changed by anything I can do now. My father always told me it was my birth that robbed her of her sanity. So as a child I had to carry the weight of my mother's madness as something that was my own doing. And I had to bear the cruelty of people who thought her kind of madness was funny—a dirty joke. So far as I am concerned, it is over, and if she dies mad, who will not say that she is better dead?"

So next morning I went on my journey in search of the truth about Uncumber, after I had made the necessary arrangements for more money. Because somebody at *Le grand Cirque* forain de St Vite had stolen my pocket-book, and everything pointed to Paul.

# 4

## Gyges and King Candaules

( 1 )

Boy Staunton made a great deal of money during the Depression because he dealt extensively in solaces. When a man is down on his luck he seems to consume all he can get of coffee and doughnuts. The sugar in the coffee was Boy's sugar, and the doughnuts were his doughnuts. When an overdriven woman without the money to give her children a decent meal must give them something bulky, sweet, and interesting to stop their crying, she probably gives them a soft drink; it was Boy's soft drink. When a welfare agency wants to take the harsh look of bare necessity off a handout basket, it puts in a bag of candies for the children; they were Boy's candies. Behind tons of cheap confectionery, sweets, snacks, nibbles, biscuits, and simple cooking sugar, and the accompanying oceans of fizzy, sweet water, disguised with chemical versions of every known fruit flavour, stood Boy Staunton, though not many people knew it. He was the president and managing director of Alpha Corporation, a much-respected company that made nothing itself but controlled all the other companies that did.

He was busy and he was adventurous. When he first went into the bread business, because a large company was in difficulties and could be bought at a rock-bottom price, I asked him why he did not try beer as well.

"I may do that when the economy is steadier," he said, "but at present I feel I should do everything I can to see that people have necessities." And we both took reflective pulls at the excellent whiskies-and-soda he had provided.

Boy's new bread company made quite a public stir with their advertisements declaring that they would hold the price of bread steady. And they did so, though the loaves seemed to be a bit puffier and gassier than they had been before. We ate them at the school, so I was able to judge.

There was filial piety, as well as altruism, in Boy's decision. Old Doc Staunton's annoyance at being outsmarted by his son had given way to his cupidity, and the old man was a large holder in Alpha. To have associated him with beer would have made trouble, and Boy never looked for trouble.

"Alpha concentrates on necessities," Boy liked to say. "In times like these, people need cheap, nourishing food. If a family can't buy meat, our vitaminized biscuits are still within their reach." So much so, indeed, that Boy was fast becoming one of the truly rich, by which I mean one of those men whose personal income, though large, is a trifling part of the huge, mystical body of wealth that stands behind them and cannot be counted, only estimated.

A few cranky politicians of the most radical party tried to estimate it in order to show that, in some way, the very existence of Boy was intolerable in a country where people were in want. But, like so many idealists, they did not understand money, and after a meeting where they had lambasted Boy and others like him and threatened to confiscate their wealth at the first opportunity, they would adjourn to cheap restaurants, where they drank his sugar, and ate his sugar, and smoked cigarettes which, had they known it, benefited some other monster they sought to destroy.

I used to hear him abused by some of the junior masters at the school. They were Englishmen or Canadians who had studied in England, and they were full of the wisdom of the London School of Economics and the doctrines of *The New Statesman*, copies of which used to limp into the Common Room about a month after publication. I have never been sure of my own political opinions (historical studies and my fondness for myth and legend have always blunted my political partisanship), but it amused me to hear these poor fellows, working for terrible salaries, denouncing Boy and a handful of others as "ca-*pittle*-ists"; they always stressed the middle syllables, this being a fashionable pronunciation of the period, and one that seemed to make rich men especially contemptible. I never raised my voice in protest, and none of my colleagues ever knew that I was personally acquainted with the ca-pittle-ist whose good looks, elegant style of life, and somewhat gross success made their own hard fortune and their leather-elbowed jackets and world-weary flannel trousers seem pitiful. This was not disloyalty; rather, it seemed to me that the Boy they hated and did not know was unrelated to the Boy I saw about once a fortnight and often more frequently.

I owed this position to the fact that I was the only person to whom he could talk frankly about Leola. She was trying hard, but she could not keep pace with Boy's social advancement. He was a genius—that is to say, a man who does superlatively and without obvious effort something that most people cannot do by the uttermost exertion of their abilities. He was a genius at making money, and that is as uncommon as great achievement in the arts. The simplicity of his concepts and the masterly way in which they were carried through made jealous people say he was lucky and people like my schoolmaster colleagues say he was a crook: but he made his own luck, and no breath of financial scandal ever came near him.

His ambitions did not rest in finance alone; he had built firmly on his association with the Prince of Wales, and though in hard fact it did not amount to more than the reception of a monogrammed Christmas card once a year it bulked substantially, though never quite to the point of absurdity, in his conversation. "He isn't joining them at Sandringham this year," he would say as Christmas drew near; "pretty stuffy, I suppose." And somehow this suggested that he had some inside information—perhaps a personal letter—though everybody who read the newspapers knew as much. All Boy's friends had to be pretty spry at knowing who "he" was, or they ceased to be friends. In a less glossily successful young man this would have been laughable, but the people Boy knew were not the kind of people who laughed at several million dollars. It was after David's birth it became clear that Leola was lagging in the upward climb.

A woman can go just so far on the capital of being a pretty girl. Leola, like Boy and myself, was now past youth; he was two months

younger than I, though I looked older than thirty-two and he somewhat less. Leola was not a full year younger than we, and her girlish-
ness was not well suited to her age or her position. She had toiled at
the lessons in bridge, maj-jongg, golf, and tennis; she had plodded
through the Books-of-the-Month, breaking down badly in *Kristin
Lavransdatter;* she had listened with mystification to gramophone
records of *Le Sacre du Printemps* and with the wrong kind of enjoyment to Ravel's *Bolero;* but nothing made any impression on her, and
bewilderment and a sense of failure had begun to possess her. She
had lost heart in the fight to become the sort of sophisticated, cultivated, fashionably alert woman Boy wanted for a wife. She loved
shopping, but her clothes were wrong; she had a passion for pretty
things and leaned toward the frilly at a time when fashion demanded
clean lines and a general air of knowingness in women's clothes. If
Boy let her shop alone she always came back with what he called
"another goddamned Mary Pickford rig-out," and if he took her
shopping in Paris the sessions often ended in tears, because he sided
with the clever shopwomen against his indecisive wife, who always
forgot her painfully acquired French as soon as she was confronted
with a living French creature. Nor did she speak English as became
the wife of one who had once hobnobbed with a Prince and might do
so again. If she positively *had* to use hick expressions, I once heard
Boy tell her, she might at least say "For Heaven's sake," and not "For
Heaven sakes." And "supper" was a meal one ate after the theatre, *not*
the meal they ate every night at half-past seven. Nor could she learn
when to refer to herself as "one," or remember not to say "between
you and I."

In the early years of their marriage Leola sometimes resented this
sort of talk and made spirited replies; she did not see why she should
become stuck-up, and talk as she had never talked before, and behave
in ways that were unnatural to her. When this happened Boy would
give her what he called "the silent treatment"; he said nothing, but
Leola's inner ear was so tuned to the silence that she was aware of the
answers to all her impertinences and blasphemies: it was *not* stuck-up
to behave in a way that accorded with your position in the world, and
the speech of Deptford was *not* the speech of the world to which they

now belonged; as for unnatural behaviour, natural behaviour was the sort of thing they hired a nurse to root out of young David—eating with both hands and peeing on the floor; let us have no silly talk about being natural. Of course Boy was right, and of course Leola gave in and tried to be the woman he wanted.

It was so easy for him! He never forgot anything that was of use to him, and his own manners and speech became more polished all the time. Not that he lost a hint of his virility or youthfulness, but they sat on him as if he were one of those marvellous English actors—Clive Brook, for instance—who was manly and gentlemanly at once, in a way Canadians as a whole could never manage.

This situation did not come about suddenly; it was a growth of six years of their marriage, during which Boy had changed a great deal and Leola hardly at all. Even being a mother did nothing for her; she seemed to relax when she had performed her biological trick instead of taking a firmer hold on life.

I never intervened when Leola was having a rough time; rows between them seemed to be single affairs, and it was only when I looked backward that I could see that they were sharp outbreaks in a continuous campaign. To be honest, I must say also that I did not want to shoulder the burdens of a peacemaker; Boy never let it be forgotten that he had, as he supposed, taken Leola from me; he was very jocose about it, and sometimes allowed himself a tiny, roguish hint that it might have been better for us all if things had gone the other way. The fact was that I no longer had any feeling for Leola save pity. If I spoke up for her I might find myself her champion, and a man who champions any woman against her husband had better be sure he means business.

I did not mean business, or anything at all. I went to the Stauntons' often, because they asked me and because Boy's brilliant operations fascinated me. I enjoyed my role as Friend of the Family, though I was unlike the smart, rich, determinedly youthful people who were their "set." It was some time before I tumbled to the fact that Boy needed me as someone in whose presence he could think aloud, and that a lot of his thinking was about the inadequacy of the wife he had chosen to share his high destiny.

Personally I never thought Leola did badly; she offset some of the too glossy perfection of Boy. But his idea of a wife for himself would have had the beauty and demeanour of Lady Diana Manners coupled with the wit of Margot Asquith. He let me know that he had been led into his marriage by love, and love alone; though he did not say so it was clear he owed Cupid a grudge.

Only twice did I get into any sort of wrangle with them about their own affairs. The first was early in their marriage, about 1926 I think, when Boy discovered Dr Emile Coué; the doctor had been very much in the public eye since 1920, but Canada caught up with him just about the time his vogue was expiring.

You remember Dr Coué and his great success with auto-suggestion? It had the simplicity and answer-to-everything quality that Boy, for all his shrewdness, could never resist. If you fell asleep murmuring, "Every day in every way, I am getting better and better," wondrous things came of it. The plugged colon ceased to trouble, the fretful womb to ache; indigestion yielded to inner peace; twitches and trembles disappeared; skin irritations vanished overnight; stutterers became fluent; the failing memory improved; stinking breath became as the zephyr of May; and dandruff but a hateful memory. Best of all it provided "moral energy," and Boy Staunton was a great believer in energy of all kinds.

He wanted Leola to acquire moral energy, after which social grace, wit, and an air of easy breeding would surely follow. She obediently repeated the formula as often as she could, every night for six weeks, but nothing much seemed to be happening.

"You're just not trying, Leo," he said one night when I was dining with them. "You've simply got to try harder."

"Perhaps she's trying too hard," I said.

"Don't be absurd, Dunny. There's no such thing as trying too hard, whatever you're doing."

"Yes there is. Have you never heard of the Law of Reversed Effort? The harder you try, the more likely you are to miss the mark."

"I never heard such nonsense. Who says that?"

"A lot of wise people have said it, and the latest is your Dr Coué. Don't clench your teeth and push for success, he says, or everything will work against you. Psychological fact."

"Bunk! He doesn't say it in my book."

"But, Boy, you never study anything properly. That miserable little pamphlet you have just gives you a farcical smattering of Couéism. You should read Baudouin's *Suggestion and Auto-Suggestion* and get things right."

"How many pages?"

"I don't count pages. It's a good-sized book."

"I haven't got time for big books. I have to have the nub of things. If effort is all wrong, why does Coué work for me? I put lots of effort into it."

"I don't suppose it does work for you. You don't need it. Every day in every way you do get better and better, in whatever sense you understand the word "better," because that's the kind of person you are. You've got ingrained success."

"Well, bring your book over and explain it to Leo. Make her read it, and you help her to understand it."

Which I did, but it was of no use. Poor Leola did not get better and better because she had no idea of what betterness was. She couldn't conceive what Boy wanted her to be. I don't think I have ever met such a stupid, nice woman. So Dr Coué failed for her, as he did for many others, for which I lay no blame on him. His system was really a form of secularized, self-seeking prayer, without the human dignity that even the most modest prayer evokes. And like all attempts to command success for the chronically unsuccessful, it petered out.

The second time I came between Boy and Leola was much more serious. It happened late in 1927, after the famous Royal Tour. Boy gave me a number of reels of film and asked me to develop them for him. This was reasonable enough, because in my saint-hunting expeditions I used a camera often and had gained some skill; at the school, as I could not supervise sports, I was in charge of the Camera Club and taught boys how to use the dark room. I was always ready to do a favour for Boy, to whose advice I owed my solvency, and when he said that he did not want to confide these films to a commercial developer I assumed they were pictures of the Tour and probably some of them were of the Prince.

So it was, except for two reels that were amateurish but pretentious "art studies" of Leola, lying on cushions, peeping through veils, sitting at her make-up table, kneeling in front of an open fire, wagging her finger at a Teddy Bear, choosing a chocolate from a large ribboned box—every sentimental posture approved by the taste of the day for "cutie" photographs, and in every one of them she was stark naked. If she had been an experienced model and Boy a clever photographer, they would have been the kind of thing that appeared in the more daring magazines. But their combined inexperience had produced embarrassing snapshots of the sort hundreds of couples take but have the sense to keep to themselves.

I do not know why this made me so angry. Was I so inconsiderable, so much the palace eunuch, that I did not matter? Or was this a way of letting me know what I had missed when Boy won Leola? Or was it a signal that if I wanted to take Leola off his hands Boy would make no objection? He had let me know that Leola had conventional ideas and that his own adventurous appetite was growing tired of her meat-and-potatoes approach to sex. Whatever it was, I was very angry and considered destroying the film. But—I must be honest—I examined the pictures with care, and I suppose with some measure of gloating, and this made me angrier still.

My solution was typical of me. I developed all the pictures as carefully as I could, enlarged the best ones (all those of Leola), returned them without a word, and waited to see what would happen.

Next time I dined with them all the pictures were brought out, and Boy went through them slowly, telling me exactly what H.R.H. had said as each one was taken. At last we came to the ones of Leola.

"Oh, don't show those!"

"Why not?"

"Because."

"Dunny's seen them before, you know. He developed them, I expect he kept a set for himself."

"No," I said, "as a matter of fact I didn't."

"The more fool you. You'll never see pictures of a prettier girl."

"Boy, please put them away or I'll have to go upstairs. I don't want Dunny to see them while I'm here."

"Leo, I never thought you were such a little prude."

"Boy, it isn't nice."

"Nice, nice, nice! Of course it isn't *nice*! Only fools worry about what's *nice*. Now sit here by me, and Dunny on the other side, and be proud of what a stunner you are."

So Leola, sensing a row from the edge in his voice, sat between us while Boy showed the pictures, telling me what lens apertures he had used, and how he had arranged the lights, and how he had achieved certain "values" which, in fact, made Leola's rose-leaf bottom look like sharkskin and her nipples glare when they should have blushed. He seemed to enjoy Leola's discomfiture thoroughly; it was educational for her to learn that her beauty had public as well as private significance. He recalled Margot Asquith's account of receiving callers in her bath though—he was always a careless reader—he did not remember the circumstances correctly.

As we drew near the end of the show he turned to me and said with a grin, "I hope you don't find it too hot in here, old man?"

As a matter of fact I did find it hot. All the anger I had felt when developing the pictures had returned. But I said I was quite comfortable.

"Oh. I just thought you might find the situation a bit unusual, as Leo does."

"Unusual but not unprecedented. Call it historical—even mythological."

"How's that?"

"It's happened before, you know. Do you remember the story of Gyges and King Candaules?"

"Never heard of them."

"I thought not. Well, Candaules was a king of Lydia a long time ago, and he was so proud of his wife's beauty that he insisted his friend Gyges should see her naked."

"Generous chap. What happened?"

"There are two versions. One is that the Queen took a fancy to Gyges and together they pushed Candaules off his throne."

"Really? Not much chance of that here, is there, Leo? You'd find my throne a bit too big, Dunny."

"The other is that Gyges killed Candaules."

"I don't suppose you'll do that, Dunny."

I didn't suppose so myself. But I think I stirred some uxorious fire in Boy, for nine months later I did some careful counting, and I am virtually certain that it was on that night little David was begotten. Boy was certainly a complex creature, and I am sure he loved Leola. What he thought of me I still do not know. That Leola loved him with all her unreflecting heart there would be no possible doubt. Nothing he could do would change that.

( 2 )

Every fortnight during the school term I made the journey to Weston on Saturday morning and had lunch with Miss Bertha Shanklin and Mrs Dempster. It took less than half an hour on a local train, so I could leave after the Saturday morning study period for boarders, which I supervised, and be back in town by three o'clock. To have stayed longer, Miss Shanklin let me know, would have been fatiguing for poor Mary. She really meant, for herself; like many people who have charge of an invalid, she projected her own feelings on her patient, speaking for Mrs Dempster as a priest might interpret a dull-witted god. But she was gentle and kind, and I particularly liked the way she provided her niece with pretty, fresh dresses and kept her hair clean and neat; in the Deptford days I had become used to seeing her in dirty disorder as she paced her room on the restraining rope.

At these meals Mrs Dempster rarely spoke, and although it was clear that she recognized me as a regular visitor, nothing to suggest any memory of Deptford ever passed between us. I played fair with Miss Shanklin and appeared in the guise of a new friend; a welcome one, for they saw few men, and most women, even the most determined spinsters, like a little masculine society.

The only other man to visit that house at any time when I was there was Miss Shanklin's lawyer, Orpheus Wettenhall. I never discovered anything about him that would explain why his parents gave him such a pretentious Christian name; perhaps it ran in the family. He invited me to call him Orph, which was what everybody called him, he said. He was an undersized, laughing man with a big walrus moustache and silver-rimmed glasses.

Orph was quite the most dedicated sportsman I have ever known. During every portion of the year when it was legal to shoot or hook any living creature, he was at it; in off-seasons he shot groundhogs and vermin beneath the notice of the law. When the trout season began, his line was in the water one minute after midnight; when deer might be shot, he lived as did Robin Hood. Like all dedicated hunters, he had to get rid of the stuff he killed; his wife "kicked over the traces" at game more than four or five times a week. He used to turn up at Miss Shanklin's now and then, opening the front door without ceremony and shouting, "Bert! I've brought you a pretty!"; then he would appear an instant later with something wet or bloody, which the hired girl bore away, while Miss Shanklin gave a nicely judged performance of delight at his goodness and horror at the sight of something the intrepid Orph had slain with his own hands.

He was a gallant little particle, and I liked him because he was so cheerful and considerate towards Miss Shanklin and Mrs Dempster. He often urged me to join him in slaughter, but I pled my wooden leg as an excuse for keeping out of the woods. I had had all the shooting I wanted in the war.

I began my visits in the autumn of 1928 and was faithful in them till February 1932, when Miss Shanklin took pneumonia and died. I did not know of it until I received a letter from Wettenhall, bidding me to the funeral and adding that we must have a talk afterward.

It was one of those wretched February funerals, and I was glad to get away from the graveyard into Wettenhall's hot little office. He was in a black suit, the only time I ever saw him in other than sporting clothes.

"Let's cut the cackle, Ramsay," he said, pouring us each a hearty drink of rye, in glasses with other people's lipmarks on the rims. "It's as simple as this: you're named as Bert's executor. Everything goes to Mary Dempster except some small legacies—one to me, the old sweetheart, for taking good care of her affairs—and a handful of others. You are to have five thousand a year, on a condition. That condition is that you get yourself appointed Mary Dempster's guardian and undertake to look after her and administer her money for her as long as she lives. I'm to see that the Public Guardian is satisfied. After Mary's death everything goes to you. When all debts and taxes are paid, Bert ought to cut up at—certainly not less than a quarter of a million, maybe three hundred thousand. You're allowed to reject the responsibility, and the legacy as well, if you don't want to be bothered. You'll want a couple of days to think it over."

I agreed, though I knew already that I would accept. I said some conventional but perfectly sincere things about how much I had liked Miss Shanklin and how I would miss her.

"You and me both," said Orph. "I loved Bert—in a perfectly decent way, of course—and damned if I know how things will be without her."

He handed me a copy of the will, and I went back to town. I did not go to see Mrs Dempster, who had not, of course, been at the funeral. I would attend to that when I had made some other arrangements.

The next day I made inquiries as to how I could be appointed the guardian of Mary Dempster and found that it was not a very complicated process but would take time. I experienced a remarkable rising of my spirits, which I can only attribute to the relief of guilt. As a child I had felt oppressively responsible for her, but I had thought all that was dissipated in the war. Was not a leg full and fair payment for an evil action? This was primitive thinking, and I had no trouble dismissing it—so it seemed. But the guilt had only been thrust away, or thrust down out of sight, for here it was again, in full strength, clamouring to be atoned, now that the opportunity offered itself.

Another element insisted on attention though I tried to put it from me: if Mrs Dempster was a saint, henceforth she would be *my* saint. Was she a saint? Rome, which alone of human agencies undertook to say who was a saint and who was not, insisted on three well-attested miracles. Hers were the reclamation of Surgeoner by an act of charity that was certainly heroic in terms of the *mores* of Deptford; the raising of Willie from the dead; and her miraculous appearance to me when I was at the uttermost end of my endurance at Passchendaele.

Now I should be able to see what a saint was really like and perhaps make a study of one without all the apparatus of Rome, which I had no power to invoke. The idea possessed me that it might lie in my power to make a serious contribution to the psychology of religion, and perhaps to carry the work of William James a step further. I don't think I was a very good teacher on the day when all of this was racing through my head.

I was a worse teacher two days later, when the police called me to say that Orpheus Wettenhall had shot himself and that they wanted to talk to me.

It was a very hush-hush affair. People talk boldly about suicide, and man's right to choose his own time of death, when it is not near them. For most of us, when it draws close, suicide is a word of fear, and never more so than in small, closely knit communities. The police and the coroner and everybody else implicated took every precaution that the truth about Orph should not leak out. And so, of course, the truth did leak out, and it was a very simple and old story.

Orph was a family lawyer of the old school; he looked after a number of estates for farmers and people like Miss Shanklin, who had not learned about new ways of doing business. Orph's word was as good as his bond, so it would have been unfriendly to ask for his bond. He had been paying his clients a good, unadventurous return on their money for years, but he had been investing that same money in the stock market for big returns, which he kept. When the crash came he was unprepared, and since 1929 he had been paying out quite a lot of his own money (if it may be called that) to keep his affairs on an even keel. The death of Bertha Shanklin had made it impossible to go on.

So the story given to the public was that Orph, who had handled guns all his life, had been cleaning a cocked and loaded shotgun and had unaccountably got the end of the barrel into his mouth, which had so much astonished him that he inadvertently trod on the trigger and blew the top of his head off. Accidental death, as clearly as any coroner ever saw it.

Perhaps a few people believed it, until a day or two later when it was known what a mess his affairs were in, and a handful of old men and women were to be met wandering in the streets, unable to believe their ill-fortune.

Nobody had time or pity for these minor characters in the drama; all public compassion was for Orph Wettenhall. What agonies of mind must he not have endured before taking his life! Was it not significant that he had launched himself into the hereafter apparently gazing upward at the large stuffed head of a moose he had shot a good forty years before! Who would have the heart to take his place on the deerhunt next autumn? When had there been his like for deftness and speed in skinning a buck? But of his ability in skinning a client little was said, except that he had obviously meant to restore the missing funds as soon as he could.

It was not positively so stated, but the consensus seemed to be that Bertha Shanklin had shown poor taste in dying so soon and thus embarrassing the local Nimrod. "There, but for the grace of God, go I," said several citizens; like most people who quote this ambiguous saying, they had never given a moment's thought to its implications. As for Mary Dempster, I never heard her name mentioned. Thus I learned two lessons: that popularity and good character are not related, and that compassion dulls the mind faster than brandy.

All the cash I could find in Miss Shanklin's house amounted to twenty-one dollars; of her bank account, into which Wettenhall had made quarterly payments, everything but about two hundred dollars had been spent on her final illness and burial. So I began then and there to maintain Mrs Dempster, and never ceased to do so until her death in 1959. What else could I do?

As executor I was able to sell the house and the furniture, but they realized less than four thousand dollars; the Depression was no time for auctions. In the course of time I was duly appointed the guardian of Mary Dempster. But what was I to do with her? I investigated the matter of private hospitals and found that to keep her in one would beggar me. All masters at Colborne had been invited to take a cut in salary to help in keeping the school afloat, and we did so; there were many boys whose parents either could not pay their fees or did not pay them till much later, and it was not in the school's character to throw them out. My investments were better than those of a great many people, but even Alpha was not paying much; Boy said it would not look well at such a time, and so there were stock splits instead, and a good deal of money was "ploughed back" for future advantage. I was not too badly off for a single man, but I had no funds to maintain an expensive invalid. So much against my will I got Mrs Dempster into a public hospital for the insane, in Toronto, where I could keep an eye on her.

It was a dark day for both of us when I took her there. The staff were good and kind but they were far too few, and the building was an old horror. It was about eighty years old and had been designed for the era when the first thing that was done with an insane patient was to put him to bed, with a view to keeping him there, safe and out of the way, till he recovered or died. Consequently the hospital had few and inadequate common rooms, and the patients sat in the corridors, or wandered up and down the corridors, or lay on their beds. The architecture was of the sort that looks better on the outside than on the inside; the building had a dome and a great number of barred windows and looked like a run-down palace.

Inside the ceilings were high, the light was bad, and in spite of the windows the ventilation was capricious. The place reeked of disinfectant, but the predominating smell was that unmistakable stench of despair that is so often to be found in jails, courtrooms, and madhouses.

She had a bed in one of the long wards, and I left her standing beside it, with a kindly nurse who was explaining what she should do with the contents of her suitcase. But already her face looked as I remembered it in her worst days in Deptford. I dared not look back, and I felt meaner than I have ever felt in my life. But what was I to do?

( 3 )

Aside from my teaching, my observation of Boy's unwitting destruction of Leola, and my new and complete responsibility for Mrs Dempster, this was the most demanding period of my life, for it was during this time I became involved with the Bollandists and found my way into the mainstream of the work that has given me endless delight and a limited, specialized reputation.

I have spent a good deal of time in my life explaining who the Bollandists are, and although you, Headmaster, are assumed by the school to know everything, perhaps I had better remind you that they are a group of Jesuits whose special task is to record all available information about saints in their great *Acta Sanctorum,* upon which they have been at work (with breaks for civil or religious uproar) since John van Bolland began in 1643; they have been pegging away with comparatively few interruptions since 1837; proceeding from the festal days of the Saints beginning in January, they have now filled sixty-nine volumes and reached the month of November.

In addition to this immense and necessarily slow task, they have published since 1882 a yearly collection of material of interest to their work but not within the scope of the *Acta,* called *Analecta Bollandiana;* it is scholarly modesty of a high order to call this "Bollandist Gleanings", for it is of the greatest importance and interest, historically as well as hagiographically.

As a student of history myself, I have always found it revealing to see who gets to be a saint in any period; some ages like wonder-workers, and some prefer gifted organizers whose attention to business produces apparent miracles. In the last few years good old saints whom even Protestants love have been losing ground to lesser figures whose fortune it was to be black or yellow or red-skinned—a kind of saintly representation by population. My Bollandist friends are the first to admit that there is more politics to the making of a saint than the innocently devout might think likely.

It was quite beyond my income to own a set of the *Acta,* but I consulted it frequently—sometimes two or three times a week—at the University Library. However, I did, by luck, get a chance to buy a run of the *Analecta,* and though it cost me a fortune by Depression reckoning, I could not let it go, and its bulk and foreign-looking binding has surprised many visitors to my study in the school.

Boys grow bug-eyed when they find that I actually read in French, German, and Latin, but it is good for them to find that these languages have an existence outside the classroom; some of my colleagues look at my books with amusement, and a few solemn asses have spread the rumour that I am "going over to Rome"; old Eagles (long before your time) thought it his duty to warn me against the Scarlet Woman and demanded rhetorically how I could possibly "swallow the Pope." Since then millions have swallowed Hitler and Mussolini, Stalin and Mao, and we have swallowed some democratic leaders who had to be gagged down without relish. Swallowing the Pope seems a trifle in comparison. But to return to 1932, there I was, a subscriber and greedy reader of the *Analecta*, and busy learning Greek (not the Greek of Homer but the queer Greek of medieval monkish recorders) so as to miss nothing.

It was then that the bold idea struck me of sending my notes on Uncumber to the editor of *Acta*, the great Hippolyte Delehaye; at worst he would ignore them or return them with formal thanks. I had the Protestant idea that Catholics always spat in your eye if they could, and of course Jesuits—crafty and trained to duplicity as they were—might pinch my stuff and arrange to have me blown up with a bomb, to conceal their guilt. Anyhow I would try.

It was little more than a month before this came in the mail:

*Cher Monsieur Ramsay,*
*Your notes on the Wilgefortis-Kummernis figure have been read with interest by some of us here, and although the information is not wholly new, the interpretation and synthesis is of such a quality that we seek your consent to its publication in the next* Analecta. *Will you be so good as to write to me at your earliest convenience, as time presses. If you ever visit Bruxelles, will you give us the pleasure of making your acquaintance? It is always a great satisfaction to meet a serious hagiographer, and particularly one who, like yourself, engages in the work not professionally but as a labour of love.*
*Avec mes souhaits sincères,*
*Hippolyte Delehaye S.J.*

*Société des Bollandistes*
*24 Boulevard Saint-Michel*
*Bruxelles*

Few things in my life have given me so much delight as this letter; I have it still. I had schooled myself since the war-days never to speak of my enthusiasms; when other people did not share them, which was usual, I was hurt and my pleasure diminished; why was I always excited about things other people did not care about? But I could not hold in. I boasted a little in the Common Room that I had received an acceptance from *Analecta;* my colleagues looked uncomprehendingly, like cows at a passing train, and went on talking about Brebner's extraordinary hole-in-one the day before.

I spoke of it to Boy when next I saw him; all he could get through his head was that I had written my contribution in French. To be fair, I did not tell him the story of Uncumber and her miraculous beard; he was no audience for such psychological-mythological gossip, which appealed only to the simple or the truly sophisticated. Boy was neither, but he had an eye for quality, and it was after this I began to be asked to dinner more often with the Stauntons' smart friends and not as a lone guest. Sometimes I heard Boy speaking of me to the bankers and brokers as "very able chap—speaks several languages fluently and writes for a lot of European publications—a bit of an eccentric, of course, but an old friend."

I think his friends thought I wrote about "current affairs," and quite often they asked me how I thought the Depression was going to pan out. On these occasions I looked wise and said I thought it was moving towards its conclusion but we might not have seen the worst of it—an answer that contained just the mixture of hope and gloom financial people find reassuring. I thought they were a terrible pack of fatheads, but I was also aware that they must be good at something because they were so rich. I would not have had their cast of mind in order to get their money, however, much as I liked money.

They were a strange lot, these moneyed, influential friends of Boy's, but they were obviously interesting to each other. They talked a lot of what they called "politics," though there was not much plan or policy in it, and they were worried about the average man, or as they usually called him "the ordinary fellow.'" This ordinary fellow had two great faults: he could not think straight and he wanted to reap where he had not sown. I never saw much evidence of straight thinking among these ca-pittle-ists, but I came to the conclusion that they were reaping where they had sown, and that what they had sown was not, as they believed, hard work and great personal sacrifice but talent—a rather rare talent, a talent that nobody, even its possessors, likes to recognize as a talent and therefore not available to everybody who cares to sweat for it—the talent for manipulating money.

How happy they might have been if they had recognized and gloried in their talent, confronting the world as gifted egotists, comparable to painters, musicians, or sculptors! But that was not their style. They insisted on degrading their talent to the level of mere acquired knowledge and industry. They wanted to be thought of as wise in the ways of the world and astute in politics; they wanted to demonstrate in themselves what the ordinary fellow might be if he would learn to think straight and be content to reap only where he had sown. They and their wives (women who looked like parrots or bulldogs, most of them) were so humourless and, except when they were drunk, so cross that I thought the ordinary fellow was lucky not to be like them.

It seemed to me they knew less about the ordinary fellow than I did, for I had fought in the war as an ordinary fellow myself, and most of these men had been officers. I had seen the ordinary fellow's heroism and also his villainy, his tenderness and also his unthinking cruelty, but I had never seen in him much capacity to devise or carry out a coherent, thoughtful, long-range plan; he was just as much the victim of his emotions as were these rich wiseacres. Where shall wisdom be found, and where is the place of understanding? Not among Boy Staunton's ca-pittle-ists, nor among the penniless scheme-spinners in the school Common Room, nor yet at the Socialist-Communist meetings in the city, which were sometimes broken up by the police. I seemed to be the only person I knew without a plan that would put the world on its feet and wipe the tear from every eye. No wonder I felt like a stranger in my own land.

No wonder I sought some place where I could be at home, and until my first visit to the Collège de Saint-Michel, in Brussels, I was so innocent as to think it might be among the Bollandists. I passed several weeks there very happily, for they at once made me free of the hall for foreign students, and as I grew to know some of the Jesuits who directed the place I was taken even more into their good graces and had the run of their magnificent library. More than one hundred and fifty thousand books about saints! It seemed a paradise.

Yet often, usually at about three o'clock in the afternoon when the air grew heavy, and scholars at nearby desks were dozing over their notes, I would think: Dunstan Ramsay, what on earth are you doing here, and where do you think this is leading? You are now thirty-four, without wife or child, and no better plan than your own whim; you teach boys who, very properly, regard you as a signpost on the road they are to follow, and like a signpost they pass you by without a thought; your one human responsibility is a madwoman about whom you cherish a maggoty-headed delusion; and here you are, puzzling over records of lives as strange as fairy tales, written by people with no sense of history, and yet you cannot rid yourself of the notion that you are well occupied. Why don't you go to Harvard and get yourself a Ph.D., and try for a job in a university, and be intellectually respectable? Wake up, man! You are dreaming your life away!

Then I would go on trying to discover how Mary Magdalene had been accepted as the same Mary who was the sister of Martha and Lazarus, and if this pair of sisters, one representing the housewifely woman and the other the sensual woman, had any real counterparts in pagan belief, and sometimes—O, idler and jackass!—if their rich father was anywhere described as being like the rich men I met at Boy Staunton's dinner parties. If he were, who would be surprised if his daughter went to the bad?

Despite these afternoon misgivings and self-reproaches I clung to my notion, ill defined though it was, that a serious study of any important body of human knowledge, or theory, or belief, if undertaken with a critical but not a cruel mind, would in the end yield some secret, some valuable permanent insight, into the nature of life and the true end of man. My path was certainly an odd one for a Deptford lad, raised as a Protestant, but fate had pushed me in this direction so firmly that to resist would be dangerous defiance. For I was, as you have already guessed, a collaborator with Destiny, not one who put a pistol to its head and demanded particular treasures. The only thing for me to do was to keep on keeping on, to have faith in my whim, and remember that for me, as for the saints, illumination when it came would probably come from some unexpected source.

The Jesuits of the Société des Bollandistes were not so numerous that I did not, in time, get on speaking terms with most of them, and a very agreeable, courteous group they were. I now realize that, although I thought I had purged my mind of nonsense about Jesuits, some dregs of mistrust remained. I thought, for instance, that they were going to be preternaturally subtle and that in conversation I would have to be very careful—about what, I did not know. Certainly if they possessed any extraordinary gifts of subtlety they did not waste them on me. I suspected too that they would smell the black Protestant blood in my veins, and I would never gain their trust. On the contrary, my Protestantism made me a curiosity and something of a pet. It was still a time when the use of index cards for making notes was not universal, and they were curious about mine; most of them made notes on scraps of paper, which they kept in order with a virtuosity that astonished me. But though they used me well in every way, I knew that I would always be a guest in this courteous, out-of-the-world domain, and I quickly discovered that the Society of Jesus discouraged its members from being on terms of intimacy with anyone, including other Jesuits. I was used to living without intimate friends, but I had a sneaking hope that here, among men whose preoccupation I shared, things might be different.

All the more reason to be flattered, therefore, when, at the conclusion of one of the two or three conversations I had with Père Delehaye, the principal editor of the *Analecta*, he said, "Our journal, as you will have observed, publishes material provided by the Bollandists and their friends; I hope you will correspond with us often, and come here when you can, for certainly we think of you now as one of our friends."

This was by way of leave-taking, for I was setting off the next day for Vienna, and I was travelling with an elderly Bollandist, Padre Ignacio Blazon.

Padre Blazon was the only oddity I had met at the Collège de Saint-Michel. He more than made up for the placidly unremarkable appearance and behaviour of the others, and I think they may have been a little ashamed of him. He was so obviously, indeed theatrically, a priest, which is contrary to Jesuit custom. He wore his soutane all the time indoors, and sometimes even in the streets, which was not regarded with favour. His battered black hat suggested that it might have begun long ago as part of Don Basilio's costume in *The Barber of Seville*, and had lost caste and shape since then. He wore a velvet skullcap, now green with whitened seams, indoors, and under his hat when outdoors. Most of the priests smoked, moderately, but he took snuff immoderately, from a large horn box. His spectacles were mended with dirty string. His hair needed, not cutting, but mowing. His nose was large, red, and bulbous. He had few teeth, so that his chaps were caved in. He was, indeed, so farcical in appearance that no theatre director with a scrap of taste would have permitted him on the stage in such a make-up. Yet here he was, a reality, shuffling about the Bollandist library, humming to himself, snuffing noisily, and peeping over people's shoulders to see what they were doing.

He was tolerated, I soon found out, for his great learning and for what was believed to be his great age. He spoke English eloquently, with little trace of foreign accent, and he jumped from language to language with a virtuosity that astonished everybody and obviously delighted himself. When I first noticed him he was chattering happily to an Irish monk in Erse, heedless of discreet shushings and murmurs of "*Tacete*" from the librarian on duty. When he first noticed me he tried to flummox me by addressing me in Latin, but I was equal to that dodge, and after a few commonplaces we changed to English. It was not long before I discovered that one of his enthusiasms was food, and after that we dined together often.

"I am one of Nature's guests," he said, "and if you will take care of the bill I shall be happy to recompense you with information about the saints you will certainly not find in our library. If, on the contrary, you insist that I should take my turn as host, I shall expect you to divert me—and I am not an easy man to amuse, Monsieur Ramezay. As a host I am exigent, rebarbative, unaccommodating. As a guest— ah, quite another set of false teeth, I assure you."

So I was always host, and we visited several of the good restaurants in Brussels. Padre Blazon was more than true to his word.

"You Protestants, if you think of saints at all, regard them with quite the wrong sort of veneration," he said to me at our first dinner. "I think you must be deceived by our cheap religious statuary. All those pink and blue dolls, you know, are for people who think them beautiful. St Dominic, so pretty and pink-checked, with his lily, is a peasant woman's idea of a good man—the precise contrary of the man she is married to, who stinks of sweat and punches her in the breast and puts his cold feet on her backside in the winter nights. But St Dominic himself—and this is a Jesuit speaking, Ramezay—was no confectionery doll. Do you know that before he was born his mother dreamed she would give birth to a dog with a lighted torch in its mouth? And that was what he was—fierce and persistent in carrying the flame of faith. But show the peasant woman a dog with a torch and she will not care for it; she wants a St Dominic who can see the beautiful soul in her, and that would be a man without passions or desires—a sort of high-minded eunuch.

"But she is too much herself to want that all the time. She would not take it in exchange for her smelly man. She gives her saints another life, and some very strange concerns, that we Bollandists have to know about but do not advertise. St Joseph, now—what is his sphere of patronage, Ramezay?"

"Carpenters, the dying, the family, married couples, and people looking for houses."

"Yes, and in Naples, of confectioners; don't ask me why. But what else? Come now, put your mind to it. What made Joseph famous?"

"The earthly father of Christ?"

"Oho, you nice Protestant boy! Joseph is history's most celebrated cuckold. Did not God usurp Joseph's function, reputedly by impregnating his wife through her ear? Do not nasty little seminarians still refer to a woman's *sine qua non* as *auricula*—the ear? And is not Joseph known throughout Italy as Tio Pepe—Uncle Joe—and invoked by husbands who are getting worried? St Joseph hears more prayers about cuckoldry than he does about house-hunting or confectionery, I can assure you. Indeed, in the underworld hagiology of which I promised to tell you, it is whispered that the Virgin herself, who was born to Joachim and Anna through God's personal intervention, was a divine daughter as well as a divine mate; the Greeks could hardly improve on that, could they? And popular legend has it that Mary's parents were very rich, which makes an oddity of the Church's respect for poverty but is quite in keeping with the general respect for money. And do you know the scandal that makes it necessary to keep apart the statues of Mary and those of St John—"

Padre Blazon was almost shouting by this time, and I had to hush him. People in the restaurant were staring, and one or two ladies of devout appearance were heaving their bosoms indignantly. He swept the room with the wild eyes of a conspirator in a melodrama and dropped his voice to a hiss. Fragments of food, ejected from his mouth by this jet, flew about the table.

"But all this terrible talk about the saints is not disrespect, Ramezay. Far from it! It is faith! It is love! It takes the saint to the heart by supplying the other side of his character that history or legend has suppressed—that he may very well have suppressed himself in his struggle toward sainthood. The saint triumphs over sin. Yes, but most of us cannot do that, and because we love the saint and want him to be more like ourselves, we attribute some imperfection to him. Not always sexual, of course. Thomas Aquinas was monstrously fat; St Jerome had a terrible temper. This gives comfort to fat men, and cross men. Mankind cannot endure perfection; it stifles him. He demands that even the saints should cast a shadow. If they, these holy ones who have lived so greatly but who still carry their shadows with them, can approach God, well then, there is hope for the worst of us.

"Sometimes I wonder why so few saints were also wise. Some were, of course, but more were down-right pig-headed. Often I wonder if God does not value wisdom as much as heroic virtue. But wisdom is rather unspectacular; it does not flash in the sky. Most people like spectacle. One cannot blame them. But for oneself—ah, no thank you."

It was with this learned chatterbox that I set out to travel from Brussels to Vienna. I was early at the station, as he had commanded, and found him already in sole possession of a carriage. He beckoned me inside and went on with his task, which was to read aloud from his breviary, keeping the window open the while, so that passers-by would hear him.

"Give me a hand with a Paternoster," he said and began to roar the Lord's Prayer in Latin as loud as he could. I joined in, equally loud, and we followed with a few rousing Aves and Agnus Deis. By dint of this pious uproar we kept the carriage for ourselves. People would come to the door, decide that they could not stand such company, and pass on, muttering.

"Strange how reluctant travellers are to join in devotions that might—who can say?—avert some terrible accident," said Blazon, winking solemnly at me as the guard's whistle blew, the engine peeped, and we drew out of the station. He spread a large handkerchief over his lap and put the big snuffbox in the middle of it, skimmed his dreadful hat into the luggage rack to join a bundle held together by a shawl strap, and composed himself for conversation.

"You have brought the refreshment basket?" said he. I had, and I had not stinted. "It might be provident to take some of that brandy immediately," he said. "I know this journey, and sometimes the motion of the train can be very distressing." So at half-past nine in the morning we began on the brandy, and soon Padre Blazon was launched into one of those monologues, delivered at the top of his voice, which he preferred to more even-handed conversation. I shall boil it down.

"I have not forgotten your questions about the woman you keep in the madhouse, Ramezay. I have said nothing on that subject during our last few dinners, but it has not been absent from my mind, you may be assured. Invariably I come back to the same answer: why do you worry? What good would it do you if I told you she is indeed a saint? I cannot make saints, nor can the Pope. We can only recognize saints when the plainest evidence shows them to be saintly. If you think her a saint, she is a saint to you. What more do you ask? That is what we call the reality of the soul; you are foolish to demand the agreement of the world as well. She is a Protestant. What does it matter? To be a Protestant is halfway to being an atheist, of course, and your innumerable sects have not recognized any saints of their own since the Reformation, so-called. But it would be less than Christian to suppose that heroic virtue may not assert itself among Protestants. Trust your own judgement. That is what you Protestants made such a dreadful fuss to assert your right to do."

"But it is the miracles that concern me. What you say takes no account of the miracles."

"Oh, miracles! They happen everywhere. They are conditional. If I take a photograph of you, it is a compliment and perhaps rather a bore. If I go into the South American jungle and take a photograph of a primitive, he probably thinks it a miracle and he may be afraid I have stolen a part of his soul. If I take a picture of a dog and show it to him, he does not even know what he looks like, so he is not impressed; he is lost in a collective of dogginess. Miracles are things people cannot explain. Your artificial leg would have been a miracle in the Middle Ages—probably a Devil's miracle. Miracles depend much on time, and place, and what we know and do not know. I am going to Vienna now to work on the Catalogue of Greek Manuscripts in what used to be the Emperor's Library. I shall be drowned in miracles, for those simple Greek monks liked nothing better and saw them everywhere. I tell you frankly, I shall be sick of miracles before I am taken off that job. Life itself is too great a miracle for us to make so much fuss about potty little reversals of what we pompously assume to be the natural order.

"Look at me, Ramezay. I am something of a miracle myself. My parents were simple Spanish people living a few leagues from Pamplona. They had seven daughters—think of it, Ramezay, seven! My poor mother was beside herself at the disgrace. So she vowed solemnly, in church, that if she might bear a son, she would give him to the service of God. She made her vow in a Jesuit church, so it was natural enough that she should add that she would make him a Jesuit. Within a year—behold, little Ignacio, so named after the saintly founder of the Society of Jesus. To a geneticist, I suppose it is not breathtaking that after seven daughters a woman should have a son, but to my mother it was a miracle. The neighbours said—you know how the neighbours always say—'Wait, the trouble is to come;

he will be a wild one, this Ignacio; the jail gapes for these sanctified children.' Was it so? Not a bit! I seemed to be a Jesuit from the womb—studious, obedient, intelligent, and chaste. Behold me, Ramezay, a virgin at the age of seventy-six! Of how many can that be said? Girls laid themselves out to tempt me; they were incited to seduce me by my sisters, who had only ordinary chastity and thought mine distasteful. I will not say I was not flattered by these temptations. But always I would say, 'God did not give us this jewel of chastity to be trampled in the dirt, my dear Dolores (or Maria or whoever it was); pray for an honourable and loving marriage, and put me from your mind.' Oh, how they hated that! One girl hit me with a big stone; you see the mark here still, just where my hair used to begin. This was a real miracle, for every morning I had unmistakable assurance that I could have been a great lover—you understand me?—but I loved my vocation more.

"I loved it so much that when the time came for me to enter the Jesuits my examiners were mistrustful. I was too good to be true. My mother's vow, my own abstentions—it worried them. They raked around, trying to discover some streak of unredeemed nature in me—some shadow, as we were saying a while ago—but I had none. Do you know, Ramezay, it stood in my way as much as if I had been a stiff-necked recalcitrant and troublemaker? Yes, my novitiate was very rough, and when I had got through that and was a formed scholastic, every dirty job was put in my way, to see if I would break. It was a full seventeen years before I was allowed to take my four final vows and become a professed member of the Society. And then— well, you see what I am now. I am a pretty useful person, I think, and I have done good work for the Bollandists, but nobody would say I was the flower of the Jesuits. If ever I was a miracle, it is done with now. My shadow manifested itself quite late in life.

"You know that Jesuit training is based on a rigorous reform of the self and achievement of self-knowledge. By the time a man comes to the final vows, anything emotional or fanciful in his piety is supposed to have been rooted out. I think I achieved that, so far as my superiors could discover, but after I was forty I began to have notions and ask questions that should not have come to me. Men have this climacteric, you know, like women. Doctors deny it, but I have met some very menopausal persons in their profession. But my ideas—about Christ, for instance. He will come again, will He? Frankly I doubt if He has ever been very far away. But suppose He comes again, presumably everybody expects He will come to pull the chestnuts out of the fire for them. What will they say if he comes blighting the vine, flogging the money-changers out of the temple one day and hobnobbing with the rich the next, just as He did before? He had a terrible temper, you know, undoubtedly inherited from His Father. Will He come as a Westerner—let us say, as an Irishman or a Texan—because the stronghold of Christianity is in the West? He certainly won't be a Jew again, or the fat will be in the fire. The Arabs would laugh their heads off if Israel produced an embarrassing Pretender. Will He settle the disagreement between Catholic and Protestant? All these questions seem frivolous, like the questions of a child. But did He not say we are to be as children?

"My own idea is that when He comes again it will be to continue His ministry as an old man. I am an old man and my life has been spent as a soldier of Christ, and I tell you that the older I grow the less Christ's teaching says to me. I am sometimes very conscious that I am following the path of a leader who died when He was less than half as old as I am now. I see and feel things He never saw or felt. I know things He seems never to have known. Everybody wants a Christ for himself and those who think like him. Very well, am I at fault for wanting a Christ who will show me how to be an old man? All Christ's teaching is put forward with the dogmatism, the certainty, and the strength of youth: I need something that takes account of the accretion of experience, the sense of paradox and ambiguity that comes with years! I think after forty we should recognize Christ politely but turn for our comfort and guidance to God the Father, who knows the good and evil of life, and to the Holy Ghost, who possesses a wisdom beyond that of the incarnated Christ. After all, we worship a Trinity, of which Christ is but one Person. I think when He comes again it will be to declare the unity of the life of the flesh and the life of the spirit. And then perhaps we shall make some sense of this life of marvels, cruel circumstances, obscenities, and commonplaces. Who can tell?—we might even make it bearable for everybody.

"I have not forgotten your crazy saint. I think you are a fool to fret that she was knocked on the head because of an act of yours. Perhaps that was what she was for, Ramezay. She saved you on the battlefield, you say. But did she not also save you when she took the blow that was meant for you?

"I do not suggest that you should fail in your duty toward her; if she has no friend but you, care for her by all means. But stop trying to be God, making it up to her that you are sane and she is mad. Turn your mind to the real problem: who is she? Oh, I don't mean her police identification or what her name was before she was married. I mean, who is she in your personal world? What figure is she in your personal mythology? If she appeared to save you on the battlefield, as you say, it has just as much to do with you as it has with her—much more probably. Lots of men have visions of their mothers in time of danger. Why not you? Why was it this woman?

"Who is she? That is what you must discover, Ramezay, and you must find your answer in psychological truth, not in objective truth. You will not find out quickly, I am sure. And while you are searching, get on with your own life and accept the possibility that it may be purchased at the price of hers and that this may be God's plan for you and her.

"You think that dreadful? For her, poor sacrifice, and for you who must accept the sacrifice? Listen, Ramezay, have you heard what Einstein says?—Einstein, the great scientist, not some Jesuit like old Blazon. He says, 'God is subtle, but He is not cruel.' There is some sound Jewish wisdom for your muddled Protestant mind. Try to understand the subtlety, and stop whimpering about the cruelty. Maybe God wants you for something special. Maybe so much that you are worth a woman's sanity.

"I can see what is in your sour Scotch eye. You think I speak thus because of this excellent picnic you have provided. 'Old Blazon is talking from the inspiration of roast chicken and salad, and plums and confectioneries, and a whole bottle of Beaune, ignited by a few brandies,' I hear you thinking. 'Therefore he urges me to think well of myself instead of despising myself like a good Protestant.' Nonsense, Ramezay. I am quite a wise old bird, but I am no desert hermit who can only prophesy when his guts are knotted with hunger. I am deep in the old man's puzzle, trying to link the wisdom of the body with the wisdom of the spirit until the two are one. At my age you cannot divide spirit from body without anguish and destruction, from which you will speak nothing but crazy lies!

"You are still young enough to think that torment of the spirit is a splendid thing, a sign of a superior nature. But you are no longer a young man; you are a youngish middle-aged man, and it is time you found out that these spiritual athletics do not lead to wisdom. Forgive yourself for being a human creature, Ramezay. That is the beginning of wisdom; that is part of what is meant by the fear of God; and for you it is the only way to save your sanity. Begin now, or you will end up with your saint in the madhouse."

Saying which, Padre Blazon spread his handkerchief over his face and went to sleep, leaving me to think.

( 4 )

It was all very well for Blazon to give me advice, and to follow it up during the years that followed with occasional postcards (usually of the rowdier Renaissance masters—he liked fat nudes) on which would be written in purple ink some such message as, "How do you fare in the Great Battle? Who is she? I pray for you. I.B., S.J." These caused great curiosity in the school, where one rarely got a postcard before two or three other people had read it. But even if I had been better at taking advice than I am, my path would have been strewn with difficulties.

My visits to Mrs Dempster weighed on me. She was not a trouble-some patient at the hospital, but she became very dull; the occasional lightening of the spirit that had shown itself when she lived with Bertha Shanklin never came now. My weekly visits were the high spots of her life; she was always waiting for me on Saturday afternoon with her hat on. I knew what the hat meant; she hoped that this time I would take her away. This was the hope of many of the patients, and when the presiding physician made his appearance there were scenes in which women clutched at his sleeves and even—I could not have believed it if I had not seen it—fell on their knees and tried to kiss his hands, for all those who had some freedom of movement knew that the power to dismiss them lay with him. A few of the younger ones tried to make a sexual association of it, and their cries were, "Aw, Doc, you know I'm your girl, Doc; you're gonna let me go this time, aren't you, Doc? You know you like me best." I couldn't have stood it, but he did. The sexual fetor in the place was hateful to me. Of course, I was known as "Mary's fella," and they assured her that every visit was sure to bring deliverance. I took her chocolates because they were something she could give the others, most of whom did not have regular visitors.

Let me say again that I was not bitter against the hospital; it was a big place in a big city, obliged to take all who were brought to it. But an hour among these friendless, distracted people was all I could bear. Many of them became known to me, and I got into the custom of telling them stories; as the stories of the saints were the bulk of my store, I told many of those, avoiding anything too miraculous or disquieting, and especially—after one bad experience—anything about wonderful deliverances from prison or bondage of any sort. They liked to be talked to, and when I was talking to a group I was at least not struggling to make conversation with Mrs Dempster alone, and seeing the unvoiced expectancy in her eyes.

Those visits rubbed deep into me the knowledge that though reason may be injured, feeling lives intensely in the insane. I know my visits gave her pleasure, in spite of the weekly disappointment about not being taken elsewhere; after all, I was her special visitor, looked on by the others as an amusing fellow with a fund of tales to tell, and I gave her a certain status. I am ashamed to say how much it cost me in resolution; some Saturdays I had to flog myself to the hospital, cursing what seemed to be a life sentence.

I should have been objective. I should have regarded it as my "good work." But my association with Mrs Dempster made that impossible. It was as though I were visiting a part of my own soul that was condemned to live in hell.

Are you wondering: Why didn't he go to Boy Staunton and ask for money to put Mrs Dempster in a better place, on the grounds that she was a Deptford woman in need, if not because of Staunton's part in making her what she was? There is no simple reply. Staunton did not like to be reminded of Deptford except as a joke. Also, Boy had a way of dominating anything with which he was associated; if I got help from him—which was not certain, for he always insisted that one of the first requirements for success was the ability to say "no"—he would have established himself as Mrs Dempster's patron and saviour and I would have been demoted to his agent. My own motives were not clear or pure: I was determined that if I could not take care of Mrs Dempster, nobody else should do it. She was mine.

Do you ask: If he couldn't afford to put the woman in a private hospital, or get her into a private patients' section of a government hospital, how did he pay for those jaunts abroad every summer? He seems not to have stinted himself there. True, but in my servitude to Mrs Dempster I was not wholly lost to my own needs and concerns. I was absorbed in my enthusiasm for the world of the saints, and ambitious to distinguish myself in explaining them to other people. And I had to have some rest, some refreshment of the spirit.

My diary tells me that I visited Mrs Dempster forty Saturdays every year and at Easter, Christmas, and on her birthday in addition. If that does not seem much to you, try it, and judge then. She was always downcast when I announced that I was off on my summer travels, but I hardened myself and promised her plenty of postcards, for she liked the pictures, and the receipt of mail gave her status among the patients. Did I do all that I could? It seemed so to me, and certainly it was not my intention to join my saint in the madhouse, as Blazon had threatened, by making myself a mere appendage to her sickness.

My life was absorbing as well. I was now a senior master in the school, and a very busy man. I had completed my first book, *A Hundred Saints for Travellers,* and it was selling nicely in five languages, though mostly in English, for Europeans do not travel as Britishers and Americans do. It was written simply and objectively, telling readers how to identify the most common saints they saw in pictures and statuary, and why these saints were popular. I avoided the Catholic gush and the Protestant smirk. I was collecting material for my next book, a much bigger piece of work, to be called *The Saints: A Study in History and Popular Mythology,* in which I wanted to explore first of all why people needed saints, and then how much their need had to do with the saintly attainments of a wide range of extraordinary and gifted people. This was biting off a very large chunk indeed, and I was not sure I could chew it, but I meant to try. I was keeping up my association with the Bollandists too, and writing for *Analecta* and also for the Royal Historical Society whenever I had anything to say.

I had become even more caught up in the life of the Stauntons. Boy liked to have me around much as he liked to have valuable pictures and handsome rugs; I gave the right tone to the place. By that I mean that it put him in a position of advantage with his friends to have someone often in his house who was from a different world, and when he introduced me as a Writer I could hear the capital letter. Of course he had other writers, and painters, musicians, and actors as well, but I was the fixture in the collection, and the least troublesome.

If this sounds like a sneering requital for the hundred-weights of excellent food and the pailfuls of good drink I consumed under his roof, let me say that I paid my way: I was the man who could be called at the last minute to come to dinner when somebody else failed, and I was the man who would talk to the dullest woman in the room, and I was the man who disseminated an air of culture at the most Philistine assemblage of sugar-boilers and wholesale bakers without making the other guests feel cheap. Having me in the dining-room was almost the equivalent of having a Raeburn on the walls; I was classy, I was heavily varnished, and I offended nobody.

Why did I accept a place that I now describe in such terms? Because I was tirelessly curious to see how Boy was getting on, to begin with. Because I really liked him, in spite of his affectations and pomposities. Because if I did not go there, where else would I meet such a variety of people? Because I was always grateful to Boy for his financial advice, which was carrying me nicely through the Depression, and which would in time make it possible for me to do better for Mrs Dempster and to arrange a broader life for myself. My motives, like those of most people, were mingled.

If his social life interested me, his private life fascinated me. I have never known anyone in whose life sex played such a dominating part. He didn't think so. He once told me that he thought this fellow Freud must be a madman, bringing everything down to sex the way he did. I attempted no defence of Freud; by this time I was myself much concerned with that old fantastical duke of dark corners, C. G. Jung, but I had read a great deal of Freud and remembered his injunction against arguing in favour of psychoanalysis with those who clearly hated it.

Sex was so much of the very grain of Boy's life that he noticed it no more than the air he breathed. Little David must be manly in all things; I remember a noisy row he had with Leola when she allowed the child to have a Highlander doll; did she want to make his son a sissy? The doll was put in the garbage pail before the weeping eyes of David, who liked to take it to bed (he was six at the time), and then he was rewarded with a fine practical steam-engine, which drove a circular saw that would really cut a matchstick in two. At eight he was given boxing gloves and had to try to punch his father on the nose as Boy knelt before him.

With little Caroline, Boy was humorously gallant. "How's my little sweetheart tonight?" he would say as he kissed her small hand. When she had been brought in by the nurse, to be shown off to a roomful of guests, Boy always followed them into the hall, to tell Caroline that she had been by far the prettiest girl in the room. Not surprisingly, David was a confused lad, pitifully anxious to please, and Caroline was spoiled rotten.

Leola was never told that she was the prettiest woman in the room. Boy's usual attitude toward her was one of chivalrous patience, with a discernible undertone of exasperation. She loved him abjectly, but she was the one person on whom he spent none of his sexual force—except in the negative form of bullying. I tried to stand up for Leola as much as I could, but as she was utterly unable to stand up for herself I had to be careful: If I was angry with Boy, as sometimes happened, she took his side. She lived her life solely in relation to him; if he thought poorly of her, it did not matter what I might say to defend her. He must be right.

Of course it was not always as black-and-white as this. I remember very well when first she discovered that he was having affairs with other women. She did so by the classic mishap of finding a revealing note in his pocket—the Stauntons rarely escaped cliché in any of the essential matters of life.

I knew of his philandering, of course, for Boy could not keep anything to himself and used to justify his conduct to me late at night, when we had both had plenty of his whisky. "A man with my physical needs can't be tied down to one woman—especially not a woman who doesn't see sex as a partnership—who doesn't give anything, who just lies there like a damned sandbag," he would say, making agonized faces so that I would know how tortured he was.

He was explicit about his sexual needs; he had to have intercourse often, and it had to be all sorts of things—intense, passionate, cruel, witty, challenging—and he had to have it with a Real Woman. It all sounded very exhausting and strangely like a sharp workout with the punching bag; I was glad I was not so demandingly endowed. So there were two or three women in Montreal—not whores, mind you, but women of sophistication and spirit, who demanded their independence even though they were married—whom he visited as often as he could. He had business associations in Montreal and it was easy.

The mention of business reminds me of another phase of Boy's sexuality of which he was certainly unconscious, but which I saw at work on several occasions. It was what I thought of as Corporation Homosexuality. He was always on the lookout for promising young men who could be advanced in his service. They must be keen apostles of sugar, or doughnuts, or pop, or whatever it might be, but they must also be "clean-cut." Whenever he discovered one of these, Boy would "take him up"—ask him to luncheon at his club, to dinner at his home, and to private chats in his office. He would explain the mystique of business to the young man and push him ahead as fast as possible in the corporation, sometimes to the chagrin of older men who were not clean-cut but merely capable and efficient.

After a few months of such an association disillusion would come. The clean-cut young man, being ambitious and no more given to gratitude than ambitious people usually are, would assume that all of this was no more than his due and would cease to be as eagerly receptive and admiring as he had been at the beginning of the affair, and might even display a mind of his own. Boy was dismayed to find that these protégés thought him lucky to have such gifted associates as themselves.

Some went so far as to marry on the strength of their new-found hopes, and Boy always asked them to bring their brides to dinner at his house. Afterward he would demand of me why a clean-cut young fellow with everything in his favour would wreck his chances by marrying a girl who was obviously a dumb cluck and would simply hold him back from real success in the corporation? One way or another, Boy was disappointed in most of these clean-cut young men; of those who survived this peril he wearied in the natural course of things, and they became well placed but not influential in his empire.

I do not suggest that Boy ever recognized these young men as anything but business associates; but they were business associates with an overtone of Jove's cup-bearer that I, at least, could not ignore. Corporation Ganymedes, they did not know their role and thus were disappointments.

Leola's awakening came at the fated Christmas of 1936. It had been an emotionally exhausting year for Boy. The old King, George V, had died in January, and in memory of that glance that had once passed between us I wore a black tie for a week. But Boy was in high feather, for "he" would at last mount the Throne; they had not met for nine years, but Boy was as faithful to his hero as ever. He reported every bit of gossip that came his way; there would be great changes, a Throne more meaningful than ever before, a wholesale ousting of stupid old men, a glorious upsurge of youth around the new King, and of course a gayer Court—the gayest, probably, since that of Charles the Second. And a gay Court, to Boy, meant an exaltation of the punching-bag attitude to sex. If he had ever read any of those psychologists who assert that a crowned and anointed King is the symbolic phallus of his people, Boy would have agreed whole-heartedly.

As everyone knows, it was not long before the news took a contrary turn. On the North American continent we got it sooner than the people of England, for our papers did not have to be so tactful. The young King—he was forty-two, but to people like Boy he seemed very young—was having trouble with the old men, and the old men with him. Stanley Baldwin, who had been with him on that visit to Canada in 1927 and whom Boy had revered as a statesman with a strong literary bent, became a personal enemy of Boy's, and he spoke of the Archbishop of Canterbury in terms that even Woodiwiss—now an archdeacon—found it hard to overlook.

When the crisis came, there was some extravagant talk of forming a group of "King's Men" who would, in an unspecified way, rally to the side of their hero and put his chosen lady beside him on the Throne. Boy was determined to be a King's Man; everybody who considered himself a gentleman, and a man who understood the demanding nature of love, must necessarily feel as he did. He lectured me about it every time we met; as an historian I was very sorry for the King but could see no clear or good way out of the mess. I believe Boy even sent a few telegrams of encouragement, but I never heard of any answers. When the black month of November came I began to fear for his reason; he read everything, heard every radio report, and snatched at every scrap of gossip. I was not with him when he heard the sad broadcast of Abdication on December 11, but I looked in at his house that evening and found him, for the only time in his life, to my knowledge, very drunk and alternating between tears and dreadful tirades against all the repressive forces that worked against true love and the expression of a man's real self.

Christmas was a dark day at the Stauntons'. Leola had had to buy all the presents for the children, and Boy found fault with most of them. The fat janitor from the Alpha offices appeared in a hired suit to play Santa Claus, and Boy told him, in front of the children, not to make a jackass of himself but to get on with his job and get out. He would not open his own gifts from Leola and the children. By the time I had made my visit to Mrs Dempster at the hospital, and turned up for midday Christmas dinner, Leola was in tears, David was huddled up in a corner with a book he was not reading, and Caroline was rampaging through the house demanding attention for a doll she had broken. I joked with David, mended the doll so that it was crippled but in one piece, and tried to be decent to Leola. Boy told me that if I had to behave like one of the bloody saints I was always yapping about, I wished I would do it somewhere else. I unwisely told him to take his Abdication like a man, and he became silently hateful and soured the food in our stomachs. He announced that he was going for a walk, and he was going alone.

Leola, grieved for him, went to fetch his overcoat and happened on the note from one of the great-spirited women in Montreal while looking for his gloves in a pocket. She was crouching on the stairs, sobbing dreadfully, when he went out into the hall, and he took in the meaning of her desolation at a glance.

"There's no reason to carry on like that," he said, picking up the fallen coat and putting it on. "Your situation is perfectly secure. But if you think I intend to be tied down to this sort of thing"—and he gestured towards the drawing-room, which was, I must say, a dismal, toy-littered waste of wealthy, frumpish domesticity—"you can think again." And off he went, leaving Leola howling.

I wish I did not have to say howling, but Leola was not beautiful in her grief. The nurse was off duty for the day, but I managed to shoo the children upstairs to their own quarters and spent a hard hour quieting her. I wish I could say I comforted her, but only one man could have done that, and he was trudging through the snow, deep in some egotistical hell of his own. At last I persuaded her to sleep, or at least to lie down, and wait to see what would happen. Nothing was ever quite so bad as it looked, I assured her. I did not really believe it, but I intended to have a word with Boy.

She went to her room, and when I thought a sufficient time had passed I went up to see how things were getting on. She had washed her face and tidied her hair and was in bed in one of the expensive nightdresses Boy liked.

"Will you be all right if I go now?"

"Kiss me, Dunny. No, not like that. That's just a peck. You used to like to kiss me."

Whether she knew it or not, this was an invitation that might lead to much more. Was the story of Gyges and Candaules to have the ending in which Gyges takes his friend's wife? No; upon the whole I thought not. But I leaned over and kissed her a little less formally.

"That's no good. Kiss me *really*."

So I did, and if my artificial leg had not given an ominous croak as I knelt on the bed I might have gone on, doubtless to cuckold Boy Staunton, which he certainly deserved. But I recovered myself and stood up and said, "You must sleep now. I'll look in later tonight and we'll talk with Boy."

"You don't love me!" she wailed.

I hurried out the door as she burst into tears again.

Of course I didn't love her. Why would I? It had been at least ten years since I had thought of her with anything but pity. I had made my bed and I intended to lie on it, and there was no room for Leola in it. On my last few visits abroad I had spent a weekend with Diana and her husband at their delightful country house near Canterbury and had enjoyed myself greatly. I had survived my boyish love for Diana, and I certainly had survived anything I ever felt for Leola. I was not to be a victim of her self-pity. The emotional upheaval caused by her disappointment about Boy's unfaithfulness had sharpened her sexual appetite; that was all. I do not suppose Boy had slept with her since the beginning of the trouble that led to the Abdication. I was not going to be the victim of somebody else's faulty chronology. I went for a walk myself, had another Christmas dinner—it was impossible to avoid heavy food on that day—and arrived back at the school at about nine o'clock, intending to do some reading.

Instead I was greeted by a message from the furnace man, who was the only person left on duty that day. I was to call the Stauntons' number at once. It was an emergency.

I called, and the children's nurse spoke. She had come back from her holiday, found the housemaid and the cook and butler still out, and had looked in on Mrs Staunton to say goodnight. Had found her in a very bad way. Did not like to explain over the phone. Yes, had called the doctor but it was Christmas night and an hour had gone by and he still had not come. Would I come at once? Yes, it was *very* serious.

The nurse was becoming a little hysterical, and I hurried to obey. But on Christmas night it is not simple to get taxis, and altogether it was half an hour before I ran upstairs to Leola's bedroom and found her in bed, white as the sheets, with her wrists bound up in gauze, and the nurse near to fits.

"Look at this," she said, gasping, and pushed me toward the bathroom.

The bath seemed to be full of blood. Apparently Leola had cut her wrists and laid herself down to die in the high Roman fashion, in a warm bath. But she was not a good anatomist and had made a gory but not a fatal job of it.

The doctor came not long after, rather drunk but fairly capable. The nurse had done all that was immediately necessary, so he redressed the wrists, gave Leola an injection of something, and said he would call again on Boxing Day.

"I sent for you at once because of this," said the nurse as soon as the doctor had gone. She handed me a letter with my name on the envelope. It read:

*Dearest Dunny:*
*This is the end. Boy does not love me and you don't either so it is best for me to go. Think of me sometimes. I always loved you.*
*Love,*
*Leola*

Fool, fool, fool! Thinking only of herself and putting me in an intolerable position with such a note. If she had died, how would it have sounded at an inquest? As it was, I am sure the nurse read it, for it was not sealed. I was furious with Leola, poor idiot. No note for Boy. No, just a note for me, which would have made me look like a monster if she had not made a mess of this, as of so much else.

However, as she began to pull around I could not reproach her, though I was very careful not to mention the note. Nor did she. It was never spoken of between us.

Boy could not be found. His business address in Montreal knew nothing of him, and he did not return until after New Year's Day, by which time Leola was on the mend, though feeble. What passed between them I do not know and was never told, but from that time onward they seemed to rub along without open disagreement, though Leola faded rapidly and looked more than her years. Indeed, the pretty face that had once ensnared both Boy and me became pudgy and empty. Leola had joined the great company of the walking wounded in the battle of life.

The people who seemed to suffer most from this incident were the children. The nurse, controlled and efficient in emergency, had broken down in the nursery and hinted broadly that Mummy had almost died. This, taken with the quarrel earlier in the day, was enough to put them on edge for a long time; David was increasingly quiet and mousy, but Caroline became a screamer and thrower of tantrums.

David told me many years later that he hated Christmas more than any other day in the calendar.

# 5

# *Liesl*

## ( 1 )

Let me pass as quickly as possible over the years of the Second World War—or World War Too, as the name my pupils give it always sounds in my ears; it is as if they were asserting firmly that the World War I remember so vividly was not the only, or the biggest, outburst of mass lunacy in our century. But I cannot leave it out altogether, if only because of the increase in stature it brought to Boy Staunton. His growth as an industrialist with, figuratively speaking, his finger in hundreds of millions of pies, not to speak of other popular goodies, made him a man of might in the national economy, and when the war demanded that the ablest men in the country be pressed into the national service, who but he was the obvious candidate for the post of Minister of Food in a coalition Cabinet?

He was very good in the job. He knew how to get things done, and he certainly knew what the great mass of people like to eat. He put the full resources of his Alpha Corporation, and all the subsidiary companies it controlled, to the job of feeding Canada, feeding its armed services, and feeding Britain so far as the submarine war would permit. He was tireless in promoting research that would produce new concentrates—chiefly from fruits—that would keep fighting men, and the children in a bombed country, going when bulkier eatables were not to be had. If the average height of the people of the British Isles is rather greater today than it was in 1939, much of the credit must go to Boy Staunton. He was one of the few men not a professional scientist who really knew what a vitamin was and where it could be found and put to work cheaply.

Of course he had to spend most of his time in Ottawa. He saw little of Leola or his children during the war years, except on flying visits during which lost intimacies could not be recaptured, not even with his adored Caroline.

I saw him from time to time because he was by now a member of our Board of Governors, and also because David was a boarder in the school. David could have lived at home, but Boy wanted him to have the experience of a community life and of being disciplined by men. So the boy spent the years from his tenth to his eighteenth birthday at Colborne, and when he got into the Upper School, at about twelve, he came under my eye almost every day.

Indeed it was my duty in 1942 to tell this unhappy boy that his mother had died. Poor Leola had become more and more listless since the outbreak of war; as Boy grew in importance and his remarkable abilities became increasingly manifest, she faded. She was not one of those politicians' wives who lets it be known that her husband's competence is kept up to the mark by the support and understanding she gives him. Nor was she of the other strain, who tell the newspapers and the women's clubs that though their husbands may be men of mark to the world, they are sorry wretches at home. Leola had no public life and wanted none.

She had completely given up any pretence at golf or bridge or any of the other pastimes in which she had attained to mediocrity in her younger days; she no longer read fashionable books or anything at all. Whenever I went to see her she was knitting things for the Red Cross—vast inner stockings for seaboots and the like—which she seemed to do automatically while her mind was elsewhere. I asked her to dinner a few times, and it was heavy work, though not so heavy as having dinner at the Stauntons' house. With Boy away and both the children in school, that richly furnished barrack became more and more lifeless, and the servants were demoralized, looking after one undemanding woman who was afraid of them.

When Leola fell ill of pneumonia I informed Boy and did all the obvious things and did not worry. But that was before the drugs for dealing with pneumonia were as effective as they now are, and after the worst of it was over a considerable period of convalescence was needed. As it was difficult to travel to any warmer climate, and as there was nobody to go with Leola, she had to spend it at home. Although I cannot vouch for this, I have always thought it suspicious that Leola opened her windows one afternoon, when the nurse had closed them, and took a chill, and was dead in less than a week.

Boy was in England, arranging something or other connected with his Ministry, and duty and the difficulty of transatlantic flights in wartime kept him there. He asked me, by cable, to do what had to be done, so I arranged the funeral, which was easy, and told the people who had to be told, which was not. Caroline made a loud fuss, and I left her with some capable schoolmistresses who bore the weight of that. But David astonished me.

"Poor Mum," he said, "I guess she's better off, really."

Now what was I to make of that, from a boy of fourteen? And what was I to do with him? I could not send him home, and I had no home of my own except my study and bedroom in the school, so I put him there and made sure one of the matrons looked in every hour or so to see that he was not utterly desolate and had anything it was in the school's power to give him. Fortunately he slept a lot, and at night I sent him to the infirmary, where he could have a room of his own.

I kept him by me at the funeral, for both the older Stauntons were now dead, and the Cruikshanks were so desolated themselves that they could only hold hands and weep. Association with the Cruikshanks had not been encouraged by Boy, so David was not really well known to them.

It was one of those wretched late autumn funerals, and though it did not actually rain everything was wet and miserable. There were not a great many present, for all the Stauntons' friends were important people, and it seemed that all the important people were so busy fighting the war in one way or another that they could not come. But there were mountains of costly flowers, looking particularly foolish under a November sky.

One unexpected figure was at the graveside. Older, fatter, and unwontedly quiet though he was, I knew Milo Papple in an instant.

As Woodiwiss read the committal, I found myself thinking that his own father had died at least twelve years before, and I had written to Milo at that time. But the Kaiser (whom Myron Papple had impersonated so uproariously at the hanging-in-effigy after the Great War) had lived, presumably untroubled by the hatred of Deptford and places like it, until 1941; had lived at Doorn, sawing wood and wondering what world madness had dethroned him, for twenty-three years after his fall. I pondered on the longevity of dethroned monarchs when I should have been taking farewell of Leola. But I well knew that I had taken leave of her, so far as any real feeling went, that Christmas afternoon when she had appealed to me for comfort and I had run away. Everything since had been a matter of duty.

Milo and I shook hands as we left the cemetery. "Poor Leola," he said in a choked voice. "It's the end of a great romance. You know we always thought her and Perse was the handsomest pair that ever got married in Deptford. And I know why you never got married. It must be tough on you to see her go, Dunny."

My shame was that it was not tough at all. What was tough was to go with David back to that awful, empty house and talk to him until the servants gave us a poor dinner; then take him back to school and tell him I thought it better that he should go to his own room, as he must some time resume his ordinary life, and the sooner the better.

Boy was always fussing that David would not be a real man. He seemed a very real man to me through all this bad time. I could not have seen as much of him as I did if I had not been temporary Headmaster. When the war began our Head had rushed off to throw himself upon the foe from the midst of the Army's education program; he stepped in front of a truck one night in the blackout, and the school mourned him as a hero. When he left, the Governors had to get a Headmaster in a hurry, but the war made good men so scarce that they appointed me, *pro tem*, without any increase in salary, as we must all shoulder our burdens without thought of self. It was taxing, thankless work, and I hated all the administrative side of it. But I bent to the task and did what I could until 1947, when I had a difficult conversation with Boy, who was now a C.B.E. (for his war work) and the Chairman of our Board of Governors.

"Dunny, you've done a superb job during the whole of the war, and long beyond. But it was fun, wasn't it?"

"No, not fun. Damned hard slogging. Endless trouble getting and keeping staff. Managing with our old men and some young ones who weren't fit for service—or teaching, if it comes to that. Problems with 'war-guest' boys who were homesick, or hated Canada, or thought they could slack because they weren't in England. Problems with the inevitable hysteria of the school when the news was bad, and the worse hysteria when it was good. The fag of keeping up nearly all my own teaching and doing the administration as well. Not fun, Boy."

"None of us had an easy war, Dunny. And I must say you look well on it. The question is, what are we to do now?"

"You're the Chairman of the Board. You tell me."

"You don't want to go on being Head, do you?"

"That depends on the conditions. It might be much pleasanter now. I've been able to get a pretty good staff during the last eighteen months, and I suppose money will be more plentiful now that the Board can think about it again."

"But you've just said you hated being Head."

"In wartime—who wouldn't? But, as I say, things are improving. I might get to like it very much."

"Look, old man, let's not make a long business of this. The Board appreciates everything you've done. They want to give you a testimonial dinner. They want to tell you in front of the whole school how greatly indebted they are to you. But they want a younger Headmaster."

"How young? You know my age. I'm not quite fifty, like yourself. How young does a Headmaster have to be nowadays?"

"It isn't entirely that. You're making this awfully tough for me. You're unmarried. A Headmaster needs a wife."

"When I needed a wife, I found that you needed her even more."

"That's hitting below the belt. Anyhow, Leo wouldn't have—never mind. You have no wife."

"Perhaps I could find one in a hurry. Miss Gostling, at our sister school, Bishop Cairncross's, has been giving me the glad eye in an academic way for two or three years."

"Be serious. It's not just the wife. Dunny, we have to face it. You're queer."

"The Sin of Sodom, you mean? If you knew boys as I do, you would not suggest anything so grotesque. If Oscar Wilde had pleaded insanity, he would have walked out of court a free man."

"No, no, no! I don't mean kid-simple, I mean queer—strange, funny, not like other people."

"Ah, that's very interesting. How am I queer? Do you remember poor old Iremonger who had a silver plate in his head and used to climb the waterpipes in his room and address his class from the ceiling? Now he was queer. Or that unfortunate alcoholic Bateson who used to throw a wet boxing glove at inattentive boys and then retrieve it on a string? I always thought they added something to the school—gave boys a knowledge of the great world that the state schools dare not imitate. Surely you do not think I am queer in any comparable way?"

"You are a fine teacher. Everybody knows it. You are a great scholarship-getter, which is quite another thing. You have a reputation as an author. But there it is."

"There is what?"

"It's this saint business of yours. Of course your books are splendid. But if you were a father, would you want to send your son to a school headed by a man who was an authority on saints? Even more, would you do it if you were a mother? Women hate anything that's uncanny about a man if they think of entrusting a son to him. Religion in the school is one thing; there is a well-understood place for religion in education. But not this misty world of wonder-workers and holy wizards and juiceless women. Saints aren't in the picture at all. Now I'm an old friend, but I am also Chairman of the Board, and I tell you it won't do."

"Are you kicking me out?"

"Certainly not. Don't be extreme. You surely understand that you are a tremendous addition to the school as a master—well-known writer on a difficult subject, translated into foreign languages, amusingly eccentric, and all that—but you would be a disaster as a peacetime Headmaster."

"Eccentric? Me!"

"Yes, you. Good God, don't you think the way you rootle in your ear with your little finger delights the boys? And the way you waggle your eyebrows—great wild things like moustaches, I don't know why you don't trim them—and those terrible Harris tweed suits you wear and never have pressed. And that disgusting trick of blowing your nose and looking into your handkerchief as if you expected to prophesy something from the mess. You look ten years older than your age. The day of comic eccentrics as Heads has gone. Parents nowadays want somebody more like themselves."

"A Headmaster created in their own image, eh? Well, you obviously have somebody virtually hired or you wouldn't be in such a rush to get rid of me. Who is it?"

(Boy named you, Headmaster. I had never heard of you then, so there can be no malice in reporting this conversation.)

We haggled a little more, and I made Boy squirm a bit, for I felt I had been shabbily used. But at last I said, "Very well, I'll stay on as chief of history and Assistant Head. I don't want your testimonial dinner, but I should like you, as Chairman, to address the school and make it very clear that I have not been demoted as soon as you could get somebody their parents like better. It will be a lie, but I want my face saved. Say the demands of my writing made me suggest this decision and I pledge my full support to the new man. And I want six months' leave of absence, on full pay, before I return to work."

"Agreed. You're a good sport, Dunny. Where will you go for your six months?"

"I have long wanted to visit the great shrines of Latin America. I shall begin in Mexico, with the Shrine of the Virgin of Guadalupe."

"There you go, you see! You go right on with the one thing that really stood between you and a Headmaster's job."

"Certainly. You don't expect me to pay attention to the opinion of numskulls like you and your Board and the parents of a few hundred cretinous boys, do you?"

( 2 )

So there I was, a few months later, sitting in a corner of the huge, nineteenth-century Byzantine basilica at Guadalupe, watching the seemingly endless crowd of men and women, old and young, as it shuffled forward on its knees to get as near as possible to the miraculous picture of the Virgin.

The picture was a surprise to me. Whether it was because I had some ignorant preconception about the tawdriness of everything Mexican, or the extravagantly Latin nature of the legend, I had expected something artistically offensive. I was by now in a modest way a connoisseur in holy pictures, ranging from catacombs and the blackened and glaring Holy Face at Lucca to the softest Raphaels and Murillos. But here was a picture reputedly from no mortal hand— not even that of St Luke—that had appeared miraculously on the inside of a peasant's cloak.

In 1531 the Virgin had appeared several times on this spot to Juan Diego and bidden him to tell Bishop Zumárraga that a shrine in her honour should be built here; when Zumárraga very naturally asked for some further evidence of Juan Diego's authority, the Virgin filled the peasant's cloak with roses though it was December; and when he opened his cloak before the Bishop, not only were the roses there, but also, on the inner side of it, this painting, before which the Bishop fell on his knees in wonderment.

As unobtrusively as possible (for I try hard not to be objectionable when visiting shrines) I examined the picture through a powerful little pocket telescope. Certainly it was painted on cloth of a very coarse weave, with a seam up the middle of it that deviated from the straight just enough to avoid the Virgin's face. The picture was in the mode of the Immaculate Conception; the Virgin, a peasant girl of about fifteen, stood on a crescent moon. The painting was skilled, and the face beautiful, if you dismiss from your mind the whorish mask that modern cosmetics have substituted for beauty and think of the human face. Why was the right eye almost closed, as though swollen? Very odd in a holy picture. But the colours were fine, and the gold, though lavish, was not barbarically splashed on. Spain might be proud of such a picture. And the proportions—the width would go about three and a half times into the length—were those of a *tilma* such as I had seen peasants wearing outside the city. A very remarkable picture indeed.

The picture was not my chief concern, however. My eyes were on the kneeling petitioners, whose faces had the beauty virtually every face reveals in the presence of the goddess of mercy, the Holy Mother, the figure of divine compassion. Very different, these, from the squinnying, lip-biting, calculating faces of the art lovers one sees looking at Madonnas in galleries. These petitioners had no conception of art; to them a picture was a symbol of something else, and very readily the symbol became the reality. They were untouched by modern education, but their government was striving with might and main to procure this inestimable benefit for them; anticlericalism and American bustle would soon free them from belief in miracles and holy likenesses. But where, I ask myself, will mercy and divine compassion come from then? Or are such things necessary to people who are well fed and know the wonders that lie concealed in an atom? I don't regret economic and educational advance; I just wonder how much we shall have to pay for it, and in what coin.

Day after day I sat in the basilica for a few hours and wondered. The sacristans and nuns who gave out little prints of the miraculous picture grew accustomed to me; they thought I must be a member of that tiny and eccentric group, the devout rich, or perhaps I was writing an article for a tourist magazine. I put something in every out-thrust box and was left alone. But I am neither rich nor conventionally devout, and what I was writing, slowly, painstakingly, and with so many revisions that the final version was not even in sight, was a sort of prologue to a discussion of the nature of faith. Why do people all over the world, and at all times, want marvels that defy all verifiable fact? And are the marvels brought into being by their desire, or is their desire an assurance rising from some deep knowledge, not to be directly experienced and questioned, that the marvellous is indeed an aspect of the real?

Philosophers have tackled this question, of course, and answered it in ways highly satisfactory to themselves; but I never knew a philosopher's answer to make much difference to anyone not in the trade. I was trying to get at the subject without wearing either the pink spectacles of faith or the green spectacles of science. All I had managed by the time I found myself sitting in the basilica of Guadalupe was a certainty that faith was a psychological reality, and that where it was not invited to fasten itself on things unseen, it invaded and raised bloody hell with things seen. Or in other words, the irrational will have its say, perhaps because "irrational" is the wrong word for it.

Such speculation cannot fill the whole of one's day. I used to rise early and go to the shrine in the morning. After luncheon I followed the local custom and slept. I explored the city until dinner. After dinner, what? I could not sit in the public rooms in my hotel for they were uncomfortable after the Spanish fashion. The writing-room was dominated by a large painting of the Last Supper, a more than usually gloomy depiction of that gloomiest of parties; apparently nobody had been able to touch a bite, and a whole lamb, looking uncomfortably alive though flayed, lay on a platter in the middle of the table with its eyes fixed reproachfully on Judas.

I tried the theatre and found myself sitting through a drama that I identified as Sardou's *Frou Frou,* heavily Hispanicized and given a further Mexican flavour. It was slow going. I went to one or two films, American pieces with Spanish sound tracks. With relief I discovered from a morning paper that a magician might be seen at the Teatro Chueca, and I booked a seat through my hotel.

Enthusiasm for magic had never wholly died in me, and I had seen the best illusionists of my time—Thurston, Goldin, Blackstone, the remarkable German who called himself Kalanag, and Harry Houdini, not long before his death. But the name of the man who was to perform in Mexico was unknown to me; the advertisement announced that Magnus Eisengrim would astonish Mexico City after having triumphantly toured South America. I assumed that he was a German who thought it impolitic to appear in the States at present.

Very soon after the curtain rose I knew that this was a magic entertainment unlike any I had ever seen. In the twentieth century stage magicians have always been great jokers; even Houdini grinned like a film star through most of his show. They kept up a run of patter designed to assure the audience that they were not to be taken seriously as wonder-workers; they were entertainers and mighty clever fellows, but their magic was all in fun. Even when they included a little hypnotism—as Blackstone did so deftly—nobody was given any cause for alarm.

Not so Magnus Eisengrim. He did not wear ordinary evening clothes, but a beautiful dress coat with a velvet collar, and silk knee breeches. He began his show by appearing in the middle of the stage out of nowhere; he plucked a wand from the air and, wrapping himself in a black cloak, suddenly became transparent; members of his company—girls dressed in fanciful costumes—seemed to walk through him; then, after another flourish of the cloak, he was present in the flesh again, and four of the girls were sufficiently ghostly for him to pass his wand through them. I began to enjoy myself; this was the old Pepper's Ghost illusion, familiar enough in principle but newly worked up into an excellent mystery. And nobody on the stage cracked a smile.

Eisengrim now introduced himself to us. He spoke in elegant Spanish, and it was clear at once that he did not present himself as a funny-man but as one who offered an entertainment of mystery and beauty, with perhaps a hint of terror as well. Certainly his appearance and surroundings were not those of the usual stage magician; he was not tall, but his bearing was so impressive that his smallness was unimportant. He had beautiful eyes and an expression of dignity, but the most impressive thing about him was his voice; it was much bigger than one would expect from a small man, and of unusual range and beauty of tone. He received us as honoured guests and promised us an evening of such visions and illusions as had nourished the imagination of mankind for two thousand years—and a few trifles for amusement as well.

This was a novelty—a poetic magician who took himself seriously. It was certainly not the role in which I had expected to re-encounter Paul Dempster. But this was Paul, without a doubt, so self-assured, so polished, so utterly unlike the circus conjurer with the moustache and beard and shabby clothes whom I had met in *Le grand Cirque forain de St Vite* more than fifteen years before, that it was some time before I could be sure it was he. How had he come by this new self, and where had he acquired this tasteful, beautiful entertainment?

It was so elegantly presented that I doubt if anyone in the Teatro Chueca but myself realized how old it was in essence. Paul did not do a single new trick; they were all classics from the past, well known to people who were interested in the history of this curious minor art and craft.

He invited members of the audience to have a drink with him before he began his serious work, and poured red and white wine, brandy, tequila, whisky, milk, and water from a single bottle; a very old trick, but the air of graceful hospitality with which he did it was enough to make it new. He borrowed a dozen handkerchiefs—mine among them—and burned them in a glass vessel; then from the ashes he produced eleven handkerchiefs, washed and ironed; when the twelfth donor showed some uneasiness, Eisengrim directed him to look towards the ceiling, from which his handkerchief fluttered down into his hands. He borrowed a lady's handbag, and from it produced a package that swelled and grew until he revealed a girl under the covering; he caused this girl to rise in the air, float out over the orchestra pit, return to the table, and, when covered, to dwindle once again to a package, which, when returned to the lady's purse, proved to be a box of bonbons. All old tricks. All beautifully done. And all offered without any of the facetiousness that usually makes magic shows so restless and tawdry.

The second part of his entertainment began with hypnotism. From perhaps fifty people who volunteered to be subjects he chose twenty and seated them in a half-circle on the stage. Then, one by one, he induced them to do the things all hypnotists rely on—row boats, eat invisible meals, behave as guests at a party, listen to music, and all the rest of it—but he had one idea that was new to me; he told a serious-looking man of middle age that he had just been awarded the Nobel Prize and asked him to make a speech of acceptance. The man did so, with such dignity and eloquence that the audience applauded vigorously. I have seen displays of hypnotism in which people were made to look foolish, to show the dominance of the hypnotist; there was nothing of that here, and all of the twenty left the stage with dignity unimpaired, and indeed with a heightened sense of importance.

Then Eisengrim showed us some escapes, from ropes and straps bound on him by men from the audience who fancied themselves as artists in bondage. He was tied up and put into a trunk, which was pulled on a rope up into the ceiling of the theatre; after thirty seconds Eisengrim walked down the centre aisle to the stage, brought the trunk to ground, and revealed that it contained an absurd effigy of himself.

His culminating escape was a variation of one Houdini originated and made famous. Eisengrim, wearing only a pair of bathing trunks, was handcuffed and pushed upside down into a metal container like a milk can, and the top of the milk can was fastened shut with padlocks, some of which members of the audience had brought with them; the milk can was lowered into a tank of water, with glass windows in it so that the audience could see the interior clearly; curtains were drawn around the tank and its contents, and the audience sat in silence to await events. Two men were asked to time the escape; and if more than three minutes elapsed, they were to order the theatre fireman who was in attendance to break open the milk can without delay.

The three minutes passed. The fireman was given the word and made a very clumsy business of getting the can out of the tank and opening the padlocks. But when he had done so the milk can was empty, and the fireman was Eisengrim. It was the nearest thing to comedy the evening provided.

The third and last part of the entertainment was serious almost to the point of solemnity, but it had an erotic savour that was unlike anything I had ever seen in a magic show, where children make up a considerable part of the audience. *The Dream of Midas* was a prolonged illusion in which Eisengrim, assisted by a pretty girl, produced extraordinary sums of money in silver dollars from the air, from the pockets, ears, noses, and hats of people in the audience, and threw them all into a large copper pot; the chink of the coins seemed never to stop. Possessed by unappeasable greed, he turned the girl into gold, and was horrified by what he had done. He tapped her with a hammer; he chipped off a hand and passed it through the audience; he struck the image in the face. Then, in an ecstasy of renunciation, he broke his magician's wand. Immediately the copper pot was empty, and when we turned our attention to the girl she was flesh again, but one hand was missing and blood was running from her lip. This spice of cruelty seemed to please the audience very much.

His last illusion was called *The Vision of Dr Faustus*, and the program assured us that in this scene, and this alone, the beautiful Faustina would appear before us. Reduced to its fundamentals, it was the familiar illusion in which the magician makes a girl appear in two widely separated cabinets without seeming to pass between them. But as Eisengrim did it, the conflict was between Sacred and Profane Love for the soul of Faust: on one side of the stage would appear the beautiful Faustina as Gretchen, working at her spinning wheel and modestly clothed; as Faust approached her she disappeared, and on the other side of the stage in an arbour of flowers appeared Venus, wearing as near to nothing at all as the Mexican sense of modesty would permit. It was plain enough that Gretchen and Venus were the same girl, but she had gifts as an actress and conveyed unmistakably the message that beauty of spirit and lively sensuality might inhabit one body, an idea that was received with delight by the audience. At last Faust, driven to distraction by the difficulties of choice, killed himself, and Mephistopheles appeared in flames to drag him down to Hell. As he vanished, in the middle of the stage but about eight feet above the floor and supported apparently on nothing at all, appeared the beautiful Faustina once more, as, one presumes, the Eternal Feminine, radiating compassion while showing a satisfactory amount of leg. The culminating moment came when Mephistopheles threw aside his robe and showed that, whoever may have been thrust down into Hell, this was certainly Eisengrim the Great.

The audience took very kindly to the show, and the applause for the finale was long and enthusiastic. An usher prevented me from going through the pass-door to the stage, so I went to the stage door and asked to see Señor Eisengrim. He was not to be seen, said the doorman. Orders were strict that no one was to be admitted. I offered a visiting card, for although these things have almost gone out of use in North America they still possess a certain amount of authority in Europe, and I always carry a few. But it was no use.

I was not pleased and was about to go away in a huff when a voice said, "Are you Mr Dunstan Ramsay?"

The person who was speaking to me from the last step of the stairs that led up into the theatre was probably a woman but she wore man's dress, had short hair, and was certainly the ugliest human creature I had ever seen. Not that she was misshapen; she was tall, straight, and obviously very strong, but she had big hands and feet, a huge, jutting jaw, and a heaviness of bone over the eyes that seemed to confine them to small, very deep caverns. However, her voice was beautiful and her utterance was an educated speech of some foreign flavour.

"Eisengrim will be very pleased to see you. He noticed you in the audience. Follow me, if you please."

The backstage arrangements were not extensive, and the corridor into which she led me was noisy with the sound of a quarrel in a language unfamiliar to me—probably Portuguese. My guide knocked and entered at once with me behind her, and we were upon the quarrellers. They were Eisengrim, stripped to the waist, rubbing paint off his face with a dirty towel, and the beautiful Faustina, who was naked as the dawn, and lovely as the breeze, and madder than a wet hen; she also was removing her stage paint, which seemed to cover most of her body; she snatched up a wrapper and pulled it around her, and extruded whatever part she happened to be cleaning as we talked.

"She says she must have more pink light in the last tableau," said Eisengrim to my guide in German. "I've told her it will kill my red Mephisto spot, but you know how pig-headed she is."

"Not now," said the ugly woman. "Mr Dunstan Ramsay, your old friend Magnus Eisengrim, and the beautiful Faustina."

The beautiful Faustina gave me an unnervingly brilliant smile and extended a very greasy hand that had just been wiping paint off her upper thigh. I may be a Canadian of Scots descent, and I may have first seen the light in Deptford, but I am not to be disconcerted by

Latin American showgirls, so I kissed it with what I think was a good deal of elegance. Then I shook hands with Eisengrim, who was smiling in a fashion that was not really friendly.

"It has been a long time, Mr Dunstable Ramsay," he said in Spanish. I think he meant to put me at a disadvantage, but I am pretty handy in Spanish, and we continued the conversation in that language.

"It has been over thirty years, unless you count our meeting in *Le grand Cirque forain de St Vite*," said I. "How are *Le Solitaire des forêts* and my friend the Bearded Lady?"

"Le Solitaire died very shortly after we met," said he. "I have not seen the others since before the war."

We made a little more conversation, so stilted and uneasy that I decided to leave; obviously Eisengrim did not want me there. But when I took my leave the ugly woman said, "We hope very much that you can lunch with us tomorrow?"

"Liesl, are you sure you know what you are doing?" said Eisengrim in German, and very rapidly.

But I am pretty handy in German, too. So when the ugly woman replied, "Yes, I am perfectly sure and so are you, so say no more about it," I got it all and said in German, "It would be a very great pleasure, if I am not an intruder."

"How can a so old friend possibly be an intruder?" said Eisengrim in English, and thenceforth he never spoke any other language to me, though his idiom was creaky. "You know, Liesl, that Mr Ramsay was my very first teacher in magic?" He was all honey now. And as I was leaving he leaned forward and whispered, "That temporary loan, you remember—nothing would have induced me to accept it if *Le Solitaire* had not been in very great need—you must permit me to repay it at once." And he tapped me lightly on the spot where, in an inside pocket, I carry my cash.

That night when I was making my usual prudent Canadian-Scots count, I found that several bills had found their way into my wallet, slightly but not embarrassingly exceeding the sum that had disappeared from it when last I met Paul. I began to think better of Eisengrim. I appreciate scrupulosity in money matters.

# ( 3 )

Thus I became a member of Magnus Eisengrim's entourage, and never made my tour of the shrines of South America. It was all settled at the luncheon after our first meeting. Eisengrim was there, and the hideous Liesl, but the beautiful Faustina did not come. When I asked after her Eisengrim said, "She is not yet ready to be seen in public places." Well, thought I, if he can appear in a good restaurant with a monster, why not with the most beautiful woman I have ever seen? Before we had finished a long luncheon, I knew why.

Liesl became less ugly after an hour or two. Her clothes were like a man's in that she wore a jacket and trousers, but her shirt was soft and her beautiful scarf was drawn through a ring. If I had been in her place I should not have worn men's patent-leather dancing shoes—size eleven at least—but otherwise she was discreet. Her short hair was smartly arranged, and she even wore a little colour on her lips. Nothing could mitigate the extreme, the deformed ugliness of her face, but she was graceful, she had a charming voice, and gave evidence of a keen intelligence held in check, so that Eisengrim might dominate the conversation.

"You see what we are doing," he said. "We are building up a magic show of unique quality, and we want it to be in the best possible condition before we set out on a world tour. It is rough still—oh, very kind of you to say so, but it is rough in comparison with what we want to make it. We want the uttermost accomplishment, combined with the sort of charm and romantic flourish that usually goes with ballet—European ballet, not the athletic American stuff. You know that nowadays the theatre has almost abandoned charm; actors want to be sweaty and real, playwrights want to scratch their scabs in public. Very well; it is in the mood of the times. But there is always another mood, one precisely contrary to what seems to be the fashion. Nowadays this concealed longing is for romance and marvels. Well, that is what we think we can offer, but it is not done with the back bent and a cringing smile; it must be offered with authority. We are working very hard for authority. You remarked that we did not smile much in the performance; no jokes, really. A smile in such a show is half a cringe. Look at the magicians who appear in night clubs; they are so anxious to be loved, to have everybody think "What a funny fellow," instead of "What a brilliant fellow, what a mysterious fellow." That is the disease of all entertainment: love me, pet me, pat my head. That is not what we want."

"What do you want? To be feared?"

"To be wondered at. This is not egotism. People want to marvel at something, and the whole spirit of our time is not to let them do it. They will pay to do it, if you make it good and marvellous for them. Didn't anybody learn anything from the war? Hitler said, 'Marvel at me, wonder at me, I can do what others can't,'—and they fell over themselves to do it. What we offer is innocent—just an entertainment in which a hungry part of the spirit is fed. But it won't work if we let ourselves be pawed and patronized and petted by the people who have marvelled. Hence our plan."

"What is your plan?"

"That the show must keep its character all the time. I must not be seen off the stage except under circumstances that carry some *cachet*; I must never do tricks outside the theatre. When people meet me I must be always the distinguished gentleman conferring a distinction; not a nice fellow, just like the rest of the boys. The girls must have it in their contract that they do not accept invitations unless we approve, appear anywhere except in clothes we approve, get into any messes with boy friends, or seem to be anything but ladies. Not easy, you see. Faustina herself is a problem; she has not yet learned about clothes, and she eats like a lioness."

"You'll have to pay heavily to make people live like that."

"Of course. So the company must be pretty small and the pay tempting. We shall find the people."

"Excuse me, but you keep saying *we* will do this and *we* will do that. Is this a royal *we*? If so, you may be getting into psychological trouble."

"No, no. When I speak of *we* I mean Liesl and myself. I am the magician. She is the autocrat of the company, as you shall discover."

"And why is Liesl the autocrat of the company?"

"That also you shall discover."

"I'm not at all sure of that. What do you want me for? My abilities as a magician are even less than when you were my audience in the Deptford Free Library."

"Never mind. Liesl wants you."

I looked at Liesl, who was smiling as charmingly as her dreadfully enlarged jaw would permit, and said, "She cannot possibly know anything about me."

"You underestimate yourself, Ramsay," she said. "Are you not the writer of *A Hundred Saints for Travellers*? And *Forgotten Saints of the Tyrol*? And *Celtic Saints of Britain and Europe*? When Eisengrim mentioned last night that he had seen you in the audience and that you had insisted on lending your handkerchief, I wanted to meet you at once. I am obliged to you for much information, but far more for many happy hours reading your delightful prose. A distinguished hagiographer does not often come our way."

There is more than one kind of magic. This speech had the effect of revealing to me that Liesl was not nearly so ugly as I had thought, and was indeed a woman of captivating intellect and charm, cruelly imprisoned in a deformed body. I know flattery when I hear it; but I do not often hear it. Furthermore, there is good flattery and bad; this was from the best cask. And what sort of woman was this who knew so odd a word as "hagiographer" in a language not her own? Nobody who was not a Bollandist had ever called me that before, yet it was a title I would not have exchanged to be called Lord of the Isles. Delightful prose! I must know more of this.

Many people when they are flattered seek immediately to show themselves very hard-headed, to conceal the fact that they have taken the bait. I am one of them.

"Your plan sounds woefully uneconomic to me," I said. "Travelling shows in our time are money-losers unless they play to capacity audiences and have strong backing. You are planning an entertainment of rare quality. What makes you think it can survive? Certainly I have no advice to give you that can be of help there."

"That is not what we ask of you," said Liesl. "We shall look for advice about finance from financiers. From you we want the benefit of your taste, and a particular kind of unusual assistance. For which, of course, we expect to pay."

In other words, no amateurish interference or inquisitiveness about the money. But what could this unusual assistance be?

"Every magician has an autobiography, which is sold in the theatre and elsewhere," she continued. "Most of them are dreadful things, and all of them are the work of another hand—do you say ghost-written? We want one that will be congruous with the entertainment we offer. It must be very good, yet popular, persuasive, and written with style. And that is where you come in, dear Ramsay."

With an air that in another woman would have been flatteringly coquettish, she laid a huge hand over one of mine and engulfed it.

"If you want me to write it over my own name it is out of the question!"

"Not at all. It is important that it appear to be an autobiography. We ask you to be the ghost. And in case such a proposal is insulting to such a very good writer, we offer a substantial fee. Three thousand five hundred dollars is not bad; I have made inquiries."

"Not good either. Give me that and a half-share in the royalties and I might consider it."

"That's the old, grasping Ramsay blood!" said Eisengrim and laughed the first real laugh I had heard from him.

"Well, consider what you ask. The book would have to be fiction. I presume you don't think the world will swallow a courtier of polished manner if he is shown to be the son of a Baptist parson in rural Canada—"

"You never told me your father was a parson," said Liesl. "What a lot we have in common! Several of my father's family are parsons."

"The autobiography, like the personality, will have to be hand-made," said I, "and as you have been telling me all through lunch, distinguished works of imagination are not simply thrown together."

"But you will not be hard on us," said Liesl. "You see, not any writer will do. But you, who have written so persuasively about the saints—slipping under the guard of the sceptic with a candour that is brilliantly disingenuous, treating marvels with the seriousness of fact—you are just the man for us. We can pay, and we will pay, though we cannot pay a foolish price. But I think that you are too much an old friend of magic to say no."

In spite of her marred face her smile was so winning that I could not say no. This looked like an adventure, and, at fifty, adventures do not come every day.


( 4 )

At fifty, should adventures come at all? Certainly that was what I was asking myself a month later. I was heartily sick of Magnus Eisengrim and his troupe, and I hated Liselotte Vitzlipützli, which was the absurd name of his monstrous business partner. But I could not break the grip that their vitality, their single-mindedness, and the beautiful mystery of their work had fastened on my loneliness.

For the first few days it was flattering to my spirit to sit in the stalls in the empty theatre with Liesl while Eisengrim rehearsed. Not a day passed that he did not go through a searching examination of several of his illusions, touching up one moment, or subduing another, and always refining that subtle technique of misdirecting the attention of his audience, which is the beginning and end of the conjurer's art.

To me it was deeply satisfying to watch him, for he was a master of all those sleights that had seemed so splendid, and so impossible, in my boyhood. "Secure and palm six half-crowns." He could do it with either hand. His professional dress coat almost brought tears to my eyes, such a marvel was it of loading-pockets, *pochettes* and *profondes*; when it was filled and ready for his appearance in *The Dream of Midas* it weighed twelve pounds, but it fitted him without a bulge.

My opinion was sought, and given, about the program. It was on my advice that the second part of his entertainment was reshaped. I suggested that he cut out the escape act entirely; it was not suitable to an illusionist, for it was essentially a physical trick and not a feat of magic. There was no romance about being stuck in a milk can and getting out again. This gave Liesl a chance to press for the inclusion of *The Brazen Head of Friar Bacon* and I supported her strongly; it was right for the character of the show they were building. But Eisengrim the Great had never heard of Friar Bacon, and like so many people who have not heard of something, he could not believe that anybody but a few eccentrics would have done so.

"It is unmistakably your thing," I said. "You can tell them about the great priest-magician and his Brazen Head that foretold the future and knew the past; I'll write the speech for you. It doesn't matter whether people have heard of Bacon or not. Many of them haven't heard of Dr Faustus, but they like your conclusion."

"Oh, every educated person has heard of Faust," said Eisengrim with something like pomposity. "He's in a very famous opera." He had no notion that Faust was also in one of the world's greatest plays.

He had virtually no education, though he could speak several languages, and one of the things Liesl had to teach him, as tactfully as possible, was not to talk out of his depth. I thought that much of his extraordinarily impressive personality arose from his ignorance—or, rather, from his lack of a headful of shallow information that would have enabled him to hold his own in a commonplace way among commonplace people. As a schoolmaster of twenty years' experience I had no use for smatterers. What he knew, he knew as well as anybody on earth; it gave him confidence, and sometimes a naïve egotism that was hard to believe.

We worked very hard on the Brazen Head, which was no more than a very good thought-reading act dressed in a new guise. The Brazen Head was "levitated" by Eisengrim and floated in the middle of the stage, apparently without wires or supports; then the girls moved through the audience, collecting objects that were sealed in envelopes by their lenders. Eisengrim received these envelopes on a tray on the stage and asked the Head to describe the objects and identify their owners; the Head did so, giving the row and seat number for each; only then did Eisengrim touch them. Next, the Head gave messages to three members of the audience, chosen apparently at random, relating to their personal affairs. It was a first-rate illusion, and I think the script I wrote for it, which was plain and literate, and free of any of the pompous rhetoric so dear to conjurers, had a substantial part in creating its air of mystery.

Rehearsal was difficult because much depended on the girls who collected the objects; they had to use their heads, and their heads were not the best-developed part of them. The random messages were simple but dangerous, for they relied on the work of the company manager, a pickpocket of rare gifts; but he had an air of transparent honesty and geniality, and as he mingled with the audience when it entered the theatre, shaking hands and pressing through the crowd as if on his way somewhere else to do something very important, nobody suspected him. Sometimes he found invaluable letters in the coats of distinguished visitors when he took these to his office to spare such grandees the nuisance of lining up at the *garderobe*. But in the case of ladies or men of no special importance it was straight "dipping," and potentially dangerous. He enjoyed it; it put him in mind of the good old days before he got into trouble and left London for Rio.

Because of a message the Brazen Head gave a beautiful lady in the very first audience before which it was shown, a duel was fought the next day between a well-known Mexican lawyer and a dentist who fancied himself as a Don Juan. Nothing could have been better publicity, and all sorts of people offered large sums to be permitted to consult the Brazen Head privately. Eisengrim, who had a perfectionist's capacity for worry, was fearful that such revelations would keep people out of the theatre, but Liesl was confident and exultant; she said they would come to hear what was said about other people, and they did.

Liesl's job was to speak for the Brazen Head, because she was the only member of the company capable of rapidly interpreting a letter or an engagement book, and composing a message that was spicy without being positively libellous. She was a woman of formidable intelligence and intuition: she had a turn for improvising and phrasing ambiguous but startling messages that would have done credit to the Oracle at Delphi.

The Brazen Head was such a success that there was some thought of putting it at the end of the show, as the "topper," but I opposed this; the foundation of the show was romance, and *The Vision of Dr Faustus* had it. But the Head was our best effort in sheer mystery.

I cannot refrain from boasting that it was I who provided the idea for one of the illusions that made Eisengrim the most celebrated magician in the world. Variety theatres everywhere abounded with magicians who could saw a woman in two; it was my suggestion that Eisengrim should offer to saw a member of the audience in two.

His skill as a hypnotist made it possible. When we had worked out the details and put the illusion on the stage, he would first perform the commonplace illusion, sawing one of his showgirls into two sections with a circular saw and displaying her with her head smiling from one end of a box while her feet kicked from the other—but with a hiatus of three feet between the two parts of the box. Then he would offer to do the same thing with a volunteer from the audience. The volunteer would be "lightly anaesthetized" by hypnosis, ostensibly so that he would not wriggle and perhaps injure himself, after which he would be put in a new box, and Eisengrim would saw him in two with a large and fearsome lumberman's saw. The volunteer was shown to be divided but able to kick his feet and answer questions about the delightfully airy feeling in his middle. Rejoined, the volunteer would leave the stage decidedly dazed, but marvelling at himself and pleased with the applause.

The high point of this illusion was when two assistants held a large mirror so that the volunteer could see for himself that he had been sawn in two. We substituted this illusion for the rather ordinary hypnotic stuff that had been in the show when first I saw it.

Working on these illusions was delightful but destructive of my character. I was aware that I was recapturing the best of my childhood; my imagination had never known such glorious freedom; but as well as liberty and wonder I was regaining the untruthfulness, the lack of scruple, and the absorbing egotism of a child. I heard myself talking boastfully, lying shamelessly. I blushed but could not control myself. I had never, so far as I can tell, been absorbed completely into the character of a Headmaster—a figure of authority, of scholarship, of probity—but I was an historian, a hagiographer, a bachelor of unstained character, a winner of the Victoria Cross, the author of several admired books, a man whose course of life was set and the bounds of whose success were defined. Yet here I was, in Mexico City, not simply attached to but subsumed in a magic show. The day I found myself slapping one of the showgirls on the bottom and winking when she made her ritual protest, I knew that something was terribly wrong with Dunstan Ramsay.

Two things that were wrong I could easily identify: I had become a dangerously indiscreet talker, and I was in love with the beautiful Faustina.

I cannot say which dismayed me the more. Almost from the earliest days of my childhood I had been close-mouthed; I never passed on gossip if I could help it, though I had no objection to hearing it; I never betrayed a confidence, preferring the costive pleasure of being a repository of secrets. Much of my intimacy with Boy Staunton rested on the fact that he could be sure I would never repeat anything I was told in confidence, and extremely little that was not so regarded. My pleasure depended on what I knew, not on what I could tell. Yet here I was, chattering like a magpie, telling things that had never before passed my lips, and to Liesl, who did not look to me like a respecter of confidences.

We talked in the afternoons, while she was working on the properties and machinery of the illusions in the tiny theatre workshop under the stage. I soon found out why Liesl dominated the company. First, she was the backer, and the finance of the whole thing rested either on her money or money she had guaranteed. She was a Swiss, and the company buzz was that she came of a family that owned one of the big watch firms. Second, she was a brilliant mechanic; her huge hands did wonders with involved springs, releases and displacements, escapements and levers, however tiny they might be. She was a good artificer too; she made the Brazen Head out of some light plastic so that it was an arresting object; nothing in Eisengrim's show was tawdry or untouched by her exacting taste. But unlike many good craftsmen, she could see beyond what she was making to its effect when in use.

Sometimes she lectured me on the beauty of mechanics. "There are about a dozen basic principles," she would say, "and if they cannot be made to do everything, they can be made to create magic—if you know what you want. Some magicians try to use what they call modern techniques—rays and radar and whatnot. But every boy understands those things. Not many people really understand clock-work because they carry it on their wrists in full sight and never think about it."

She insisted on talking to me about the autobiography of Eisengrim I was preparing. I had never been used to talking to anyone about a work in progress—had indeed a superstitious feeling that such talk harmed the book by robbing it of energy that should go into the writing. But Liesl always wanted to know how it was getting on, and what line I meant to take, and what splendid lies I was concoct-ing to turn Paul Dempster into a northern wizard.

We had agreed in general terms that he was to be a child of the Baltic vastnesses, reared perhaps by gnomelike Lapps after the death of his explorer parents, who were probably Russians of high birth. No, better not Russians; probably Swedes or Danes who had lived long in Finland; Russians caused too much trouble at borders, and Paul still kept his Canadian passport. Or should his parents perish in the Canadian vastnesses? Anyhow, he had to be a child of the steppes, who had assumed his wolf-name in tribute to the savage animals whose midnight howls had been his earliest lullaby, and to avoid revealing his distinguished family name. I had worked on the lives of several northern saints, and I had a store of this highly coloured material at my fingers' ends.

As we discussed these fictions, it was not surprising that Liesl should want to know the facts. In spite of her appearance, and the mistrust of her I felt deep within me, she was a woman who could draw out confidences, and I heard myself rattling on about Deptford, and the Dempsters, and Paul's premature birth, though I did not tell all I knew of that; I even told her about the sad business in the pit, and what came of it, and how Paul ran away; to my dismay I found that I had told her about Willie, about Surgeoner, and even about the Little Madonna. I lay awake the whole night after this last piece of blathering, and got her alone as soon as I could the next day, and begged her not to tell anyone.

"No, Ramsay, I won't promise anything of the sort," said she. "You are too old a man to believe in secrets. There is really no such thing as a secret; everybody likes to tell, and everybody does tell. Oh, there are men like priests and lawyers and doctors who are supposed not to tell what they know, but they do—usually they do. If they don't they grow very queer indeed; they pay a high price for their secrecy. You have paid such a price, and you look like a man full of secrets—grim-mouthed and buttoned-up and hard-eyed and cruel, because you are cruel to yourself. It has done you good to tell what you know; you look much more human already. A little shaky this morning because you are so unused to being without the pressure of all your secrets, but you will feel better quite soon."

I renewed my appeal again that afternoon, but she would give no promise, and I don't think I would have believed her if she had done so; I was irrationally obsessed with an ideal of secrecy that I had carried for fifty years, only to betray it now.

"If a temperamental secret-keeper like you cannot hold in what he knows about Eisengrim, how can you expect it of anyone you despise as you despise me?" she said. "Oh yes, you do despise me. You despise almost everybody except Paul's mother. No wonder she seems like a saint to you; you have made her carry the affection you should have spread among fifty people. Do not look at me with that tragic face. You should thank me. At fifty years old you should be glad to know something of yourself. That horrid village and your hateful Scots family made you a moral monster. Well, it is not too late for you to enjoy a few years of almost normal humanity.

"Do not try to work on me by making sad faces, Ramsay. You are a dear fellow, but a fool. Now, tell me how you are going to get the infant Magnus Eisengrim out of that dreadful Canada and into a country where big spiritual adventures are possible?"

If the breakdown of character that made me a chatterbox was hard to bear, it was a triviality beside the tortures of my love for the beautiful Faustina.

It was a disease, and I knew it was a disease, I could see plainly everything that made her an impossible person for me to love. She was at least thirty years younger than I, to begin, and she had nothing that I would have recognized as a brain in her head. She was a monster of vanity, venomously jealous of the other girls in the show, and sulky whenever she was not being admired. She rebelled against the company rule that she might not accept invitations from men who had seen her on the stage, but she delighted in having them surge forward when she left the stage door, to press flowers, sweets, and gifts of all kinds on her as she stepped into a hired limousine with Eisengrim. There was one wild-eyed student boy who thrust a poem into her hand, which, as it was writing, I suppose she took for a bill and handed back to him. My heart bled for the poor simpleton. She was an animal.

But I loved her! I hung about the theatre to see her come and go. I lurked in the wings—to which I had been given the entrée, for large screens were set up to protect the illusions from stage hands who were not members of the company—to watch her very rapid changes from Gretchen to Venus and back again, because there was an instant when, in spite of the skilled work of two dressers, she was almost naked. She knew it, and some nights she threw me a smile of complicity and on others she looked offended. She could not resist admiration from anyone, and although I was something of a mystery to most of the company, she knew that I had a voice that was listened to in high places.

There were whole nights when I lay awake from one o'clock till morning, calling up her image before my imagination. On such nights I would suffer, again and again, the worst horror of the lover: I would find myself unable to summon up the adored one's face and—I write it hardly expecting to be believed except by someone who has suffered this abjection of adoration—I would shake at the blasphemy of having thus mislaid her likeness. I plagued myself with fruitless questions: would the promise of a life's servitude be enough to make her stoop to me? And then—for common sense never wholly left me—I would think of the beautiful Faustina talking to curious, gaping boys at Colborne College, or meeting the other masters' wives at one of their stupefying tea parties, and something like a laugh would shake me. For I was so bound to my life in Canada, you see, that I always thought of Faustina in terms of marriage and the continuance of my work.

My work! As if she could have understood what education was, or why anyone would give a life to it! When I wrestled with the problem of how it could be explained to her I was further shaken because, for the first time in my life, I began to wonder if education could be quite the splendid vocation I had, as a professional, come to think it. How could I lay my accomplishments at her beautiful feet when she was incapable of knowing what they were? Somebody—I suppose it was Liesl—told her I knew a lot about saints, and this made a kind of sense to her.

One happy day, meeting me in the corridor of the theatre after I had been watching her transformations in *The Vision of Dr Faustus,* she said, "Good evening, St Ramsay."

"St Dunstan," said I.

"I do not know St Dunstan. Was he a bad old saint who peeps, eh? O-o-h, shame on you, St Dunstan!" She made a very lewd motion with her hips and darted into the dressing-room she shared with Eisengrim.

I was in a melting ectasy of delight and despair. She had spoken to me! She knew I watched her and probably guessed that I loved her and longed for her. That bump, or grind, or whatever they called it, made it very clear that—yes, but to call me St Dunstan! What about that? And "bad old saint"—she thought me old. So I was. I was fifty, and in the chronology of a Peruvian girl who was probably more than half Indian, that was very old. But she had spoken, and she had shown awareness of my passion for her, and—

I muddled on and on, most of that night, attributing subtleties to Faustina that were certainly absurd but that I could not fight down.

Officially she was Eisengrim's mistress, but they were always quarrelling, for he was exquisitely neat and she made a devastation of their dressing-room. Further, it was clear enough to me that his compelling love affair was with himself; his mind was always on his public personality, and on the illusions over which he fussed psychologically quite as much as Liesl did mechanically. I had seen a good deal of egotism in my life, and I knew that it starved love for anyone else and sometimes burned it out completely. Had it not been so with Boy and Leola? Still, Eisengrim and the beautiful Faustina shared quarters at the hotel. I knew it, because I had left my own place and moved into the even more Spanish establishment that housed the superior members of the company. They shared a room, but did it mean anything?

I found out the day after she called me St Dunstan. I was in the theatre about five o'clock in the afternoon and chanced to go down the corridor on which the star's dressing-room lay. The door was open, and I saw Faustina naked—she was always changing her clothes—in the arms of Liesl, who held her close and kissed her passionately; she had her left arm around Faustina, and her right hand was concealed from me, but the movement of Faustina's hips and her dreamy murmurs made it clear, even to my unaccustomed eyes, what their embrace was.

I have never known such a collapse of the spirit even in the worst of the war. And this time there was no Little Madonna to offer me courage or ease me into oblivion.

( 5 )

"Well, dear Ramsay, you are looking a little pale."

It was Liesl who spoke. I had answered a tap on my door at about one o'clock in the morning, and there she stood in pyjamas and dressing-gown, smiling her ugly smile.

"What do you want?"

"To talk. I love to talk with you, and you are a man who needs talk. Neither of us is sleeping; therefore we shall talk."

In she came, and as the little room offered only one uncompromising straight-backed chair, she sat down on the bed.

"Come and sit by me. If I were an English lady, or somebody's mother, I suppose I should begin by saying, 'Now what is the matter?'—but that is just rhetoric. The matter is that you saw me and Faustina this afternoon. Oh yes, I saw you in the looking-glass. So?"

I said nothing.

"You are just like a little boy, Ramsay. Or no, I am forgetting that only silly men like to be told they are like little boys. Very well, you are like a man of fifty whose bottled-up feelings have burst their bottle and splashed glass and acid everywhere. That is why I called you a little boy, for which I apologize; but you have no art of dealing with such a situation as a man of fifty, so you are thrown back to being like a little boy. Well, I am sorry for you. Not very much, but some."

"Don't patronize me, Liesl."

"That is an English word I have never really understood."

"Don't bully me, then. Don't know best. Don't be the sophisticated European, the magic-show gypsy, the wonderfully intuitive woman, belittling the feelings of a poor brute who doesn't know any better than to think in terms of decency and honour and not taking advantage of people who may not know what they're doing."

"You mean Faustina? Ramsay, she is a wonderful creature, but in a way you don't begin to grasp. She isn't one of your North American girls, half B.A. and half B.F. and half good decent spud—that's three halves, but never mind. She is of the earth, and her body is her shop and her temple, and whatever her body tells her is all of the law and the prophets. You can't understand such a person, but there are more of them in the world than of the women who are tangled up in honour and decency and the other very masculine things you admire so much. Faustina is a great work of the Creator. She has nothing of what you call brains; she doesn't need them for her destiny. Don't glare at me because I speak of her destiny. It is to be glorious for a few years: not to outlive some dull husband and live on his money till she is eighty, going to lectures and comparing the attractions of winter tours that offer the romance of the Caribbean."

"You talk as if you thought you were God."

"I beg your pardon. That is your privilege, you pseudo-cynical old pussy-cat, watching life from the sidelines and knowing where all the players go wrong. Life is a spectator sport to you. Now you have taken a tumble and found yourself in the middle of the fight, and you are whimpering because it is rough."

"Liesl, I am too tired and sick to wrangle. But let me tell you this, and you may laugh as loud and as long as you please, and babble it to everybody you know because that is your professed way of dealing with confidences: I loved Faustina."

"But you don't love her now because of what you saw this afternoon! Oh, knight! Oh, saint! You loved her but you never gave her a gift, or paid her a compliment, or asked her to eat with you, or tried to give her what Faustina understands as love—a sweet physical convulsion shared with an interesting partner."

"Liesl, I am fifty, and I have a wooden leg and only part of one arm. Is that interesting for Faustina?"

"Yes, anything is for Faustina. You don't know her, but far worse you don't know yourself. You are not so very bad, Ramsay."

"Thank you."

"Oooh, what dignity! Is that a way to accept a compliment from a lady? I tell him he is not so very bad, and he ruffles up like an old maid and makes a sour face. I must do better; you are a fascinating old fellow. How's that?"

"If you have said what you came to say, I should like to go to bed now."

"Yes, I see you have taken off your wooden leg and stood it in the corner. Well, I should like to go to bed now too. Shall we go to bed together?"

I looked at her with astonishment. She seemed to mean it.

"Well, do not look as if it were out of the question. You are fifty and not all there: I am as grotesque a woman as you are likely to meet. Wouldn't it have an unusual savour?"

I rose and began to hop to the door. Over the years I have become a good hopper. But Liesl caught me by the tail of my pyjama coat and pulled me back on the bed.

"Oh, you want it to be like Venus and Adonis! I am to drag you into my arms and crush out your boyish modesty. Good!"

She was much stronger than I would have supposed, and she had no silly notions about fighting fair. I was dragged back to the bed, hopping, and pulled into her arms. I can only describe her body as rubbery, so supple yet muscular was it. Her huge, laughing face with its terrible jaw was close to my own, and her monkeylike mouth was thrust out for a kiss. I had not fought for years—not since my war, in fact—but I had to fight now for—well, for what? In my genteel encounters with Agnes Day, and Gloria Mundy, and Libbie Doe, now so far in the past, I had always been the aggressor, insofar as there was any aggression in those slack-twisted amours. I certainly was not going to be ravished by a Swiss gargoyle. I gave a mighty heave and got a handful of her pyjama coat and a good grip on her hair and threw her on the floor.

She landed with a crash that almost brought down plaster. Up she bounced like a ball, and with a grab she caught up my wooden leg and hit me such a crack over my single shin that I roared and cursed. But when next she brought it down—I had never considered it as a weapon, and it was terrible with springs and rivets—I had a pillow ready and wrenched it from her.

By this time someone downstairs was pounding on his ceiling and protesting in Spanish, but I was not to be quieted. I hopped toward Liesl, waggling the leg with such angry menace that she made the mistake of retreating, and I had her in a corner. I dropped the leg and punched her with a ferocity that I should be ashamed to recall; still, as she was punching back and had enormous fists, it was a fair enough fight. But she began to be afraid, for I had a good Highland temper and it was higher than I have ever known. Tears of pain or fright were running from her deep-set eyes, and blood was dribbling from a cut lip. After a few more smart cuffs, keeping my legless side propped against the wall, I began to edge her toward the door. She grasped the handle behind her, but as she turned it I got a good hold on the bedhead with one hand, and seized her nose between the fingers of the other, and gave it such a twist that I thought I heard something crack. She shrieked, managed to tug the door open, and thundered down the passage.

I sank back on the bed. I was worn out, I was puffing, but I felt fine. I felt better than I had done for three weeks. I thought of Faustina. Good old Faustina! Had I trounced Liesl to avenge her? No, I decided that I had not. A great cloud seemed to have lifted from my spirit, and though it was too soon to be sure, I thought that perhaps my reason, such as it was, had begun to climb back into the saddle and that with care I might soon be myself again.

I had eaten no dinner in my misery, and I discovered I was hungry. I had no food, but I had a flask of whisky in my briefcase. I found it and lay back on the bed, taking a generous swig. The room was a battlefield, but I would tidy it in the morning. Liesl's dressing-gown and a few rags from her pyjamas lay about, and I left them where they were. Honourable trophies.

There came a tap on the door.

"What is it?" I called out in English.

"Señor," hissed a protesting voice, "zis honeymoon—oh, very well, very well for you, señor, but please to remember there are zose below who are not so young, if you please, señor!"

I apologized elaborately in Spanish, and the owner of the voice shuffled back down the passage. Honeymoon! How strangely people interpret sound!

In a few minutes there was another tap, even gentler. I called out, "Who is it?"—in Spanish this time.

The voice was Liesl's voice. "You will be so kind as to allow me to recover my key," it said thickly and very formally.

I opened the door, and there she stood, barefooted and holding what was left of her pyjama coat over her bosom.

"Of course, señora," said I, bowing as gracefully as a one-legged man can do and gesturing to her to come in. Why I closed the door after her I do not know. We glared at each other.

"You are much stronger than you look," said she.

"So are you," said I. Then I smiled a little. A victor's smile, I suppose; the kind of smile I smile at boys whom I have frightened out of their wits. She picked up the dressing-gown, taking care not to turn her back on me.

"May I offer you a drink," said I, holding out the flask. She took it and raised it to her lips, but the whisky stung a cut in her mouth and she winced sharply. That took all the lingering spite out of me. "Sit down," I said, "and I'll put something on those bruises."

She sat down on the bed, and not to make a long tale of it, I washed her cuts and put a cold-water compress on her nose, which had swollen astonishingly, and in about five minutes we were sitting up in the bed with the pillows behind us, taking turn and turn about at the flask.

"How do you feel now?" said I.

"Much better. And you? How is your shin?"

"I feel better than I have felt in a very long time."

"Good. That is what I came to make you feel."

"Indeed? I thought you came to seduce me. That seems to be your hobby. Anybody and anything. Do you often get beaten up?"

"What a fool you are! It was only a way of trying to tell you something."

"Not that you love me, I hope. I have believed some strange things in my time, but that would test me pretty severely."

"No. I wanted to tell you that you are human, like other people."

"Have I denied it?"

"Listen, Ramsay, for the past three weeks you have been telling me the story of your life, with great emotional detail, and certainly it sounds as if you did not think you were human. You make yourself responsible for other people's troubles. It is your hobby. You take on the care of a poor madwoman you knew as a boy. You put up with subtle insult and being taken for granted by a boyhood friend—this big sugar-man who is such a power in your part of the world. You are a friend to this woman—Leola, what a name!—who gave you your *congé* when she wanted to marry Mr Sugar. And you are secret and stiff-rumped about it all, and never admit it is damned good of you. That is not very human. You are a decent chap to everybody, except one special somebody, and that is Dunstan Ramsay. How can you be really good to anybody if you are not good to yourself?"

"I wasn't brought up to blow a trumpet if I happened to do something for somebody."

"Upbringing, so? Calvinism? I am a Swiss, Ramsay, and I know Calvinism as well as you do. It is a cruel way of life, even if you forget the religion and call it ethics or decent behaviour or something else that pushes God out of it.

"But even Calvinism can be endured, if you will make some compromise with yourself. But you—there is a whole great piece of your life that is unlived, denied, set aside. That is why at fifty you can't bear it any longer and fly all to pieces and pour out your heart to the first really intelligent woman you have met—me, that's to say—and get into a schoolboy yearning for a girl who is as far from you as if she lived on the moon. This is the revenge of the unlived life, Ramsay. Suddenly it makes a fool of you.

"You should take a look at this side of your life you have not lived. Now don't wriggle and snuffle and try to protest. I don'tmean you should have secret drunken weeks and a widow in a lacy flat who expects you every Thursday, like some suburban ruffian. You are a lot more than that. But every man has a devil, and a man of unusual quality, like yourself, Ramsay, has an unusual devil. You must get to know your personal devil. You must even get to know his father, the Old Devil. Oh, this Christianity! Even when people swear they don't believe in it, the fifteen hundred years of Christianity that has made our world is in their bones, and they want to show they can be Christians without Christ. Those are the worst; they have the cruelty of doctrine without the poetic grace of myth.

"Why don't you shake hands with your devil, Ramsay, and change this foolish life of yours? Why don't you, just for once, do something inexplicable, irrational, at the devil's bidding, and just for the hell of it? You would be a different man.

"What I am saying is not for everybody, of course. Only for the twice-born. One always knows the twice-born. They often go so far as to take new names. Did you not say that English girl renamed you? And who was Magnus Eisengrim? And me—do you know what my name really means, Liselotte Vitzlipützli? It sounds so funny, but one day you will stumble on its real meaning. Here you are, twice-born, and nearer your death than your birth, and you have still to make a real life.

"Who are you? Where do you fit into poetry and myth? Do you know who I think you are, Ramsay? I think you are Fifth Business.

"You don't know what that is? Well, in opera in a permanent company of the kind we keep up in Europe you must have a prima donna—always a soprano, always the heroine, often a fool; and a tenor who always plays the lover to her; and then you must have a contralto, who is a rival to the soprano, or a sorceress or something; and a basso, who is the villan or the rival or whatever threatens the tenor.

"So far, so good. But you cannot make a plot work without another man, and he is usually a baritone, and he is called in the profession Fifth Business, because he is the odd man out, the person who has no opposite of the other sex. And you must have Fifth Business because he is the one who knows the secret of the hero's birth, or comes to the assistance of the heroine when she thinks all is lost, or keeps the hermitess in her cell, or may even be the cause of somebody's death if that is part of the plot. The prima donna and the tenor, the contralto and the basso, get all the best music and do all the spectacular things, but you cannot manage the plot without Fifth Business! It is not spectacular, but it is a good line of work, I can tell you, and those who play it sometimes have a career that outlasts the golden voices. Are you Fifth Business? You had better find out."

This is not a verbatim report, Headmaster; I said a good deal myself, and I have tidied Liesl's English, and boiled down what she said. But we talked till a clock somewhere struck four, and then fell happily asleep, but not without having achieved the purpose for which Liesl had first of all invaded my room.

With such a gargoyle! And yet never have I known such deep delight or such an aftermath of healing tenderness!

Next morning, tied to my door handle, was a bunch of flowers and a message in elegant Spanish:

Forgive my ill manners of last night. Love conquers all and youth must be served. May you know a hundred years of happy nights. Your Neighbour in the Chamber Below.

# 6

# The Soirée of Illusions

## ( 1 )

The Autobiography of Magnus Eisengrim was a great pleasure to write, for I was under no obligation to be historically correct or to weigh evidence. I let myself go and invented just such a book about a magician as I would have wanted to read if I had been a member of his public; it was full of romance and marvels, with a quiet but sufficient undertone of eroticism and sadism, and it sold like hot-cakes.

Liesl and I had imagined it would sell reasonably well in the lobbies of theatres where the show was appearing, but it did well in book stores and, in a paperback edition that soon followed, it was a steady seller in cigar stores and other places where they offer lively, sensational reading. People who had never done an hour's concentrated work in their lives loved to read how the young Magnus would rehearse his card and coin sleights for fourteen hours at a stretch, until his body was drenched in nervous sweat, and he could take no nourishment but a huge glass of cream laced with brandy. People whose own love-lives were pitched entirely in the key of C were enchanted to know that at the time when he was devoting himself entirely to the study of hypnotism, his every glance was so supercharged that lovely women forced themselves upon him, poor moths driven to immolate themselves in his flame.

I wrote about the hidden workshop in a Tyrolean castle where he devised his illusions, and dropped hints that girls had sometimes been terriby injured in some device that was not quite perfect; of course Eisengrim paid to have them put right again; I made him something of a monster but not too much of a monster. I also made his age a matter of conjecture. It was a lively piece of work, and all I regretted was that I had not made a harder bargain for my share of the profit. As it was, it brought me a pleasant annual addition to my income and does so still.

I wrote it in a quiet place in the Adirondacks to which I went a few days after my noctural encounter with Liesl. Eisengrim's engagement at the Teatro Chueca was drawing to an end, and the show was to visit a few Central American cities before going to Europe, where a long tour was hoped for. I gave the beautiful Faustina a handsome and fairly expensive necklace as a parting present, and she gave me a kiss, which she and I both regarded as a fair exchange. I gave Eisengrim a really expensive set of studs and links for his evening dress, which staggered him, for he was a miser and could not conceive of anybody giving anything away. But I had talked earnestly with him and wrung from him a promise to contribute to the maintenance of Mrs Dempster; he did not want to do it, swore that he owed her nothing and had indeed been driven from home by her bad reputation. I pointed out to him, however, that if this had not been the case, he would not have become the Great Eisengrim but would probably be a Baptist parson in rural Canada. This was false argument and hurt his vanity, but it helped me gain my point. Liesl helped too. She insisted that Eisengrim sign a banker's order for a sum to be paid to me monthly; she knew that if he had to send me cheques he would forget very soon. The studs and links were something to soothe his wounded avarice. I gave nothing to Liesl; by this time she and I were strong friends and took from each other something that could find no requital in presents.

That money from Eisengrim was not entirely necessary, but I was glad to get it. Within a month of the end of the war I had been able to transfer Mrs Dempster from the public wards of that hateful city asylum to a much better hospital near a small town, where she could have the status of a private patient, enjoying company if she wanted it and gaining the advantages of better air and extensive grounds. I was able to work this through a friend who had some influence; the asylum doctors agreed that she would be better in such a place, and that she was unfit for liberty even if there had been anywhere for her to go. It meant a substantial monthly cost, and though my fortunes had increased to the point where I could afford it, my personal expenditures had to be curtailed, and I was wondering how often in future I would be able to travel in Europe. I would have thought myself false to her, and to the memory of Bertha Shanklin, if I had not made this change in her circumstances, but it meant a pinch, considering that I was trying to build up a fund for my retirement as well. My position was a common one; I wanted to do the right thing but could not help regretting the damnable expense.

So, as I say, I was glad to get a regular sum from Eisengrim, which amounted to about a third of what was needed, and my sense of relief led me into a stupid error of judgement. When first I visited Mrs Dempster after returning from my six months' absence I told her I had found Paul.

Her condition at this time was much improved, and the forlorn and bemused look she had worn for so many years had given place to something that was almost like the sweet and sometimes humorously perceptive expression l remembered from the days when she lived at the end of a rope in Deptford. Her hair was white, but her face was not lined and her figure was slight. I was very pleased by the improvement. But she was still in a condition to which the psychiatrists gave a variety of scientific names but which had been called "simple" in Deptford. She could look after herself, talked helpfully and amusingly to other patients, and was of use in taking some of the people who were more confused than herself for walks. But she had no ordered notion of the world about her, and in particular she had no sense of time. Amasa Dempster she sometimes recalled as if he were somebody in a book she had once read inattentively; she knew me as the only constant factor in her life, but I came and went, and now if I were absent for six months it was not greatly different in her mind from the space between my weekly visits. The compulsion to visit her regularly was all my own and sprang from a sense of duty rather than from any feeling that she missed me. Paul, however, held a very different place in her confused world, as I soon discovered.

Paul, to her, was still a child, a lost boy—lost a distance of time ago that was both great and small—and to be recovered just as he had run away. Not that she really thought he had run away; surely he had been enticed, by evil people who knew what a great treasure he was; they had stolen him to be cruel, to rob a mother of her child and a child of his mother. Of such malignity she could form no clear picture, but sometimes she spoke of gypsies; gypsies have carried the burden of the irrational dreads of stay-at-homes for many hundreds of years. I had written a passage in my life of Eisengrim in which he spent some of his youth among gypsies, and as I listened to Mrs Dempster now I was ashamed of it.

If I knew where Paul was, why had I not brought him? What had I done to recover him? Had he been ill used? How could I tell her that I had news of Paul if I havered and temporized and would neither bring her child to her or take her to him?

In vain I told her that Paul was now over forty, that he travelled much, that he had a demanding career in which he was not his own master, that he would surely visit Canada at some time not now very far in the future. I said that he sent his love—which was a lie, for he had never said anything of the kind—and that he wanted to provide her with comfort and security. She was so excited, and so unlike herself, that I was shaken and even said that Paul was maintaining her in the hospital, which God knows was untrue, and proved to be another mistake.

To say that a child was keeping her in a hospital was the most ridiculous thing she had ever heard. So that was it? The hospital was an elaborately disguised prison where she was held to keep her from her son! She knew well enough who was her jailer. I was the man. Dunstan Ramsay, who pretended to be a friend, was a snake-in-the-grass, an enemy, an undoubted agent of those dark forces who had torn Paul from her.

She rushed at me and tried to scratch my eyes. I was at a great disadvantage, for I was alarmed and unnerved by the storm I had caused, and also my reverence for Mrs Dempster was so great that I could not bear to be rough with her. Fortunately—though it scared the wits out of me at the moment—she began to scream, and a nurse came on the run, and between us we soon had her powerless. But what followed was a half-hour of confusion, during which I explained to a doctor what the trouble was, and Mrs Dempster was put to bed under what they called light restraint—straps—with an injection of something to quiet her.

When I called the hospital the next day the report was a bad one. It grew worse during the week, and in time I had to face the fact that I seemed to have turned Mrs Dempster from a woman who was simple and nothing worse, into a woman who knew there was a plot to deprive her of her little son, and that I was its agent. She was under restraint now, and it was inadvisable that I should visit her. But I did go once, driven by guilt, and though I did not see her, her window was pointed out to me, and it was in the wing where the windows are barred.

( 2 )

Thus I lost, for a time, one of the fixed stars in my universe, and as I had brought about this great change in Mrs Dempster's condition by my own stupidity I felt much depressed by it. But I suffered another loss—or at least a marked change—when Boy Staunton married for the second time, and I did not meet with the approval of his wife.

During the war Boy acquired a taste for what he believed to be politics. He had been elected in easy circumstances, for he was a Conservative, and in their plan for a coalition Cabinet the Liberals had not nominated anybody to oppose him. But in the years when he had great power he forgot that he had been elected by acclamation and came somehow to think of himself as a politician—no, a statesman—with a formidable following among the voters. He had all the delusions of the political amateur, and after the war was over he insisted that he detected an undertone, which grew in some parts of the country to a positive clamour, that he should become leader of the Conservative party as fast as possible and deliver the people of Canada from their ignominious thralldom to the Liberals.

He had another delusion of the political novice: he was going to apply "sound business principles" to government and thereby give it a fine new gloss.

So he attempted to become Conservative leader, but as he was a newcomer he had no chance of doing so. It seemed to me that everything about Boy was wrong for politics: he was very rich and could not understand that very rich men are not loved by the majority; he was handsome, and handsome men are not popular in politics, even with women; he had no political friends and could not understand why they were necessary.

In spite of his handicaps he was elected once, when a by-election opened a Parliamentary seat traditionally Conservative. The voters remembered his services during the war and gave him a majority of less than a thousand. But he made a number of silly speeches in the Commons, which caused a few newspapers to say that he was an authoritarian; then he abused the newspapers in the Commons, and they made him smart for it. Boy had no idea what a mark he presented to jealous or temperamentally derisive people. However, he gained some supporters, and among them was Denyse Hornick.

She was a power in the world of women. She had been in the W.R.N.S. during the war and had risen from the ranks to be a lieutenant commander and a very capable one. After the war she had established a small travel agency and made it a big one. She liked what Boy stood for in politics, and after a few meetings she liked Boy personally. I must not read into her actions motives of which I can have no knowledge, but it looked to me as if she decided that she would marry him and make him think it was his own idea.

Boy had always been fond of the sexual pleasure women could give him, but I doubt if he ever knew much about women as people, and certainly a determined and clever woman like Denyse was something outside his experience. He was drawn to her at first because she was prominent in two or three groups that worked for a larger feminine influence in public affairs, and thus could influence a large number of votes. Soon he discovered that she understood his political ideas better than anybody else, and he paid her a compliment typical of himself by assuring everybody that she had a masculine mind.

The by-election gave him a couple of years in Parliament before a general election came along to test his real strength. By that time any public gratitude for what he had done as a war organizer had been forgotten, the Conservative party found him an embarrassment because he was apt to criticize the party leader in public, the Liberals naturally wanted to defeat him, and the newspapers were out to get him. It was a dreadful campaign on his part, for he lost his head, bullied his electors when he should have wooed them, and got into a wrangle with a large newspaper, which he threatened to sue for libel. He was defeated on election day so decisively that it was obviously a personal rather than a political rejection.

He made an unforgettable appearance on television as soon as his defeat had been conceded. "How do you feel about the result in your riding, Mr Staunton?" asked the interviewer, expecting something crisp, but not what he got. "I feel exactly like Lazarus," said Boy, "licked by the dogs!"

The whole country laughed about it, and the newspaper he thought had libelled him read him a pompous little editorial lecture about the nature of democracy. But there were those who were faithful, and Denyse was at the top of that list.

In the course of time the press tired of baiting him, and there were a few editorials regretting that so much obvious ability was not being used for the public good. But it was no use. Boy was through with politics and turned back to sugar, and everything sugar could be made to do, with new resolve.

Denyse had other ambitions for him, and she was a wilier politician than he. She thought he would make a very fine Lieutenant-Governor of the Province of Ontario and set to work to see that he got it.

Necessarily it was a long campaign. The LieutenantGovernorship was in the gift of the Crown, which meant in effect that the holder of the office was named by the Dominion Cabinet. A Lieutenant-Governor had only recently been appointed, and as he was in excellent health it would be five years and possibly longer before Boy would have a chance. On his side was one strong point; it cost a lot of money to be Lieutenant-Governor, for the duties were ample and the stipend was not, so candidates for the post were never many. But a

Liberal Government at Ottawa would not be likely to appoint a former Conservative parliamentarian to such a post, so there would have to be a change of government if Boy were to have a chance. It was a plan full of risks and contingencies, and if it were to succeed it would be through careful diplomacy and a substantial amount of luck. It was characteristic of Denyse that she decided to get busy with the diplomacy at once, so as to be ready for the luck if it came.

Boy thought the idea a brilliant one. He had never lost his taste for matters connected with the Crown; he had no doubt of his ability to fill a ceremonial post with distinction, and even to give it larger dimensions. He had everything the office needed with one exception. A Lieutenant-Governor must have a wife.

It was here that Denyse's masculinity of mind showed itself with the greatest clarity. Boy told me exactly what she said when first the matter came up between them. "I can't help you there," she said; "you're on your own so far as that goes." And then she went straight on to discuss the rationale of the Lieutenant-Governor's office—those privileges which made it a safeguard against any tyrannous act on the part of a packed legislature. It was by no means a purely ceremonial post, she said, but an agency through which the Crown exercised its traditional function of safeguarding the Constitution against politicians who forgot that they had been elected to serve the people and not to exploit them. She had informed herself thoroughly on the subject and knew the powers and limitations of a Lieutenant-Governor as well as any constitutional lawyer.

Boy had been aware for some time that Denyse was attractive; now he saw that she was lovable. Her intelligent, cool, unswerving devotion to his interests had impressed him from very early in their association, but her masculinity of mind had kept him at a distance. Now he became aware that this poor girl had sacrificed so much of her feminine self in order to gain success in the business world, and to advance the cause of women who lacked her clarity of vision and common sense, that she had almost forgotten that she was a woman, and a damned attractive one.

When love strikes the successful middle-aged they bring a weight of personality and a resolution to it that makes the romances of the young seem timid and bungling. They are not troubled by doubt; they know what they want and they go after it. Boy decided he wanted Denyse.

Denyse was not so easily achieved. Boy told me all about his wooing. Matters between us were still as they had been for thirty years, and the only difference was that Liesl had taught me that his confidences were not wrung from him against his will but gushed like oil from a well, and that I as Fifth Business was his logical confidant. Denyse at first refused to hear his professions of love. Her reasons were two: her business was her creation and demanded the best of her, and as a friend of Boy's she did not want him to imperil a fine career by an attachment that contained dangers.

What dangers? he demanded. Well, she confided, rather unwillingly, there had been Hornick. She had married him very early in the war, when she was twenty; it had been a brief and disagreeable marriage, which she had terminated by a divorce. Could a representative of the Crown have a wife who was a divorcee?

Boy swept this aside. Queen Victoria was dead. Even King George was dead. Everybody recognized the necessity and humanity of divorce nowadays, and Denyse's splendid campaigns for liberalizing the divorce laws had put her in a special category. But Denyse had more to confess.

There had been other men. She was a woman of normal physical needs—she admitted it without shame—and there had been one or two other attachments.

Poor kid, said Boy, she was still a victim of the ridiculous Double Standard. He told Denyse about his dreadful mistake with Leola, and how it had driven him—positively driven him—to seek outside marriage qualities of understanding and physical response that were not to be found at home. She understood this perfectly, but he had to argue for a long time to get her to see that the same common-sense view applied to herself. It was in such things as this, Boy told me with a fatuous smile, that Denyse's masculinity of mind failed her. He had to be pretty stern with her to make her understand that what was sauce for the gander was certainly sauce for the goose. Indeed, he called her Little Goose for a few days but gave it up because of the ribald connotation of the word.

Then—he smiled sadly when he explained the absurdity of this to me—there was her final objection, which was that people might imagine she married him for his money and the position he could give her. She was a small-town girl, and though she had gained a certain degree of know-how through her experience of life (I am not positive but I think she even went so far as to say that she was a graduate of the School of Hard Knocks), she doubted if she was up to being Mrs Boy Staunton, and just possibly the Lieutenant-Governor's lady. Suppose—just suppose for a moment—that she were called upon to entertain Royalty! No, Denyse Hornick knew her strengths and her weaknesses and she loved Boy far too well ever to expose him to embarrassment on her account.

Yes, she loved him. Had always done so. Understood the fiery and impatient spirit that could not endure the popularity-contest side of modern politics. Thought of him—didn't want to seem highbrow, but she did do a little serious reading—as a Canadian Coriolanus. "You common cry of curs, whose breath I hate." She could imagine him saying it to those sons-of-bitches who had turned on him at the last election. Yearned towards him in her heart as a really great man who was too proud to shake hands and kiss babies to persuade a lot of riffraff to let him do what he was so obviously born to do.

Thus the masculinity of mind that had made Denyse Hornick a success in her world was swept aside, and the tender, loving woman beneath was discovered and awakened by Boy Staunton. They were married after appropriate preparations.

As a wedding it was neither a religious ceremony nor a merrymaking. It is best described as A Function. Everybody of importance in Boy's world was there, and by clever work on Denyse's part quite a few Cabinet Ministers from Ottawa were present and the Prime Minister sent a telegram composed by the most eloquent of his secretaries. Bishop Woodiwiss married them, being assured that Denyse had not been the offending party in her divorce; he demurred even then, but Boy persuaded him, saying to me afterward that diocesan care and rumours of the death of God were eroding the Bishop's intellect. The bride wore a ring of unusual size; the best man was a bank president; the very best champagne flowed like the very best champagne under the care of a very good caterer (which is to say, not more than three glasses to a guest unless they made a fuss). There was little jollity but no bitterness except from David.

"Do we kiss the bride?" a middle-aged guest asked him.

"Why not?" said he. "She's been kissed oftener than a police-court Bible and by much the same class of people."

The guest hurried away and told somebody that David was thinking of his mother.

I do not think this was so. Neither David nor Caroline liked Denyse, and they hated and resented her daughter, Lorene.

Not much attention had been paid to Lorene during the courtship, but she was an element to be reckoned with. She was the fruit of the unsatisfactory marriage with Hornick, who may, perhaps, have had the pox, and at this time she was thirteen. Adolescence was well advanced in Lorene, and she had large, hard breasts that popped out so close under her chin that she seemed to have no neck. Her body was heavy and short, and her physical coordination was so poor that she tended to knock things off tables that were quite a distance from her. She had bad vision and wore thick spectacles. She already gave rich promise of superfluous hair and sweated under the least stress. Her laugh was loud and frequent, and when she let it loose, spittle ran down her chin, which she sucked back with a blush. Unkind people said she was a half-wit, but that was untrue; she went to a special boarding-school where her teachers had put her in the Opportunity Class, as being more suited to her powers than the undemanding academic curriculum, and she was learning to cook and sew quite nicely.

At her mother's wedding Lorene was in tearing high spirits. Champagne dissolved her few inhibitions, and she banged and thumped her away among the guests, wet-chinned and elated. "I'm just the luckiest kid in the world today," she whooped. "I've got a wonderful new Daddy, my Daddy-Boy—he says I can call him Daddy-Boy. Look at the bracelet he gave me!"

In the goodness of her innocent heart Lorene tried to be friendly with David and Caroline. After all, were they not one family now? Poor Lorene did not know how many strange gradations of relationship the word "family" can imply. Caroline, who had never had a pleasant disposition, was extremely rude to her. David got drunk and laughed and made disrespectful remarks in an undertone when Boy made his speech in response to the toast to the bride.

Rarely is there a wedding without its clown. Lorene was the clown at Boy's second marriage, but it was not until she fell down— champagne or unaccustomed high heels, or both—that I took her into an anteroom and let her tell me all about her dog, who was marvellously clever. In time she fell asleep, and two waiters carried her out to the car.

( 3 )

Denyse had the normal dislike of a woman for the friends her husband has made before he married her, but I felt she was more than usually severe in my case. She possessed intelligence, conventional good looks, and unusual quality as an intriguer and politician, but she was a woman whose life and interests were entirely external. It was not that she was indifferent to the things of the spirit; she sensed their existence and declared herself their enemy. She had made it clear that she consented to a church wedding only because it was expected of a man in Boy's position; she condemned the church rite because it put women at a disadvantage. All her moral and ethical energy, which was abundant, was directed towards social reform. Easier divorce, equal pay for equal work as between men and women, no discrimination between the sexes in employment—these were her causes, and in promoting them she was no comic-strip feminist termagant, but reasonable, logical, and untiring.

Boy often assured me that underneath this public personality of hers there was a shy, lovable kid, pitifully anxious for affection and the tenderness of sex, but Denyse did not choose to show this aspect of herself to me. She had a fair measure of intuition, and she sensed that I regarded women as something other than fellow-citizens who had been given an economic raw deal because of a few unimportant biological differences. She may even have guessed that I held women in high esteem for qualities she had chosen to discourage in herself. But certainly she did not want me around the Staunton house, and if I dropped in, as had been my habit for thirty years, she picked a delicate quarrel with me, usually about religion. Like many people who are ignorant of religious matters, she attributed absurd beliefs to those who were concerned with them. She had found out about my interest in saints; after all, my books were not easy to overlook if one was in the travel business. The whole notion of saints was repugnant to her, and in her eyes I was on a level with people who believed in teacup reading or Social Credit. So, although I was asked to dinner now and then, when the other guests were people who had to be worked off for some tiresome reason, I was no longer an intimate of the household.

Boy tried to smooth things over by occasionally asking me to lunch at his club. He was more important than ever, for as well as his financial interests, which were now huge, he was a public figure, prominent in many philanthropic causes, and even a few artistic ones, as these became fashionable.

I sensed that this was wearing on him. He hated committees, but they were unavoidable even when he bossed them. He hated inefficiency, but a certain amount of democratic inefficiency had to be endured. He hated unfortunate people, but, after all, these are one's raw material if one sets up shop as a philanthropist. He was still handsome and magnetic, but I sensed grimness and disillusion when he was at his ease, as he was with me. He had embraced Denyse's rationalism—that was what she called it—fervently, and one day at the York Club, following the publication and varied reviews of my big book on the psychology of myth and legend, he denounced me petulantly for what he called my triviality of mind and my encouragement of superstition.

He had not read the book and I was sharp with him. He pulled in his horns a little and said, as the best he could do in the way of apology, that he could not stand such stuff because he was an atheist.

"I'm not surprised," said I. "You created a God in your own image, and when you found out he was no good you abolished him. It's a quite common form of psychological suicide."

I had only meant to give him blow for blow, but to my surprise he crumpled up.

"Don't nag me, Dunny," he said. "I feel rotten. I've done just about everything I've ever planned to do, and everybody thinks I'm a success. And of course I have Denyse now to keep me up to the mark, which is lucky—damned lucky, and don't imagine I don't feel it. But sometimes I wish I could get into a car and drive away from the whole damned thing."

"A truly mythological wish," I said. "I'll save you the trouble of reading my book to find out what it means: you want to pass into oblivion with your armour on, like King Arthur, but modern medical science is too clever to allow it. You must grow old, Boy; you'll have to find out what age means, and how to be old. A dear old friend of mine once told me he wanted a God who would teach him how to grow old. I expect he found what he wanted. You must do the same, or be wretched. Whom the gods hate they keep forever young."

He looked at me almost with hatred. "That's the most lunatic defeatist nonsense I've ever heard in my life," he said. But before we drank our coffee he was quite genial again.

Although I had been rather rough I was worried about him. As a boy he had been something of a bully, a boaster, and certainly a bad loser. As he grew up he had learned to dissemble these characteristics, and to anyone who knew him less well than I it might have appeared that he had conquered them. But I have never thought that traits that are strong in childhood disappear; they may go underground or they may be transmuted into something else, but they do not vanish; very often they make a vigorous appearance after the meridian of life has been passed. It is this, and not senility, that is the real second childhood. I could see this pattern in myself; my boyhood trick of getting off "good ones" that went far beyond any necessary self-defence and were likely to wound, had come back to me in my fifties. I was going to be a sharp-tongued old man as I had been a sharp-tongued boy. And Boy Staunton had reached a point in life where he no longer tried to conceal his naked wish to dominate everybody and was angry and ugly when things went against him.

As we neared our sixties the cloaks we had wrapped about our essential selves were wearing thin.

## ( 4 )

Mrs Dempster died the year after Boy's second marriage. It came as a surprise to me, for I had a notion that the insane lived long and had made preparations in my will for her maintenance if I should die before her. Her health had been unimpaired by the long and wretched stay in the city asylum, and she had been more robust and cheerful after her move to the country, but I think my foolish talk about Paul broke her. After that well-meant piece of stupidity she was never "simple" again. There were drugs to keep her artificially passive, but I mistrusted them (perhaps ignorantly) and asked that so far as possible she be spared the ignominy of being stunned into good conduct. This made her harder to care for and cost more money. So she spent some of her time in fits of rage against me as the evil genius of her life, but much more in a state of grief and desolation.

It wore her out. I could not talk to her, but sometimes I looked at her through a little spy-hole in her door, and she grew frailer and less like herself as the months passed. She developed physical ailments— slight diabetes, a kidney weakening, and some malfunctioning of the heart—which were not thought to be very serious and were controlled in various ways; the doctors assured me, with the profes- sional cheeriness of their kind, that she was good for another ten years. But I did not think so, for I was born in Deptford, where we were very acute in detecting when someone was "breaking up," and I knew that was what was happening to her.

Nevertheless it was a surprise when I was called by the hospital authorities to say she had had a serious heart seizure and might have another within a few hours. I had known very little of life without Mrs Dempster, and despite my folk wisdom about "break- ing up" I had not really faced the fact that I might lose her. It gave me a clutching around my own heart that scared me, but I made my way to the hospital as quickly as I could, though it was some hours after the telephone call when I arrived.

She was in the infirmary now, and unconscious. The outlook was bad, and I sat down to wait—presumably for her death. But after perhaps two hours a nurse appeared and said she was asking for me. As it was now some years since she had seen me without great distress of mind I was doubtful about answering the call, but I was assured it would be all right, and I went to her bedside.

She looked very pale and drawn, but when I took her hand she opened her eyes and looked at me for quite a long time. When she spoke her speech was slack and hardly audible.

"Are you Dunstable Ramsay?" she said.

I assured her. Another long silence.

"I thought he was a boy," said she and closed her eyes again.

I sat by her bed for quite a long time but she did not speak. I thought she might say something about Paul. I sat for perhaps an hour, and then to my astonishment the hand I held gave a little tug, the least possible squeeze. It was the last message I had from Mrs Dempster. Soon afterward her breathing became noisy and the nurses beckoned me away. In half an hour they came to tell me she was dead.

It was a very bad night for me. I kept up a kind of dismal stoicism until I went to bed, and then I wept. I had not done such a thing since my mother had beaten me so many years before—no, not even in the worst of the war—and it frightened and hurt me. When at last I fell asleep I dreamed frightening dreams, in some of which my mother figured in terrible forms. They became so intolerable that I sat up and tried to read but could not keep my mind on the page; instead I was plagued by fantasies of desolation and wretchedness so awful that I might as well not have been sixty years old, a terror to boys, and a scholar of modest repute, for they crushed me as if I were the feeblest of children. It was a terrible invasion of the spirit, and when at last the rising bell rang in the school I was so shaken I cut myself shaving, vomited my breakfast half an hour after I had eaten it, and in my first class spoke so disgracefully to a stupid boy that I called him back afterward and apologized. I must have looked stricken, for my colleagues were unusually considerate towards me, and my classes were uneasy. I think they thought I was very ill, and I suppose I was, but not of anything I knew how to cure.

I had arranged for Mrs Dempster's body to be sent to Toronto, as I wanted it to be cremated. An undertaker had it in his care, and the day after her death I went to see him.

"Dempster," he said. "Yes, just step into Room C."

There she was, not looking very much like herself, for the embalmer had been generous with the rouge. Nor can I say that she looked younger, or at peace, which are the two conventional comments. She just looked like a small, elderly woman, ready for burial. I knelt, and the undertaker left the room. I prayed for the repose of the soul of Mary Dempster, somewhere and somehow unspecified, under the benevolence of some power unidentified but deeply felt. It was the sort of prayer that supported all the arguments of Denyse Staunton against religion, but I was in the grip of an impulse that it would have been spiritual suicide to deny. And then I begged forgiveness for myself because, though I had done what I imagined was my best, I had not been loving enough, or wise enough, or generous enough in my dealings with her.

Then I did an odd thing that I almost fear to record, Head-master, for it may lead you to dismiss me as a fool or a madman or both. I had once been fully persuaded that Mary Dempster was a saint, and even of late years I had not really changed my mind. There were the three miracles, after all; miracles to me, if to no one else. Saints, according to tradition, give off a sweet odour when they are dead; in many instances it has been likened to the scent of violets. So I bent over the head of Mary Dempster and sniffed for this true odour of sanctity. But all I could smell was a perfume, good enough in itself, that had obviously come out of a bottle.

The undertaker returned, bringing a cross with him; seeing me kneel, he had assumed that the funeral would be of the sort that required one. He came upon me sniffing.

"Chanel Number Five," he whispered, "we always use it when nothing is supplied by the relatives. And perhaps you have noticed that we have padded your mother's bosom just a little; she had lost something there, during the last illness, and when the figure is reclining it gives a rather wasted effect."

He was a decent man, working at a much-abused but necessary job, so I made no comment except to say that she was not my mother.

"I'm so sorry. Your aunt?" said he, desperate to please and be comforting but not intimate.

"No, neither mother nor aunt," I said, and as I could not use so bleak and inadequate a word as "friend" to name what Mary Dempster had been to me, I left him guessing.

The following day I sat quite alone in the crematory chapel as Mary Dempster's body went through the doors into the flames. After all, who else remembered her?

( 5 )

She died in March. The following summer I went to Europe and visited the Bollandists, hoping they would pay me a few compliments on my big book. I am not ashamed of this; who knew better than they if I had done well or ill, and whose esteem is sweeter than that of an expert in one's own line? I was not disappointed; they were generous and welcoming as always. And I picked up one piece of information that pleased me greatly: Padre Blazon was still alive, though very old, in a hospital in Vienna.

I had not meant to go to Vienna, though I was going to Salzburg for the Festival, but I had not heard from Blazon for years and could not resist him. There he was, in a hospital directed by the Blue Nuns, propped up on pillows, looking older but not greatly changed except that his few teeth were gone; he even wore the deplorable velvet skull-cap rakishly askew over his wild white hair.

He knew me at once. "Ramezay!" he crowed as I approached. "I thought you must be dead! How old you look! Why, you must be all kinds of ages! What years? Come now, don't be coy! What years?"

"Just over the threshold of sixty-one," I said.

"Aha, a patriarch! You look even more though. Do you know how old I am? No, you don't, and I am not going to tell. If the Sisters find out they think I am senile. They wash me too much now; if they knew how old I am they would flay me with their terrible brushes—flay me like St Bartholomew. But I will tell you this much—I shall not see one hundred again! How much over that I tell nobody, but it will be discovered when I am dead. I may die any time. I may die as we are talking. Then I shall be sure to have the last word, eh? Sit down. You look tired!

"You have written a fine book! Not that I have read it all, but one of the nuns read some of it to me. I made her stop because her English accent was so vile she desecrated your elegant prose, and she mispronounced all the names. A real murderer! How ignorant these women are! Assassins of the spoken word! For a punishment I made her read a lot of *Le Juif errant* to me. Her French is very chaste, but the book nearly burned her tongue—so very anticlerical, you know. And what it says about the Jesuits! What evil magicians, what serpents! If we were one scruple as clever as Eugène Sue thought we should be masters of the world today. Poor soul, she could not understand why I wanted to hear it or why I laughed so much. Then I told her it was on the Index, and now she thinks I am an ogre disguised as an old Jesuit. Well, well, it passes the time. How is your fool-saint?"

"My what?"

"Don't shout; my hearing is perfectly good. Your fool-saint, your madwoman who dominates your life. I thought we might get something about her in your book but not a word. I know. I read the index first; I always do. All kinds of saints, heroes, and legends but no fool-saint. Why?"

"I was surprised to hear you call her that because I haven't heard that particular expression for thirty years. The last man to use it about Mary Dempster was an Irishman." And I told him of my conversation with Father Regan so long ago.

"Ah, Ramezay, you are a rash man. Imagine asking a village priest a question like that! But he must have been a fellow of some quality. Not all the Irish are idiots; they have a lot of Spanish blood, you know. That he should know about fool-saints is very odd. But do you know that one is to be canonized quite soon? Bertilla Boscardin, who did wonders—truly wonders—during the First World War with hospital patients; many miracles of healing and heroic courage during air-raids. Still, she was not quite a classic fool-saint; she was active and they are more usually passive—great lovers of God, with that special perception that St Bonaventura spoke of as beyond the power of even the wisest scholar."

"Father Regan assured me that fool-saints are dangerous. The Jews warn against them particularly because they are holy meddlers and bring ill-luck."

"Well, so they do, sometimes, when they are more fool than saint; we all bring ill-luck to others, you know, often without in the least recognizing it. But when I talk of a fool-saint I do not mean just some lolloping idiot who babbles of God instead of talking filth as they usually do. Remind me about this Mary Dempster."

So I did remind him, and when I had finished he said he would think about the matter. He was growing weary, and a nun signalled to me that it was time to leave.

"He is a very dear and good old man," she told me, "but he does so love to tease us. If you want to give him a treat, bring him some of that very special Viennese chocolate; he finds the hospital diet a great trial. His stomach is a marvel. Oh, that I might have such a stomach, and I am not even half his massive age!"

So next day I appeared with a lot of chocolate, most of which I gave to the nun to be rationed to him; I did not want him to gorge himself to death before my eyes. But the box I gave him was one of those pretty affairs with a little pair of tongs for picking out the piece one wants.

"Aha, St Dunstan and his tongs!" he whispered. "Keep your voice down, St Dunstan, or all these others will want some of my chocolate, and it probably would not be wholesome for them. Oh, you saintly man! I suppose a bottle of really good wine could not be got past the nuns? They dole out a thimbleful of some terrible belly-vengeance they buy very cheap, on their infrequent feast days.

"Well, I have been thinking about your fool-saint, and what I conclude is this: she would never have got past the Bollandists, but she must have been an extraordinary person, a great lover of God, and trusting greatly in His love for her. As for the miracles, you and

I have looked too deeply into miracles to dogmatize; you believe in them, and your belief has coloured your life with beauty and goodness; too much scientizing will not help you. It seems far more important to me that her life was lived heroically; she endured a hard fate, did the best she could, and kept it up until at last her madness was too powerful for her. Heroism in God's cause is the mark of the saint, Ramezay, not conjuring tricks. So on All Saints' Day I do not think you will do anything but good by honouring the name of Mary Dempster in your prayers. By your own admission you have enjoyed many of the good things of life because she suffered a fate that might have been yours. Though a boy's head is hard, Ramezay, hard—as you, being a schoolmaster, must surely know. You might just have had a nasty knock. Nobody can say for sure. But your life has been illuminated by your fool-saint, and how many can say so much?"

We talked a little further of friends we shared in Brussels, and then suddenly he said, "Have you met the Devil yet?"

"Yes," I replied, "I met Him in Mexico City. He was disguised as a woman—an extremely ugly woman but unquestionably a woman."

"Unquestionably?"

"Not a shadow of a doubt possible."

"Really, Ramezay, you astonish me. You are a much more remarkable fellow than one might suppose, if you will forgive me for saying so. The Devil certainly changed His sex to tempt St Anthony the Great, but for a Canadian schoolmaster! Well, well, one must not be a snob in spiritual things. From your certainty I gather the Devil tempted you with success?"

"The Devil proved to be a very good fellow. He suggested that a little compromise would not hurt me. He even suggested that an acquaintance with Him might improve my character."

"I find no fault with that. The Devil knows corners of us all of which Christ Himself is ignorant. Indeed, I am sure Christ learned a great deal that was salutary about Himself when He met the Devil in the wilderness. Of course, that was a meeting of brothers; people forget too readily that Satan is Christ's elder brother and has certain advantages in argument that pertain to a senior. On the whole, we treat the Devil shamefully, and the worse we treat Him the more He laughs at us. But tell me about your encounter."

I did so, and he listened with a great show of prudery at the dirty bits; he sniggered behind his hand, rolling his eyes up until only the whites could be seen; he snorted with laughter; when I described Liesl and the beautiful Faustina in the dressing-room he covered his face with his hands but peeped wickedly between his fingers. It was a virtuoso display of clerical-Spanish modesty. But when I described how I had wrung Liesl's nose until the bone cracked he kicked his counterpane and guffawed until a nun hurried to his bedside, only to be repelled with full-arm gestures and hissing.

"Oho, Ramezay, no wonder you write so well of myth and legend! It was St Dunstan seizing the Devil's snout in his tongs, a thousand years after his time. Well done, well done! You met the Devil as an equal, not cringing or frightened or begging for a trashy favour. That is the heroic life, Ramezay. You are fit to be the Devil's friend, without any fear of losing yourself to Him!"

On the third day I took farewell of him. I had managed to arrange for some chocolate to be procured when he needed more, and as a great favour the nuns took six bottles of a good wine into their care to be rationed to him as seemed best.

"Good-bye," he cried cheerfully. "We shall probably not meet again, Ramezay. You are beginning to look a little shaky."

"I have not yet found a God to teach me how to be old," I said. "Have you?"

"Shhh, not so loud. The nuns must not know in what a spiritual state I am. Yes, yes, I have found Him, and He is the very best of company. Very calm, very quiet, but gloriously alive: we *do*, but He *is*. Not in the least a proselytizer or a careerist, like His sons." And he went off into a fit of giggles.

I left him soon after this, and as I looked back from the door for a last wave, he was laughing and pinching his big copper nose with the tiny chocolate tongs. "God go with you, St Dunstan," he called.

He was much in my mind as I tasted the pleasures of Salzburg, and particularly so after my first visit to the special display called *Schöne Madonnen,* in the exhibition rooms in the Cathedral. For here, at last, and after having abandoned hope and forgotten my search, I found the Little Madonna I had seen during my bad night at Passchendaele. There she was, among these images of the Holy Mother in all her aspects, collected as examples of the wood and stone carver's art, and drawn from churches, museums, and private collections all over Europe.

There she was, quite unmistakable, from the charming crown that she wore with such an air to her foot set on the crescent moon. Beneath this moon was what I had not seen in the harsh light of the flare—the globe of the earth itself, with a serpent encircling it, and an apple in the mouth of the serpent. She had lost her sceptre, but not the Divine Child, a fat, reserved little person who looked out at the world from beneath half-closed eyelids. But the face of the Madonna—was it truly the face of Mary Dempster? No, it was not, though the hair was very like; Mary Dempster, whose face my mother had described as being like a pan of milk, had never been so beautiful in feature, but the expression was undeniably hers—an expression of mercy and love, tempered with perception and penetration.

I visited her every day during my week in Salzburg. She belonged, so the catalogue told me, to a famous private collection and was considered a good, though late, example of the Immaculate Conception aspect of the Madonna figure. It had not been considered worthy of an illustration in the catalogue, so when my week was up I never saw it again. Photography in the exhibition was forbidden. But I needed no picture. She was mine forever.

( 6 )

The mysterious death of Boy Staunton was a nine days' wonder, and people who delight in unsolved crimes—for they were certain it must have been a crime—still talk of it. You recall most of the details, Headmaster, I am sure: at about four o'clock on the morning of Monday, November 4, 1968, his Cadillac convertible was recovered from the waters of Toronto harbour, into which it had been driven at a speed great enough to carry it, as it sank, about twenty feet from the concrete pier. His body was in the driver's seat, the hands gripping the wheel so tightly that it was very difficult for the police to remove him from the car. The windows and the roof were closed, so that some time must have elapsed between driving over the edge and the filling of the car with water. But the most curious fact of all was that in Boy's mouth the police found a stone—an ordinary piece of pinkish granite about the size of a small egg—which could not possibly have been where it was unless he himself, or someone unknown, had put it there.

The newspapers published columns about it, as was reasonable, for it was local news of the first order. Was it murder? But who would murder a well-known philanthropist, a man whose great gifts as an organizer had been of incalculable value to the nation during the war years? Now that Boy was dead, he was a hero to the press. Was it suicide? Why would the President of the Alpha Corporation, a man notably youthful in appearance and outlook, and one of the two or three richest men in Canada, want to kill himself? His home-life was of model character; he and his wife (the former Denyse Hornick, a figure of note in her own right as an advocate of economic and legal reform on behalf of women) had worked very closely in a score of philanthropic and cultural projects. Besides, the newspapers thought it now proper to reveal, his appointment by the Crown to the office of Lieutenant-Governor of Ontario was to have been announced within a few days. Was a man with Boy Staunton's high concept of service likely to have killed himself under such circumstances?

Tributes from distinguished citizens were many. There was a heartfelt one from Joel Surgeoner, within a few hundred yards of whose Lifeline Mission the death occurred—a Mission that the dead man had supported most generously. You wrote one yourself, Headmaster, in which you said that he had finely exemplified the school's unremitting insistence that much is demanded of those to whom much has been given.

His wife was glowingly described, though there was little mention of "a former marriage, which ended with the death of the first Mrs Staunton, nee Leola Crookshanks, in 1942." In the list of the bereaved, Lorene took precedence over David (now forty, a barrister and a drunk) and Caroline (now Mrs Beeston Bastable and mother of one daughter, also Caroline).

The funeral was not quite a state funeral, though Denyse tried to manage one; she wanted a flag on the coffin and she wanted soldiers, but it was not to be. However, many flags were at half-staff, and she did achieve a very fine turnout of important people, and others who were important because they represented somebody too important to come personally. It was agreed by everyone that Bishop Woodiwiss paid a noble tribute to Boy, whom he had known from youth, though it was a pity poor Woodiwiss mumbled so now.

The reception after the funeral was in the great tradition of such affairs, and the new house Denyse had made Boy build in the most desirable of the suburbs was filled even to its great capacity. Denyse was wonderfully self-possessed and ran everything perfectly. Or almost perfectly; there was one thing in which she did not succeed.

She approached me after she had finished receiving the mourners—if that is the right way to describe the group who were now getting down so merrily to the Scotch and rye—and, "Of course you'll write the official life," said she.

"What official life?" I asked, startled and clumsy.

"What official life do you suppose?" she said, giving me a look that told me very plainly to brace up and not be a fool.

"Oh, is there to be one?" I asked. I was not trying to be troublesome; I was genuinely unnerved, and with good cause.

"Yes, there is to be one," she said, and icicles hung from every word. "As you knew Boy from childhood, there will be a good deal for you to fill in before we come to the part where I can direct you."

"But how is it official?" I asked, wallowing in wonderment. "I mean, what makes it official? Does the government want it or something?"

"The government has had no time to think about it," she said, "but I want it, and I shall do whatever needs to be done about the government. What I want to know now is whether you are going to write it or not." She spoke like a mother who is saying "Are you going to do what I tell you or not?" to a bad child. It was not so much an inquiry as a flick of the whip.

"Well, I'll want to think it over," I said.

"Do that. Frankly, my first choice was Eric Roop—I thought it wanted a poet's touch—but he can't do it, though considering how many grants Boy wangled for him I don't know why. But Boy did even more for you. You'll find it a change from those saints you're so fond of." She left me angrily.

Of course I did not write it. The heart attack I had a few days later gave me an excellent excuse for keeping free of anything I didn't want to do. And how could I have written a life of Boy that would have satisfied me and yet saved me from murder at the hands of Denyse? And how could I, trained as a historian to suppress nothing, and with the Bollandist tradition of looking firmly at the shadow as well as the light, have written a life of Boy without telling all that I have told you, Headmaster, and all I know about the way he died? And even then, would it have been the truth? I learned something about the variability of truth as traditional people see it from Boy himself, within an hour of his death.

You will not see this memoir until after my own death, and you will surely keep what you know to yourself. After all, you cannot prove anything against anyone. Nor was Boy's manner of death really surprising to anyone who knows what you now know about his life.

It was like this.

( 7 )

Magnus Eisengrim did not bring his famous display of illusions to Canada until 1968. His fame was now so great that he had once had his picture on the cover of *Time* as the greatest magician in history. *The Autobiography* sold quite well here, though nobody knew that its subject (or its author) was a native. It was at the end of October he came to Toronto for two weeks.

Naturally I saw a good deal of him and his company. The beautiful Faustina had been replaced by another girl, no less beautiful, who bore the same name. Liesl, now in early middle age and possessed of a simian distinction of appearance, was as near to me as before, and I spent all the time I could spare with her. She and

Blazon were the only people I have ever met with whom one resumed a conversation exactly where it had been discontinued, whether yesterday or six years earlier. It was through her intercession—perhaps it would be more truthful to call it a command—that I was able to get Eisengrim to come to the school on the Sunday night in the middle of his fortnight's engagement, to talk to the boarders about hypnotism; schoolmasters are without conscience in exacting such favours.

He was a huge success, of course, for though he had not wanted to come he was not a man to scamp anything he had undertaken. He paid the boys the compliment of treating them seriously, explaining what hypnotism really was and what its limitations were. He emphasized the fact that nobody can be made to do anything under hypnotism that is contrary to his wishes, though of course people have wishes that they are unwilling to acknowledge, even to themselves. I remember that this concept gave trouble to several of the boys, and Eisengrim explained it in terms, and with a clarity, that suggested to me that he was a much better-informed man than I had supposed. The idea of the hypnotist as an all-powerful demon, like Svengali, who could make anybody do anything, he pooh-poohed; but he did tell some amusing stories about odd and embarrassing facets of people's personalities that had made their appearance under hypnotism.

Of course the boys clamoured for a demonstration, but he refused to break his rule of never hypnotizing anyone under twenty-one without written consent from their parents. (He did not add that young people and children are difficult hypnotic subjects because of the variability of their power of concentration.) However, he did hypnotize me, and made me do enough strange things to delight the boys without robbing me of my professional dignity. He made me compose an extemporary poem, which is something I had never done before in my life, but apparently it was not bad.

His talk lasted for about an hour, and as we were walking down the main corridor of the classroom building Boy Staunton came out of the side door of your study, Headmaster. I introduced them, and Boy was delighted.

"I saw your show last Thursday," he said. "It was my stepdaughter's birthday, and we were celebrating. As a matter of fact, you gave her a box of sweets."

"I remember perfectly," said Eisengrim. "Your party was sitting in C21-25. Your stepdaughter wears strong spectacles and has a characteristic laugh."

"Yes, poor Lorene. I'm afraid she became a bit hysterical; we had to leave after you sawed a man in two. But, may I ask you a very special favour?—how did your Brazen Head know what was implied in the message it gave to Ruth Tillman? That has caused some extraordinary gossip."

"No, Mr Staunton, I cannot tell you that. But perhaps you will tell me how you know what was said to Mrs Tillman, who sat in F32 on Friday night, if your party came to the theatre on Thursday?"

"Mightn't I have heard it from friends?"

"You might, but you did not. You came back to see my Exhibition on Friday night because you had missed some of it by reason of your daughter's over-excitement. I can only assume my exhibition offered something you wanted. A great compliment. I appreciated it, I assure you. Indeed, I appreciated it so much that the Head decided not to name you and tell the audience that your appointment as Lieutenant-Governor would be announced on Monday. I am sure you understand how much renunciation there is in refusing such a scoop. It would have brought me wonderful publicity, but it would have embarrassed you, and the Head and I decided not to do that."

"But you can't possibly have known! I hadn't had the letter myself more than a couple of hours before going to the theatre. I had it with me as a matter of fact."

"Very true, and you have it now; inside right-hand breast pocket. Don't worry. I haven't picked your pocket. But when you lean forward, however slightly, the tip of a long envelope made of thick creamy paper can just be seen; only governments use such ostentatious envelopes, and when a man so elegantly dressed as you are bulges his jacket with one of them, it is probably—you see? There is an elementary lesson in magic for you. Work on it for twenty years and you may comprehend the Brazen Head."

This took Boy down a peg; the good-humoured, youthful chuckle he gave was his first step to get himself on top of the conversation again. "As a matter of fact," he said, "I've just been showing it to the Headmaster; because, of course, I'll have to resign as Chairman of the Board of Governors. And I was just coming to talk to you about it, Dunny."

"Come along then," I said. "We were going to have a drink."

I was conscious already that Boy was up to one of his special displays of charm. He had put his foot wrong with Eisengrim by asking him to reveal the secret of an illusion; it was unlike him to be so gauche, but I suppose the excitement about his new appointment blew up his ego a little beyond what he could manage. It seemed to me that I could already see the plumed, cocked hat of a Lieutenant-Governor on his head.

Eisengrim had been sharp enough with him to arouse hostility, and Boy loved to defeat hostility by turning the other cheek—which is by no means a purely Christian ploy, as Boy had shown me count-less times. Eisengrim further topped him by the little bit of observa-tion about the letter, which had made Boy look like a child who is so besotted by a new toy that it cannot let the toy out of its grasp. Boy wanted a chance to right the balance, which of course meant making him master of the situation.

It was clear to me that one of those sympathies, or antipathies, or at any rate unusual states of feeling, had arisen between these two which sometimes lead to falling in love, or to sudden warm friend-ships, or to lasting and rancorous enmities, but which are always extraordinary. I wanted to see what would happen, and my appetite was given the special zest of knowing who Eisengrim really was, which Boy did not, and perhaps would never learn.

It was like Boy to seek to ingratiate himself with the new friend by treating the old friend with genial contempt. When the three of us had made our way to my room at the end of the top-floor corri-dor—my old room, which I have always refused to leave for more comfortable quarters in the newer buildings—he kicked the door open and entered first, turning on the lights and touring the room as he said, "Still the same old rat's nest. What are you going to do when you have to move? How will you ever find room anywhere else for all this junk? Look at those books! I'll bet you don't use some of them once a year."

It was true that several of the big volumes were spread about, and I had to take some of them out of an armchair for Eisengrim, so I was a little humbled.

But Eisengrim spoke. "I like it very much," said he. "I so seldom get to my home, and I have to live in hotel rooms for weeks and months on end. Next spring I go on a world tour; that will mean something like five years of hotels. This room speaks of peace and a mind at work. I wish it were mine."

"I wouldn't say old Dunny's mind was at work," said Boy. "I wish all I had to do was teach the same lesson every year for forty years."

"You are forgetting his many and excellent books, are you not?" said Eisengrim.

Boy understood that he was not going to get what he wanted, which cannot have been anything more than a complicity with an interesting stranger, by running me down, so he took another tack. "You mustn't misunderstand if I am disrespectful towards the great scholar. We're very old friends. We come from the same little village. In fact I think we might say that all the brains of Deptford—past, present, and doubtless to come—are in this room right now."

For the first time in Boy's company, Eisengrim laughed. "Might I be included in such a distinguished group?" he asked.

Boy was pleased to have gained a laugh. "Sorry, birth in Deptford is an absolute requirement."

"Oh, I have that already. It was about my achievements in the world that I had doubt."

"I've looked through your *Autobiography*—Lorene asked me to buy a copy for her. I thought you were born somewhere in the far north of Sweden."

"That was Magnus Eisengrim; my earlier self was born in Deptford. If the *Autobiography* seems to be a little high in colour you must blame Ramsay. He wrote it."

"Dunny! You never told me that!"

"It never seemed relevant," said I. I was amazed that Paul would tell him such a thing, but I could see that he, like Boy, was prepared to play some high cards in this game of topping each other.

"I don't remember anybody in the least like you in Deptford. What did you say your real name was?"

"My real name is Magnus Eisengrim; that is who I am and that is how the world knows me. But before I found out who I was, I was called Paul Dempster, and I remember you very well. I always thought of you as the Rich Young Ruler."

"And are you and Dunny old friends?"

"Yes, very old friends. He was my first teacher of magic. He also taught me a little about saints, but it was the magic that lingered. His specialty as a conjurer was eggs—the Swami of the Omelette. He was my only teacher till I ran away with a circus."

"Did you? You know I wanted to do that. I suppose it is part of every boy's dream."

"Then boys are lucky that it remains a dream. I should not have said a circus; it was a very humble carnival show. I was entranced by Willard the Wizard; he was so much more skilful than Ramsay. He was quite clever with cards and a very neat pickpocket. I begged him to take me, and was such an ignorant little boy—perhaps I might even call myself innocent, though it is a word I don't like—that I was in ecstacy when he consented. But I soon found out that Willard had two weaknesses—boys and morphia. The morphia had already made him careless or he would never have run the terrible risk of stealing a boy. But when I had well and truly found out what travelling with Willard meant, he had me in slavery; he told me that if anybody ever found out what we did together I would certainly be hanged, but he would get off because he knew all the judges everywhere. So I was chained to Willard by fear; I was his thing and his creature, and I learned conjuring as a reward. One always learns one's mystery at the price of one's innocence, though my case was spectacular. But the astonishing thing is that I grew to like Willard, especially as morphia incapacitated him for his hobby and ruined him as a conjurer. It was then he became a Wild Man."

"Then he was *Le Solitaire des forêts*?" I asked.

"That was even later. His first decline was from conjurer to Wild Man—essentially a geek."

"Geek?" said Boy.

"That is what carnival people call them. They are not an advertised attraction, but word that a geek is in a back tent is passed around quietly, and money is taken without any sale of tickets. Otherwise the Humane Societies make themselves a nuisance. The geek is represented as somebody who simply has to have raw flesh, and especially blood. After the spieler has lectured terrifyingly on the psychology and physiology of the geek, the geek is given a live chicken; he growls and rolls his eyes, then he gnaws through its neck until the head is off, and he drinks the spouting blood. Not a nice life, and very hard on the teeth, but if it is the only way to keep yourself in morphia, you'd rather geek than have the horrors. But geeking costs money; you need a live chicken every time, and even the oldest, toughest birds cost something. Before Willard got too sick even to geek, he was geeking with worms and gartersnakes when I could catch them for him. The rubes loved it; Willard was something even the most disgusting brute could despise.

"There was trouble with the police, at last, and I thought we would do better abroad. We had been over there quite a time, Ramsay, before you and I met in the Tyrol, and by then Willard was in very poor health, and *Le Solitaire des forêts* was all he could manage. I doubt if he even knew where he was. So that is what running away with a circus was like, Mr Staunton."

"Why didn't you leave him when he was down to geeking?"

"Shall I answer you honestly? Very well, then; it was loyalty. Yes, loyalty to Willard, though not to his geeking or his nasty ways with boys. I suppose it was loyalty to his dreadful, inescapable human need. Many people feel these irrational responsibilities and cannot crush them. Like Ramsay's loyalty to my mother, for instance. I am sure it was an impediment to him, and certainly it must have been a heavy expense, but he did not fail her. I suppose he loved her. I might have done so if I had ever known her. But, you see, the person I knew was a woman unlike anybody else's mother, who was called 'hoor' by people like you, Mr Staunton."

"I really don't remember," said Boy. "Are you sure?"

"Quite sure. I have never been able to forget what she was or what people called her. Because, you see, it was my birth that made her like that. My father thought it his duty to tell me, so that I could do whatever was possible to make it up to her. My birth was what robbed her of her sanity; that sometimes happened, you know, and I suppose it happens still. I was too young for the kind of guilt my father wanted me to feel; he had an extraordinary belief in guilt as an educative force. I couldn't stand it. I cannot feel guilt now. But I can call up in an instant what it felt like to be the child of a woman everybody jeered at and thought a dirty joke—including you, the Rich Young Ruler. But I am sure your accent is much more elegant now. A Lieutenant-Governor who said 'hoor' would not reflect credit on the Crown, would he?"

Boy had plenty of experience in being baited by hostile people, and he did not show by a quiver how strange this was to him. He prepared to get the attack into his own hands.

"I forget what you said your name was."

Eisengrim continued to smile, so I said, "He's Paul Dempster."

This time it was my turn for surprise. "Who may Paul Dempster be?" asked Boy.

"Do you mean to say you don't remember the Dempsters? In Deptford? The Reverend Amasa Dempster?"

"No. I don't remember what is of no use to me, and I haven't been in Deptford since my father died. That's twenty-six years."

"You have no recollection of Mrs Dempster?"

"None at all. Why should I?"

I could hardly believe he spoke the truth, but as we talked on I had to accept it as a fact that he had so far edited his memory of his early days that the incident of the snowball had quite vanished from his mind. But had not Paul edited his memories so that only pain and cruelty remained? I began to wonder what I had erased from my own recollection.

We had drinks and were sitting as much at ease as men can amid so many strong currents of feeling. Boy made another attempt to turn the conversation into a realm where he could dominate.

"How did you come to choose your professional name? I know magicians like to have extraordinary names, but yours sounds a little alarming. Don't you find that a disadvantage?"

"No. And I did not choose it. My patron gave it to me." He turned his head towards me, and I knew that the patron was Liesl. "It comes from one of the great northern beast fables, and it means Wolf. Far from being a disadvantage, people like it. People like to be in awe of something, you know. And my magic show is not ordinary. It provokes awe, which is why it is a success. It has something of the quality of Ramsay's saints, though my miracles have a spice of the Devil about them—again my patron's idea. That is where you make your mistake. You have always wanted to be loved; nobody responds quite as we would wish, and people are suspicious of a public figure who wants to be loved. I have been wiser than you. I chose a Wolf's name. You have chosen forever to be a Boy. Was it because your mother used to call you Pidgy Boy-Boy, even when you were old enough to call my mother 'hoor'?"

"How in God's name did you know that? Nobody in the world now living knows that!"

"Oh yes, two people know it—myself and Ramsay. He told me, many years ago, under an oath of secrecy."

"I never did any such thing!" I shouted, outraged. Yet, even as I shouted, a doubt assailed me.

"But you did, or how would I know? You told me that to comfort me once, when the Rich Young Ruler and some of his gang had been shouting at my mother. We all forget many of the things we do, especially when they do not fit into the character we have chosen for ourselves. You see yourself as the man of many confidences, Ramsay. It would not do for you to remember a time when you told a secret. Dunstan Ramsay—when did you cease to be Dunstable?"

"A girl renamed me when I had at last broken with my mother. Liesl said it made me one of the twice-born. Had you thought that we are all three of the company of the twice-born? We have all rejected our beginnings and become something our parents could not have foreseen."

"I can't imagine your parents foreseeing that you would become a theorizer about myth and legend," said Elsengrim. "Hard people—I remember them clearly. Hard people—especially your mother."

"Wrong," said I. And I told him how my mother had worked and schemed and devised a nest to keep him alive, and exulted when he decided to live. "She said you were a fighter, and she liked that."

Now it was his turn to be disconcerted. "Do you mind if I have one of your cigars?" he said.

I do not smoke cigars, but the box he took from a shelf on the other side of the room might easily be mistaken for a humidor—rather a fine one. But as he took it down and rather superciliously blew dust from it his face changed.

He brought it over and laid it on the low table around which our chairs were grouped. "What's this?" he asked.

"It is what it says it is," said I.

The engraving on the silver plaque on the lid of the box was beautiful and clear, for I had chosen the script with care:

Requiescat in pace
MARY DEMPSTER
1888-1959
Here is the patience
and faith of the saints.

We looked at it for some time. Boy was first to speak.

"Why would you keep a thing like that with you?"

"A form of piety. A sense of guilt unexpiated. Indolence. I have always been meaning to put them in some proper place, but I haven't found it yet."

"Guilt?" said Eisengrim.

Here it was. Either I spoke now or I kept silence forever. Dunstan Ramsay counselled against revelation, but Fifth Business would not hear.

"Yes, guilt. Staunton and I robbed your mother of her sanity." And I told them the story of the snowball.

"Too bad," said Boy. "But if I may say so, Dunny, I think you've let the thing build up into something it never was. You unmarried men are terrible fretters. I threw the snowball—at least you say so, and for argument's sake let that go—and you dodged it. It precipitated something which was probably going to happen anyhow. The difference between us is that you've brooded over it and I've forgotten it. We've both done far more important things since. I'm sorry if I was offensive to your mother, Dempster. But you know what boys are. Brutes, because they don't know any better. But they grow up to be men."

"Very important men. Men whom the Crown delighteth to honour," said Eisengrim with an unpleasant laugh.

"Yes. If you expect me to be diffident about that, you're wrong."

"Men who retain something of the brutish boy, even," said I.

"I don't think I understand you."

Fifth Business insisted on being heard again. "Would this jog your memory?" I asked, handing him my old paperweight.

"Why should it? An ordinary bit of stone. You've used it to hold down some of the stuff on your desk for years. I've seen it a hundred times. It doesn't remind me of anything but you."

"It is the stone you put in the snowball you threw at Mrs Dempster," I said. "I've kept it because I couldn't part with it. I swear I never meant to tell you what it was. But, Boy, for God's sake, get to know something about yourself. The stone-in-the-snowball has been characteristic of too much you've done for you to forget it forever!"

"What I've done! Listen, Dunny, one thing I've done is to make you pretty well-off for a man in your position. I've treated you like a brother. Given you tips nobody else got, let me tell you. And that's where your nice little nest-egg came from. Your retirement fund you used to whine about."

I hadn't thought I whined, but perhaps I did. "Need we go on with this moral bookkeeping?" I said. "I'm simply trying to recover something of the totality of your life. Don't you want to possess it as a whole—the bad with the good? I told you once you'd made a God of yourself, and the insufficiency of it forced you to become an atheist. It's time you tried to be a human being. Then maybe something bigger than yourself will come up on your horizon."

"You're trying to get me. You want to humiliate me in front of this man here; you seem to have been in cahoots with him for years, though you never mentioned him or his miserable mother to me— your best friend, and your patron and protector against your own incompetence! Well, let him hear this, as we're dealing in ugly truths: you've always hated me because I took Leola from you. And I did! It wasn't because you lost a leg and were ugly. It was because she loved me better."

This got me on the raw, and Dunstable Ramsay's old inability to resist a cruel speech when one occurred to him came uppermost. "My observation has been that we get the women we deserve, King Candaules," I said, "and those who eat jam before breakfast are cloyed before bedtime."

"Gentlemen," said Eisengrim, "deeply interesting though this is, Sunday nights are the only nights when I can get to bed before midnight. So I shall leave you."

Boy was all courtesy at once: "I'm going too. Let me give you a lift," said he. Of course; he wanted to blackguard me to Eisengrim in the car.

"Thank you, Mr Staunton," said Eisengrim. "What Ramsay has told us puts you in my debt—for eighty days in Paradise, if for nothing in this life. We shall call it quits if you will drive me to my hotel."

I lifted the casket that contained Mary Dempster's ashes. "Do you want to take this with you, Paul?"

"No thanks, Ramsay. I have everything I need."

It seemed an odd remark, but in the emotional stress of the situation I paid no heed to it. Indeed, it was not until after the news of Boy's death reached me next morning that I noticed my paperweight was gone.

( 8 )

Because of the way he died, the consequent police investigations, and the delays brought about by Denyse's determination to make the most of the nearly official funeral, Boy was not buried until Thursday. The Saturday evening following I went to see Eisengrim's *Soirée of Illusions*, as he now called it, at its last performance, and though I spent much of the evening behind the scenes with Liesl, I went into the front of the house during *The Brazen Head of Friar Bacon*. Or rather, I hid myself behind the curtains of an upper box so that I could look down into the auditorium of our beautiful old Royal Alexandra Theatre and watch the audience.

Everything went smoothly during the collecting and restoration of borrowed objects, and the faces I saw below me were the usual studies in pleasure, astonishment, and—always the most interesting—the eagerness to be deceived mingled with resentment of deception. But when the Head was about to utter its three messages to people in the audience and Eisengrim had said what was to come, somebody in the top balcony shouted out, "Who killed Boy Staunton?"

There was murmuring in the audience and a hiss or two, but silence fell as the Head glowed from within, its lips parted, and its voice—Liesl's voice, slightly foreign and impossible to identify as man's or woman's—spoke.

"He was killed by the usual cabal: by himself, first of all; by the woman he knew; by the woman he did not know; by the man who granted his inmost wish; and by the inevitable fifth, who was keeper of his conscience and keeper of the stone."

I believe there was an uproar. Certainly Denyse made a great to-do when she heard of it. Of course she thought "the woman he knew" must be herself. The police were hounded by her and some of her influential friends, but that was after Eisengrim and his *Soirée of Illusions* had removed by air to Copenhagen, and the police had to make it clear that they really could not investigate impalpable offences, however annoying they might be. But I knew nothing about it, because it was there, in that box, that I had my seizure and was rushed to the hospital, as I was afterward told, by a foreign lady.

When I was well enough to read letters I found one—a postcard, to my horror—that read:

*Deeply sorry about your illness which was my fault as much as most such things are anybody's fault. But I could not resist my temptation as I beg you not to resist this one: come to Switzerland and join the Basso and the Brazen Head. We shall have some high old times before The Five make an end of us all.*

*Love,*
*L.V.*

And that, Headmaster, is all I have to tell you.

*Sankt Gallen*
1970

# THE DEPTFORD TRILOGY

ROBERTSON
FIFTH BUSINESS
DAVIES

ROBERTSON
THE MANTICORE
DAVIES

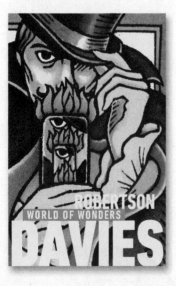

ROBERTSON
WORLD OF WONDERS
DAVIES

"One of the splendid literary enterprises of this decade."
— *Newsweek*

penguinrandomhouse.ca